THE DOWN DEEP

DEEP

BAEN BOOKS
by CATHERINE ASARO

Sunrise Alley
Alpha

Skolian Empire: Dust Knights
The Down Deep

Skolian Empire: Major Bhaajan
Undercity
The Bronze Skies
The Vanished Seas
The Jigsaw Assassin

The Saga of the Skolian Empire
The Ruby Dice
Diamond Star
Carnelians

THE DOWN DEEP

DEEP

CATHERINE ASARO

THE DOWN DEEP

A Baen Books Original

Baen Publishing Enterprises
P.O. Box 1403
Riverdale, NY 10471
www.baen.com

ISBN: 978-1-9821-9350-8

Cover art by Kurt Miller

First printing, July 2024
Distributed by Simon & Schuster
1230 Avenue of the Americas
New York, NY 10020

Library of Congress Cataloging-in-Publication Data

Names: Asaro, Catherine, author.
Title: The down deep / Catherine Asaro.
Description: Riverdale, NY : Baen Publishing Enterprises, 2024. | Series: Skolian Empire, Dust Knights ; 1
Identifiers: LCCN 2024005642 (print) | LCCN 2024005643 (ebook) | ISBN 9781982193508 (hardcover) | ISBN 9781625799692 (e-book)
Subjects: LCGFT: Fantasy fiction. | Novels.
Classification: LCC PS3551.S29 D69 2024 (print) | LCC PS3551.S29 (ebook) | DDC 813/.54—dc23/eng/20240212
LC record available at https://lccn.loc.gov/2024005642
LC ebook record available at https://lccn.loc.gov/2024005643

Printed in the United States of America

10 9 8 7 6 5 4 3 2 1

DEDICATION

To Aly Parsons, Martin Wooster, and
J.G. "Huck" Huckenpöhler
With fond memory

ACKNOWLEDGMENTS

I would like to thank the many people who helped put together this book. Their input has been invaluable. My thanks to my Patreon subscribers for their invaluable support and encouragement, to Mary Lou Mendum, Elaine Kant, and especially to Tamara Wiens for her insights. To Kurt Miller for creating such a wonderful cover. To all the excellent folks at Baen Books, including my publisher and editor, Toni Weisskopf and David Afsharirad, also to Alex Bear, Ben Davidoff, Carol Russo, Jason Cordova, Joy Freeman, Leah Brandtner, Marla Ainspan, Rabbit Boyett, Thom Ketring, and everyone else there who helped make this book possible. A special thanks to the Ethan Ellenberg Literary Agency for their excellent work on my behalf, including Ethan Ellenberg, Bibi Lewis, Raelene Gorlinsky, Evan Gregory, Ezra Ellenberg, and Maria Santos. Most of all to my daughter, Catherine Kendall Asaro Cannizzo, with all my love.

CHAPTER I
Visit. Or Not.

⬦

"If you go with them, you will die." The General of the Pharaoh's Army scowled at her sister Lavinda. "That is unacceptable."

Bhaaj stayed back from the arguing sisters and kept her mouth shut. The chamber where they stood practically oozed serenity, from its sky-blue walls to its many windows. Yah, sure. Right now, it felt about as calm as someone shouting, "No way!"

General Vaj Majda stood taller than everyone else in the room, indeed taller than most anyone alive, even her imposing sisters, Lavinda and Corejida. All three had the black hair and dark eyes of Skolian royalty, a trio of inexcusably wealthy human beings with enough power to crash a few planets together if they got angry enough. Not that planet-bashing technology existed, but what the hell. If they'd actually wanted to do it, instead of just sounding like they did, they'd have found a way. Majda always triumphed.

Colonel Lavinda Majda met her sister's glare without a flinch. As an army officer, she served in Vaj's chain of command. The middle sister, Corejida, had remained a civilian; she ruled the financial empire the House of Majda had built over the millennia, since the age when their ancestors rode as conquering warrior queens and inflicted enough barbarism on the universe to last an eon. These days, the Majdas increased their holdings in a more civilized manner—like taking over the economies of entire worlds. Why bother with bloodthirsty armies? Just buy everything on the fucking planet.

1

"Or maybe these people you want to visit won't murder you," Vaj continued, relentless. "They'd benefit more by taking you hostage. We never bargain with kidnappers, but you are my sister and heir, which means we'd have to negotiate." She crossed her arms. "So no. You will not visit the Undercity."

Bhaaj wanted to curse to the sky. Would this mission die before it started? She'd come with her protégé Angel to discuss Lavinda's visit. Or so they'd thought. Angel waited at her side, taciturn and still, as if they could vanish into their silence. Good luck with that. They stood out like throbbing thumbs someone had slammed in an old-fashioned door. With their curly hair and subtle differences in features, anyone would know they came from the Undercity, which supposedly meant they might go wild and beat up everyone in sight. Never mind that Bhaaj had served in the army for twenty years and then as a private investigator for the elite of an empire.

It was true, though, that Angel looked as angelic as a jackhammer. Strong and powerful, gorgeous in her vibrant youth, she made no attempt to hide the tattoos, scars, and circuit-diagrams that covered her muscled biceps. She'd run with a dust gang since childhood, with all the angelic behaviors that implied, like beating up rival gangs. Despite her upscale clothes today, she obviously didn't come from the City of Cries.

Goddess, what a name. Seriously, *Cries*? What did they have to weep about? Sure, they lived on a world that had been dying for millennia, until even in its kindest regions it threatened to barbecue its human settlers. Except the Majdas lived here, and they wanted a nice place for their palace. Like paradise. Sorry, Cries, you can't die yet. Not that anyone objected to it existing as one of the most starkly beautiful cities in an interstellar empire. They just chose to forget the Undercity, that so-called slum hidden in ruins beneath the desert.

"I'll have protection." Lavinda motioned at Bhaaj and Angel. "Major Bhaajan and her Dust Knights."

Vaj gave Bhaaj the slightest nod, her only acknowledgement that Bhaaj had worked on retainer to the House of Majda for over four years now. She barely glanced at Angel.

Don't disrespect my protégé, Bhaaj thought. Angel didn't look offended, though. More than anything, she seemed curious about the sisters.

"It's still too risky," Vaj told Lavinda.

"I'm willing to take the risk," Lavinda said. "This visit is too important to cancel. We aren't getting anywhere with people in Undercity." She indicated Angel. "She's the only one who has agreed to take a job with the government, and she's joining as a civilian."

Angel remained impassive, but Bhaaj felt her interest spark. Her protégé was far savvier than anyone outside the Undercity gave her credit for, except perhaps Lavinda.

Corejida Majda spoke up. "She's right, Vaj. We need to meet the people of the Undercity on their own terms if we're going to establish better relations. Hell, *any* relations."

Vaj motioned toward Bhaaj without glancing at her. "That's Major Bhaajan's job. I see no reason to send my sister."

"General, permission to speak?" Bhaaj asked. Although she'd retired from the army ten years ago, she instinctively reverted to military behavior with the general.

Vaj turned to her. "Go ahead."

"I'm happy to act as a liaison with the Undercity," Bhaaj said. "I appreciate the chance to improve relations. However, the gap between our cultures is large." She was the queen of understatement today. "We've existed as separate worlds for so long that my people don't trust the government." Why would they? For millennia, Cries had ignored them. Now the Undercity had something everyone wanted, and suddenly the authorities were all about "relationships" and "mutual benefit." Bhaaj had no intention of letting them take advantage of her people. She could act on their behalf, but she didn't want to alienate the powers of the Imperialate in the process, with who knew what disasters that might create.

She spoke carefully. "Colonel Majda's visit would go a long way toward establishing more trust with my people." Lavinda needed only to meet folks, be diplomatic, and *listen* to them. That alone would offer a big step forward, the first time anyone with influence had reached out to the Undercity.

Vaj snorted. "What, they don't trust us because we're offering them a higher wage than they've ever seen, with actual benefits, a decent standard of living, and access to education so they can better themselves? They'd rather be a bunch of lazy thugs, take drugs, and live in squalor?"

For fuck's sake, Bhaaj thought. Angel tensed at her side, and Bhaaj spoke quickly, cutting off any response Angel felt inspired to bestow on the Majda queen. "General, I mean no offense. But my people don't live in squalor, and we value a strong work ethic." How did Vaj think they survived? As for the drug use, yah, it was a problem, but they needed solutions, not dismissal. "Both of our peoples could benefit from coming to understand each other better."

"Well, that was tactful," Lavinda said. "Vaj, you have no idea how much you just insulted them. I've encountered only hints of their culture, and already I can see it's incredible. Beautiful. We need to get one of us down there, not only to show the Undercity we genuinely want better relations but so we can educate ourselves as well." She met her sister's intransigent gaze. "We have to meet them on their terms, or they will never trust us. And we *need* them. They can make the difference between our surviving as a free civilization and conquest by the Trader Empire."

Vaj spoke tightly. "I won't risk your life."

Lavinda tilted her head toward Bhaaj and Angel. "I'll have protection."

For an instant, Bhaaj glimpsed something under Vaj's iron exterior, something unexpected, maybe even impossible. *Vulnerability?* The general feared for the sister she loved.

As quickly as that reveal came, Vaj recovered her control. She said only, "Yes, Major Bhaajan and her martial arts fighters do excellent work. But it isn't enough."

"Send a squad of Majda guards with me." Lavinda glanced at Bhaaj. "Would the Undercity accept their presence?"

They'll hate it, Bhaaj thought. Given that she'd doubted Vaj would agree to anything less, though, she'd prepared her people for this possibility. "Three Majda guards can come. No uniforms. They should dress like us, simple clothes designed for durability."

Angel spoke in the terse Undercity dialect. "Maybe not bring weapons." Her gaze glinted. "Gangers steal."

Bhaaj almost swore. Sure, high-powered guns would be more tempting to her people than gold, but they'd deal with it. They didn't need Vaj finding another reason to get worried. "We shouldn't have a problem. Three Dust Knights led by the man Ruzik will also escort Colonel Majda. My people hold them in the highest regard. It will be a sign of honor to Lavinda that they give her protection. All the Dust Knights will uphold that vow, not just those who work with Ruzik."

"Ruzik?" Vaj motioned at Angel. "Are you talking about her husband's *gang*?"

Well, yah. That was another factoid better avoided. "The Dust Knights are the martial arts circle I established. It includes both young students and adults earning higher-level belts. Angel and her husband received their first-degree black belts last year." Bhaaj nodded to Vaj as one martial arts teacher to another, even though Vaj didn't teach anyone anything martial except how to obey orders. "One of their testers was Randall Miyashiro, your tykado master here at the palace."

"Ah, yes." Vaj sounded a fraction less recalcitrant. "Randall speaks well of your students."

What amazed Bhaaj most wasn't the General's nod to Miyashiro's high position, but the cognitive dissonance of hearing the most conservative matriarch alive speak with respect for a man's judgment in matters of combat. The days when barbaric queens kept their men in seclusion had long ago vanished, replaced by a supposedly egalitarian society where men had equal rights. Employers, politicians, influencers, and most everyone else gave at least lip service to the idea because they wanted to avoid becoming the mesh-media's favorite hate object. The Majdas, however, didn't give a rat's ass about controversy. They still secluded their princes, unrepentant in their conviction that men should stay hidden while women ran the universe, and if people didn't like it, tough.

Except.

The general served as a joint commander for a male Imperator. Almost as many men as women served under her, and if she acted against them, the backlash could threaten even her position. So Vaj dealt with it, the "it" being that she had to treat the men as equal to the women. Besides, she was no idiot. When she decided to hire a tykado expert to train her security forces, she wanted the best. That he happened to be male was, in her view, an unfortunate anomaly, but that didn't stop her. She offered him an unprecedented salary, and Randall Miyashiro became the only male tykado master in the history of Majda.

"I'm glad Master Miyashiro thinks well of them," Bhaaj said.

Vaj frowned at her. She frowned at her sisters, first Lavinda, then Corejida, then Lavinda again for good measure. Finally she said, "Very well. Three Majda guards."

Glancing at Bhaaj, Lavinda gave the barest nod. Good. They'd passed the first hurdle.

As the Majda sisters discussed the visit, Bhaaj considered their next step. They had to face the Undercity, which the rest of the Imperialate considered the lowest of the low. The media loved to make villains out of her people, who had no voice to protest. They wouldn't have known how to object even if they'd realized the rest of humanity despised them. They hid their true culture, a world of great beauty that existed within their crushing poverty.

Bhaaj wanted to improve matters.

This trip had resulted from her attempts. Her people would never accept charity, so a few years ago, she'd arranged an exchange; in return for a day of free medical care and food, they'd let the military test them as *Kyle operators*. Not that people in the Undercity cared what "Kyle" meant. Bhaaj had given up trying to explain that it referred to humans with the neurological mutations needed to operate tech from the ancient Ruby Empire. In truth, *no one* understood those rare machines that had survived the Ruby collapse. Scholars wrote no end of papers about the subject which, when stripped to basics, said, *What the hell? How can you mash neuroscience, math, and mysticism into one discipline?*

No matter. The Imperialate could use the few remaining Ruby machines that still worked. The result? Almost instant communication across star-spanning distances. It created their sole advantage over the other empire that dominated the stars—the Traders, those narcissistic psychopaths who viewed galactic domination as their gods-given right. Traders had no Kyle tech or trained operators, which meant their interstellar communications crawled compared to the Imperialate. For that reason—and only that reason—the Imperialate survived against them.

The Undercity had no idea. Their ancestors had taken their introverted selves underground, choosing isolation over the sunlight. They'd left the rest of humanity to rampage in barbaric splendor until the Ruby Empire exploded in the flames of war and plunged into five thousand years of dark ages. Now humans had spread across the stars again. To survive, the Imperialate needed Kyles, but for reasons science hadn't yet solved, they were almost impossible to clone. Not that most people wanted that dubious honor. The neurological changes that defined Kyles also made their minds painfully sensitive. They were empaths. Only one in ten thousand humans qualified as a full Kyle, driving the military to seek them anywhere. No one expected to find many in the ruins beneath the desert, but the government was desperate enough to try.

On that day, they learned the truth.

One in three Undercity citizens was an empath.

Bhaaj finally understood. Her ancestors had retreated underground because they couldn't bear the mental pressure of their brutal ancestors. They chose isolation instead, living, dying, and loving in the dark. It concentrated their traits until now they gave birth to Kyles at a rate three thousand times that of normal populations. Suddenly the Imperialate—which had dismissed, ridiculed, and ignored the Undercity for centuries—said, *Hey, let's be friends.*

Convincing General Majda to allow this visit had proved difficult, but doable. They now had a more difficult task, maybe an impossible one.

They had to convince the Undercity.

CHAPTER II
The Statue

Bhaaj stood with Lavinda inside the cave known as the Foyer, both of them pretending they didn't notice all the other people hulking there, three guards from the Majda police and all four members of Ruzik's dust gang, including Angel. Rippled walls surrounded them, and the ceiling arched high over their heads, lost in small stalactites that hung down like stone icicles.

"This is part of the Undercity?" Lavinda asked. "It's beautiful."

One of Ruzik's gang gave a dismissive snort, the man Byte-2, named after his father Byte. The fourth member of Ruzik's gang, a woman called Tower for her height, smirked at Lavinda. Standing by the wall with his muscular arms crossed, Ruzik scowled at Tower and Byte-2. Their posture changed almost invisibly, just enough to show they didn't miss his silent reproach: *Quit dissing our guest.*

Although Lavinda acted as if she didn't notice, Bhaaj had no doubt the colonel realized she'd managed to start her visit by saying something her reluctant hosts considered stupid.

Pretending it hadn't happened, Bhaaj spoke in a conversational voice. "This isn't actually the Undercity." She motioned to the archway where they'd entered the Foyer. Beyond it, they could see the narrow street they'd taken to this cave. The lane stretched away into the mist, bordered on either side by faded vendor stalls. The merchants in those booths worked here because they couldn't afford a better location farther up the street. They peddled cheap food and trinkets to the few tourists who ignored the signs warning them away from this area. Farther up, the lane turned into a luxurious tourist attraction called the Concourse, with trendy cafés, glitzy nightclubs, and boutiques. Visitors thronged the boulevard, thrilled for that supposed taste of the most notorious slum in the Imperialate, everyone spending huge sums on fake "Undercity" goods, making the Cries merchants rich while the people who actually lived in the Undercity died in the dark.

"The Tourist Bureau claims the Concourse is part of the Undercity," Bhaaj said. "It isn't, though. This entrance is—" She thought for a moment. "It's like an air lock that separates the Undercity from the above-city."

Lavinda nodded and left it at that. Her guards watched Ruzik's gang like they wanted to whack them over the head and toss them in jail. Standing together, Ruzik and Byte-2 looked like copies, Byte-2 leaner and with a sharper face. They were brothers, Byte-2 three years older than Ruzik, nearly twenty-five, the same as Angel. Ruzik led their gang despite his youth, mainly because he was smarter than most anyone else anywhere.

The tats on his biceps showed his namesake, the giant ruziks that roamed the desert above. People from Earth had reacted with surreal delight when they saw images of the big lizards. *T. rex!* they'd cried. Bhaaj had to admit, a ruzik did look like a *Tyrannosaurus rex*. Scales covered a ruzik's hide, though, and they wielded more powerful front arms than their dino relatives. Maybe whoever stranded humans here had engineered them from DNA they'd found on Earth. Bhaaj didn't see the point, except that ruziks were more suited to Raylicon than softer species like, say, the obstinate humans who insisted on living in this desolate place. In any case, the badass lizards suited Ruzik and his gang.

Lavinda gestured, taking in the entire Foyer. "This place doesn't look like people use it."

"We don't," Bhaaj said.

Lavinda squinted at her. "Then how do you leave the Undercity?"

Behind Lavinda, Tower started to laugh, then shut her mouth when Ruzik glowered. Angel showed no reaction, just stayed impassive. Ruzik knew Lavinda from previous cases he'd worked with Bhaaj, and he seemed to like the colonel. It didn't surprise Bhaaj. He'd always been a good judge of character.

Bhaaj said only, "The cops throw my people in jail if they catch them on the Concourse."

"The police?" Lavinda glanced at the three Majda officers, all women, of course, given that Vaj had appointed them. They'd dressed in black today, with nothing to hint at their authority except the heavy guns holstered on their hips. "You do this?" Lavinda asked. "Imprison people just for leaving the Undercity?"

"No, ma'am," one of the guards said, Captain Morah if Bhaaj remembered correctly. "We don't patrol here. Major Bhaajan is talking about the Concourse police force."

Lavinda turned her laser focus on Bhaaj. "You're saying the Concourse police make anyone who lives here stay underground?"

Well, they tried. No one could stop her people from sneaking out. Of course they used hidden exits, secret places where they went back and forth to the Concourse. They sure as hell never came through this too-obvious portal into forbidden territory.

Bhaaj spoke blandly. "The Concourse police protect the shoppers." She had so much more to say, but she held back. Harsh words would just blow up this visit and ruin their chances to improve the brutal poverty that fueled her anger. Lavinda didn't push. It was one reason Bhaaj had begun to trust her; the colonel picked up cues that her sisters had no idea even existed.

"Need to go," Angel said in the taciturn Undercity dialect. She switched to accented but otherwise perfect Cries speech. "I have my first day of work for the Kyle Division in the city today. I don't want to be late."

"You go," Bhaaj told her. "We're good."

Angel nodded, then turned and gave Ruzik the barest hint of a smile. His impassive look softened as he met her gaze. With that swooning declaration of love finished, she considered the Majda security officers, who looked ready to clap her in power-cuffs. Bhaaj could imagine her thought: *Tough for you, key clinkers.* That Angel held back saying it boded well. Today she'd even dressed like a slick, and she carried city ID. Bhaaj's wrecking ball of a protégée was learning to give a convincing appearance of civilized behavior.

With a glint of satisfaction, Angel walked past the Majda guards, leaving the Foyer through an archway bordered by exquisite carvings that few people even knew existed, let alone appreciated for their great archeological value. And so she headed on her way, setting a new benchmark, becoming the first civilian to gain employment in Cries straight out of the Undercity.

Lifting her hand, Bhaaj invited Lavinda to an exit across from the one Angel had used. A second archway stood there, another marvel of ancient architecture. They headed through it, following a dirt path that widened beyond the arch. Bhaaj and Lavinda walked together, both of them carrying packs, with guards and Dust Knights before and behind them.

A lamppost stood up ahead, a pole of antiqued metal topped by a curved hook. Old-fashioned and well-wrought, the lantern hanging from the hook spread its light across the path.

"That's lovely," Lavinda said. "It looks like the Concourse lamps."

"The city installed it." Bhaaj's voice cooled. "It's the only thing they've provided here."

"They don't light the Undercity?"

"For fuck's sake," Byte-2 said up ahead. He glanced back to add more, then stopped when Ruzik gave him a look that threatened mayhem. Closing his mouth, Byte-2 turned forward again.

"We have an agreement with Cries," Bhaaj said. "If we maintain this lamp and the sign they put on it"—she motioned toward a plaque on the pole of the lamppost—"they won't send police here."

Lavinda went to the pole and read the plaque, a burnished piece of artwork engraved with blunt words: *Do not go beyond this point. If you have come this far, you have entered the most dangerous area of the Undercity. This region is off-limits to visitors. You continue at risk to your life.* It was written both in the Cries dialect and in Skolian Flag, a second language for all Skolians, the official tongue of the Imperialate.

The colonel stared at the plaque far longer than she needed to read its words. She finally turned to Bhaaj. "Your people agreed to post that notice?"

"My ancestors, actually. That plaque has been here for centuries." Bhaaj shrugged. "We suggested the wording, just to make sure no one misunderstood."

"But why?" Lavinda asked. "Do you all *want* to keep out everyone else?" She paused. "I understand that my initial suggestions to help, years ago, were idiotic. You don't need your children dumped in state-sponsored schools, offered work as low-paid laborers in the desert or menial jobs in the city. But those aren't the only ways for outsiders to help."

Bhaaj blinked, at a loss for words. Majdas never called themselves idiotic. Period.

"I realize we have a long way to go with your people," Lavinda added. "If we do the work, though, our interactions could help us both."

"My hope, too." Bhaaj nodded to her, then continued down the path accompanied by Lavinda and their squad of human punching machines.

Mercifully, Lavinda let it go, which was fortunate, because Bhaaj doubted she could say more without giving offense. None of her people wanted intruders from the above-city here. Hell, many of her people didn't even believe Cries existed, at least not the images they'd found of a glorious city with towers sparkling in all that impossible light. *She* hadn't believed it either, not until that day, at age fifteen, when she'd snuck all the way to the end of the Concourse, over a kilometer distant from the Foyer. She'd stepped through a shimmering film that filled the archway there—

Into sunlight.

Bhaaj would never forget that moment when she stood under the endless blue sky. No way could she absorb it all: wind on her face, sun on her skin, wide-open spaces, desert stretching everywhere. She'd turned in a circle, struggling to take it in—and a new sight had come into view, distant and bathed in the limitless sunshine.

The City of Cries.

Those shining towers were *real*.

Somehow she'd walked to the city. Finding the army recruitment center was harder than she expected, even after she'd looked up how to get there. The sights, sounds, smells, the *sky* so overwhelmed her, she barely managed to think. Yet despite it all, she reached her goal and enlisted. Or she tried. They said she was too young, that they could only take her at sixteen. Even then, she'd have to spend two more years in school, which they considered a good thing, because she failed all their arcane "academic exams" except math. They didn't know what to make of her intelligence tests, which listed her as brilliant. When they talked about finding her a foster family, after she stupidly told them that she had no parents to stop her from enlisting, she'd walked out.

Bhaaj went back the day she turned sixteen. She'd spent that year stealing time on the Cries education meshes, enough that she passed all her exams, including top marks in math. The army stuck her in school anyway because of her age, but eventually she shipped out into a universe that hated her Undercity origins, that called her subhuman. She'd taken great pleasure in proving them wrong, especially in making the supposedly impossible climb into the officer ranks. Twenty years later, she came home with the dream of improving life for her people. So yah, she was an idealist. Or an idiot. No matter. She tried anyway.

Of course she told Lavinda none of that. Too personal. They remained silent, following the path with its slight downward slope. When they'd gone beyond the light from the lamppost, the Majda guards switched on their gauntlet lamps.

Bhaaj stopped, turning to them. "Lights off."

The Majda captain stared at her, impassive. Damn. Bhaaj wished they'd sent Captain Duane Ebersole instead. She and Duane had a lot in common, both always having to prove themselves. He offered a perfect example of the saying that a man had to be twice as good as a woman for the Majdas to consider him equal. Duane had done it and then some. Even so. When it came to protecting her sister, Vaj Majda considered it better to send women. The captain of that illustrious trio met Bhaaj's gaze with an implacable stare and left her lamp glowing.

Bhaaj sensed Ruzik tensing to fight. He didn't give two shits about the sex of his opponents. No one in the Undercity cared. You didn't survive poverty by telling half the population they couldn't do squat. Only the wealthy could afford such irrationally restrictive customs.

Lavinda spoke quickly, before anyone punched anyone else. "All right. But how do we continue without light?"

Diplomacy, Bhaaj reminded herself. "My apology." She even gave Captain Morah a respectful nod. "I should have explained."

The captain squinted, seeming more confused than anything else. Her tensed posture eased.

"We do use lights," Bhaaj told them. "But only a certain type." In other words, whatever they could scrounge or steal, nothing like the high-end tech carried by Majda forces. "If you arrive with tech beyond anything we use, people will react as if you're intruders." And they'd like nothing better than to beat up what they saw as rich, boastful trespassers.

Captain Morah didn't look convinced. "You have an alternative?"

"Like this." Bhaaj flicked on the light stylus hanging by a chain around her neck. A sphere of radiance surrounded her, dimmer and more golden than the harsh light from the Majda lamps.

Morah laughed. "You're kidding, right?"

Bhaaj wanted to get pissed off, except she could tell the captain meant well. She *felt* the guard's reaction. Damn it, she had no desire to be an empath. She had enough trouble figuring out her own emotions without dealing with other people's moods. Growing up in the Undercity, crushed under the weight of sickness, starvation, violence and death—no. She couldn't bear to absorb all that pain. In her youth, to survive, she'd buried her Kyle ability. The army, however, had other ideas. Their brain-benders woke up her brain and now they wanted to train her. Bah.

Bhaaj glanced at Lavinda and found her smiling, just barely, but enough to make Bhaaj scowl. Lavinda's face immediately became neutral. It made no difference. Going to those brain-benders did have one advantage: they'd taught Bhaaj how to refine the instinctive mental protections she'd learned in her youth without realizing it. Now she "slammed down" her mental walls. It spurred her brain to produce more of the neurotransmitters that blocked other empaths from detecting her moods.

Lavinda winced, then gave her a look that anyone, Kyle or not, could read: *That wasn't necessary.*

Sorry, she thought. Lavinda couldn't detect thoughts, but she'd probably get a sense of Bhaaj's intent, that she hadn't meant to use so much force.

"Are you sure you want us to turn off our lights?" Captain Morah was saying.

Lavinda tilted her head at Bhaaj. "Follow her lead."

Morah motioned to the other Majda guards, and they switched off their lights, leaving only the sphere of light around Bhaaj. Ruzik tapped on a scavenged piece of tech-mech hanging around his neck, and a dim, golden light glowed around him as well.

That done, they headed along the path again. The top of a spiral staircase soon appeared out of the darkness. Memories flooded Bhaaj. She'd stood here the day she turned sixteen, facing Dig, her closest friend, the girl she'd loved like a sister. Dig had wanted her to stay. They'd said so little, but a world of pain lay beneath their taciturn words. As much as Bhaaj regretted leaving the people she loved, she *needed* to go. Wanderlust had pulled her like a steel cord. Yet the Undercity would always live within her, even now when she could move among circles she'd never known existed in her youth.

Bhaaj stopped at the stairs, next to an ancient statue. It showed Azu Bullom, a god worshipped thousands of years ago in the Ruby Empire. He had a man's head, with horns that spiraled around his ears and the body of a great cat. Stone wings lifted from his back in a huge span of chiseled feathers, like motion frozen into stone.

As everyone gathered at the stairs, Lavinda said, "That's a remarkable figure. Who carved it?"

"We don't know." Bhaaj fought her ingrained tendency to say nothing. On principle, her people told outsiders zilch about the Undercity. She'd invited Lavinda here, though, and she needed to offer more than zilch. "It's been here longer than any of us knows. Our sculptors maintain it. We have no weather underground, and we don't often use these stairs, so it doesn't get much wear."

Lavinda spoke quietly. "It's one of the most striking examples of early Ruby Empire sculpture I've come across outside of a museum. And it just sits here, unseen?"

"Yah." Bhaaj spoke carefully. "We feel it's safer if Cries doesn't know about it."

Lavinda exhaled. "Yes, I can see that. People in Cries would either want to remove it or else invite tourists to visit it here, causing damage."

Bhaaj hadn't expected Lavinda to understand. She nodded with respect to the colonel, then headed down the stairs, aware of the others following. Their footsteps scratched on the gritty stone, sending swirls of dust into the air that rose at first, and then drifted downward.

Halfway to the next level, Bhaaj came to a place where just a few days ago, no stairs had existed, just broken pieces of stone sticking out in jagged angles. True to their word, the Knights had completed their repairs, working with one of the best builders in the Undercity.

She continued on.

Down and around.

Down and around.

At the bottom, Bhaaj stepped onto a flat area at the base of the stairs. Light surrounded her, with darkness beyond that dim glow. She moved aside so the others could gather around her.

Byte-2 glanced at Ruzik. When Ruzik nodded, Byte-2 took off, jogging into the darkness.

"Where is he going?" Captain Morah asked.

Wait for it, Bhaaj thought.

After a moment, Lavinda said, "Major Bhaajan?"

Wait for it, Bhaaj thought.

A light flared in the distance. An instant later, more lights flared, filling their world with radiance—and revealing a wonderland. Light from every direction struck crystals, mica, and reflective grains of sand, all of it embedded in stone, creating hundreds, thousands, *millions* of points sparkling like a host of stars, a nebula created underground. The world glittered.

"Saints almighty," one of the Majda guards murmured.

Yah, Bhaaj thought. As a child, she'd taken this spectacular display for granted, but in the years since, nothing she'd seen anywhere else could match this hidden world.

The air felt cool, maybe another reason her people had chosen to live in these ruins, the remains of an alien civilization that had long ago vanished. Go deep enough, and the temperature became livable even when the eighty-hour days scorched the surface.

Bhaaj waited, letting their visitors take in the view. They'd reached what her people called the *aqueducts,* though she'd never figured out why. These canals seemed too large to act as a water transportation system. Hell, Raylicon didn't have enough water *anywhere* to flow through such giant conduits. This tunnel measured twenty meters across and forty high, supported by a system of braced arches designed by long-dead architects. Her group stood on a midwalk, a path against the wall about three meters wide and halfway up the canal.

Some thirty paces away, Byte-2 stood by a torch in a wall sconce. His light had flared first; the rest had come from the Dust Knights waiting for his signal, all stationed by torches along the midwalks.

They wore darks tops and trousers, also heavy boots. Their gauntlets glinted in the torchlight, creations utterly different from the sanitized smart bracelets sold in Cries. Many had tattoos, cyber implants, and battle scars. Silent and unsmiling, terrifying without even trying, they stood guard on the Undercity. Bhaaj knew them, understood them. She'd *been* them in her youth. Never had she lost that heart, not even now when she pretended to be civilized for her upscale clients.

Yet for all their impressive appearance, the Knights played second-fiddle to the canal itself. Towering columns supported the tunnel, some natural rock formations, others created by ancient builders. Human sculptors had carved them into statues of the deities Bhaaj's ancestors worshipped during the Ruby Empire. Another figure of Azu Bullom rose by the stairs, his body that of an animal that had existed only in myth—

Until eighty years ago.

On that day, a Skolian battle cruiser encountered a tiny scout ship exploring the stars. The cruiser's evolving intelligence, or EI, easily breached the helpless scout's systems. Its terrified crew had good reason for their fear; the officers onboard the massive cruiser assumed the scout had come to survey territory for potential conquerors. They prepared to imprison the invaders—

And then they found an image in the scout's library that changed human history forever.

A jaguar.

Azu Bullom.

It took the cruiser's invading EI only moments to verify that the animal—this *jaguar*—originated on a world independent of any Skolian or Trader colony, a world with a documented human history going back hundreds of thousands of years. In that instant, a six-thousand-year-old myth became reality.

Earth existed.

Humanity found her lost children that day, six millennia after an unknown race had stranded Bhaaj's ancestors on Raylicon. The reality, however, wasn't the idyll they'd had imagined. Earth's people had nearly destroyed their sublime world in what they called the Virus Wars. It had decimated the population, wiping out entire cultures and corrupting a substantial portion of their records. Desperate, they'd reached for the stars, searching for new worlds where they could live.

Bhaaj would never forget the incredulous words of a much younger Vaj Majda during the first summit between the Imperialate and Earth's emissaries. *You destroyed humanity's home world, and now you think you can just find more? We have no more! We fight for every slice of celestial real estate we can coax into livable territory. You had paradise—and you idiots threw it away.*

Those words hadn't made her popular on Earth, and the Imperialate diplomats had quickly withdrawn her from the talks. Even so. Vaj had given voice to what many of Earth's lost children thought, one of the few things the Imperialate and the Traders had ever agreed about.

Yah, right, Bhaaj thought. *Who are we to criticize?* Despite the lack of Earthlike planets, her displaced children had multiplied into the trillions, flinging their overpopulated selves across thousands of planets and habitats. And what had they done with that great achievement? Created world-slagging armies that could destroy humanity. While the Trader Aristos committed genocide, both human and planetary, and the Imperialate sought to crush their empire, Earth was recovering, tended by an ashamed populace that sought to heal their world from the crucible of their own violence.

The Virus Wars had obliterated any clue to the origins of the humans who settled Raylicon. Neither the Skolians nor Traders had any success when they compared their ancient stories to what remained of Earth's historical records.

Bhaaj wondered, though, if the Undercity might offer clues that other comparisons missed. The first humans on Raylicon had created this artwork. Byte-2 stood by a sculpture of the fire goddess Ixa Quelia carved into the wall. Larger than life, she rose more than three heads taller than him. Her hair streamed along the stone like an untamed celebration of freedom, and a sword hung from her belt, glittering with embedded crystals. She had the chiseled features, high cheekbones, and large eyes associated with the nobility. Hell, she could have been Lavinda's sister, if Lavinda had looked wild instead of civilized. Beyond her, a statue of the war goddess Chaac brandished the axe of lightning and carried a shield painted with gold, red, and white rings. Across the canal, Izam Na Quetza, the winged god of transcendence and flight, stood with his spirit companion Na-quetz, a bird with green and yellow feathers. The statues existed as a haunting memorial to an ancient time preserved only in the hidden byways of the aqueducts, lost to the rest of humanity.

Newer sculptures stood in the lower half of the canal. The one across from them showed four modern-day warriors, two women and two men, all facing forward. One woman held up a knife, poised to strike. The man next to her had a massive gun, what looked like a military power rifle, a weapon that supposedly no one here knew about, at least not legally. The other two had smaller guns, and they all looked ready for combat. Muscled and powerful, they were barely more than children by Skolian standards. In the Undercity, where you grew up fast or died, they ranked as battle-scarred adults.

Lavinda spoke quietly. "This is incredible."

"Yah," one of her guards murmured. Although most of them continued to look around with undisguised amazement, one had turned to watch Bhaaj. In fact, so had Ruzik and Tower, both with a sense of waiting. Odd. They seemed expectant, even worried. The Majda guard was staring at a patch on Bhaaj's tank top just above the waist, a circular emblem of the Pharaoh's Army. Bhaaj had picked up the shirt at an army surplus store, but she saw no reason to gape at it. Plenty of people in Cries wore army surplus clothes.

Bhaaj squinted at Ruzik. "What?"

He tilted his head toward the other side of the canal, up ahead rather than across from them. Bhaaj turned—

The statue stood on the floor of the canal, one of the taller-than-life variety carved into the stone. The last time Bhaaj had come here, nothing but a wall had existed in that place. This new image showed a woman with her arms raised in perfect tykado form, ready to fight, a warrior with long legs and muscled arms. She lifted her head in defiance, her curls streaming along the wall in a mirror of the Ixa Quelia statue across the canal. The woman in the new sculpture had a strong face, beautiful and powerful. She wore a muscle shirt, trousers, boots, and heavy gauntlets.

The emblem of the Pharaoh's Army showed on her shirt just above the waist.

Not only was it the only statue in the Undercity that displayed a modern military insignia, but it was also the only one with a fighter in a tykado stance. No one here had known tykado existed prior to four years ago, when Bhaaj founded the Dust Knights. The Knights studied the martial art, both the fighting moves and its philosophies of balance, with violence as a last resort. Their teacher worked with them almost every day.

Their teacher. Bhaaj.

"Well, fuck me," Bhaaj said, ever the soul of articulate discourse.

The hint of a smile showed on Ruzik's face. He, Tower, and Byte-2 looked satisfied, as if she had made some pithy statement. Actually, it was pithy by Undercity standards.

"New," Ruzik explained. "Artists finish today."

Bhaaj nodded to them. Enough said. The Undercity had given her one of its greatest honors, more than she'd ever expected or deserved. The story of her reaction here, her open mouth, her three words, it would all go into the Whisper Mill and spread everywhere, nothing too much, but yah, more than the usual. A good and fitting reaction.

Only Bhaaj would know the truth, that in the privacy of her home when no one could see, she would shed tears in her gratified disbelief that they honored her this way, that somehow, her efforts to improve life for her recalcitrant, beautiful, violent, gifted people was making a difference.

CHAPTER III
Beyond the Wall

Lit only by the lamps Bhaaj and Ruzik carried, the narrow passage wound through the labyrinth of the Maze. The trip felt endless, like one of those frustrating dreams that offered riches at the end of a journey you could never finish. Eventually, though, the path widened into a chamber where natural columns of stone held up the ceiling. On the left, rocky ledges rose into shadows in a staircase created by nature instead of humans, including that it ended at a blank wall. Almost no one else knew about this place. Why would they? Stairs that led to a dead end had no use.

Maybe.

Bhaaj walked up the stairs to the wall and knelt. Running her fingers along the bottom of the barrier, she pushed in several places, using a code she knew by heart. It remained only in her mind, hidden from any strangers who might seek the true Undercity, a mythical world no outsiders could even find, let alone enter. The bang of stone hitting stone sounded somewhere, loud in the silence. An instant later, the wall in front of her shifted, grinding rock against rock as it rose upward. When it finished, an open space a few handspans wide showed between its bottom edge and the ground.

Standing up, Bhaaj faced the group at the bottom of the stairs, Lavinda and her guards with Ruzik and his Knights. She indicated the space. "We go."

Lavinda squinted at her. "You want us to crawl under that wall?"

Bhaaj doubted Lavinda had ever crawled in her life. Hell, as a baby she'd probably just stood up one day and strode around, confident in her dominion over her playroom.

"Yah," Bhaaj said. "We go."

Lavinda came forward, looking intrigued. "You're speaking your language with me. You've never done that before."

Huh. Bhaaj hadn't realized she'd slipped into the terse Undercity dialect. Most times, she spoke to Lavinda in either Skolian Flag, the universal tongue of the Imperialate, or Iotic, a language used only by royalty and nobility. Interesting. Apparently, she trusted the Majda colonel more than she'd have believed possible a few years ago, when they'd first met.

"You come. See Undercity," Bhaaj told her. "So I speak Undercity."

Lavinda nodded, no excess words. Maybe she was learning to communicate in their dialect. Or maybe she was just being Lavinda, with that legendary Majda restraint.

Bhaaj dropped to the ground and slid under the barrier, scraping along the ground. On the other side, she stood up and brushed the grit off her clothes. One by one, everyone else followed. Lavinda seemed more bemused than anything else. No surprise there. Over the past few years, Bhaaj had realized the colonel never expected special treatment. In the military Lavinda had used her first two names only, without the Majda surname. No one had known her identity, so they treated her like any other soldier, including sending her into battle. Years later, when the brass promoted her to lieutenant colonel, General Vaj Majda finally revealed the truth. Lavinda had risen high enough by then to interact with people who knew the general. Anyone with half a brain could see their resemblance.

The Majda guards looked royally pissed about dragging their butts under a wall, far more than the actual royal. Even so. They did what they had to do. After everyone gathered around Bhaaj, she pushed the wall back into place and resumed the climb, leading her pack up and around the curving staircase. At the top, they entered a foyer with a stone floor, walls and ceiling. An archway stood across from them, one bordered with tessellated carvings that looked modern, but had a style similar to the ancient work they'd seen elsewhere.

Two people waited in that archway. Dara and Weaver.

Relief washed over Bhaaj. They'd come to greet Lavinda, verifying their approval of the visit. The woman, Dara, was Bhaaj's closest friend. Dara worked as a bartender in the casino run by the notorious Mean Jak, a glitzy hideaway he called the Black Mark. Normally it was the only way city slicks could visit the Undercity, and then only with an invite harder to finagle than a trip to the wealthiest mansion in Cries. They had to come blindfolded, led by Undercity guides, with sound-deadening tech for their ears and blockers for their tech-mech, to make sure they had no idea how to come and go from the casino. Even with that, Jak periodically moved his establishment, using high-end nanobots he'd purchased with his ill-gotten gains. They could tear down his casino in less than an hour and rebuild it elsewhere almost as fast.

The Black Mark served the elite of an empire, illegal as all hell on Raylicon, where gambling violated a slew of laws, but who cared? As long as Jak kept his biz hidden, the authorities in Cries would never crack down on him. Too many of them frequented his sensual den of vice.

Today, Dara hadn't worn her glittering casino outfit. She looked far more prosaic in trousers, a tank top, and boots. Weaver, Dara's husband, stood at her side, both of them dark haired and dark eyed. They looked *healthy*, a rarity for Bhaaj's people. How? Because Dara worked for Jak. He hired only from the Undercity, and he paid well in filtered water, food, and health services. He took whatever money the decadent wealthy of an empire chose to squander in his casino and used it to help their people step out of poverty. It didn't matter how vile the Cries authorities considered him. The Undercity called him a hero.

Even so. Bhaaj sometimes wanted to hit Jak over the head for taking so many damn risks. Goddess only knew why she'd married him. Maybe she had rocks in her head, because for some inexplicable reason, she loved his exasperating self.

Dara nodded to them. "Eh, Bhaaj." Two words for one greeting. She was talkative today. She also nodded to Lavinda and said, "Eh."

Fortunately, Lavinda didn't know enough of their dialect to realize Dara had showed Bhaaj more honor than a royal Majda heir. Regardless, she'd given Lavinda respect, and that was what mattered.

Then again, maybe Lavinda did realize. She nodded first to Dara, then to Dara's husband Weaver. She didn't inflict any Cries verbosity on them, none of the *My greetings. How goes your day?* business that people took for granted everywhere else in the universe.

Dara raised her arm, inviting them to the archway. Bhaaj and crew followed her into a large room, a welcoming space filled with Weaver's art. He'd carved benches out of rock formations in the walls and sculpted them with dragons, their wings curving along the stone in pleasing patterns. Rose cushions softened the furniture. His tapestries glowed with scenes of life in the aqueducts, all in vivid threads of blue, purple, red, and green, with metallic accents. So far, he was the only Undercity native who'd tackled the onerous process of getting a permit to sell his work on the Concourse. It turned out to be worth the trouble. He sold true Undercity art, not the junk created by above-city vendors, and the tourists loved his creations.

Recently Weaver had sold his first large tapestry. It earned him many credits, what most people called byte-bucks, or bykes for short. He had no idea what it meant; the Undercity economy worked on bargains and trade. You couldn't *see* bykes, so they meant nothing to most people here. His teenaged daughter Darjan, however, kenned them just fine. With Bhaaj's help, she set up an account for him at a Cries bank and sent his bykes rolling into his savings.

Those earnings brought in a long-term supply of filtered water for his family and circle, and smaller amenities, too, like the lamp with its graceful stained-glass shade that stood in one corner of this room, shedding light in frequencies that helped plants grow without sunlight. Potted flowers set about the room sported pink blossoms, bred by self-taught Undercity botanists to survive in the aqueducts. Curtains of blown-glass beads sparkled in archways to the left and right, and handwoven rugs softened the floor. But wait—what had happened to the water purifier? It usually sat in one corner. Weaver must have moved it to another room, freeing up more space here in the family room. He created this beauty, looking after the home while Dara tended bar in Jak's infamous casino.

Sixteen-year-old Darjan was seated on cushions at a table with the preteen Crinkles, both girls playing a game where they swiped at holo-gems floating in the air. As Bhaaj entered, the girls jumped up and bowed from the waist, the greeting of tykado students to their *sabneem*, a Skolian word for fighting mentor. With the Dust Knights, it took on meanings never intended elsewhere. The Undercity considered Bhaaj a gang leader, one who headed all the Knights instead of the usual quartet of two women and two men. Bhaaj could just imagine what the Interstellar Tykado Federation would say to that idea. She nodded to her students, giving them permission to be at ease, or whatever non-military thing you did for adolescent gang members.

You need a new name for the dusters, Max thought to Bhaaj. **Something other than gang.**

Ho! Sometimes she forgot Max, the EI in her gauntlets. He linked to her brain via sockets in her wrist and bio-threads in her body.

You've been quiet today, she thought to him, tech-created telepathy courtesy of bio-electrodes that fired her neurons in response to his signals and sent him messages from her brain in the reverse process.

You haven't had many thoughts strong enough to initiate contact. Max's response took on an amused quality. **Except that one about Jak.**

I'm glad you find my love life so entertaining, Bhaaj mentally growled.

I'm an EI. I don't experience a sense of entertainment, Max informed her, despite sounding thoroughly entertained.

As Bhaaj stepped aside to let Lavinda come forward, both Darjan and Crinkles bowed to their royal guest. Bhaaj released a breath she hadn't realized she was holding. Good. They showed respect to the Majda queen. Well, technically Lavinda wasn't a queen, but people called her that anyway and referred to Vaj as the Matriarch to distinguish her higher rank from her sisters.

Dara indicated the plushest set of cushions on the carpeted floor and spoke to Lavinda. "For you." For the rest of them, she motioned to other pillows strewn around the room, plump cushions brocaded in rose, purple, and blue. The air smelled good, from both the incense sticks in the corner and from the faint scent of the nontoxic aromatic chemicals in Undercity dust. The sticks sent up tendrils of smoke that curled into the air and escaped through air vents in the ceiling. Darjan and Crinkles settled on the floor by their table, watching their elders with undisguised fascination.

Their seating arrangements didn't faze Lavinda. Ironically, unlike most people in Cries, who used civilized chairs, the Majdas liked to relax on ornate pillows around low tables in their palace, as had their ancestors. Lavinda and Bhaaj settled into the cushions with Dara's family while one of the Majda guards and Byte-2 stood by the entrance. Ruzik, Captain Morah, and the other two guards took up positions in the foyer, the only way into this secret haven.

After sliding off her pack, Lavinda took out two large bottles of filtered water. She offered them to Dara and Weaver, speaking in the Undercity dialect. "My thanks for your invite." Her accent wasn't great, but she used the right number of syllables, one for most words, saying "invite" with two to stress the honor Dara and her family showed her. A three-syllable word indicated either ridicule or great respect. Any more syllables in one word became a joke or an insult, except the names *Undercity* and *aqueducts*, which deserved the high honor of their four syllables. Bhaaj had given up trying to explain to the army why her people found it hilarious when reps talked about "recruiting" them into the "Imperialate military."

Dara nodded to Lavinda, accepting the bargain; her family hosted the queen and in return she gave them water. When Bhaaj first suggested it, Lavinda had been mortified at the idea that two large bottles of water offered equitable thanks for their hospitality. No matter. She'd understand soon. In a world where naturally occurring water could kill you, the purified form had more worth than gold.

Taking the bottles, Weaver left the room via an inner archway. His passage through its curtain set the beads swinging until they sparkled in the lamplight, making soft music as the beads clinked together. He'd not only designed the curtains to please the eyes, but also the ears. Now he'd fill the handblown glasses he created with filtered water, offering his guests invaluable works of art to drink an invaluable liquid.

Dara spoke to Lavinda in an accented version of the above-city dialect, which she'd learned for her job in the casino. "Welcome to our home, Your Highness." She even smiled.

Lavinda loosened up enough to smile back, sort of, which was good, because by smiling Dara had just shown her a trust that no one else down here would bestow on their above-city invaders. Then again, Dara's teenaged daughter might if she felt like defying tradition, which Darjan tended to do all the time lately. The Undercity considered Darjan an adult at sixteen; in the general

Imperialate culture, she wouldn't reach her majority for another nine
years, at twenty-five.

Bhaaj, we have a problem, Max thought.

What's up?

Jak is on his way here.

What the hell? Jak knew he'd throw a monster wrench into the
already strained détente of this visit by showing up. It did him no
good, either. The last thing he wanted was to draw Majda attention
to his shady casino dealings. Bhaaj stood up fast.

"What's wrong?" Lavinda asked.

Bhaaj spoke in dialect. "Got more people."

"You can't go in there," someone said in the foyer. It sounded like
Captain Morah. "I said, stop! NOW."

Jak's voice came into the room as plainly as a growling dust-dino.
He spoke in the above-city dialect, his Undercity accent heavy but
his grammar perfect. "I need to see Major Bhaajan." He almost
sounded polite. Almost.

Morah spoke sharply. "Stay where you are!"

As Bhaaj reached the archway, the captain appeared in the
opening, and they both stopped with a jerk. Bhaaj could hear
everyone else getting up in the room behind her.

"He's my husband," Bhaaj told Morah.

The captain stared at her, all sign of her earlier thaw vanished.
"You're married to one of the worst crime lords on the planet?"

"For fuck's sake," Jak said from the foyer. His reaction might have
had more effect if he hadn't sounded so wickedly pleased by her
description. He was standing a few paces beyond the captain, a lean
man in black clothes with guards on either side of him, both
Lavinda's officers and Ruzik's gang.

Bhaaj kept her gaze on Captain Morah as she spoke in an even
voice. "I'm going to step past you so I can talk to him." She lifted her
hands. "I have no weapons."

Morah didn't move, just stood with her hand on the grip of her
holstered gun.

"Captain, let her by," Lavinda said.

Morah's clenched look suggested she'd rather shoot Jak and maybe
Bhaaj as well. After the barest pause, however, she stepped aside.

Bhaaj entered the foyer, keeping her hands down and visible. Of course she was armed, but none of it showed, neither the knife in her ankle sheath nor the mini-gun hidden in a small holster under her shirt. She watched Jak and he watched her, both of them silent. Tilting her head toward the far wall of the foyer, she walked in that direction. Jak joined her there, and they stood by a bench carved into a great lizard with its tail coiling around the legs of the seat.

"What?" Bhaaj asked in a low voice.

"Got ears to ground. Hear whisper." He regarded her steadily. "Vakaar make problem."

Bloody hell. Vakaar. That name belonged to one of the two Undercity drug cartels. Captain Morah had it wrong. Jak didn't rank among the worst crime bosses here. Raylicon was one of the few worlds that considered gambling illegal. Yah, Bhaaj had her issues with Jak's choice of career, which could involve addictions just as much as the drug trade, but when it came to breaking the law, the cartel queens had him beat by a brutal, murderous light-year.

Bhaaj spoke tightly. "What Vakaar want?"

"Break bargain," Jak said. "Want Majda."

"Damn it!" She didn't even try to lower her voice. Every guard in the foyer stiffened, and Lavinda's guards reached for their guns.

Bhaaj strode back to where Lavinda waited. "We've leaving. Now!"

"Why?" Lavinda asked. "We just got here."

Dara spoke firmly. "Cries queen welcome. My home, her home."

"I ken. We thank." Bhaaj's voice grated. "Vakaar not like. Want Majda."

Weaver stared at her. "Vakaar gave word. Agreed to visit."

"They lied," Bhaaj said.

"You mean the Vakaar drug cartel?" Lavinda asked. "I'd think the last thing they want is to draw attention to themselves from the Cries authorities." Dryly she added, "Especially my family."

"That's putting it mildly," Bhaaj said. "No one wants a war with Majda."

"Then why grab me?" Lavinda asked.

"I've no idea," Bhaaj admitted. "Maybe for a ransom."

"Not make sense," Ruzik said. "Cartels crazy, not stupid."

Bhaaj didn't get it either. Neither cartel wanted open warfare with Cries. Although the police periodically organized campaigns to rid the Undercity of drugs, it rarely worked except as a cosmetic measure. The cartels had bought off too many cops. Their tentacles extended everywhere, beyond the Undercity, even offworld. They also knew their uneasy balance with the Cries authorities could collapse if they pushed it even a little.

If either cartel killed Lavinda, all bets were off. General Vaj Majda hated betrayal of her family more than she hated the cartels, even more than she wanted détente with the Undercity. She'd descend like a nightmare on the shadowy world beneath her glistening empire. Obliterating the cartels would spread metaphorical earthquakes throughout both the Undercity and Cries, threatening the precarious balance humanity maintained with the killing biosphere of this world. The only way to finish the cartels was to destroy anything they could touch, above the ground as well as below, including resource-intensive measures needed to make this small part of the planet habitable. Only the Majdas had the wealth and influence to support those measures. If they withdrew their support, the City of Cries—a leading governmental center—would suffer, maybe even collapse. Everyone would lose.

The cartels *knew* that. Yah, the Vakaar boss was a sociopath, but she also had an intellect as sharp as the snap of a whip, a mind she kept clear of the shit she sold to the rest of the universe. She knew that crushing this visit would destroy her trade far more than any ransom could bring her.

Bhaaj glanced Jak, a silent invitation that he join them. The moment he stepped forward, all three Majda guards drew their guns. He stopped and raised his eyebrows at Captain Morah, but he didn't look at all fazed to have three trained killers ready to explode his sensuous self with bullets.

Bhaaj scowled at the captain. "He came to help."

Morah didn't relax.

"Captain, let him approach," Lavinda said.

Clenching her hand on the stock on her gun, Morah nodded to the other two guards. None of them holstered their weapons, but they did lower them until Jak no longer stood in their sights. As he walked to Bhaaj, he kept his empty hands visible with no hint showing of any other weapons he carried.

"This Vakaar plan," Bhaaj asked him. "Real? You sure?"

"Yah." He paused, then said, "Ears hear Cutter say."

Cutter Vakaar. That meant it came from the cartel queen herself. "Just hear? Not see?"

"Both."

Bhaaj scowled, pissed to high hell. "Not make sense."

"Yah. Cutter knows this." Jak grimaced. "Take Majda, more stupid than stupid." Turning to Lavinda, he switched into Cries speech. "I'm sorry to bring this news. For what it's worth, none of us expected it, either."

"Maybe it's fake," Lavinda said.

Bhaaj wondered that, too. Someone might have impersonated the drug queen, hoping to stir trouble. "Jak, did your spies see Cutter close up when she was making these plans? Could it have been someone disguised as her?"

He shook his head. "See close up."

"Maybe it was holo." That came from Darjan, Dara's oldest daughter.

"It seems unlikely," Captain Morah said. "Holos look translucent up close. To get one that appears solid even a short distance away, you'd need technology beyond any you have down here."

Jak got one of his Looks, a subtle reaction Bhaaj suspected only she recognized. He'd just decided Captain Morah was an idiot. Darjan wasn't anywhere near so subtle with her loud snort. Weaver frowned at her with that *behave yourself* look fathers had used with teenagers since time immemorial.

It was actually Lavinda who said, "Captain, the best tech-mech here is as advanced as anything we know. It's just put together ways we don't understand by people who didn't learn design in what we consider a standard manner."

Ho! Bhaaj hadn't realized Lavinda figured that out. Not good. They didn't need the above-city realizing the genius of the Undercity cyber-riders, that they created all sorts of bizarre and useful devices unknown to Cries. Some city authority might try to regulate their work.

Weaver spoke in the Cries dialect. "I use holos to model my art. I can make them look almost solid. You need to be close to see it's just light." He motioned at Jak. "Closer than you are to me now."

"I suppose what my sources saw could have been faked," Jak said. "But it would take a lot of work, and for what? No one benefits."

Dara was watching Bhaaj with a hard gaze. "Kajada benefit. Make trouble for Vakaar."

Bhaaj crossed her arms and scowled. Sure, Dara spoke a truth, that the Kajada cartel could benefit from anything that blew back on the Vakaar cartel. Kajada and Vakaar had fought for generations, responsible for so much mayhem, cruelty, and death that it made Bhaaj ill. But this was different. She spoke coldly to Dara. "Not Kajada."

"Yah, Kajada," Dara told her. "Bhaaj blind."

"Fuck you," Bhaaj said. Everyone gaped at her, Darjan especially. None of them ever heard her speak that way to Dara. Even so. Dara had just stepped over an invisible line they never touched.

Lavinda looked between the two of them. "What's going on?"

"Nothing," Bhaaj said.

Lavinda spoke carefully. "You wrote a reference letter for the daughter of the previous Kajada cartel boss when the girl applied to the Dieshan Military Academy. My understanding was that the Kajada girl had no link to her mother's cartel."

Bhaaj answered tightly. "It wasn't 'her mother's' cartel."

Jak spoke, his voice low and harsh. "I live. Bhaaj lives. Gourd lives. Why? Because of Dig Kajada."

"Uh, excuse me," one of the Majda guards said. "Could someone tell us what's going on? Who are Dig and Gourd?"

Bhaaj took a deep breath, then slowly released it. She spoke evenly. "When I was a kid, I ran with a dust gang. The gangs act as protectors here, taking care of what we call our circle. It's an extended family, though often many of its people aren't related by blood. A gang protects their supplies and territory against other gangs. In return, the circle makes a home life for everyone. Most gangs consist of two women and two men." She struggled with the memories, so full of pain and joy, love and grief. "I should say two girls and two boys. Dust gangs rarely survive into adulthood."

Morah spoke coldly. "You look alive to me."

Jak's voice turned to ice. "Yah. We survived. All of us except Dig."

"Who is this Dig?" Lieutenant Warrick asked.

"Dig led our gang," Bhaaj said. "Me, Jak, and also Gourd, a boy who could do anything with tech-mech." She regarded them steadily. "Dig Kajada was like my sister."

"Dig *Kajada*?" The other Majda guard, the one who hadn't yet spoken, gaped at her. "Your *sister* was the worst cartel monster in known history?"

Jak opened his mouth, and Bhaaj spoke fast, jumping in before he could say something that would destroy what remained of their uneasy alliance with their Majda visitors. "No. She wasn't the head of any cartel. That was her mother, Jadix Kajada. Dig hated what her mother did." Hell, Dig had hated her mother, too, who had no use for her except for any advantage a strong daughter could give her business.

Captain Morah looked as if she couldn't decide whether to be incredulous or disgusted. "Are you seriously trying to deny that Dig Kajada ran the Kajada cartel?"

"Bhaaj." Dara's voice finally gentled. "Tell them."

Damn it, Bhaaj thought. *I hate this.*

She's right, Max answered, even though she hadn't asked his opinion. **If you want this visit to work, you need to be open about everything.**

Bhaaj tried to speak, but the words wouldn't come. She held up her hand and walked away while the memories flooded her. She'd hated Jadix, not only for the grief the cartel boss had inflicted on the universe, but also for how she treated Dig. Being a stupid adolescent, all fire and defiance, Bhaaj had let Jadix know exactly how she felt. It never went well. If she hadn't left to enlist in the army, Jadix would have eventually killed her.

All her life, Dig had tried to reach her mother. Then the previous Vakaar boss had murdered Jadix, taking the one thing Dig wanted above all else—the chance to convince her mother to love her. And in that, the Vakaar cartel queen made the worst mistake of her life. Dig vowed to destroy her, and if it meant she had to do what she swore would never happen—take over the Kajada cartel and all its unholy power—then so be it. She and Vakaar went to war, bringing both cartels to their knees before the two crime bosses killed each other. Dig's last act had been to protect her own children, dying herself to save them.

In the years since, the cartels had flailed, and the cops they hadn't bribed were moving against them. It left neither Vakaar nor Kajada in any position to survive a showdown with Majda.

Bhaaj took a deep breath, then went back to the group. With a pain that never faded, she said, "I didn't lose Dig the day I left the Undercity to enlist. I lost her years later when she took over the cartel to avenge her mother's death." She turned to Lavinda. "And yes, Dig kept the people she loved separate from her trade, especially her family. Her oldest child *wasn't* her mother's daughter."

They all just looked at her. No one seemed to know how to react. Then Lavinda said, "I'm sorry. It sounds difficult."

Bhaaj pushed her hand through the tendrils of hair curling around her face. "This trip is over. We'll take you back to the Foyer and escort you to Cries."

"It's not that easy," Jak said. "Vakaar has eyes everywhere in the aqueducts."

"Aqueducts?" Captain Morah asked.

"It means everywhere people live here," Jak said. "Undercity, Down Deep, any place."

"Vakaar watch every exit," Ruzik said. "Secret or not."

Darjan said, "Not the Maze."

Her mother frowned at her. "Nahya. Maze not have out place."

"What are they saying?" Captain Morah asked. "I can't follow it."

Bhaaj turned to her. "If the Vakaars really do have a plan against Colonel Majda, they'll have all the exits from the Undercity watched. However, a Maze exists deeper down that almost no one can navigate." She glanced at Dara's daughter. "You say Maze has way out?"

"Not sure," Darjan admitted. "Not ken Maze."

Her mother glowered at her. "Then why say?"

Darjan hesitated. "Maybe know ruz-pup who kens."

"Did you say ruz-pup?" Captain Morah snorted. "A pup couldn't find its own tail."

Darjan gave her a look that could incinerate rock.

"It's slang," Bhaaj said. "It means a desirable young man."

Weaver scowled at his daughter. "Who this ruz-pup?"

"Not mine." Darjan sounded disappointed.

"You say this boy know Maze?" Bhaaj asked.

"Not boy," Darjan informed her. "Man."

Man, woman, boy, girl, Bhaaj didn't care. "How he know Maze?"

Darjan lifted her hands in the Undercity equivalent of a shrug. "Live there."

"Not live there," Bhaaj said. "He die." He'd have no food, no water, no nothing.

Darjan crossed her arms. "He live in Maze."

"So how we find?" Bhaaj asked.

"Not know," the girl admitted.

"How you know him, then?"

"Healer know him."

"You mean Doctor Rajindia?" Bhaaj asked. A few years ago, the Ruby Pharaoh had sent Karal Rajindia to set up a health clinic for the Undercity, the first and only of its kind. Born into the House of Rajindia, Karal belonged to Skolian nobility, but you'd never know. She worked alongside the people here like anyone else.

"This man hurt?" Dara asked her daughter.

"Sick." Darjan sounded evasive again. "Get help. Red rash."

"He go see Kar?" Bhaaj asked. The disease called carnelian rash had killed many of her people. No doctor in Cries would offer their services to the Undercity, but Karal regularly treated and vaccinated people against the illness.

"Maybe. Maybe not." Darjan shrugged. "Not my biz."

Bhaaj regarded her with exasperation. "Then how we find him?"

"Ask Healer Kar."

Huh. Why would a Rajindia noblewoman know those private details about an Undercity man? Yah, that was *interesting*. "One of us needs to visit Doctor Rajindia," Bhaaj said. "Find out more about this Maze exit." She spoke to Dara and Weaver. "Okay if queen stay here?"

"Yah," Dara said. "Long as needs."

"Why here?" Lavinda asked.

"It's one of the safest places for you to wait while we figure out what to do," Bhaaj said. "Almost no one knows how to get here, and those few who do, I trust. It's also easy to guard. I'll send more Dust Knights while I'm gone, just in case."

"You're going?" Jak scowled at her. "Where the hell to?"

Bhaaj met his gaze. "Talk to Kajada."

CHAPTER IV
Kajada

Bhaaj sat at Dig's grave.

It was hard to believe that four years had passed since she, Jak, and Gourd had brought Dig's cremated remains here, after the brutal finish of the cartel war. They'd spread her ashes across the ground, letting them mix with the dust. Hundreds of people had gathered to watch, standing back, leaving the three of them alone. More crammed the midwalks above them on either side of the canal. Many held tech-mech lamps or torches, their lights like fire-dragons in the darkness. Others came armed, including enough military hardware to get half of them thrown in prison. Yet no one attacked anyone else. On that day, and that day only, they kept a truce, dust gangers, drug punkers, cyber-riders, merchants, children, parents, guardians, and the surviving combatants of the cartel war.

They came to bear witness to Dig's passing.

The Vakaar punkers showed up to make sure Dig really had died. Behind their impassive faces, inside the shadowed cavities of their souls, Bhaaj had no doubt they rejoiced. The Kajada punkers paid tribute to a leader they'd feared but also respected. They'd seen the difference between Dig and her mother. Jadix had ruled by fear, forcing desperate people to work for her through threats, blackmail, and violence. Yah, Dig was smarter than her mother, but that wasn't what cemented her rule of the Kajada empire. She knew how to lead, how to build loyalty, how to make people *want* to work for her. In a different life, she could've turned into a great leader.

Instead, she became a nightmare.

Her enemies had felt the force of her vengeance with a power even Jadix had never managed. When Hammer Vakaar murdered Dig's husband, the father of her children, a man she'd loved beyond all else, that rammed the final nail into the coffin of Dig's transformation. Legends of her infamy spread across the aqueducts, across Cries, even across the Imperialate. In the end, she destroyed Hammer Vakaar in the chaos of war, bringing both cartels to their knees with her fury.

Of all the people who came to the memorial, no one had mourned—

Except Jak, Gourd, and Bhaaj.

In their youth, when Dig led their gang, she'd sworn they would know the universe *wanted* them. It didn't matter that they had no parents. They had Dig, and she had the resources of her mother's empire. They'd never starved, never felt alone, never lived the terror of a child with no one to care if they died. In those days, none of them fully appreciated the trade-off it demanded from Dig, that she had to work for her mother's cartel, the drug trade she hated. Dig paid the ultimate price so her circle could have lives worth living. She gave up her soul for the people she loved.

None of Dig's four children came to her memorial. They'd remained secreted with people Dig chose before she died, the few she trusted to keep them safe. Unlike her mother, Dig never let the drug trade touch her family. She had one last demand for Digjan, her eldest daughter. As Dig died, while Digjan knelt at her side and Bhaaj on the other, she told her daughter, *"You see this Bhaajan person? You be like her, Digjan. Like HER. Not me."*

Like her? Bhaaj had thought Dig hated her for deserting the Undercity. She'd blamed herself for what Dig became. If she'd stayed as the sister Dig needed, would Dig have denied the cartel? Or would Jadix have killed Bhaaj one day, ridding herself of Bhaaj's defiance? In retaliation, Dig would've gone after Jadix, probably killing her own mother. With the Vakaar cartel free to run rampant over the Undercity, Dig would have taken over the Kajada cartel anyway, to protect her people. Bhaaj saw no way their lives could have led to anything but a chasm they couldn't cross. Never in a thousand years had she expected Dig's dying words.

Suffocating with guilt, Bhaaj had done her best to give Dig's daughter a better life, the life the girl wanted. Bhaaj helped her gain acceptance to the academy that trained starfighter pilots.

Now Bhaaj sat alone on a stump of rock by the wall where they'd held the memorial. She, Jak, and Gourd had carved a mural here, an image of four dust gangers, their faces too vague to identify, but their heights and clothes just like the four of them in adolescence. Those stone gangers stood together, forever at guard over Dig's final resting place, four youths with their lives still full of promise. It was no great sculpture; none of them were artists. That didn't matter. It stood witness to a legacy they would never forget.

Now a sphere of light surrounded Bhaaj, with darkness beyond. The canal stretched out in both directions, silent and thick with dust that looked red in brighter light but now showed as a black carpet. Caught by Bhaaj's light, though, specks of azurite glinted blue in the dust. Thirty years ago, this territory had belonged to the circle her dust gang protected. Another gang claimed it now, one that earned both fear and respect because they ruled the territory that decades ago had belonged to Dig Kajada and also to Bhaaj, who now led the Dust Knights.

Max, Bhaaj thought. *Crank up my ear augs.*

Done.

Her hearing ramped up until she caught the whisper of moving air, courtesy of her biomech web. Bio-threads networked her body, as did bio-hydraulics, enhanced musculature and an augmented skeletal system. It gave her more than double the speed, reflexes, and strength of a normal person, all powered by a microfusion reactor within her body. The army had implanted her first biomech web, and she'd upgraded it several times after she retired despite the great expense and many clearances it required. In her job, it proved invaluable.

However, it didn't provide what she needed today. She had no doubt watchers were spying on her, but she heard nothing except the faint air currents, which circulated via conduits that networked these canals like blood vessels created from stone.

Bhaaj waited.

Shall I activate your optics? Max asked.

No. I can see well enough.

A rustle came from above, hardly more than a whisper.

Bhaaj got to her feet, slow and easy. She didn't reach for the EM pulse gun she wore in a shoulder holster over her muscle shirt.

Smooth and efficient, a woman jumped down from the midwalk and landed a few meters away, sending dust spraying into the air. Bending her legs, she absorbed the impact of that drop with an expertise Bhaaj had rarely seen even when she'd trained soldiers. Tech-mech packed her gauntlets, including a lamp that shed light around her like the halo of a demonic angel. She watched Bhaaj with a cold stare and carried a machine gun, holding it in one hand despite its weight. Her tank top had ripped at the waist, showing her hardened abs, also the tattoos and embedded circuits that covered her body. One scar snaked from her forehead down her face to her neck. Whoever had tried to kill her had failed, and they'd no doubt paid a fatal price for that mistake.

Damn. This wasn't Cutter Kajada, the current Kajada boss. The woman did have the Kajada insignia of a lizard engraved in her right gauntlet, identifying her as a punker for the cartel. Her left gauntlet displayed a knife with drops of blood on its tip. Great. Just great. A Kajada assassin had come to meet her.

"What you want?" the woman asked.

"Talk to Cutter," Bhaaj said.

"Nahya."

Bhaaj waited.

"Why?" Hostility hardened the assassin's voice.

"Heard jib. Vakaar."

"Fuck Vakaar."

"Yah." Bhaaj agreed, but she didn't think much of Kajada, either.

A rustle came from her left, toward the center of the canal. In her side vision, she glimpsed a man in the shadows creeping toward her, slow and stealthy.

Max, do you register that guy sneaking up on me? she asked.

Yes, Max answered. **And yes, I'd say he's about to attack.**

Combat mode on.

Done.

The world jumped into sharp relief as her body went into overdrive. Everything seemed to slow down, each second stretched into eons. The guy was a meter away, moving with what he probably thought was silence. To Bhaaj, he sounded like a giant stomping through loose gravel.

"You got no biz here," the woman in front of her said.

Bitch, you not distract me, Bhaaj thought at the assassin—and whirled toward the guy. Despite her hyped-up speed, she felt as if she moved through invisible molasses. She brought up her knee, keeping her foot flexed, in the same moment that the assassin threw her knife. Bhaaj leaned to the side as she kicked out her leg, shifting enough that the knife whizzed past her head, slicing off a tendril of hair but missing her neck. Unleashing a roundhouse kick, she slammed her boot into the guy's stomach and threw out her arm for balance. Normally she'd have bashed him in the head, but with her enhanced strength, that blow could kill him. She had no wish to end anyone, besides which, she'd be an idiot to whack Cutter Kajada's minions.

Even as the guy doubled over and staggered back, the assassin was sprinting toward them. While Bhaaj spun to the woman, raising her fists, the assassin came at her with whip-fast strikes—what the hell? She was wielding her machine gun like a huge, misshapen truncheon. Why not just shoot? If she could catch Bhaaj with even a few bullets from that baby, it'd pulverize her. Its weight and weird shape had to make it hell to control as a bat, but that didn't slow the assassin. At normal speed, that barrage would've been a flurry of motion. To Bhaaj, it seemed to crawl, letting her evade or block the strikes.

As Bhaaj danced away, her other attacker climbed to his feet despite the force of the kick she'd landed on him. Ho! This dude had cred with the rough-and-rumble. She moved fast, keeping both fighters in front of her so they couldn't come at her from both sides. The man had a knife on his belt, but with the fight going so fast, he hadn't drawn it yet.

For an instant, the assassin left an opening on her right side. Bhaaj lunged in and grabbed the woman's wrist, hitting her elbow to weaken her grip on the machine gun. Throwing her body into the move, Bhaaj forced her to drop the weapon. Even as the gun fell, Bhaaj caught it and jumped back. At the same time, she drew her own revolver, yanking it out of its holster so fast that the motion blurred even in her slowed timescape. She hefted up the machine gun in one hand and activated it with a flick of her finger, a move she'd perfected in the army. Aiming the big gun at the woman and her revolver at the man, Bhaaj stood with her feet planted wide and her arms outstretched, each of the punkers in her sights, each of them too far away to reach her.

"Not move, assholes," Bhaaj said. "Or you die."

Both punkers froze.

"Enough." A woman's gravelly voice came from the darkness beyond the reach of their lamps. "Not kill my punkers." She walked out of the shadows behind the two Kajada fighters.

Bhaaj would've known this newcomer anywhere. Yah, Cutter Kajada loomed large in the aqueducts. Hardened and scarred, older than her lieutenants, with a powerful, muscled body and black hair buzzed close to her head, she looked like a throwback to the barbaric queens who had rampaged across the desert above during the Ruby Empire.

Cutter aimed her gun at the ground in front of Bhaaj, a tangler, a gruesome weapon that could fry the neural connections in your brain, sending you into massive seizures that didn't end until you died. Bhaaj kept her guns trained on the two punkers, with Cutter between them. Given her enhanced speed, she could get all of them before they stopped her, and they knew it. They also knew they could probably finish her as well, even as they died.

"You want talk?" Cutter's voice sounded like rocks scraping together. "So talk."

"Hear buzz," Bhaaj told her. "It say shit. Vakaar want Majda queen." She shifted the machine gun just enough to put Cutter directly in her sights.

Cutter didn't look surprised. "Not want queen. Want meeting with queen."

"Fuck meeting," Bhaaj said.

"Then fuck visit," Cutter asked. "Queen meet with Kajada and Vakaar. Same time. Same place. Or leave."

Bhaaj stared at her, certain she'd heard wrong. Meet with Kajada *and* Vakaar? Punkers from the two cartels did only one thing if they ended up in the same place: murder each other.

"Lie," Bhaaj told her. "Kajada and Vakaar meet?" She spat to the side to let Cutter know what she thought of that claim.

"Not lie," Cutter told her. "Queen meet us. Both."

"Why?" This made so little sense, Bhaaj almost forgot to be pissed about Cutter sending two minions to beat her up or test her resolve or whatever.

"Queen come," Cutter said. "We talk."

"You screw with Majda queen," Bhaaj told her, "then Majda screw with you. Big time."

"Got no biz with Majda," Cutter said. "Queen ask to come here. We not want." Her gaze never wavered. "She want visit? Then she visit us. Kajada. Vakaar. Both." Her voice hardened. "Or she goes."

Bhaaj couldn't imagine taking Lavinda to meet even one cartel, let alone both in the same place. "She leave aqueducts, you not stop her?"

"Not stop," Cutter said. "But if leave, not come back. Come back, we kill."

Well, bloody hell. Bhaaj had no idea what to say. She had to do something, though; her arm holding the machine gun was tiring, even with her augmented strength.

Cutter glanced right and left at her two lieutenants, and they responded by lowering their fists. They all snapped off their lamps, leaving them in shadows at the edge of the light around Bhaaj.

"We go," Cutter said.

That done, they melted away into the shadows, leaving her alone with Dig's grave.

Bhaaj walked up the stairs to Dara and Weaver's home. She made no attempt to hide her approach. Sure enough, within moments, Captain Morah appeared at the top of the staircase.

"That was fast," the captain said.

"Yah." Bhaaj joined her, the two of them standing like combatants. "I need to talk to Lavinda."

Morah frowned at her. "What the hell happened to you?"

"Nothing." Bhaaj knew she had bruises, but she barely felt them. She walked past the captain, entering the foyer beyond. Her biz with Cutter Kajada couldn't have been *that* fast; Byte-2 was back, already returned from his visit with Doctor Rajindia.

Lavinda was sitting on a bench, socializing with Dara and her daughters, and Jak stood by the far wall, talking to Weaver. They all fell silent as Bhaaj entered. One guard stayed posted by the entrance while the other Majda officers and all three Dust Knights remained in the foyer.

Jak came over to her. "You got beat up."

She touched his arm, one tap, nothing more, but he'd know what she meant. *Be wary.*

Lavinda joined them. "Are you all right?"

"Yah, fine," Bhaaj said.

"I take it your meeting with the Kajadas didn't go so well," Lavinda said.

"Nothing unexpected." Bhaaj spoke bluntly. "Both Kajada and Vakaar want to meet with you. Your guards can come, but they can't bring their weapons."

"Like hell." Captain Morah joined them. "Is this a joke?"

"No." Bhaaj kept her focus on Lavinda. "If you don't want to do it, neither cartel will stop you from leaving the Undercity. But you *will* leave."

"Good," Morah said. "This visit was a mistake."

"No." Lavinda frowned at her, then turned back to Bhaaj. "What do they want?"

"Hell if I know." Bhaaj lifted her hands, then let them drop. "I've never heard of the cartels cooperating."

One of the Majda guards snorted, a woman with the black hair, black eyes, and the aristocratic features that suggested she had relatives among the nobility. "Cooperation, hell. To do what? Murder Colonel Majda, I'd wager."

"Lieutenant Warrick, enough," Lavinda told her. She studied Bhaaj as if she were a puzzle to solve. "What's your take on this meeting?"

"It's hard to say." The cartels knew she made the Dust Knights swear off drugs, which won her exactly zero friends among them. "The leaders of both cartels want to meet with you. They'll come in force, because neither wants to risk the other using this meeting to, uh, remove obstacles to their trade." They'd love the chance to smash as many rival punkers as they could corral together. "Hell, I don't know if they can even exist in the same place without it turning into a blood bath. If you do this, you could get hurt."

"And if I don't?"

"They'll let you leave." Bhaaj met her gaze. "And you can never return, neither you nor any other emissary. They're making a stand, asserting that this is their world. They don't want you here."

Lavinda frowned. "Then why ask me to meet them?"

"I don't know." Bhaaj had gnawed at that question like a lizard with a dead wasp-rat. She glanced at Jak. In his casino, he had an ear to just about everything. "Any whispers on this?"

"Small whispers. Cartels not want Majda to notice them." He lifted his hands, then dropped them again. "So why meet queen?"

"To hold her for ransom," Captain Morah said.

Jak switched into Cries speech. "They know that if Majda gets their colonel back through ransom, their next step will be to pulverize both cartels."

Ruzik stepped forward. "It's a test."

"You think?" Bhaaj asked.

"Makes sense," he said.

"To test what?" Lavinda asked. "If I'll let them continue breaking the law? They'd be fools to draw this much attention if that's what they want."

"Maybe they're testing your intent," Bhaaj said. "Your courage." It seemed an odd way, though, both cartels coming together.

Captain Morah spoke. "Do you think they're lying about allowing Colonel Majda passage out of the Undercity if she won't meet with them?"

"I'd say they mean it." Bhaaj spoke dryly. "Everyone here will be glad to see you all leave."

"I'd rather not go," Lavinda said. "If that means I have to meet with them, I will."

"Ma'am, we can't allow that." Although Captain Morah sounded calm, Bhaaj felt her tension like an invisible cord stretched tight.

"You don't have the authority to stop me," Lavinda said.

"That's true." Morah didn't sound the least bit conciliatory. "But General Majda does."

Well, shit. They would have to invoke Vaj.

"My sister approved this mission," Lavinda said.

"Contingent on your safety," Morah said. "I'm required to contact her if it that safety appears compromised."

"I don't know if it's compromised," Bhaaj admitted. "Cutter claims they'll keep a truce with Vakaar for the meeting."

Morah snorted. "Right. And I have some property in the desert I'd like to sell you."

"Captain, listen," Lavinda said. "We knew this trip involved risks. Well, this is a risk. In my judgment, it's not enough to end the visit when we've barely started. If we let any possible threat scare us off, we'll never develop a relationship with the Undercity."

"Why would we care?" Morah seemed genuinely baffled.

Lieutenant Warrick spoke up. "Yes, we've heard it, that we should have better relations with the only other city on the planet, but I mean, what the hell? This *isn't* a city. Why are we dancing around here as if we don't dare insult a bunch of slow-witted drug addicts, gangsters, and homeless people who have nothing to offer the rest of us?"

Ho! As many times as Bhaaj had heard that bull-crapalooza, she'd never stopped wanting to turn whoever said it into a smear of plasma.

"Yah, and fuck you too," Tower said. Apparently she had no trouble speaking the Cries dialect when she wanted to.

"Enough," Bhaaj told her. To Lavinda, she said, "My apologies."

"You've nothing to apologize for." Lavinda turned to Warrick. "What the hell is wrong with you, talking that way about our hosts?"

Warrick changed her tone. "I'm sorry, ma'am. Permission to speak?" Although Warrick wasn't active military, it didn't surprise Bhaaj that Majda security followed similar protocols.

"Go ahead," Lavinda said. "But take care, Lieutenant."

Warrick spoke carefully. "Colonel, I don't understand why you are endangering your life. It's honorable that you'd like to meet people here on their own terms, but surely better ways exist to integrate the Undercity into Cries culture than risking your life."

Lavinda's voice cooled. "We didn't come here to assimilate anyone into our way of life." She turned to Dara, Weaver, and their oldest daughter, who had stayed a few steps back from them, wary and waiting. The two younger children stood in the archway to their home, watching everyone with obvious fascination. "My deepest apology for any offense we have caused," Lavinda said to Dara and Weaver. "We thank you for opening your beautiful home to us and mean no disrespect."

Dara glanced at her daughter.

"Queen say good home, good invite," Darjan told her parents. "Say loud guard is ass-bat."

"Ah." Dara and Weaver nodded to Lavinda, accepting her apology.

Captain Morah spoke to Lavinda. "Ma'am, Officer Warrick should never have spoken as she did. But she has a point. Surely a better way exists to improve contact here than meeting with drug dealers."

Bhaaj practically had to bite the inside of her mouth to keep from speaking. Despite her differences with General Majda, she agreed with the decision to keep secret the full extent of why the government wanted better relations with the Undercity. The less people knew, the less chance that unscrupulous, treasonous, or enemy agents would try to exploit the people here.

Lavinda met the captain's gaze. Everyone waited.

"Colonel?" Captain Morah finally asked.

"You and your officers received an upgraded security clearance before we left, yes?" Lavinda asked.

"That's right, ma'am."

Glancing at Bhaaj, Lavinda motioned to Ruzik, who stood flanked on one side by his brother and on the other by Tower. "Do they understand the clearance they received?"

Ruzik answered in the Cries dialect. "Yes, we understand it."

Lavinda glanced at Dara. "And you? Your family?"

"We ken," Darjan said. "Already talk with Bhaaj."

Lavinda looked around at them all. "What I'm going to tell you is secured. None of you can speak of this beyond myself, Major Bhaajan, and my sister, General Majda. To betray that security is treason. If you do, you will be prosecuted to the full extent of the law. Do you understand?"

"Yes, ma'am," Captain Morah said, echoed by her two officers.

"Yah, ken," Ruzik said. "We talk, we die."

Lavinda spoke dryly. "That about sums it up." She turned to Captain Morah. "One third of the population here are Kyle operators with enough strength to work the Kyle net. In the population below the Undercity, what they call the Down Deep, half of the people are full Kyle operators."

The Majda guards gaped at her. Ruzik, Byte, and Tower already knew, but Bhaaj doubted they realized the full significance of Lavinda's words.

"Holy fuck," Lieutenant Warrick said.

"But *how*?" Captain Morah asked.

"We think it's why our ancestors retreated to live underground," Bhaaj said. "They couldn't take the pressure of other human minds. The methods that Kyles use to protect their minds come from modern-day science. My ancestors had nothing. So they withdrew here." Hints existed of other reasons, too, but for now, this explanation was enough.

"How was that possible?" Morah asked. "Wouldn't they die?"

"Why would we die?" Bhaaj asked. "Being empaths doesn't make us physically weaker."

"But the mortality rate here." That came from the other Majda guard. "It's huge."

"Yah." Bhaaj fought down the resentment that never left her, not even after decades. "It used to be the highest in the Imperialate. Poverty, starvation, violence, and no formal medical care does that to you. Kyle traits have nothing to do with it. But just leaving or making drastic changes isn't a viable option. The environment here, everything about the way we live—it interacts with our brains in ways we can't yet explain." They'd only begun to understand how the fragile lives they'd built nurtured their minds. Like the music. Her people sang all the time, and their songs echoed throughout the canals. It even affected the operation of their bizarre tech-mech creations.

Morah spoke carefully. "I understand why you want to continue, Colonel. But we need to let someone up the chain of command know what's happening."

Lavinda scowled at her. "If we do, they'll report to my sister, and Vaj will pull us out."

"Lavinda, she has a point," Bhaaj said. In her side vision, she saw Morah stiffen as if Bhaaj had threatened them, which was odd since she'd just agreed with the captain.

"You must have a better idea." Lavinda spoke wryly. "You usually do."

Morah breathed out, her tensed posture easing. It hit Bhaaj then. She'd addressed Lavinda—not just a colonel but also a royal Majda heir—by her first name. A great insult. Lavinda reacted with no offense, though, business as usual, obviously no problem. It wouldn't occur to either of them to be upset, only to pretty much everyone else in the universe.

So DO I have a better idea? Bhaaj asked herself.

Are you addressing me? Max asked.

What? Oh. No, just thinking hard.

Because I do have an idea.

Really? What?

Use Angel as your go-between. She's up in the city, so what happens here won't affect her. She also won't report to General Majda unless you ask her to.

Majda will know if we contact her.

Um.

That didn't sound good. *What, Max?*

Ask Ruzik.

How would you know anything about private talk between Ruzik and Angel?

I pick up traces of chatter. From their, uh, comm links.

Max, for flaming sake. Her EI wasn't supposed to violate their privacy. Besides, Ruzik and Angel had protections on their gauntlets that could block even the nosiest snoop-spiders. *How can you do that? They have top-notch security.*

They do indeed. Max paused. **Mine is better.**

So. He admitted it. Bhaaj already knew he could update himself with dark-mesh tech most people had never even heard of, let alone put in their EI. She spoke to Ruzik. "You and Angel. Talk secret? Majda not know?"

His expression turned neutral, no trace of reaction. "Eh? Not ken."

"Fine," Bhaaj said. "While you not kenning what I say, you talk to Angel private, yah? Say what goes here. Say we have check-in. We not check-in, she tell Majda."

Ruzik met her gaze with no trace of a reaction, like a mask had dropped over his face. After a moment, though, he said, "How often check-in?"

"Every hour," Bhaaj said. "Until after meet with punkers."

Ruzik nodded. Done.

Lavinda looked from Ruzik to Bhaaj. "I didn't get all that."

"He'll stay in contact with Angel," Bhaaj said. "If we need help or don't check back with her, she'll contact your people."

Lavinda frowned. "The moment he contacts Angel, my 'people'

will know." She didn't even try to hide the fact that Majda security was spying on them.

Bhaaj met her gaze with the blandest look she could manage. "They won't know."

"They have the best intel on this planet," Lavinda told her. "Hell, the best available to the General of the Pharaoh's Army."

"Yah." Bhaaj said nothing more. The less the colonel knew, the better. Plausible deniability and all that. Besides, Lavinda already knew what they could do. Except for this visit, Bhaaj always hid from Majda sensors during her work in the Undercity. If her people thought she was letting Majda spy on them, they'd never talk to her.

After a moment, Lavinda said, "All right, I get it." She glanced at Captain Morah. "His wife, Angel Ruzik, will be the go-between with Majda security."

"Just Angel," Ruzik said. "I am here."

Bhaaj couldn't help but smile. "Thinks you take your name from Angel." She glanced at Lavinda. "Ruzik isn't named for Angel. He's just Ruzik. Angel is just Angel. One name."

"Ah." Lavinda spoke to Ruzik in the Undercity dialect. "Good name." He inclined his head to her.

Bhaaj turned to Dara and Weaver. "I go. Set up cartel meet." She motioned to their younger children. "I send Dust Knights to take little dusters. Make them safe."

"Agree," Dara said. Weaver nodded.

Dara's eldest daughter stood taller. "I get Knights."

"Yah," Bhaaj said. "Go."

As Darjan took off, Bhaaj spoke to Ruzik. "Send Tower, yah? Check exits." They needed a good escape route in case Lavinda had to leave fast.

When Ruzik glanced at Tower, she nodded and left the foyer, her long legs eating up distance, her loose curls shaking around her shoulders. It bemused Bhaaj that people thought she and Tower looked alike. They did both have those wild curls. She'd cut hers off in the army, exasperated by her inability to make them behave, but now her heavy braid reached her waist.

Lavinda was speaking to Ruzik. "You talk to Angel now?"

"Eh?" Ruzik asked.

"You go," Bhaaj said. He'd never talk to Angel in front of them. "Come back later, eh?"

"Yah, good." With that, he also left, the scarred Dust Knight striding off to speak with his warrior goddess of a wife who, at least for today, was being civilized.

Bhaaj headed off then as well, to set up their meeting with the killers of the Undercity.

CHAPTER V
Kyle Center Four

Strange place.

Angel looked around the lobby. The Majda slicks who'd "briefed" her at the palace called this place Selei Tower, named for Dyhianna Selei, the Ruby Pharaoh of the Imperialate. Apparently above-city types chose names for their buildings the way gangers created dust sculptures in the canals, so you knew who claimed that territory. Except this building existed above the ground. Skyscraper. That had made no sense until Angel had walked here through the city and discovered that yah, that mirrored tower did indeed look like a needle scraping the sky.

The *endless* sky. Even after all the times she'd come above the ground this past year, she still marveled at the open space, full of light and wind and wicked new odors, like the scent of "genuine Earth expresso-coffee with cinnamon." Whatever those rudely multisyllabic words meant, that drink smelled fucking *good*. And yah, she knew how to use all those absurd words with too many syllables. She thought them plenty when it suited her mood. Fortunately for the verbiage-saturated universe, she chose not to inflict the talky-talk in her mind on the rest of creation.

She walked around the lobby, taking in the sights. Glass panels formed its walls, and sunlight poured through the tinted barriers, flooding the place with light. She approved. The symbols here all came from above-city dust gangs. On one wall, the insignia of the

Pharaoh's Army glowed, a red pyramid within a gold circle. Other walls had icons for the Imperial Fleet, Advanced Services Corp, and Jagernaut Force. The Fleet used a "sailing ship" floating in water for its symbol, which made no sense. Ships sailed in space. When Angel and Ruzik had gone offworld to help Bhaaj with a case, they "embarked' on a starship here and "disembarked" on Parthonia, a world so different, it seemed unreal. In a place there called Selei City (yah, Selei again), you could turn on a spout and drinkable water came out. *Any time you wanted.* Angel had liked that case. It also got her this "job," even if she still wasn't convinced she wanted a job.

The best part of the visit to Parthonia, though, had been the Selei City Open Marathon. She liked to run. Hell, she loved it. Of course they rarely used vehicles in the Undercity, which damaged the ruins; instead, they ran everywhere. Angel also ran for the sheer joy of it, every day. She had since she was old enough to walk, speeding through her life to escape the starvation, sickness, violence—the lack of everything always nipping at her heels.

So she ran in the Selei City Open. And she won the damn thing. Hah!

Angel didn't know what to do with the medal they gave her, but having it felt good, like when she earned honors for some online school thing. Although she claimed she didn't like schooling, she actually enjoyed sneaking onto the Cries meshes to learn stuff. Like "politics." At first she'd thought it was a form of comedy, but she soon kenned the reality. Slicks went to war over it. As a civilian working for the army, she'd be helping them fight their enemies. Her enemies, too, apparently. The Trader Aristos. A bunch of raggedy-assed losers if she'd ever heard of any. They enslaved billions, took their territory, tortured people, committed genocide against rebels, and in general inflicted their lizard-crap selves on the universe.

Before she'd agreed to the army job, though, she'd talked to Bhaaj. *These Aristos real? Or slicks make them up?* When Bhaaj went quiet, Angel felt cold. Bhaaj just said, *Yah, real. Worse than you could know.* That had been enough.

Now today Angel went to work for the army, a huge dust gang that had no dust.

After she finished walking around the lobby, getting the feel of the place, she went to a circular counter in the center where a man sat watching her. He had no smile. Good. Slicks smiled too much. You only did that when you trusted someone, and she didn't trust these people worth bull-beans.

The man spoke coldly. "Can I help you?"

"Yah," Angel told him. "Got job."

"What?" He frowned as if she were a bug on the floor. "I can't understand you."

Angel switched into slick talk. "I'm reporting for my job with the army Kyle center on the twenty-third floor. Today is my first day."

He looked her over as if she wore tattered rags or something. Weird. She'd dressed like someone from Cries today, in the gray tunic and trousers Bhaaj suggested, silly clothes since the red dust would easily show on them. Then again, as deprived as slicks were up here, they didn't have any dust.

"Where are you from?" he asked in a haughty voice. He made it sound like she came from the lowest of the low, a pest scuttling on the ground.

Angel spoke coldly. "Ruzik circle."

"What?" He tapped the console in front of him. "Look, lady, you have to leave."

"I am expected to report to my job for processing," she told him. "I suggest you comm my contact."

He blinked, his hand poised above a panel that had just turned red. "Who is your contact?"

"Colonel Lavinda Majda." But no, the Majda queen wasn't here, she'd gone to the Undercity with Bhaaj. "Or her office."

"Majda. Right." The man acted like she'd spoken a flood of five-syllable words, all for ridicule rather than honor. He pressed the red panel. "If you don't leave, security will escort you from the building."

Angel considered him, taking in his appearance. He wouldn't survive five seconds in the Undercity. "It's true," she commented. "You could have your security escort me from the building. Of course, you'll have to explain why to Colonel Majda."

He stared at her, his face pale behind what he probably intended as a neutral expression. Anyone with a hint of the mind-feeling biz could sense his anger and uncertainty. It jumped out like a punch.

A woman spoke behind her. "Is there a problem here?"

Angel turned to see two women in green security uniforms. Huh.

Not drones like most slicks used in the city. This Selei Tower had real people. Angel wondered if it meant they had lower status, like the Undercity. Somehow, she didn't think so. Robots were easy. You didn't have to feed them, for one. Humans took more resources.

She just said, "No problem. I'm trying to report to my first day at work."

The security guard looked her over with the same frown as the counter dude. Bhaaj had warned her this might happen. *You'll be wearing clothes appropriate for your job, but there's no hiding that we come from the Undercity, even if you wear long sleeves and a high neck to cover your tats and scars. We look wild to them. It doesn't matter. Regardless of what they say or do, just stay polite and speak their language.* Angel wore the conservative clothes, but the hell with long sleeves and a neck so high it felt like she'd choke. It was *hot* outside. Besides, she'd earned her tats and scars.

The guard spoke to the guy behind the counter. "I take it her information isn't in the system?"

"Well it's, uh, I didn't check." He glanced at Angel. "Do you have ID?"

Angel pulled the card out of her pocket, a glossy square with a holo-pic of her. She handed it to the counter dude.

"Oh." He squinted at the picture, then at her, then at the picture again. Finally he swiped the card across one of his panels. Green lights lit up and a voice said, "Angel Ruzik, employee Kyle center four, grade three clearance." A hum came from the panel and a new card snapped out, this one larger than Angel's ID, with a bigger picture of her and writing that gave her name, even if they got the Ruzik part wrong. The Majdas seemed to think that as her husband, he took his name from hers. She ran with Ruzik's gang, though, so if they wanted to tack his name on after hers, she'd take it. The new card also showed the soaring hawk logo that the Majdas put on anything they could touch.

"Holy shit." The guy looked up at her. "You *are* sponsored by Majda."

Angel shrugged. So what?

The security woman spoke again, the frown still in her voice as well as on her face, but this time she gave it to the counter guy. "It sounds like everything is in order to me."

"Um, yes, I guess so." He gave Angel both her ID and the new card. "Wear your badge at all times while you're in the building." He motioned to a glass-enclosed room in a wall across the lobby. "Your card will get you access to that lift, so you don't have to check in here every time."

Well, good. Took him long enough. Angel was tempted to growl and swing her fists, just to see them jump like startled sandmites. Hah! That'd be entertaining. It'd probably also get her tossed out of this breakable lobby, though. She behaved herself and just nodded, first at the counter dude and then to the security officers. With that, she took off, striding across the lobby.

At the glass-enclosed room, she stood wondering what to do. A light flashed over her face, her body, and the card the guy had given her. "Access granted," a woman said, doing that thing slicks liked so much, having disembodied voices talk. EIs. Evolving intelligences. Angel thought at least some of them still had a lot of evolving to do, but never mind. Bhaaj had Max in her gauntlets and Jak had Royal Flush. Angel had no problem with those EIs. She included them among the people she respected even if they weren't people. For one thing, they didn't talk too much.

"You may enter the south tower lift," the room added. "Please watch you step," The glass wall in front of her opened in the middle, the two halves sliding apart. Intrigued, Angel walked into the chamber beyond the doors. As she turned to look out at the lobby, the doors closed, shutting her into the glass room.

"Eh?" Angel didn't like being closed in when she couldn't see an obvious way out.

"I would suggest you fasten your badge to your tunic," the room told her. "You don't want to lose it. Also, it is easier for sensors to read it if you face the badge outward."

Angel scowled, but after fooling with the badge, she figured out how to make it stay on the waistband of her tunic. In the meantime, the room went *up*. Weird. As it rose along the wall, the lobby receded below. How did it do that? The room kept going up, past the ceiling of the lobby until she saw no more than a wall. Wait, now they'd passed the top of the wall—

Ho!

They'd reached the needle portion of the tower, rising along the outside of the building. She could see the entire city. Angel stared in disbelief. She'd never traveled so high in her life. Cries spread out below, basking in the sunlight. The buildings shimmered, their mirrored towers reflecting the blue sky. A few fly-cars soared among them. She could make out people walking on the boulevards below, though they grew smaller with every moment as the lift continued up the tower. Green stuff showed everywhere in parks and along the wide streets. Plants. In a desert. That meant someone had to water them. A *lot* of water. Naturally occurring liquids killed those kinds of plants, which meant they needed filtered water. These slicks used one of the most valuable resources on the entire planet to grow their fucking decorations.

"Nahya," Angel said. It felt so wrong, she didn't have the words.

"Did you need something?" the lift asked.

Angel switched to the Cries language. "No. I'm fine."

"I am glad to hear that," the lift told her. "We are almost to your destination."

A moment later, the lift stopped. Angel squinted at the city below. What did this room expect her to do, step through the glass and plunge to her death? It rattled her, as did a lot of what these indecipherable people did, all six syllables deserved, but she never let them see how she felt. Snarking about them in her mind worked much better than giving even a hint of fear.

A woosh came from behind Angel. Turning, she saw that the back wall of the chamber had opened down the middle, offering her an escape that didn't involve dying. Relieved, she walked into the wide corridor beyond the exit. The hall stretched out ahead of her, its walls displaying widely spaced pictures, except they moved, showing winged lizards flying through the sky or wind blowing sand in the desert, all that beautiful, heartbreaking *space*.

A small table to her right stood like an invitation. Three glasses rested there, along with a spouted vase full of water and fat drops condensing on its glass sides. Or maybe its crystal sides. Angel had a hard time telling the difference; she just knew that cyber-riders used crystal in some of their creations. Given that the slicks had made this display, she'd bet someone had even filtered this water. What they were thinking, leaving something so valuable just sitting here, with *glasses*? Didn't it occur to them that people would steal their water? Maybe they considered this art, like the images on the walls. Yah, torture people with beauty. It seemed a slick thing to do.

In her youth, Angel would have drunk the entire vase, or decanter, or whatever you called that thing. Then she would have spritzed-off before anyone caught her pinching their stuff. Today she stayed on her best behavior and headed down the hall, ignoring the blatant temptation.

A woman was walking toward her from the far end of the hall. Angel couldn't see much about her yet, just that she wore a yellow tunic and trousers similar to the gray stuff Angel had inflicted on herself today. The woman had black hair and dark skin like everyone else, except for the few offworlders who did menial jobs the robots hadn't already taken. The only Raylican natives available to do those jobs lived in the Undercity, and they'd rather eat lizard shit than clean up after slicks.

Angel knew about the places in the desert where they farmed water from below the ground and filtered it. They gave the farming jobs to her people because robots got too much sand in their parts. It meant you spent hours in the burning sun with no rest. No one cared if you ate sand because you had no food, or if you drank unfiltered water because they wouldn't give you what they fucking purified *right there*, until finally you fell down and died. How inconvenient. It was still cheaper than using robots. Supposedly anyone from the Undercity could get work as a laborer on the farms. You could also bash your head against the wall until your brains fell out, but why would you do either?

Anyway, this woman seemed like everyone else in Cries, which meant she looked rich. As they neared each other, Angel realized the woman was smiling like they were trusted friends. Seriously? She'd never met this person in her life. Angel schooled her face to neutrality, rather than the *I'm going to punch that smile off your face* look she would have used with someone who challenged her this way in the Undercity. Apparently, as hard as she found it to believe, people from the City of Cries didn't know they were being offensive when they showed their teeth to strangers.

The woman lifted her hand in a greeting Angel had seen other people here use. So Angel lifted her hand, too.

The woman stopped in front of her. "My greetings, Goodwoman

Angel." She continued with that smile of hers. "Welcome to the Pharaoh's Army Kyle Division. I'm Gabrial Tanson."

Angel really, really wanted to dislike this Gabrial person. Unfortunately, she also sensed the woman's mood. Gabrial felt nervous, wanted to make a good impression, and earnestly meant to treat her visitor well. She'd even revealed her name. Well, damn. Angel could hardly return that honor by acting like an asshole. She nodded to the woman, not smiling of course, but not beating her up, either. "Thank you," she said in the Cries dialect. Two words, more than needed, but no matter. Slicks showed respect by being talky.

Gabrial raised her hand, inviting Angel to walk with her. As they headed down the hall, the woman said, "I can show you to your office and get you started on the orientation materials. We're having a division get-together this afternoon where you can meet everyone. After that, you'll talk with your supervisor about the specifics of your work. Tomorrow you'll see a Rajindia neurologist for an analysis of your Kyle rating." She gave Angel an apologetic look. "The orientation has a lot of material. I'm sorry about that. It can get tedious, but it's important to read it all."

Angel nodded, accepting the challenge. She decided she liked Gabrial after all. The woman assumed she could read, and in Cries-speak too. Although Angel could read just fine, many people in the Undercity didn't bother to learn. It hadn't taken Angel long to realize that most above-city types assumed her people were incapable even of rational thought let alone literacy. Bhaaj in one of her more annoying decisions had decreed that if you wanted to be a Dust Knight you had to get "schooling," like reading, writing, math, all that biz. Angel didn't see what it had to do with fighting, but no matter. She enjoyed finding out absurd things about the universe. It was *interesting*.

She liked math, too, especially when it helped her figure out odds at cards. It got her into fights when she won too much, but tough. Even before she joined the Knights, she'd had a rep in the rough-and-tumble, what Bhaaj called "street fighting," never mind that they had no streets, only canals. It had taken Angel time to learn tykado, what with all its odd rules, moves, and other stuff, but she liked it. So yah, now she had black belt in tykado, only first degree, but she was working on her second. She could crush any pissed-off poker bitches who wanted to smash her for counting cards.

Gabrial stopped at a tall archway and stepped back, inviting her to enter, but still looking as nervous as a jump-kit. Angel had the impression that she terrified the woman. She couldn't see why. She'd done nothing except walk with her and say a few words. Odd. She'd have to—

Ho! Angel stopped pondering Gabrial, poker, or anything else as she entered the office. The room could easily fit twenty people standing side-by-side without even touching each other, yet only one desk stood to the left. *One?* Didn't they put the number of desks in an office to match the number of people who used the place? Maybe she had to share the desk. The size of the room meant nothing, though, compared to its windows. The entire wall across from her, from waist height to the ceiling, consisted of glass. The panels were tinted, probably to mute all that sunlight pouring everywhere in the sky outside, but they still let her look out at the world.

Angel walked to the windows and stood there, staring. She could see for a long, long way, past the towers of Cries to the desert beyond, a rolling expanse of red sand and rock that went on forever, all the way to the horizon in every direction. Almost every direction. On her right, the mountains towered beyond the city, stark peaks with nothing green. Somewhere up there, hidden from view, the Majdas lived in their spectacular, golden palace surrounded by imported green stuff that would die anywhere else on this parched ball of rock they called home.

"I'm sorry the office is so small," Gabrial said.

Small? Angel turned to see her host standing in the doorway, framed by its giant keyhole shape, vertical sides that ended in what people called an "onion-shaped" arch far above her head. A stained-glass circle in the onion showed the insignia of Pharaoh's Army. Gabrial still looked nervous and apologetic.

When Angel had first heard the way above-city people said, "I'm sorry," she'd thought they were too naive to realize how much those words invited attack. Apologizing looked weak, and weakness got you killed. However, she'd soon realized that in Cries, "I'm sorry" offered a shorthand explanation, like what she sensed from Gabrial, a way of saying, "I'm sorry we gave you an office smaller than everyone else, but you're new and we only have so many to spare, not that we have many Kyle operators to give offices to, but this is the smallest division in the building." Angel approved of any attempts by the slicks to say more with less words, besides which, the office was huge. So she just said, "It's fine."

"Well. Good." Gabrial smiled again, and this time it didn't look offensive, mainly because Angel had decided she liked her shy host. She could sense Gabrial's intentions better than she could with most people. The woman meant well.

Gabrial showed her the desk with its shiny tech, including a holoscreen. When her host touched a panel, the screen raised up and displayed a menu with holographic icons, or holicons, reminding Angel of the screens that cyber-riders played with in their dens. This one looked new, though, instead of cobbled together from salvage and black-market tech.

"Pretty," Angel commented, her version of above-city "small talk."

"The orientation module is here somewhere...." Gabrial's forehead furrowed as she flicked her fingers through holicons. The screen responded by showing displays, none of which made sense, like one of a brain neuron and another of people looking happy for no reason. "Where is it . . . ah, here we go." A screen came up with intelligent-looking people gathered in a big room. It said *Orientation, Kyle Center Four, Pharaoh's Army Division, Selei Tower.*

Gabrial motioned to the desk chair, which resembled some sort of cyber artwork with glossy tech-mech along its arms and back. "You can sit here while you go through the materials."

Angel sat and surprise! The chair-art felt comfortable. She flicked her finger through the holicon of a door floating in front of the screen with the word ENTRANCE.

"Welcome to the Pharaoh's Army Kyle Center orientation," a woman said. "In this orientation, we will walk you through the purpose, history, and functions of the Kyle division."

"Eh," Angel told it. She already knew the purpose, history, and functions of the Kyle division. The army used it to pound Traders. Then again, having more details could be useful.

"I can go through it with you," Gabrial said at her side.

Angel glanced at her with no comment. When Gabrial just stood there, waiting, Angel realized she didn't understand. So Angel spoke in Cries dialect. "Thank you. But I'll go through it myself. I'm looking forward to learning about the division." So many words! She sounded like an idiot. It had the desired effect, though. Gabrial nodded as if Angel had answered in a reasonable, courteous manner. She even looked relieved.

After Gabrial left, Angel scrolled through the orientation. They wanted her to learn the duties of a *telop*, one of the Kyle operators who linked to the Kyle mesh in Kyle space and allowed non-Kyle people to use the Kyle network. A lot of Kyle, and who knew what it meant.

She soon got the gist of it, though. In the Undercity, word spread through the Whisper Mill. Tell someone your message, news, gossip, or whatever, and they'd tell someone else, who'd tell more people, and soon everyone knew. Things got changed sometimes, but usually not too much. The Kyle mesh acted like a mental Whisper Mill. You thought your business instead of speaking. It wasn't that easy, though. You couldn't just think to the receiver. Nothing happened. You needed a person—a telop—to link you to Kyle space, a place "located outside spacetime." A network existed in that outside place, one built by the two people in the normal universe who were better at being Kyle than anyone else alive, said persons being the Ruby Pharaoh and her nephew the Imperator, the dude who commanded all the Imperialate gangs.

It baffled Angel that they had one high boss over the Pharaoh's Army, Imperial Fleet, Jagernaut Force, Allied Services, and all the other Skolian gangs. It'd be like having a super boss in charge of the cartels and all their drug punkers. Never work. Then again, the cartel bosses were shitholes who murdered people and destroyed lives. Maybe this Imperator was more like Bhaaj, in charge of all the Dust Knights even though they came from different gangs, even a few punkers who'd wanted out of the cartels and needed the backing of the Knights so they didn't get whacked by a cartel queen for leaving.

A buzz sounded in the room.

"Eh?" Angel lifted her head to survey the office. She saw no one.

The buzz sounded again.

Huh. It came from the desk. She squinted at its glossy panels. No lights showed on any of them. She looked under the desk, but nothing showed there, either, except the underside of a desk.

Another buzz.

Angel sat up. "What the fuck?"

"Are you addressing me?" a woman asked.

"Not know," Angel said. "Who the fuck are you?"

"The profanity is unnecessary," the voice said. "I am Aide 142, the EI for this office."

"You make that buzz?"

"The sound is your comm," Aide 142 informed her. "Someone is trying to contact you."

"Who?"

"I don't know." The buzz came again. "I suggest you answer the comm."

"How?"

"You can either tell me to answer it," the EI said, "or you can tap it on your desk."

"Where on desk?"

"The menu is to your right. Do you see the narrow strip of platinum metal?"

She peered at the desk. Its panels all looked the same.

The buzz came again.

"What color is platinum?" Angel asked.

"It looks silver."

"All look silver."

"Can you read?"

"For fuck's sake," Angel said. Besides, none of the panels had words or icons.

"Does that mean no?"

"Means yah, I can read. Means stop being an asshole."

"I am incapable of functions that involve the administration of human excrement."

Angel couldn't help but laugh. "Fooled me."

"I have no wish to fool you."

"Good." The annoying buzz sounded yet again. "What message I got?"

"Here you are," Aide 142 said.

A new voice rose into the air, a man this time. "My greetings. I'm trying to reach Angel Ruzik. Can you put me through to her?"

Angel winced. Slicks gave their names so easily. Telling someone your name meant you trusted them even more than if you smiled at them. You *never* revealed your name to strangers. Except up here, they threw around names like they were giving candy to kids. It sucked. This unknown person knew her name, how to reach her, and who knew what else.

"Why you want her?" Angel asked.

A pause. Then the guy said, "Whom am I speaking to?"

Whom indeed. "You want Angel," she said, "you tell me why."

"You don't sound like an EI. Or anyone at the Kyle division."

"Tough."

Another pause. Then the slick, who was apparently smarter than he sounded, spoke again. "Are you Angel Ruzik? That's who I'm trying to reach."

"Angel," she said. "Not Ruzik."

"Oh." He sounded confused. "Ruzik isn't your last name?"

"Not got last name."

"Ah," the guy said.

Be polite, Angel reminded herself. She switched into the Cries dialect. "What can I do for you, Goodman—" She let the title hang without a name, an obvious pressure for him to reveal what people called him. By Undercity standards, that got as rude as you could get. Bhaaj hadn't said she had to be cool by Undercity standards, though, only according to the above-city.

And sure enough, not only did he offer his name, he apologized. "Ah, of course. I'm sorry for the confusion. I'm Mason Qazik. I coach the Raylicon Track and Field Olympic team and run the tryouts in the City of Cries." Goddess, now he sounded even *more* apologetic. "I'm not trying to be grandiose here. I'll be honest with you, Raylicon has one of the worst Olympic teams in the Imperialate. It's because we draw on only one city, Cries, which only has a few million people. Other teams draw on entire worlds or habitats. However, we do usually manage to qualify."

Huh. Angel had no clue what he meant.

After a moment, he added, "I'm sorry if I'm blathering. I've never been good with this recruiting business."

Another apology. She wondered how this man had managed to survive into adulthood without getting flattened into the ground.

"It's just that I saw the recordings of you running in the Selei City Open on Parthonia," he continued. "It was *beautiful.* We've a couple of great runners on the team right now, but I don't think either could beat your time. Your style is, well, unconventional. With some coaching, I'll bet you could improve your times even more. As it is, your finish at the Open qualifies you for the classic Greek marathon in the Olympics. I mean, it's not a medal-worthy Olympic time, sure, but it's a start. Hell, it would qualify you for the Imperial marathon. Just barely, but that's all it takes. I know, seventy kilometers and all that climbing, but it's the most prestigious track and field event." He took a breath. "That is, um, if you're, uh, interested."

Angel blinked. Amazing. Truly. How could he string together so many syllables and make so little sense? She ought to respond, though, given his efforts to show respect. She appreciated that, particularly after what had happened in the lobby.

"You want me to run?" she asked.

"Yes!" Enthusiasm bubbled in his voice. "I'd also like to talk to the fellow who came in fifth. Ruzik? Was that his name? He came in a fraction ahead of your coach, Major Bhaajan. Hell, I wish I could ask her to run. I'd heard she was an Olympic *medalist* decades ago in the classic marathon. I can't, though. She's got biomech in her body. I mean, I know, she deactivated it for the Open. But they don't let you into the Olympics if you're augmented, not even if you can turn it off."

Angel had no idea how to respond to this earnest and excited guy. So she told him a truth, an obvious one everyone knew. "Like to run."

"Good! We'd love to have you join the team."

"I think about, yah?"

"I'm sorry. I didn't get that."

She switched into Cries-speak. "I will think about it, yes?"

"Ah, yes! Of course. I'll leave my contact info with your EI. The official tryouts aren't for a while, but you could meet the other people preparing to compete. Get to know everyone." Dryly he added, "It's not a huge group. Not even medium sized. Hell, it's probably the smallest group of Olympic track-and-field hopefuls anywhere. They're a good bunch, though. I think you'll like them."

Angel needed to ask someone about this before she committed to anything. Remembering her promise to Bhaaj, she said, "I will let you know. And thank you for thinking of me. I appreciate your interest." There. Lots of words to make him happy. He seemed like a good dude.

"You're welcome! I look forward to hearing from you."

"Eh." Angel waited. When nothing more happened, she said, "EI 142?"

"What can I do for you?" 142 asked.

"Am I done with the comm?"

"Goodman Qazik has signed off, if that's what you mean. He gave me his contact data."

"Good. If I get any more buzzes, you find out who is buzzing and let me know. Then I'll decide if I want to answer."

"Very well. I will update my protocols."

Angel was about to turn back to the intriguing, albeit talky, orientation, when another buzz came, this one a discreet, barely audible hum from her own gauntlet.

"You have received a buzz," Aide 142 said helpfully. "However, it is on a private, secured, and hidden system that I have no way to access."

And I'm not giving you access. Angel tapped a panel on her gauntlet. "Ruzik?"

"Eh." His voice came out of her comm. "Got problem."

"With Majda?"

"Yah. And cartels."

Angel stiffened. "What goes?"

"Want to meet Majda queen."

"Fuck."

"Yah."

"You want me get help?"

"Nahya. We deal." He paused. "We check in each hour. With you. No check, you call Majda. Use secret line to Matriarch." He said all three syllables of her title with respect, indicating honor. "Tell Majda we need help."

"I ken." Angel hesitated, worried for him. "You good?"

His voice softened the barest amount. "Yah, good. You?"

"Yah. Good."

With that great outpouring of love, they signed off.

Angel checked to make sure she still had the Majda link hidden in her comm codes. Satisfied, she went back to the Kyle orientation to learn more about the things she could do with her Kyle brain, which apparently almost no one else in the universe could manage despite their wealth, heritage, power, titles, and words. She couldn't wait to figure out everything she could get away with as a telop, or no, she meant all the support she could give the slicks. Really. She meant support.

Learning to do what slicks couldn't do just might be fun.

CHAPTER VI
A New Wind

The cartels came in force, Kajada and Vakaar alike, gathered in one place with enough punkers to massacre each other if they changed their minds about acting human for this meeting.

Bhaaj and crew also arrived en masse, or at least as much mass as eight people could muster. They walked onto a peninsula of rock that jutted out at midwalk level in a large canal. The canal, which was over twenty meters wide and even taller from ground to ceiling, ended at the jutting finger of rock. Cartel punkers waited on the dusty floor below, on the midwalks, and undoubtedly spying from within the walls and ceiling, which were riddled with caves, passages, and breaks, all made from eons of poisonous, mineral-rich water dripping through the nooks and crannies of their world.

"Not good," Ruzik said at Bhaaj's side.

Bhaaj grimaced. "Yah." She'd chosen this place from three suggested by the cartels because it offered the easiest way out of their territory if her group had to run. They all stood at the end of the peninsula with a tunnel exit in the sheer wall at their backs, the only obvious escape from this end of the canal. Wide spaces separated their section of rock from the midwalks on either side, so only Bhaaj's group had access to the tunnel exit. She hoped.

Their light came from torches or lamps that people held. The Vakaars waited on the left and the Kajadas on the right. They didn't need the tunnel exit behind Bhaaj; any of them could take off in the other direction, running down into the canal or along its midwalks. So yah, everyone had a way out—except Bhaaj had to take her people down into the canal to meet with the cartels.

Too many punkers waited down there. About twenty had come with each cartel, and probably another ten from each hid in the walls, spying on the meeting. They'd brought pulse revolvers, blast-pistols, and machine guns, including military-issue weapons from the black market. Knives, maces, daggers, and other instruments of mayhem glinted everywhere. Cutter Kajada and Hammerjan Vakaar had both come, each surrounded by their lieutenants, their groups separated by only a few precarious meters. In the dim light, with the flickering torches and the sea of darkness beyond, the scene looked like an artist's depiction of hell.

"Goddess," Lavinda said in a low voice.

"We can still leave," Bhaaj told her.

"No, we should stay." Lavinda paused. "How do meetings like this usually go?"

"Hell if I know," Bhaaj said. "It's never happened before." The only other time she'd seen punkers from both cartels in one place without fighting was at Dig's memorial.

"Have you figured out what they want?" Lavinda asked.

"Not a clue," Bhaaj admitted.

"Unless they plan to kidnap a royal heir," Captain Morah said, her voice tight.

"This can't be a grab," Bhaaj said. "Better ways exist if that's what they want, besides which, they'd never cooperate for it."

Lavinda looked out over the waiting cartel. "You see anyone you trust?"

"No." Bhaaj tilted her head to where the Kajada cartel queen stood on the left below, her gaze intent on them. "I've known Cutter Kajada for years, since before she took over the cartel. She's Dig's cousin. Most of the time, she's crazy pissed at the world. She knows Dig and I were like sisters, though. In her mind, I'm family." With a shrug, Bhaaj added, "Yah, she'd kill me if I challenged her. As long as neither of us pushes it, though, we get along. Sort of."

"Not exactly an overwhelming endorsement." Lavinda nodded toward the other side of the canal, where the top Vakaar punkers surrounded Hammerjan. "What about them?"

Bhaaj snorted. "They'd love to finish me. They know if they do, though, the Dust Knights will turn against them in full force, starting another war, this time between Vakaar and the gangs. As soon as Kajada saw any sign of Vakaar weakening, they'd take advantage. It'd be chaos. Vakaar hates Kajada even more than they hate me, so they keep peace with my Knights."

Lavinda stared at her. "Why the blazes do you come down here all the time, if you're dealing with all this? We gave you a penthouse in the city, for saints' sake. You could live there."

"This is my home. I give back what I can." Although the Vakaars would never admit it, that was probably another reason they didn't take her on. They benefited as much as anyone else from the changes she was helping bring to the aqueducts.

A restless wave of mutters rolled through the gathered watchers.

"We have to do something," Bhaaj said.

"Then let's go meet them," Lavinda said.

"You sure?" Bhaaj asked.

"Yes. Do you have a way down there?"

Bhaaj motioned at a staircase carved into the sheer wall of the peninsula that led down to the bottom of the canal. "There."

"Colonel, wait," Captain Morah said. "You can't go down there."

Lavinda's gaze never wavered. "Captain, I understand your concern. But we won't get this chance again. These groups have power. If they decide they don't want us here, we aren't getting détente with the Undercity. Period." Bitterly she said, "We need the Undercity, regardless of anything you may have heard, read, or seen. We need the people here. But if they think I'm a coward, they'll never deal with us."

Ruzik spoke with respect to the colonel. "We all come with you."

Lavinda inclined her head to him. Enough said.

Morah gave her own reluctant nod and turned to her guards. "You flank Colonel Majda at all times."

"Yes, ma'am," Lieutenant Warrick answered in the same moment that the still unnamed guard said, "Understood, Captain."

With that done, they headed to the steps. The staircase was carved into the peninsula and ran from left to right down to the floor of the canal. It was narrow enough that they had to descend single-file, Bhaaj in front and Lavinda in the middle with guards in front and behind her. The stairs had no railing, nothing protecting them from the drop-off, so they took it one slow step at a time, always watched by the silent cartels.

It felt like it took forever to reach the bottom, but Bhaaj finally stepped onto flat ground, stirring the dust into eddies that drifted in the air and settled on her clothes. She never took her gaze off the cartels, which meant she couldn't look back to see if the others followed her. She heard them with her augmented senses, though, the scrape of feet, the clink of a pebble falling down the wall, the rustle of their clothes.

As Bhaaj walked forward, the punkers shifted position, forming an aisle bordered on one side by Kajada and on the other by Vakaar. She walked down that gauntlet, acutely aware of them watching her. Both cartels had brought their best fighters, muscled hulks with embedded tech-mech glinting on their arms, hands, and hardened abs. Some boasted cyber implants in their faces, replacing a lost eye, a shredded ear, or anything else they wanted. It was all as illegal as badass-bytes, created from black market parts by cyber-riders who gave exactly zero shits about above-city laws.

Slow and easy, Bhaaj thought. She kept going as if it were perfectly normal to walk past two lines of killers bristling with weapons. They studied her with no outward reaction, which meant the others in her group must be following, no one provoking their hosts either by acting like a threat or by showing weakness.

She felt naked without her pulse revolver. No way could they carry weapons here, not even hidden, since the cartel's cyber-riders could scan for them. However, she'd put two drones in her jacket pocket, her red and blue beetle-bots. Red acted as a snoop bot, optimized for spying. Technically, Blue was the same, but she'd weaponized its buzz-bug self. Although it could squirt ink into someone's eyes or blast digitized nonsense into a cyber-spy, neither ability would register as a weapon. Normally it also carried two sedative darts, but today she'd left those with Dara.

Bhaaj, your pulse is too high, Max thought.

Yah, big surprise there. *You getting anything you don't like from these punkers?*

They're armed to the teeth, literally in some cases. Not just what you see, but explosives in their cybernetics, poison capsules,

dart throwers in their gauntlets, knives of every kind of metal and composite I can detect. And guns. A *lot* of guns.

And yet, they aren't fighting.

No. They aren't. He sounded as baffled as she felt.

Cutter came toward Bhaaj from the left and Hammerjan from the right, both flanked by their lieutenants. The other punkers shifted position to form an opening in their midst. As Bhaaj slowed to a stop, aware of her group gathering around her, the cartels formed a circle, leaving Bhaaj's crew in the center with the two cartel bosses, cutting off all escape.

Cutter and Hammerjan stared at each other, two scarred warriors, both in their early thirties yet looking far older. Although they stayed impassive, Bhaaj felt their animosity like a fire in the air. Neither spoke; no threats, no violence, nothing. Instead, they each gave the barest nod you could offer a person without it being impossible to see. Whatever they wanted from Lavinda ranked even higher on their bucket lists than butchering each other.

They turned to the colonel.

"You Majda?" Cutter asked.

"I am," Lavinda said.

Hammerjan's voice hardened. "You come to pinch our people."

Damn! They thought Lavinda intended to kidnap Kyles from the Undercity? Bhaaj started to answer, but Lavinda shook her head, then spoke to Hammerjan in passable dialect. "Not *take* people. Ask people."

Cutter waved her hand in dismissal. "Ask, take. You want us to serve you. Make us your byte-bitches."

"Not serve," Lavinda said. "We give jobs. Good bargain. Good trades."

Cutter snorted and the Vakaar boss crossed her arms, her muscled biceps ridged with tension. Neither bothered to ask what "bargain."

Instead, Cutter spoke to Bhaaj. "Majda queen lie?"

"Nahya," Bhaaj said. "Is truth."

Hammerjan narrowed her gaze at Bhaaj. "You lie."

"Nahya. Not lie." Bhaaj doubted she'd fully convince a Vakaar, but they knew she had a rep for straight-talk.

Cutter motioned at Lavinda as she spoke to Bhaaj. "You vouch?"

"Yah," Bhaaj said. "I vouch."

Hammerjan's lips curled with disgust. "For Majda." She made the name sound like mud on the wall.

"For *this* Majda." No way would Bhaaj bring any other Majda here.

Cutter studied the colonel, then turned to her Vakaar rival. Hammerjan met her gaze.

"We go," Hammerjan said to Cutter. "You?"

"Yah," Cutter said. "We go."

Bhaaj blinked. Go where? Did they plan to leave now that she'd vouched for Lavinda? That made no sense. Why go to all this trouble? They knew she'd never bring Lavinda here if she couldn't vouch for her. Maybe they meant to take the colonel hostage after all, not for ransom but as insurance, to make sure Lavinda kept her word when she claimed the army wouldn't kidnap anyone. The Concourse cops sometimes rounded up whatever "dust rats" they could find sneaking out on the boulevard and forced the kids to work on the water farms, vicious labor that could grind you down until you died. Maybe the cartels wanted to ensure the army didn't inflict the same on anyone who followed up on their offers for jobs.

Except—they knew the Dust Knights had committed to looking out for anyone approached by the army. The cartels might not trust Bhaaj, but however much they wanted to whack her for cracking down on drugs, they knew her Knights would make good on their vow to protect the Undercity.

Maybe it has nothing to do with protection, Max thought. **It could be a challenge to the Knights, a way to establish cartel dominance over them using Lavinda.**

Good point, Bhaaj thought. *I hope you're wrong.* The last thing anyone needed was a war where Kajada and Vakaar joined forces against the Dust Knights.

With no other comment, Cutter motioned to her people. In the same moment, Hammerjan raised her hand in a signal. Bhaaj instinctively went for the gun she usually wore in her shoulder holster, which of course she didn't have today, damn it.

Whatever she might have expected, though, it didn't come close to what happened. The crowd of Kajada punkers rippled like water stirred by some invisible effect. What—? There! Several children were walking through the crowd, which shifted as people moved aside to let them pass. Same with the Vakaars; three kids were making their way through the protective ocean of muscle. The cartels had brought their *children*? No wonder they wanted to make sure they thoroughly outnumbered and outgunned Lavinda's people.

Cutter and Hammerjan offered no explanation. Their hostility felt tangible, like embers ready to ignite, yet they just stood, watching each other and Lavinda.

The Vakaars at the edge of the circle parted, and the three kids stepped into the open space. One boy seemed about sixteen and the girl was a younger teen. The other boy looked seven or eight. All three came to stand with Hammer, watching Bhaaj and Lavinda. The Kajadas moved aside to let three of their own come forward, a girl in her late teens and two younger kids, a boy and a girl.

Bhaaj looked from Cutter to Hammer, at a complete and utter loss. "Eh?"

Neither answered. Instead, Cutter spoke to Lavinda. "You get mooders?"

Lavinda squinted at her, then glanced at Bhaaj.

Don't interfere, Max warned. **Their business is with Colonel Majda.**

Yah, well, the esteemed colonel doesn't know what the hell they're saying.

I might be able to link with her EI, Max thought.

No, don't. With all the cyber muscle here, someone would probably sense that you sent a signal to Raja. It would look like we're plotting.

Then think at Colonel Majda.

What?

Don't use a cyber link. Just think.

Bhaaj doubted it would work, but what the hell. Lavinda was a Kyle operator. So Bhaaj tried what she'd made it a policy never to do, in part because she didn't know how but also because she was usually too busy denying her Kyle ability. She sent Lavinda a mental message.

Hammerjan is asking if you're looking for empaths, Bhaaj thought, adding as much force as she could to the idea.

Although Lavinda showed no reaction, Bhaaj had an odd sense, as if the Majda queen gave her a mental nod. The colonel spoke, directing her words to both Cutter and Hammerjan. "We look for people who feel what other people feel." Although she wasn't using pure Undercity dialect, her speech had the right cadences.

"From any in Undercity?" Hammerjan demanded. "Or just fucking Dust Knights."

"For all," Lavinda said. "With or without fucks."

No, shut up! Bhaaj wanted to shout. This was *not* the time for bad jokes.

Fortunately, Hammer almost smiled, just barely, yah, but down here that equated to a belly laugh. For one fraction of a second, she'd actually found Lavinda funny. Cutter didn't look any more pissed than usual, so apparently the joke hadn't ticked her off.

No more jokes! Bhaaj thought at Lavinda. *Don't risk it.*

Cutter motioned to the children who'd come forward, both Kajada and Vakaar. "For them?"

"They mooders?" Lavinda asked.

"Yah." Cutter and Hammer spoke at almost the exact same moment.

Holy shit, Bhaaj thought.

"Yah." Lavinda kept her voice firm, but Bhaaj sensed her puzzlement. "Children, too."

"Even cartel jans and sons?" Cutter asked.

"Majda call cartel cri-min-al." Hammer made her last word an insult.

"They come *as* cartel?" Lavinda asked.

"Nahya," Hammer told her. "Not as cartel. As kid."

"As selves," Cutter said.

"Then, yah," Lavinda said. "For all. Any person. From any place."

"For med too?"

Lavinda looked confused, but before Bhaaj could react, light dawned in the colonel's expression. "Yah," she told the cartel queens. "Can get med help. Can go to clinic with healer Kar. Always, even if not go to army. True for all."

Bhaaj felt as if a roaring filled her ears, maybe from her sudden surge of adrenalin or maybe from shock. The cartels didn't want to *stop* Lavinda. They hadn't come to fight, kill, assert dominance or peddle their seductive death. They wanted something else, wanted it so much they risked forming a united front and—for this one time— even denied their brutal trade.

They wanted their children to have a chance at what Lavinda offered.

Although it wasn't unheard of for punkers to be Kyles, it warped them. Horribly. To be an empath and soak up the violence, cruelty, and malevolence dealt by the cartels—to take that in *every day* of their lives—it destroyed a person. No one here taught empaths to defend their minds. They didn't know how. Either they repressed their "gift," as Bhaaj had done, or else they fell to the agony. She'd seen Cutter change over the years, turning a curious child into a sociopathic adult. Yet incredibly, both Cutter and Hammer saw the value in what Lavinda offered, a way out for their youth who hadn't yet become so twisted by their lives that they lived beyond redemption.

"We send whisper," Cutter told Lavinda.

"Through Bhaaj." Hammerjan tilted her head at the three Vakaar kids. "For pups."

Cutter motioned at her trio. "If they want."

Both cartel bosses went silent, then, waiting.

Lavinda exhaled, her breath so low it was almost inaudible. "I ken."

"Good," Hammer said. "We go now."

"Send whisper later," Cutter said.

With that, the cartels melted away as if their mutual repulsion finally drove them apart. First the most distant punkers vanished into the shadows, then those closer in, and finally those in the circle around Bhaaj and Lavinda, including Cutter and Hammerjan. Within moments, Bhaaj's group were the only ones in the canal.

"Gods," Ruzik said.

"That's it?" Lavinda said.

Bhaaj stared at her. Ruzik stared at her. Tower and Byte stared at her. The Majda guards still looked ready to fight, as if they'd prepared for mayhem and didn't know what to do with vanishing cartels instead.

After a moment, Lavinda said, "I don't get it."

Bhaaj finally found her voice. "What don't you get?"

"Everyone made a big deal about this meeting." Lavinda gestured at Bhaaj and Ruzik's gang. "You all especially. Then nothing happened. I mean, a lot of people showed up to ask me a couple of questions, but that's it."

"They not kill anyone," Byte-2 said.

"Not fight," Tower said.

"Not stop you," Ruzik said.

Bhaaj spoke as the roaring in her mind eased. "Do you remember Dark Singer, the Vakaar assassin who turned herself in last year and told the Cries authorities everything she knew about the cartels?"

Lavinda frowned. "You told us she was a Dust Knight, that she'd left the cartel."

"Yah. She became a Knight." Bhaaj regarded her steadily. "She could have taken over the Vakaar cartel, Lavinda. They would have gladly followed her."

"You convinced her to give herself up instead."

"No. I didn't. She came to me on her own. Why? Because she was an *empath*."

"Yes. I know." The colonel seemed baffled by this new direction. "That's why we gave witness protection to her and her family and let her serve her sentence in a military internment center instead of a high-security prison. She's learning to work for us."

"Yah." Bhaaj met her gaze. "She also used to be the worst assassin in the Undercity. Why do you think she wanted an out, even if it meant going to prison?"

"Being an empath in the cartels twists you," Ruzik said. "It destroys you." He tapped his temple. "Angel and I, we help each other. Make haven. Singer, the assassin—she had husband. Daughter. Both Kyle. They kept her from dying in the darkness."

"If she'd taken over the Vakaar cartel," Bhaaj said, "she'd have become a far deadlier crime boss than Hammerjan. Singer is damn smart, Lavinda. Most Kyles are, with all those extra neural structures in their brains."

"I get it." Lavinda looked as if she didn't get it at all. "And?"

"The cartels don't *have* Kyles," Bhaaj said.

"It kills them," Tower said.

"Or they turn into killers," Ruzik told her.

"They go crazy," Byte-2 said.

After a pause, Lavinda said, "There were times in the army, during combat—" She spoke with difficulty. "Being a Kyle, soaking it all in during battles, especially up-close combat—it changes you."

"Yah." Bhaaj met her gaze. "And you had the resources of a

military trained to protect its Kyles, the guidance of the military doctors if you had problems, and the support of one of the most powerful families in the Imperialate. Our people have *nothing*. Those few Kyles in the cartels rarely survive. If they do, they become so warped that they end up as assassins, sadists, or gibbering idiots." Even Bhaaj, despite her circle of loved ones, had needed to suppress her ability so she could survive. "It would've happened to Singer if she'd stayed here. It was *already* happening. Somehow she had enough insight—and enough drive to protect the family she loved—to seek a way out, first by joining the Knights, and then, when that wasn't enough, by giving herself up to the Cries authorities."

"Yah," Tower said. "The cartels, they like their crazy mooders, but not for good."

Byte-2 grimaced, drawing furrows in the cyber implants along his neck. "Cartels use mooders."

"Make them killers," Ruzik said.

Lavinda spoke carefully. "Are you saying they'll want to use any Kyle work they do with the army to profit their drug trade?"

Good question. It wouldn't surprise Bhaaj. More was going on here, though. "They always want to maximize profits. But Lavinda, they all know about Singer, that she lost her freedom, her home, even her world. She almost lost her life." The Cries authorities had wanted her executed even after she made her deal with the army.

Lavinda scowled. "Of course she lost her freedom. She was a murderer." When Bhaaj started to speak, Lavinda held up her hand. "Yes, I know, she was killing other drug dealers. *Kajada* dealers, in service to the Vakaar cartel. Who does that help? And it's still murder, Bhaaj, with the intent of furthering a drug trade that's destroying all our peoples." She spoke with a bitter edge. "Until a few years ago, addictions were the sum total of the interaction between your people and Cries. Drugs and your husband's charming trade. Gambling."

Bhaaj had no intention of going there with anyone. She had many issues with what Jak did for a living, but that was between the two of them and no one else. "The point," she told Lavinda, "is that as far as the cartels know, any empaths who go to the authorities are lost to the cartel. It offers them nothing."

"Then why would they ask me about it?" Lavinda said. "And why would both Kajada and Vakaar come together to see me? Isn't that unusual?"

"Unusual?" Bhaaj gave a harsh laugh. "It's *unheard* of. They'd rather have a bloodbath."

"So what you're claiming," Lavinda said, "is that they came together in force, both Kajada and Vakaar, in a manner that drew immense attention to their trade at a time when they most want to avoid it, when the Cries authorities are conducting their largest drug crackdown in history, when both cartels are weakened from the war and the data we got from Singer, yet they still wanted to risk meeting with one of the most powerful authorities in the city, all to ask for something that has no benefit to them."

"No benefit to the *cartels.*" Bhaaj took a breath. "It does have a benefit, one that many people, even some drug punkers, put beyond greed and power."

Lavinda considered her for a long moment. "It benefits the people they love."

The people we love. If Bhaaj hadn't considered Dig Kajada her sister—if she hadn't known Dig's capacity for human decency—she'd never have believed the cartels could act for anything beyond their own greed. Dig's mother, Jadix, had never put love ahead of self-interest. Whatever in the human brain allowed a person to feel love had burned out of Jadix long before she gave birth to Dig.

And yet . . .

Jadix's granddaughter, Dig's oldest daughter, was a strong Kyle operator, abilities that came from recessive traits passed by biological parents to their children. Recessive. It meant the traits had to come from *both* parents to manifest. If Dig's daughter was a Kyle, then both Dig and her husband had carried at least some of the genes, which meant, incredibly, that either the monster Dig called mother or the dead punker who'd fathered her, or both of them, gave her the genes. Could Jadix Kajada have been an *empath*? Had she represented the horrific end result of surrounding empaths with the worst of human nature?

Dig had loved and protected her children. Eighteen years later, her oldest daughter became the first Undercity native to qualify for admission into the Dieshan Military Academy. And now, incredibly, these new versions of the cartels sought better lives for their children.

They wanted it enough to present a united front, a challenge to Lavinda, sure, to test her resolve and bravery, but that wasn't the main reason. Today they'd put love for their children ahead of their trade.

What did that mean for the Undercity? Everyone in the aqueducts lived in the shadow of the crime empires that shared their world. It hardened the lives of an already poverty-stricken population. If the cartels took a new direction, even for just a few of their children, could that offer hope that they might make other positive changes?

Hope, my ass, Bhaaj thought. If Kajada and Vakaar joined forces, they'd become that much more powerful, since they wouldn't be fighting each other anymore. It could turn into a nightmare beyond any the Undercity had previously faced.

"Bhaaj?" Lavinda asked.

With a start, Bhaaj realized she'd just been standing there, staring at them. She glanced at Ruzik, and he nodded, just barely, but enough to let her know he understood.

"We need to check in with Doctor Rajindia," Bhaaj said. "Make sure she knows the cartels may send their children to the clinic." It sounded like Cutter and Hammerjan didn't realize that going to Doctor Rajindia differed from what Lavinda offered. They saw the struggles of their Kyle children as an illness. "We should get going," she added. "We have work to do."

CHAPTER VII
Rajindia

Med-clinic.

Such an innocuous name for such a deep-seated change. Bhaaj still remembered the day Doctor Karal Rajindia set up her clinic in the Undercity. No one came near it. No one bothered her, either, because the Dust Knights gave her protection, but they'd all have rather seen her get lost—until they discovered she really could heal them.

It also didn't take long for people to realize she cared about her patients. Although officially Karal lived in the City of Cries and only came to her clinic during work hours, she often slept here. Gradually people warmed. Eventually they created beautiful living quarters for her in the clinic, polished rooms with carved walls and exquisite art, an exchange in return for her care.

When Bhaaj told the Ruby Pharaoh that her people had no real medical care, only self-taught healers, she hadn't expected much response. Even at her wildest imaginings, she'd never have thought that Dyhianna Selei Skolia, titular ruler of the Skolian Imperialate, would send one of her own physicians. Technically the pharaoh no longer governed, only served the elected Assembly, but no one doubted the immense power she wielded. She was one of only two Kyles strong enough to build and maintain the Kyle web used by the rest of the telops. It made sense that Karal Rajindia served as her doctor. Karal specialized in Kyle medicine, which involved the neurological mutations that let humans use the Kyle network, what many people called the psiberweb. And the pharaoh had sent her here, to the Undercity.

A curtain of blue and green beads created by a glass blower hung in the clinic entrance. When Bhaaj shook the curtain, its beads jingled together, creating a sparkling wash of music.

"Come," a voice called from somewhere within.

Bhaaj pushed aside the beads and entered, aware of Ruzik and Tower holding the curtain open behind her. Their entire party trooped into the waiting room beyond, filling the delicate place with their overly muscled and armed selves. Bhaaj felt like a wrecking ball in a glass shop. No one greeted them; whoever had called out had remained deeper within the clinic.

Weavings softened the walls, cool swaths of blue and green with gold accents. Bhaaj wondered if the artists who created these works had any idea they evoked the oceans that no longer existed on Raylicon. Gold rugs warmed the floor, with accents of blue and green. Sculptures of winged reptiles stood in the wall nooks, dragons glazed in blue, green and gold, with red accents and rubies for eyes. Another curtain hung in an archway across from them, and Bhaaj heard people talking beyond that sparkling drape of beads.

"Saints almighty," Lavinda murmured. "Are these works genuine?"

"Genuine what?" Bhaaj asked, preoccupied with the distant voices.

Lavinda indicated a tapestry on the wall. "My family has one of those in a dining room of our home. It looks like that, except its colors aren't as vivid."

Bhaaj squinted at her. "You have an Undercity rug hanging in your palace?"

"Our 'rug' is nearly six thousand years old." Lavinda motioned again, her gesture taking in the entire room. "These weavings, and the ones created by that man whose home we visited earlier—Bhaaj, they look like those few works of art that have survived from the Ruby Empire. Except these are *better*." She spoke with incredulity. "I've only visited two places here where people live, and both have decorations that anthropologists would consider priceless."

Bhaaj had no idea what to say. True, even she could tell that Weaver's tapestries were better than the imitations sold by the vendors from Cries. But priceless? The Majda tapestry probably had that great worth because of its age. You could find modern versions of such art everywhere in the Undercity. Lavinda's response suggested Weaver could ask even more for the works he sold on the Concourse. He had to be careful, though. If he and the other Undercity artists flooded the market with "priceless" works of art, they wouldn't remain priceless for long.

She spoke thoughtfully. "The techniques used by our weavers come down more directly from the Ruby Empire than what you see in the city. I wouldn't be surprised if modern textile producers have lost those methods. My people do it all by hand." She shrugged. "To us, drinkable water is more valuable than these tapestries."

"Water?" Lavinda blinked. "Why?"

"Pure," Ruzik said.

"Oh. Yes, of çourse," Lavinda said. "I imagine the water that occurs naturally down here is poisonous. But your people can go to the city and get purified bottles from a filtration facility."

Bhaaj gave a bitter laugh. "You're kidding, right?"

"Well, no. Why do you say that?"

"They won't sell to us," Ruzik answered, his voice tight. "Never."

"We show up, they call cops," Byte-2 said. "Cops throw us in clinker. Lose key."

"Even if they didn't call the police," Bhaaj said, "my people can't pay for water or food."

"Filtered water isn't a luxury product," Lavinda said. "The prices are low."

Bhaaj struggled to cap her anger. "We have *no* credit here. Most don't even know what it means. Hell, only three people in the Undercity even have a Cries bank account: myself, Jak, and Weaver. Probably Angel too, or she will soon."

Lavinda didn't respond at first, she just stood, taking it in. After a moment, she asked, "Can you filter the water yourself?"

"With what?" Bhaaj asked. "Leftover scraps of tech we salvage from Cries dumps?"

Tower said, "Not all salv—"

"That's right," Bhaaj said quickly, cutting her off. "Sometimes we can't even get salvage." The last thing she needed was for Tower to inform an army colonel that their cyber-riders stole most of the supplies they needed to cobble together filtration equipment. They couldn't buy the systems; water itself might be a low-priced product in Cries, but filtration equipment came at an appalling cost, its expense driven by a monopoly from the most powerful company on the planet, a corporation the Majdas owned stock in, maybe even had family members on the board of directors.

Lavinda looked from her to Tower. Instead of prying into how they built their systems, she said, "Do you have enough filtration equipment to serve your population?"

"Eh?" Tower turned to Bhaaj. "Say what?"

"Ask about water," Bhaaj said. "Good water. Have enough?"

Byte-2 snorted. "Majda queen make jib. Bad jib."

Lavinda glanced at Bhaaj. "I didn't catch that. Did I offend him?"

"He thinks you're making fun of us, asking if we have enough water." Bhaaj rolled her shoulders, trying to relax her tension. "Lavinda, we do have filtration systems, small ones that we patch together. But they have to serve over a thousand people. It's not enough. The biggest causes of fatality here, after violence and murder, is desperate people drinking unfiltered water and dying from the poisons it carries."

Lavinda stared at her. "Can't you get help from the City of Cries?"

"No. If we can't pay, we can't drink. Period." Bhaaj spoke bluntly. "Oh no, wait. I forgot. They'll 'allow' us to work on the water farms for a wage even less than the maintenance costs for your *robots*." She took a breath, calming her surge of anger. "Weaver recently bought a filtration system for this clinic and gave Doctor Rajindia bottles of filtered water, in return for Karal treating our people who had nothing to trade with her. He could do it because his work sells for good prices, and his daughter knows how to manage the income." She breathed out, letting her pulse slow. "This way, more of my people will accept healing. It's not charity. The Undercity gave Doctor Rajindia a water filtration system and looks after her home. The Dust Knights protect her. In return, she heals them, including offering pure water if they need it to survive."

Lavinda's forehead furrowed. "Karal Rajindia could easily get the funds—"

Bhaaj laid her hand on Lavinda's shoulder. When the colonel stiffened, Bhaaj withdrew her hand, knowing she'd gone too far. No one touched a Majda without permission. Her action had the desired effect, however. Lavinda shut up. Yes, Karal Rajindia could get funds to install a filtration plant, but no one here would accept water that way, with nothing given in return. Weaver and his daughter had come up with the solution. Bhaaj had no doubt that Karal also upgraded and maintained the system without letting anyone know, so she could continue to provide filtered water for a desperate but proud people who refused to accept charity.

Lavinda spoke quietly. "Have your people always lived like this?"

"It's better than it used to be. Centuries ago, less than half our population reached adulthood." Bhaaj's voice roughened. "By adulthood, I mean the age of fifteen or sixteen. We don't have the luxury of a prolonged youth." She took a moment, then added, "The situation has improved."

A woman spoke in a pronounced Iotic accent. "Mostly in the past few years. You have Major Bhaajan to thank for that."

Bhaaj and Lavinda both turned with a start. The woman stood in the inner archway, holding a few strings of beads to the side. She wore her straight dark hair pulled back, but a few locks had escaped to frame her face. She was a striking woman, with large eyes, high cheekbones, and elegant features.

Lavinda spoke with respect. "My greetings, Lady Rajindia."

Doctor Karal Rajindia bowed to Lavinda and spoke in Iotic, the language of royalty. "My greetings, your Highness."

Bhaaj looked between the two of them. They both came from the noble or royal Houses. With Lavinda in the room as a contrast, though, it struck Bhaaj how much Karal had changed. The doctor's three years of working with the Undercity had gentled her in a way hard to describe. She seemed more . . . open. When Bhaaj had first met her, Karal kept her hair shorter, not even shoulder length, a professional style that gave her a sophisticated appearance, in charge and ready to work. Since then, it had grown out until the dark mane flowed around her shoulders and down her back in the Undercity style.

The beads stirred and a man appeared, joining the doctor. Although Bhaaj didn't recognize him, he clearly came from the aqueducts. He had that shape to his face, the high cheekbones, tousled black curls, large eyes, an overall look most people would recognize as Undercity. Unlike most, though, he had no scars. No one had ever broken his nose. No lines of strain marred his exceptional features. In a Skolian entertainment center, he could easily have found work as a model. This man came by his looks naturally, however; no way existed here for him to get the body sculpting that many theatrical artists paid a fortune for nowadays, fighting the competition they faced from digital "actors" animated by EI brains.

"Eh." Tower gaped at the fellow. Bhaaj almost smiled. Even a hardened warrior could find herself thrown off balance by a handsome man. The fellow said nothing. Of course no one asked for his name, not even Lavinda, who would have expected an introduction in the above-city.

Instead Lavinda spoke to the doctor. "Thank you for taking time to meet with us, Lady Rajindia."

"Call me Karal, please." The doctor tilted her head toward Byte-2 and continued in Iotic. "Your messenger said you needed a guide for the Maze."

"Not need," Byte-2 said. "We fix that problem. Got new one."

Karal blinked at him, then spoke in the Undercity dialect. "You ken the queen's talk?"

"Nahya," Byte-2 said. "Only ken talk from down here."

"But you ken what we just say," Karal said.

"Yah." Byte-2 seemed baffled. "You say in Undercity talk." He gave the barest nod to both Lavinda and the doctor, a sign of respect. "You learn it well."

"My thanks." Lavinda looked more confused than thankful.

Bhaaj spoke. "I think our Undercity dialect descends more from ancient Iotic than modern languages. We've lived in comparative isolation, so it hasn't evolved as much."

Lavinda spoke in modern Iotic. "Can you understand what I am saying right now?"

"I ken," Byte-2 said.

"Mostly," Tower added.

Ruzik spoke in Skolian Flag. "I understand most of what you say in Iotic, sometimes better than in Flag. Except you have an accent."

"Interesting," Lavinda mused. She glanced at Bhaaj. "According to your army records, you learned Iotic in only a few months."

It had actually only taken Bhaaj a couple of tendays to teach

herself, but she hadn't let on at first because it seemed useful when
people didn't know she understood them. She'd stopped hiding it
after she realized many of them considered her an uneducated idiot.
Goddess, it had felt gratifying to see the shock on their faces when
she answered in Iotic.

She said only, "I figured I'd get promoted faster that way."

The man with Karal shifted his weight like a runner who needed
to sprint away. To Karal, he said, "We go?"

"Yah," she murmured.

Interesting, Bhaaj thought. He and Karal stood closer than either
Undercity natives or Skolian nobility normally tolerated. Their heads
leaned toward each other by the barest amount. Small, almost
unreadable signs, but she recognized them. Hah! Love reared its
ever-present head. But Karal was a Skolian noble. To say it would
shock her House if she had a relationship with an Undercity man was
like saying the galaxy had a few stars. How delightfully scandalous,
or it would be if it didn't threaten the Undercity's good fortune in
having Karal as doctor. Bhaaj hoped they stayed discreet.

Lavinda spoke to the man. "Are you the guide?"

"Maze guide," he told her. "But it not help you. Maze not have a
path out of Undercity."

Bhaaj said nothing. The Maze *did* offer a way to leave the
Undercity, an exit into the ruins of the ancient city Ixa Yaxlan out in
the desert. The military kept it a secret. Bhaaj knew about it from a
previous case, but even with Max helping her, she couldn't find it on
her own. Too much interference from cyber-rider tech hid the route.

"Not need guide anymore," Ruzik told the man.

"Cartels let Majda queen visit after all," Byte-2 said. To Karal, he
added, "Punkers want come here, too. Part of bargain."

Karal regarded him uneasily. "I've never treated the cartels
before."

"We protect you," Ruzik added.

"They want to bring their children," Bhaaj said. If Karal turned
away the cartels, it would scuttle their precarious bargain with
Lavinda.

Karal was watching her closely. She took a deep breath and
nodded. "Of course I'll treat them. I wouldn't turn away anyone, child
or adult."

"We done now?" the man with her asked. "We must go. Fast!"

"Go?" Bhaaj asked. "Where?"

"The Down Deep." Karal nodded to the man. "He came to tell me."

"Med problem?" Bhaaj asked.

"Yah." Worry etched lines across the doctor's face. "Two die. One more sick. Red rash."

Bhaaj grimaced. For people beyond the aqueducts, the carnelian rash amounted to no more than a childhood illness, one easily conquered. Not so here, where it often proved fatal.

"You go," she told Karal. "We're fine."

Lavinda was watching them closely. "What is it?" she asked Bhaaj.

"An outbreak of carnelian rash." Bhaaj stopped, caught by a crushing memory. As a child, she'd lost one of her circle-sisters to the rash. The small girl had died in her arms while Bhaaj desperately tried to soothe her. Although Karal had convinced people in the Undercity to get the vaccine she offered, she had more trouble reaching the Down Deepers, who avoided anyone outside their insular world.

"Do you need help?" Lavinda asked Karal. "I could bring more doctors."

"Nahya!" Tower said.

"That would be a disaster," Ruzik said in Flag.

"Why?" Lavinda asked. "We can treat carnelian rash."

"No one will see it as help," Karal told her. "It will look like the above-city thinks they can trespass on the Undercity just because the people here agreed to let you visit."

Bhaaj spoke. "It's a balance, Lavinda. My people accepted your visit. Even the punkers let you pass. But that's just you and your guards. Four of you, like a dust gang." When Captain Morah opened her mouth, no doubt to protest that portrayal, Bhaaj held up her hand. "Yes, I know, you're Majda security, not a gang. But that's how we do it here, protecting people. The four of you form a unit just as do our dust gangs." She spoke firmly. "If you bring in anyone else, people will think you lied, that your visit is a precursor to betraying their trust. The Knights might reconsider the support they've given your visit. The cartels will withdraw what is already only a grudging acceptance."

"Seriously?" Lavinda asked. "When we're offering life-saving treatment?"

"Not take charity." Tower practically spat the three-syllable word *charity.*

"It's fine," Karal told Lavinda. "I can treat the rash. I have plenty of medicine."

"Will you be safe going to the Deep?" Lavinda asked.

"Of course." Karal seemed surprised by the question. "Carnelian rash isn't contagious, especially if you have health meds in your body. You only risk catching it if you drink infected water. The virus dies in other environments." She exhaled, sounding tired. "Unfortunately, people here don't have even the simplest health precautions we take for granted."

"Goddess," Lavinda muttered. "Someone in Cries ought to clean up the water here."

"Yah, right," Ruzik said with an edge. "Because the above-city so wants to use their precious resources on us."

Tower spoke coldly to Lavinda. "This is *our* home. We take care of. Not slicks."

Lavinda considered them. "What if we offered a bargain, say equipment to help filter the underground lakes here in return for your people letting us train them to use their Kyle abilities. Like with Angel."

Ruzik met her gaze with an impassive look. "We see what Angel says."

Good answer, Bhaaj thought. Although he offered no agreement, neither did he dismiss the offer. Until Angel weighed in about her new job, however, no one would do squat with these nebulous abilities none of them understood anyway.

"Can we visit the Down Deep with Doctor Rajindia?" Lavinda asked.

Bhaaj blinked. She hadn't intended to go that deep. Lavinda had come here to make connections, though, and the Deep had the highest concentration of Kyles. Her presence offered a powerful message, that the above-city was willing to meet the people of the aqueducts on their terms. Instead of waiting, perhaps they should go with Karal. The Rajindia noblewoman understood Lavinda better than anyone else here, and she also knew the aqueducts. She could offer a bridge between their two worlds.

Bhaaj spoke to Karal. "We come with?"

"Do you all have nanomeds to deal with the rash?" Karal asked. "It's unlikely you'd catch it even if you don't, but it's best to be safe."

"All of us," Lavinda said, her motion including herself and her guards.

At the same time Bhaaj and Ruzik both said, "Yah. We have."

"All right. Come with." Karal tilted head toward her friend. "He take us."

Bhaaj nodded. They could use a guide. Reaching the Down Deep was no trivial matter.

The passage of time saturated the ruins.

Ruzik stayed alert as he brought up the rear of the Majda queen's company. They followed a tunnel wide enough for their group to go two or three at a time, and he scanned the area as they walked. They numbered ten now, including Doctor Rajindia and her friend, the man called Paul Franco. Ruzik had heard of Franco, enough even to know his name. Franco earned fame because he lived in the Maze, this dense and tangled region that separated the Undercity from the Deep.

Although Ruzik wasn't ready to trust the stranger, he kenned why someone might retreat to the Maze, staying away from everyone else. Hell, he'd thought about it himself as a kid, those times when the misery around him pressed on his mind until he had to escape. Instead of retreating, though, he gave the people in his circle the best life he could manage, enough so that sometimes, they felt happiness instead of pain.

Up ahead, Bhaaj was walking with the Majda queen, pretending to maintain their distant formality. Odd that. Neither of them seemed to realize they considered each other a friend. No matter. They'd figure it out.

Darkness lurked beyond the glow of their lamps, as if time had left ever-thickening shadows in this buried world. The chilly air had a faint scent, what normal people called "rocky sweet," and Earth books called "cinnamon." Ruzik had looked it up during one of his secret forays into the digitized records of the hilariously named "Cries University Chemistry Department Library." That scent came from a molecule called cinnamaldehyde. Who the hell named this stuff? They actually said all those words out loud instead of just in their head.

He liked the learning, though, bad-mannered names and all. Traces of cinnamaldehyde showed up in the rocks, all that remained of the long-ago time when a sea had stretched across the land above. No one seemed to know what plants or other biz had existed then. It seemed like a story, a fable for telling small kids late at night, but never mind. He enjoyed the subject.

Ruzik let himself fall behind, out of earshot from the others, and tapped his gauntlet. Angel's voice rose into the air. "Eh?"

"Check in," Ruzik said.

"You good?"

"Yah. Done with punkers."

"What'd they want?"

"Let their kids do Kyle riz."

"Odd." Her tone lightened. "Good."

"Yah. Not need more check-ins," Ruzik added. "Majda do them." They no longer had to hide their actions from the colonel's hard-assed sister now that they'd finished with the punkers.

"If need again," Angel said, "Say to me."

"Yah." Ruzik let himself smile. "Good say."

Her voice warmed. "Yah."

With that, they cut the link.

Ruzik continued to monitor the area, alert and intrigued. It was one reason he liked being Bhaaj's second; it meant trying new things, like this visit to the Deep. He even enjoyed the reading she inflicted on them, or at least he did after he figured out how to sneak onto the university meshes, those treasure troves of knowledge forbidden to his people. Ho! He delved into any subject that interested him, especially philosophy. Amazing. All those crassly polysyllabic words had an actual use, letting you talk about the ideas that spun and spun in your mind, never spoken.

Ruzik kenned it now, that because many of his people were empaths, they shared a sense of complex ideas instead of saying them. Except it always felt vague, besides which, not everyone could do it. When you had enough words, however, you could tell anyone exactly what you meant. All that learning also helped him find ways to improve life for his circle beyond the obvious solution of beating the shit out of other gangs and taking what had belonged to them.

He couldn't get enough of military history. The strategies used by battle leaders fascinated him. The more he learned, though, the more fucked it seemed. All that sweat humans put into killing each other, and for what? Yah, you needed to survive, and he'd learned to stay on top, for his circle, his gang, and himself. Even so. The endless wars humanity wreaked on itself seemed like a miserable waste. A better way had to exist. Not that he had any ideas to offer, but he pondered it anyway.

So much had changed in the four years since he'd met Bhaaj. Rumors had swirled back then about a ganger who'd spent decades fighting for the "army" and then come home. Some kids claimed she'd taught them some sweet moves for the rough-and-tumble. They called themselves dust knights. Yah, cute. Maybe they could go hug some dust pups.

Then the cartel war came, crashing through the Undercity. He'd fought the punkers, killing several. He didn't want the remorse that came to him in the night when even Angel couldn't soothe his nightmares. Fuck the cartels. They'd smashed people he loved.

By the time the war ended, they'd all heard about how Bhaaj fought—faster, stronger, and smarter than anyone else. They wanted, *needed* to learn how she crushed her enemies. Ruzik kenned now that some of her abilities came from changes in her body, the "biomech web." Even without it, though, like in the race in Selei City, she slayed.

After the war, more than the usual kids came to train with Bhaaj. Adult gangers, cyber-riders, even a cartel assassin. Before that session, Ruzik had known his power, known that no one could slam him in the rough-and-tumble. That day, he'd learned otherwise. He fought like crap. To master tykado, he had to relearn everything. He'd also finally recognized Bhaaj. In her youth, her dust gang had protected the circle where he and Byte-2 lived. Although she'd left the Undercity when he was small, some of his earliest memories included how well she'd treated them.

The rep of the Knights had spread fast, even up to Cries. When Ruzik and Angel placed in the Selei City Open on the world Parthonia, people asked their names. They just answered, "Dust Knight," and the title spread into the offworld version of a Whisper Mill, what slicks called the interstellar networks.

A scrape came from the darkness behind him.

Ruzik stopped and turned, putting his back to the wall of the tunnel.

Listening.

There! A scrape.

Tower, he thought.

She sent him a sense of questioning.

Come. She'd been just ahead of him in their group. If she slipped back here, no one would notice except maybe Bhaaj, and she knew she could trust his instincts.

As Tower appeared out of the shadows, Ruzik held up his hand, cautioning silence.

They stood and listened.

Yah, again, boots scraping on stone, faint but there.

Tower took up position across the tunnel, and Ruzik touched his gauntlet, slowly fading his light. A sense of agreement came from Tower, followed by the dimming of her light. They kept it gradual, as if they were moving away. In a few moments, the darkness became complete. He couldn't see his hand when he held it in front of his face.

Listening.

More scrapes nearby, stealthy footsteps.

Unease came from Tower. Concentrating, Ruzik picked up her mood, something about not bashing people they knew nothing about. Yah, right, their followers had a good reason for skulking around this remote, isolated place. *They creep,* he thought with enough force to reach her. *They hide.* He had one priority above all else: protect the Majda visit. Attack now, ask questions later.

A sense of agreement came from Tower.

They waited.

The footsteps came closer.

Three people, Ruzik decided.

Yah. Tower's actual thought came to him that time, a rarity.

Closer still—he heard breathing—

Now! Ruzik hit a panel on his gauntlet.

Light flooded the tunnel, blinding after the darkness. Ruzik was ready. He had two seconds to see what they faced: a woman with a giant dagger, a tall man with a knife, and a smaller man with a knife sheathed on his belt. Ruzik lunged at the tall man.

The big guy took a second too long to ken what had happened with the light; by the time he reacted, thrusting his blade, Ruzik had already blocked the strike. At the same time, he kicked *hard*, whamming his boot into the man's knee. His opponent shouted and stumbled backward, staggering while Ruzik came at him with a series of tykado punches. Although the guy sort of countered his blows, he couldn't move worth shit. Ruzik pivoted away, grabbed the guy, and yanked him around, twisting his arm behind his back. Wrapping his other arm around the man's neck, he squeezed until his opponent gasped for breath. Locked in that stance, he kept up the pressure, trying to cut off the man's breath enough to make him pass out. Damn! This guy had control. Ruzik forced him to the ground—the guy dropped his knife—Ruzik kicked it away—

An attack came from the side, a blow that hurtled Ruzik across the ground. Moving by instinct, he rolled and jumped to his feet. The woman he'd seen earlier came at him, stabbing at his chest. He spun on one foot, evading the worst of her attack, but her knife slashed his arm. As blood spurted up, he gritted his teeth. He kept moving, hard and fast, raising his fist—

Tower barreled into the woman. In that same instant, another blow came at Ruzik from behind. Pivoting, he found the dude he'd knocked down was up again, swaying but still going. The man lunged, but mistimed his faltering steps, making him easy to evade. With a grunt, Ruzik socked him hard. As the guy staggered, Tower grabbed him, then dropped him to the ground on his stomach and yanked his arms behind his back.

Whirling, Ruzik saw—damn! The dagger chick was up again, wielding her knife even as blood leaked from a gash on her side. He grabbed her bicep, blocking her thrust, and pushed her face first against the wall while he pulled her arms behind her back. Holding her wrists with one hand, he forced the knife out of her hand, then pulled off the cloth he used as a belt. Uncowed, she continued to fight even as he tied her wrists behind her back. Heaving in a breath, he glanced around—yah, there, Tower had tied up the taller guy. The smaller one lay motionless on the ground, either unconscious or dead.

Ruzik pulled his prisoner away from the wall and shoved her toward Tower. As the woman stumbled forward, she cursed at him, and then fell, catching herself on one knee.

"Sit," Ruzik said. "Stay put. Or you get dead."

The woman eased into a sitting position, staring like she could incinerate him with her gaze.

"You too." Tower hefted up the taller man and pushed him over to the woman. He sat next to her while he glowered at Tower. For good measure, he gave Ruzik the same look. So they stayed, a surly duo with their hands bound behind their backs.

Ruzik glanced at Tower, and she nodded, kenning his intent. While she made sure the duo remained secured, Ruzik went to where the third man lay by the wall.

"You alive?" Ruzik asked.

The man groaned and opened his eyes. "Fuck, no."

"Eh," Ruzik told him, more relieved than he'd ever reveal. He had no wish to kill them. He turned the guy over and pulled off the man's ragged belt. It worked far better for tying his wrists than for holding up his ugly-assed trousers.

"What you doing?" the guy mumbled.

"Stand up," Ruzik told him.

"Can't," the guy muttered.

"Yah, can." Ruzik put his hand under his prisoner's large bicep and pulled upward, helping him climb to his feet. The man grunted at him.

"Here." Ruzik took him over to his companions, who sat unmoving under Tower's cold stare. With an unceremonious push, Ruzik sat him next to the other two.

"Fuck you and your kids and your kid's kids," the woman told Ruzik, followed by some of the most inspired cussing he'd heard, like *Go drown your ugly crap holes in rotting gas-slug corpses.* Hah! Next time he got pissed, that'd be a good one to use. He stood in front of the hapless trio with his arms crossed, letting his biceps bulge. Blood ran over his arm from where the woman had sliced him.

Tower moved behind the trio so they couldn't see her. That way, she and Ruzik could see into the tunnel beyond in either direction in case anyone else came skulking around.

"Why you creep after us?" Ruzik asked, his voice deceptively mild.

They all scowled at him.

"Thieves," Tower decided.

"Yah." Ruzik considered them. "Want to pinch our stuff, eh?"

The woman spoke in a harsh voice. "Majda queen got more than she needs."

Well, shit. They *had* meant to rob the colonel. His voice hardened. "Queen got bargain with us."

"Yah," Tower told them. "You screwed up."

"Yah, well, fuck you," the woman told her.

Ruzik glanced at Tower over their heads. "They break bargain. Go after queen."

Tower snorted. "Leave 'em tied up, eh? Feet, too."

Ruzik motioned at the walls. "Tie to holes in rock. Leave here." He had no intention of stranding them alone without a way to escape, but they didn't need to know that.

"Wait!" the woman said.

"Not leave us," the tall man said.

"Not got water," the woman said.

"Not got food," the tall man added.

The muscular man grunted. "Not got shit."

Ruzik spoke to Tower. "Maybe we just cut throat. Not leave to starve."

She pretended to consider the thought. "More kind, eh?"

"Nahya!" The woman stared at Ruzik. "Not kill."

He met her gaze. "You spit on bargain with queen. With Dust Knights."

The beefy man said, "Got no tumble with Dust Knights."

Ruzik tapped his own temple. "Knight." He pointed to Tower. "Knight."

"Eh?" The guy's face paled.

"Gangers always rough-and-tumble," the woman said. "We lose, we leave. Not kill!"

Ruzik knew exactly what she meant. Dust gangs battled to protect their territory. You never killed your challengers, at least not on purpose. The losers gave up the contested stuff. Done.

"This not same," he said. "You go against Majda. They get pissed, we all pay price."

The thieves had the brains to look scared, at least the woman and the taller guy.

"Stupid to fight Dust Knights," Tower added from behind them.

"Not know you Knights," the muscular man claimed.

"That lizard crap," Ruzik told him. Everyone knew they protected the Majda visit.

"We go." The woman made it sound like an oath written in blood. "Not mess with queen."

"Not come back," the taller man promised.

"We swear," the woman added.

"Yah, well, all people swear," Ruzik told her. "Then here you come. We let you go, you try pinch Majda again."

"Nahya!" the taller man said.

"You got any good stuff?" the beefy man asked Ruzik. "We pinch yours."

"For fuck's sake," the woman told him. "Shut mouth."

Ruzik glanced at Tower, and she nodded, her agreement hidden from the thieves. He scowled for a while as if he were waging a mental battle. Finally he said, "So, yah. Okay. Got prop."

The thieves sat up straighter, hope flashing across their faces. "We listen," the woman said.

"We keep hands tied," Ruzik said. "Take boots. Then let you go. You keep lights. Go out way you come in. Not bother us again. Never." He shouldn't have added that last; proposals didn't include forever demands. He was pissed enough, though, that he didn't care.

"Yah." The woman didn't even try to negotiate. "We go. Not come back. Never."

Ruzik made a show of looking at Tower over their heads. "What think?"

She waited long enough to make the thieves sweat more. "Maybe."

"Why maybe?" Ruzik asked.

"Not like them," Tower said.

"Yah," Ruzik agreed.

"We swear!" the woman said.

"On honor!" the taller man said.

"Got pinched stuff at home," the beefy man informed them. "Need get back, or some bit-kit pinch it back from me."

"Goddess all-fucking-mighty." The woman glared at him. "*Shut* mouth!"

"You not helping," the other man told him.

Ruzik just looked at Tower. They let the moment stretch out until it became excruciating.

Tower finally said, "What the hell. Let them go."

The thieves visibly sagged, the taller man letting out a whoosh of breath.

Ruzik and Tower made quick work of taking the boots from their prisoners and flicking on their lamps. That done, they hefted the three thieves back up to their feet.

"Go." Ruzik shoved the woman in the direction the trio had come, back toward the Undercity. "Not come back."

"Yah." Tower pushed the taller man. "Never."

"Or we whack," Ruzik added.

"Not want that," the beefy man informed them.

"Enough," the woman told him. The trio set off, limping back home.

Ruzik watched until the light of their lamps faded. "Stupid," he muttered.

"You trust them not to come back?" Tower asked.

"Mostly." Given the beating they'd taken, Ruzik doubted they'd have tried going after the Majda party again even if he and Tower hadn't threatened to kill them. "But we keep look out."

"Yah." Tower touched his arm. "Better fix that, eh?"

Ruzik looked down. The blood from the gash across his bicep had dripped down his torso. As much as he hated to use their good water for anything besides drinking, he needed to clean the wound. He could bind it with a strip of cloth torn from his shirt.

"I take care of." He motioned toward the tunnel in the direction of the Deep. "We get back to Majda."

"What?" Bhaaj said.

Lavinda glanced at her. "I didn't say anything."

Bhaaj frowned as they walked along the tunnel. The Majda guards were up ahead with Karal and their unnamed guide. Byte-2 came next, then Lavinda and Bhaaj, with Ruzik and Tower to bring up the rear.

"It's nothing." Bhaaj fell silent, concentrating. Ruzik and Tower had fallen behind and were up to something. Both were . . . doing their job, guarding the group.

"Eh," Bhaaj muttered.

"What's up?" Lavinda asked.

"Just thinking." Whatever Ruzik had found, she trusted his ability to deal with it.

"I should check in with Majda security," Lavinda said.

"Good idea." The more open they kept their comms, the better.

"Raja," Lavinda said.

A woman answered with an elegant Iotic accent. "Do you wish me to contact the palace?"

Up ahead, Byte-2 whirled around, drawing the knife at his belt, fast and efficient.

"Ho!" Tower said behind them. "Who the hell said that?"

Bhaaj glanced back with a start. Tower was following them again, with Ruzik coming up behind her.

"Not problem," Ruzik called to his brother. "Just queen's talky."

Byte-2 scowled, but after a pause, he sheathed his knife, keeping his hand on the hilt.

"Raja, identify yourself," Lavinda said.

"My greetings," Raja said. "I am the EI for Her Royal Highness."

Bhaaj wondered if Lavinda realized Raja had an Iotic accent. You couldn't buy an EI that way; they came with a neutral template. However, true to their name, EIs evolved with their users.

"Raja, contact Duane Ebersole in palace security," Lavinda said.

"One moment," the EI answered.

While they waited for Duane to come online, Bhaaj fell back, giving Lavinda privacy. Joining Tower and Ruzik, she spoke in a quiet voice. "Problem?"

"Nahya." Ruzik kept his voice low. "Thieves come. We deal. Send home."

"Beat them up," Tower said, her voice barely audible.

"Tell them we cut throats," Ruzik added.

"For fuck's sake," Bhaaj said. "Not kill people."

"Not do it," Ruzik allowed. "Just scare them."

Tower smirked. "A lot."

"We keep look out," Ruzik said. "Just in case."

Knowing Ruzik and Tower, Bhaaj suspected they'd terrified the would-be thieves. Ruzik was another matter, though, with that bloody cloth on his arm. "You hurt?" she asked.

"Nahya," he told her.

"Get healer for it," Bhaaj said.

"Not need," he growled. "Is fine."

Bhaaj scowled at him. "Always you say fine. You die, still say fine."

Tower gave a silent laugh. "Like Bhaaj, eh?"

"Nahya," Bhaaj told them, even though Tower spoke the truth. Sometimes her Dust Knights learned her ways too well. "Healer Karal look at."

Ruzik grunted, but then said, "Yah. At Deep."

From up ahead, Raja spoke at a normal volume, which they could hear back here. "I have Captain Ebersole on the line."

As Bhaaj caught up with Lavinda, Duane's voice came over her comm, professional and friendly. "My greetings, Colonel Majda. How is the visit?"

"It's good," Lavinda said. "We've met with some families, with Doctor Rajindia, and with uh—" She squinted at the air. "Other citizens who have an interest in the Kyle program."

"I'll let General Majda know it's going well." Although Duane said nothing about Lavinda's pause, Bhaaj had no doubt he'd noticed. He missed very little. He was also the only member of the Majda police force—hell, *any* police force—that people from the aqueducts tolerated. Or at least, they no longer tried to whack him if he came here.

Bhaaj glanced at Lavinda and motioned at her comm. With a nod, Lavinda said, "Captain Ebersole, Major Bhaajan would like to talk to you."

"Of course," Duane said. "My greetings, Major."

"My greetings," Bhaaj answered. "I was wondering if you knew anything about someone named Mason Qazik. Angel said he contacted her about his sports team."

"Sorry," Duane said. "Never heard of him."

"Hah!" Lavinda grinned. "I can answer that one. He coaches the Olympic track-and-field team. I suggested he look at the recording of the Selei Open, the race that Angel won." She spoke in a confiding voice. "My niece Azarina is a runner. She hopes to make the Olympic team. She's quite good."

Bhaaj smiled, then realized she'd never responded that way to a royal. Well, never mind. If her subconscious thought the time had come with Lavinda, who was she to argue.

"Oh, I know who you mean," Duane said. "I didn't recognize his name, but I've seen him on a few sportscasts."

"Angel is meeting him at the sports complex today," Bhaaj said. "Eighth hour after Midday Sleep. I'm worried they won't let her in." It was one of many places in Cries that forbade entrance to her people. Not that anyone from the Undercity wanted to go there. They didn't even know it existed. Even so. Someone had felt the need to decree that none of her people could invade their precious sports fiefdom, never mind that such an exclusion wasn't legal for buildings supported by city funds.

Lavinda spoke. "Captain Ebersole, why don't you meet her there? Make sure no problems come up."

"I'd be happy to." If it bothered him that he got relegated to the arena while the less senior Captain Morah had the prestigious assignment of guarding an heir to the Majda throne, no sign of it showed in his voice. Although Bhaaj doubted he missed the slight, he wouldn't have reached his high position in a female-dominated profession if he didn't know how to deal with it. She'd learned fast in her youth that she'd never survive in the army if she couldn't control her urge to beat up people who bad-mouthed her Undercity background. And Duane could run circles around her with his restraint.

"Thank you, Captain," Lavinda said. "I'll check in with you again later."

"Will do, Colonel."

After Lavinda signed off, she scowled at Bhaaj. "Don't give me that look."

Bhaaj blinked, baffled. "What look?"

"That 'What the hell is wrong with your idiot sister, not sending him here' look."

Bhaaj spoke blandly. "I would never speak with disrespect about the General of the Pharaoh's Army."

"Listen, Bhaaj. She *knows* she's from another era." Lavinda exhaled. "She may not like the way customs have changed, but she adapts as best she can. Surely you've seen your own people struggling to deal with similar cultural conflicts."

"Not at all." An edge came into Bhaaj's voice. "We don't have the luxury of telling half our population that they can't step outside roles supposedly dictated by their sex."

A call came from Captain Byte-2 up ahead. "One by one."

Lavinda glanced at her.

"He means go single file." Bhaaj motioned toward the path ahead. "This way narrows."

Lavinda grimaced. "It's a good thing I don't get claustrophobia."

"Yah." Bhaaj gave her the truth. "These tunnels are ancient. We don't dig new ones or widen them because we don't want to threaten their stability." She trailed her hand along the wall. The rock felt smooth. "The architects who built this place were geniuses. These ruins have lasted for millennia. They aren't indestructible, though. Sometimes they collapse." Hence, the Maze.

Lavinda spoke dryly. "Vaj would have a royal fit if she knew what I was doing."

"It should be safe." Bhaaj stopped as Byte-2 held back, letting the doctor's mystery friend go ahead of him, probably so he could keep watch on the man. Once they started again, Lavinda followed and Bhaaj came next along the narrowed tunnel.

Nothing broke the silence except their muffled footsteps and the distant dripping of water. Their party stretched out, well separated as they walked. Eventually the path widened again, but Bhaaj held back, sensing Lavinda's wish to take in their eerily beautiful surroundings alone. Delicate stone hangings appeared out of the darkness, their crystals glittering like constellations brought here from the night sky. These caves predated the ruins by eons. Over the ages, they had become a wonderland of rocky lacework and rippled stone curtains, all formed as mineral-rich water trickled through the rock from underground streams and lakes. Bhaaj hoped the Deepers hadn't become desperate enough to drink the unfiltered water. It could spread carnelian rash wicked fast.

Karal Rajindia fell back to walk with Bhaaj. "I never knew about this route to the Deep."

"I doubt many people do," Bhaaj said. "Your friend seems to know the Maze well."

"He lives here," Karal said. "He's like a nomad wandering through the outer edges of the Maze." She spoke dryly. "This is some labyrinth. If my EI wasn't mapping our route, I'd never find my way out."

"Even that might not be enough." Bhaaj thought of her previous attempts to trace a path here. "The Maze is huge, maybe even hundreds of square kilometers. It's crisscrossed by all sorts of tech-mech signals. It'll interfere with your EI." She paused, then added what she'd normally never tell someone from Cries. With Karal, it was different, though. "The signals come from the cyber-riders. They hide us from the above-city."

"Paul mentioned something like that."

"Paul?" Bhaaj didn't recognize the name. It sounded like Caul, one of the most common Skolian names, but she liked this variation.

Karal motioned toward her friend. "Paul Franco." She winced. "Ah, damn. Don't tell him I said his name." Her look turned rueful. "It's hard to change a lifetime of customs."

Bhaaj spoke wryly. "I had a terrible time when I enlisted. I kept fighting people for asking my name." She glanced at Paul. "How'd you meet him?"

"After he broke his arm, he came to my clinic for help." The hint of a smile touched her face. "We hit it off well. We're both empaths."

"Ah." Bhaaj had no idea how to respond. Imperialate royalty never "hit it off well" with even highly placed commoners. With someone in the Undercity? Unheard of. Then again, the bond that formed between empaths could defy even the strongest customs.

"We got to know each other by playing the Doppelganger game," Karal added. "It's fun."

Bhaaj grimaced. "I hate that game."

"Really? Why?" Karal regarded her with curiosity. "Did it come up with someone you didn't want to look like?"

"The opposite." Bhaaj spoke with a longing that she usually repressed. Down here, though, in the darkness surrounded by a glittering fantasy world, it felt more distant. "I tried every database I could access, and I never got a single match."

"Not even a relative?"

"I don't have any." Bhaaj pushed away her sense of loss. "After I enlisted, the army checked to see if they could locate anyone who carried even a small amount of the same DNA as me. They didn't find anything."

Karal spoke thoughtfully. "Before I started working here, I thought the government had DNA records for just about everyone. That was before I realized how thoroughly your people stay off the grid."

Bhaaj shrugged as if she didn't care about her lack of relatives, which was a lie, but not one she'd admit. "That's what the army docs told me. All my ancestors must come from the Undercity. Back then, the military had no records on our population."

"We have a few now, from my clinic."

Bhaaj stiffened. "You're spying on us?"

"Well, no. It's just for my patients." Karal paused. "It's confidential. I always let them know I keep records. I'm not trying to trick anyone."

"They don't know what 'keep records' means." Bhaaj scowled at her. "They have no idea the above-city can identify them from those records."

"Bhaaj, I explain it, I swear. In detail. Some agree and some don't. For those who don't, I respect their wishes."

Bhaaj still didn't like it. After all this time, though, she knew Karal well enough to trust her word. Besides, it benefited the people of the Undercity to know more about their genetics. "Did you and Paul find any doppelgangers for yourselves?"

"A few." A smile warmed her face. "Our favorites are from Earth. He looks like a man called Dario Franchitti who raced cars in the twenty-first century. I look like an actress from that era named Alana De La Garza, but with darker coloring."

Bhaaj wondered how it felt to know that people existed who looked enough like you that they might share some of your ancestry, even as distant as Earth relatives. She'd never had that gift.

"You're lucky." Bhaaj hesitated. "One time, I sort of found one. She wasn't real, though. It was a digital painting called 'Warrior' by an artist named Luis Royo from Earth. It appeared on the cover of the magazine *Heavy Metal* in the year 2005. The picture looked like me when I was young."

"Were you happy with it?"

"I guess." Bhaaj shrugged. "You could see through her clothes. I never dressed that way." Then she amended, "But yah, she otherwise looked like me. Her face, the other stuff she wore, her hair, her shape, it could have been me. She just wasn't a real person."

"Maybe the artist used a real model for the painting," Karal offered.

"Maybe." Bhaaj felt too embarrassed to admit just how thoroughly she'd searched. She'd never found anything about any woman who might have posed for the picture. That didn't say much, though. Earth had lost a huge amount of data during its Virus Wars, which decimated both the living and digital spheres, wiping out a significant portion of the human population and their records. Even if the data had existed, Bhaaj doubted it would've helped. Genetically her people had diverged from Earth's populations long ago. Any similarities, like the ones Karal and her friend Paul found, probably happened more by chance than any close genetic connection.

Karal was watching her closely. "You have ancestors. Somewhere."

"I'll never know, I guess."

"Someone must have witnessed your birth."

Bhaaj spoke bitterly. "Yah. My mother." She *really* didn't want to talk about this. It hurt too much. Her mother had come from the Deep. Maybe. Probably. Hell, who knew. For most of her life, Bhaaj had denied the Deep existed. Yah, she was an idiot. Everyone in the aqueducts knew about it. Deepers almost never visited the Undercity, though, so she'd let herself "forget."

No one knew what happened during her birth beyond a vague tale that someone found a dead woman in a cave with her newborn baby squalling for help. For some reason, they took the infant to the orphanage in Cries. *Why?* Women here often died giving birth, especially before Karal had come. The mother's circle always found a place for the baby. No one would strand a child in that blighted orphanage. Yet some monster had left her in a basket by its door with a message tucked into her swaddling, its words scrawled in the Undercity dialect: *Parents dead. Bhaaj's jan.*

Bhaaj's jan. The daughter of someone named Bhaaj. That message remained her sole legacy.

She'd lived in the orphanage for three years, until the day Dig Kajada freed her. The cops had caught Dig stealing food on the Concourse and dumped her in the orphanage. She ran away, of course, back to the Undercity, and she took the younger Bhaaj with her. Dig, Jak, and Gourd became Bhaaj's family, a ragged gang of kids with no supervision except Dig's demon of a mother who didn't give two shits about them. In her youth, Bhaaj had dreamed her father came from the above-city. That fantasy died when the army found exactly zilch about her heritage. She'd lived with that loneliness ever since.

She said only, "My mother died giving me birth. I saw it."

"I'm sorry." Karal's forehead wrinkled with puzzlement. "How could you see it as a newborn?"

"Not see, exactly." It was a moment before Bhaaj continued. "I'm an empath. Apparently, my mother was too. You know how that works, yes? The parents and unborn child form a bond. My mind linked with my mother. Maybe my father, too." Father. Some unknown stranger held the dubious honor of that title. Maybe he had died, maybe not. If he'd lived, he obviously hadn't wanted her. She'd rather believe he chose to abandon her, though, than what the note left in her basket said, that both her parents had died.

"You mean your mind was linked to your mother's during the birth?" Karal asked. "That can be traumatic. I hope the doctor or midwife monitored the process to protect you."

"What doctor or midwife? I was born in a fucking *cave*."

Bhaaj, she has no way to know, Max thought. **It's not her fault.**

Bhaaj took a breath, then spoke more evenly. "The Kyle docs think I experienced every moment of my mother's labor, linked to her mind. And then I—I died with her."

Karal spoke softly. "I'm sorry."

"I don't remember, of course." Bhaaj gave up trying to pretend she didn't care. "The neurologists think that's part of why I repressed my Kyle abilities."

Karal spoke with compassion. "Many of your people do."

"It's a survival mechanism." When the doctor started to speak again, Bhaaj held up her hand. She couldn't talk about it anymore.

Someone spoke up ahead, and they all slowed down, gathering into a group.

"What's wrong?" Karal asked.

"Too much light," Paul told her.

"Too much?" Lavinda seemed perplexed. "We hardly have any at all."

"Close to Deep now?" Bhaaj asked.

Paul nodded. "Lamps too bright for Deepers." He switched off his light, followed by everyone else. Darkness closed around them— except it wasn't truly dark. The stone everywhere glowed, an effect too faint to see when their lights were on. A blue sheen spiraled across the walls, and the lacy rock formations shimmered as if dusted by an ephemeral blue glitter.

"Good gods," Lavinda said. "What is that?"

"Bioluminescence," Karal said. "I think."

"Bi-what?" Tower asked.

"Living thing that makes light," Karal said.

"Bio jibber," Byte-2 muttered, unimpressed.

Tower went to the wall and peered at the swirls of light. "Rock glow blue. Not alive."

"This light lives," Bhaaj said. It was some sort of algae, though different from what floated in seas. It needed less moisture to survive.

Tower turned, then jerked, her face barely visible in the blue light. "Bhaaj! Got bio stuff."

Lavinda spoke uneasily. "She's right, Bhaaj. You're glowing."

Already? The only other time Bhaaj had come here, it had taken longer for the chemicals in the air to react with whatever they activated in her skin. She glanced at her arms. Her skin already showed a faint blue luminance.

I don't like it, Max thought. **Last time, this algae mucked up my systems.**

I thought you updated your tech to fix that, Bhaaj thought.

Yes, and it will help. However, I can't guarantee it won't eventually affect me.

We won't stay here long.

All right. I'll let you know if any problems start.

Good. Bhaaj spoke to the others. "It's a genetic trait of the Deepers. Their skin reacts with the algae in the air."

"But you aren't a Deeper," Lavinda said. "You're Undercity."

"I have some Deeper DNA." Bhaaj shifted her weight from foot to foot. "Not both parents. If I was pure Deeper. I couldn't go aboveground without protection. The sunlight would scorch my skin. Even living in the Undercity would be difficult."

"Enough talky." Paul looked ready to jump back into motion. "We go."

"How far?" Karal asked.

"Not much." A curl fell into Paul's face, and he pushed it aside. With that done, he headed into the blue-tinged darkness. The rest of them followed, spreading out again.

Lavinda walked with Bhaaj. "Raja, my EI, says the algae are getting into her systems. I don't want to lose my line to Captain

Ebersole." With a scowl, she added, "The last thing I need is Vaj deciding she needs to 'rescue' me."

"Raja should be all right. We won't be here for long." Bhaaj tapped her gauntlet. "Max can deal with it better. If you ever can't reach Captain Ebersole, I can contact him. I also have two of my beetle-bots." She still had the little spy drones in the pocket of her jacket. "I could send one of them."

"Good." Lavinda thought for a moment. "It wouldn't hurt if we also had a person to relay messages, just in case our tech fails."

Bhaaj raised her voice. "Byte?"

Ruzik's brother glanced back. "Eh?"

"Need Tam," Bhaaj said. "You get?" No one could run like Tam Wiens, especially in long distances. Byte-2 and Tam had remained friends for years, even after Tam left the circle protected by Ruzik's gang and joined her own dust gang.

Byte-2 slowed to walk with them. "How get? No whispers here."

Bhaaj raised her gauntleted arm. "I call. You talk?"

"Tam not got comm," Byte-2 said.

Ruzik said, "Ask Hack."

"Oh. Yah." Bhaaj nodded. As a cyber-rider in Ruzik's circle, Hack also knew Tam, and Hack had all sorts of tech-mech he could use to contact people.

"Hack find him, no problem," Ruzik said.

Byte-2 scowled at his brother. "Find her. Not him."

Ruzik squinted at him. "Uh, okay. Her."

Ruzik's confusion didn't surprise Bhaaj. Tam hadn't transitioned until after she left his circle, and mostly she just kept in touch with Byte-2. Born only two days apart, they'd been like twins.

After leaving a message with Hack, they continued on, heading for a world with no light, only blue swirls that glistened as if ghosts had brushed through the Deep.

CHAPTER VIII
Izu Yaxlan

Sports complex.

Angel snorted. *Sports?* Who'd come up with that idea, to turn survival into a game? Still, she approved of contests. Dust gangs did it all the time, besting other gangs when they could. Mostly it involved beating up people, but running faster than your enemy certainly helped. Slicks did contests to win round pieces of metal. No matter. She knew better, that winning kept you alive, and that gave her an edge against her above-city opponents.

She didn't know what to think of this Izu Yaxlan Sports Complex where the coach wanted to meet. People at the Kyle center claimed the name Izu Yaxlan came from an ancient city in the desert, one that lay in ruins. Strange. Anyone who knew the original Undercity dialect could tell you that city's real name was Itza Yaxchilan, shortened from Itzanám Yaxchilan. Then again, almost no one spoke the ancient dialect. Angel knew because Bhaaj insisted they do this "schooling" biz. Angel had decided to make it less boring by learning stuff no one else could do, like figuring out how to read the ancient dialect. At first, it seemed impossible, because no one else could read it, either. Then Bhaaj suggested she study ancient Iotic, which turned out to be almost the same, so that took care of that.

The word Yaxchilan felt *right*. No one used it now except a few Undercity folk-singers. Angel loved those old songs. For her "history class," she decided to sleuth out the origins of the folk stories. No one remembered the earliest versions, but surprise! Learning to read had a use after all. She could interpret symbols all over the aqueducts, the hieroglyphs everyone else called art instead of writing. Within the Maze, she found plenty of the ancient glyphs.

The oldest songs were delightfully weird, even claiming that whoever kidnapped humans from Earth moved them in *time* as well as space, shifting them by thousands of years. No one cared about the old stories except Bhaaj, who for some reason felt proud of her even when Angel didn't do squat, but what the hell. It felt good. Bhaaj told her the research project would've earned her "top grades at Uni," which Angel gathered was a good thing. She even tried to sing the ballads for Bhaaj. Although she could only guess at the melodies, it didn't matter; she couldn't carry a tune worth shit, and her voice sounded like metal scraping metal. Bhaaj listened anyway, until Angel took pity on her and stopped singing.

A few times, Angel tried to tell above-city types, speaking rather than singing the stories, but they just gave her that patronizing smile as if she were a barely literate fool. In truth, she wasn't sure herself if it mattered. Even if no one else cared, though, she got a kick out of knowing that at least some of their ancestors called themselves the Maya and came from a city named Yaxchilan on Earth.

Now here she was, heading for another place with the mangled name Izu Yaxlan. She walked past the largest mansions in Cries, huge places where only a few people lived. She couldn't fathom what they did with all that territory. The sunlight beat down on her like a fire. Too bright. She needed lotion to shield her skin. Tomorrow the doctors at work planned to give her "health nanomeds" that would help protect her Undercity self from the sun. Angel didn't want strange things swimming in her body, but Bhaaj kept telling her to get them and her job required it, so what the hell.

The sports complex turned out to be a huge building surrounded by trees, lawns, and great stretches of white stuff that looked like stone but gave when she walked on it. The place was bigger than she expected, enough that she had no idea where to meet the running guy. She walked up a white pathway with plants on either side. So much *green*. It made her queasy. She went to a white stone bench and sat there, letting her mind adjust to this place.

A hum came from her left. Turning, she discovered a floating white ball about twice the size of her head with a smaller ball on top of it.

"Eh," Angel said.

"Are you all right?" the smaller ball asked.

"Fine." She felt like an idiot talking to a ball.

"Can I help you?" it asked.

"Nahya."

"I'm sorry, I don't understand," the ball said.

Huh. Even not-alive objects here talked too much.

The ball tried again. "Do you need directions to the Undercity?"

"Nahya."

"Why are you at the Izu Yaxlan Sports Complex?"

"Got meeting," Angel said.

"I'm sorry. You can't meet anyone here."

Maybe it had problems with its hearing tech. "Meet running coach."

"You are from the Undercity, yes?"

"Yah."

"Undercity natives aren't allowed on the grounds of the complex."

She blinked. "Why not?"

"The Safety and Security force sets the rules. That is one of them."

Someone needed to fix this bot so it could handle unexpected stuff. Angel just stood up. "Got meeting," she clarified, and then headed along the path toward the complex.

"Stop!" The ball whirred next to her, stirring the air with its fans or whatever kept it floating. "You cannot go further."

"Go away," Angel told it. Bhaaj hadn't told her she had to be polite to bots.

The ball kept pace with her. "I am notifying security."

"Good." Maybe it would leave then. She doubted it, though.

At the end of the path, Angel found a circular plaza paved in white tiles. Leafy trees bordered the area, bright with blue flowers. An entrance to the sports complex stood across the plaza, two tall glass doors that let her see the interior of the building. Sort of. The bright sunlight made it hard to see much beyond the glass. From a distance, the complex had looked circular, but this close up, the walls seemed straight. The curve of the building showed only if she looked right or left.

"Big place," she commented to the whirring ball.

"You must leave," it answered.

"I told you. I got meeting."

"Security is on their way," the ball said. "They will escort you off the grounds."

Angel shook her head, baffled, then crossed the plaza to the double doors. She peered through the glass. It didn't look like much inside, just a lot of open space. It reminded her of the Concourse, but without all those stalls, cafes, and tourists.

Angel pushed against the door. Nothing happened.

"Can I do something for you?" a male voice asked.

Angel looked around, but saw no one. "Door, you speak to me?" Everything else in Cries seemed to talk.

"Yes. Do you wish me to open? I'm not allowed to admit Undercity natives."

"Not make sense." Why would this Mason Qazik person ask her to come here if the building and its batty balls wouldn't let her inside?

A woman spoke sharply behind her. "You there! Get away from that door."

Angel turned to see two women in uniforms, though they wore blue instead of the gray used by the Concourse cops. She switched to Cries talk, staying on her best behavior. "My greetings. I'm sorry for the trouble." That was a lie, since she hadn't done anything, but never mind. Bhaaj had gone on forever telling her how she should act with any authorities she encountered, all about courtesy and no fights and on and on. It all boiled down to *Don't piss them off.*

"I have a meeting this afternoon with Mason Qazik, the track-and-field coach," Angel said. "However, I don't seem able to enter the building."

"A meeting. Yeah, sure." The guard on Angel's right pulled a big stick off her belt, what slicks called a truncheon. The guard on the left had already drawn her pulse gun. If one of its bullets hit Angel dead-on, it could explode her body.

The first guard motioned with her truncheon. "Move on now."

"If I leave," Angel said. "I'll miss my meeting."

The guards advanced on her. "Are you refusing to comply with the law?"

"Uh, no." Angel tensed, ready to fight.

"Turn around," one of the women said. "Put your hands behind your back."

"Why?" Angel asked. Who'd turn their back on a threat? That'd be quite a feat back home, to make her rivals give up just by saying *Turn around please so I can smash you more easily.*

"I said turn around!" the woman with the truncheon shouted.

What the hell? Angel kept her back to the complex, keeping both guards in sight, but she put up her hands to show that she had no weapons, at least none they could see. "I don't want trouble."

The guard with the gun suddenly came at her from the left while the other lunged forward and grabbed her arm. When they swung Angel around and slammed her against the wall, Angel's head hit the glass so hard, her vision blurred. She reacted on instinct, twisting away to face them. The guard with the gun was raising her weapon, ready to shoot—holy shit, did they mean to *kill* her? Angel spun in a tykado move and kicked the weapon out of her hand, making it fly through the air. The other guard tried to tackle her, but the woman couldn't fight worth batcrap. Although Angel easily threw her off, she held back her punches. Damn, she wished she hadn't promised Bhaaj not to hit anyone.

A man shouted. With her adrenaline surging, Angel couldn't tell what he said. It made no sense unless the wall had decided to yell. The guard with the big stick swung at her, and Angel easily dodged her clumsy attack. She raised her fist—

"I said stop!" the man shouted. "She's under the Majda umbrella."

Ho! Angel froze, her arm raised, her gaze on the big-stick bitch. The woman had also stopped moving, her face twisted with hatred, her club only a handspan from Angel's head. The other guard was getting to her feet. She glanced around, probably looking for her gun.

A tall man in the black uniform of a Majda cop stood a few paces back from them, his hands raised as if to calm everyone down. He looked familiar.

"What the fuck?" The truncheon guard lowered her weapon, her gaze raking over the Majda newcomer. Angel didn't need Kyle abilities to figure out that she recognized him, or at least his uniform. She spoke in a harsh voice. "This is a city matter. She's resisting arrest."

"She didn't do anything," the man said. "I saw the whole thing."

Huh. Angel decided she liked this guy.

The other guard picked up her gun and spoke to the Majda dude. "You have no jurisdiction here." She gestured at Angel. "She attacked. Went after my weapon. This is a matter for the Cries police."

"For flaming sake." The man looked ready to punch the guards himself. "My EI recorded the entire incident. You two grabbed her with no provocation and slammed her head against the door. And you activated that pulse revolver, ma'am. If you had fired it, you would have killed her."

Neither guard responded to his accusation. Angel could feel their anger. They'd expected this new clinker to support them.

The woman with the gun spoke more carefully. "You're Majda police."

He tapped a glinting disk on his belt, where all the Majda cops wore their badges. "Captain Duane Ebersole."

"A man as a captain?" The truncheon bitch snorted. "On the Majda force? You expect us to believe that?" She raised her bat. "Are you working with this dust rat?"

"Dust Knight," Angel muttered, though not loud enough for anyone to hear.

"Uh, Trey, wait." The other woman was reading a screen on her gauntlet. "He's who he claims." She glanced at the truncheon guard, Trey apparently. "I verified his badge ID with our Majda database."

Trey looked thoroughly pissed. Her anger came on so strong that it hit Angel like a body slam. This Trey person wanted to beat her into a flat, bloody mess. She wanted Angel to pay a price for daring to come here, for daring to come aboveground, for daring to fucking *exist*.

Although the other guard didn't like Angel, she didn't hate her, either. Angel was breaking the rules, so she tried to deal with it. If that included shooting her, the guard didn't like it, but she would do whatever necessary to protect her territory. Seeing Duane, though, changed matters. She felt confused, stupid even. As much as she didn't like anything Undercity, she feared Majda even more.

Trey just stood, with no outward response. She probably had no idea Angel could sense the battle going on within her as she resisted accepting that a Majda guard wasn't supporting her story about what had happened.

Trey spoke curtly to Duane. "You claim this woman is sponsored by Majda?"

"That's right," Duane said. "She has a meeting with the track-and-field coach. He set it up."

The other guard frowned. "He should have notified security for the complex. We could have warned him that they'd have to meet elsewhere."

"Elsewhere?" Duane's forehead furrowed. "What do you mean?"

"She can't come here," the guard said. "It's against the law."

"What law?" Duane sounded more baffled than anything else.

Angel scowled, pissed that they were talking about her as if she wasn't right here. Then again, the talking she wanted to do involved telling these bitches what she thought about them. She'd promised Bhaaj to be polite no matter what, and this definitely qualified as a "what," so maybe she ought to let Duane do the speechifying.

"The law for the, um—the complex—just a moment." The guard with the gun tapped her gauntlet few times, squinted at its tiny screen, then tapped more. Finally she looked up. "It's a policy instituted by the sports arena."

Duane didn't try to hide his annoyance. "This is a public facility supported by city funds. Forbidding someone access based on where they live is illegal."

"Screw that." Trey's voice got louder. "We're doing the job we were hired to do. Period."

"Like I said," Duane told them. "Forbidding entry is illegal." He spoke with that tone the Majda queens got when they wanted to assert dominance. "Legally, a citizen of the Undercity has as much right to come here as anyone else." His voice hardened. "Are you asking me to break the law by telling a future member of the Raylicon Olympic Track and Field team she can't train with the team?"

"Actually," Angel said. "I haven't agreed to join the team yet." If she had to put up with this shit every time she came here, why would she bother?

"Train with the Olympic team?" The guards regarded him blankly, as if he'd just suggested Angel planned on growing wings and flying. "She can't."

"Why not?" Angel asked. Whether or not she decided to join this "team" was her decision, not theirs.

The guard with the gun turned to her and spoke awkwardly. "You have to, uh, well—you need preparation. Discipline. Access. The right background. You don't have any of that."

Angel had no idea what she meant. "I run fine," she told them. "Better than you, I'd bet."

"I'll escort Angel to her meeting," Duane said quickly, before they could respond.

Trey scowled like she needed to hit someone with her stick. She started to speak, stopped, started, then stopped again. Finally she said, "You're claiming Majda takes responsibility for her presence here?"

"Yes." Duane's voice could have chilled ice. "If you object, you can register a complaint with the House of Majda."

The other guard spoke fast. "That won't be necessary." She gave Trey a warning glance, then turned back to Duane. "We have no quarrel with Majda."

Glancing at Angel, Duane tilted his head toward the building. Enough said. As soon as he came over, a glass portal in the wall slid open. Apparently this door could listen as well as speak. The moment they stepped inside, it closed behind them, leaving the guards outside.

"That sucked," Angel said.

"Sorry." Duane had the good sense to leave it at that. Instead, he lifted his hand, inviting her to walk along the wide corridor that curved around the sports complex.

Angel went with him, giving her battle-ready body time to settle down. The hallway reminded her of a large canal in the Undercity, though it boasted neither midwalks nor dust. The floor was smoother, too, and tiled by gray squares. The ceiling rose high over their heads, far enough to hold two canals stacked up, but no walkways showed up there, either. They just wasted all that space. Stuff bordered the hall, banners with pictures of animals or bands of color. Places labeled "water station" stood at regular intervals, with glasses, fountains, and ice. Angel avoided them like the carnelian rash. More cops would probably show up if she dared drink their precious water.

They passed a few people striding along or gathered in groups. Everyone looked fit, more so than most of the other slicks she'd met. It felt right.

After a while, when her urge to punch people eased, Angel spoke, using above-city speech to show Duane respect. "That guard might have shot me."

"I'd certainly hope not." He spoke tightly. "Killing someone for coming here is beyond the pale even in Cries."

Even in Cries. Great. This running biz sounded less appealing by the second. "She didn't want to fire, but she thought she might have to." Her fist clenched at her side. "The other one wanted to smash me to a pulp."

"You picked all that up from them?"

"Yah." Anyone could have felt reactions that strong, at least the people she knew. "It's good you came. But why were you here?"

"I was waiting for you." He gave her an apologetic look. "At the track entrance. It wasn't until notification of an 'incident' came over my police channel that I realized you'd gone to the wrong door."

That made sense. A smart duster always had extra ways to enter places. "But how'd you know to wait for me?"

"Bhaaj asked me to."

"Eh." A new thought came to Angel. "Duane—about Bhaaj."

"Yes?"

"She enlisted at sixteen."

"Well, yes." He paused. "You can't ship out until you're eighteen. They'll take you at sixteen, but you have to spend two years in school. They sent her out with the ground troops then."

Ground troops. After reading through her work orientation, Angel better understood how things worked, maybe even more than whoever wrote that boring introduction had meant to reveal. "Ground troops are lowest of the low, yah?"

Duane spoke tightly. "Never let anyone tell you that. In my book, any soldier who puts their life on the line to defend the Imperialate is the highest of the high."

"Yah." Angel agreed with him. But still. "People think it's lowest, though."

After a moment, he said, "Yes, most do."

"So Bhaaj enlists as a kid." An adult in the Undercity, sure, but not according to these slicks. "She has no help. No Majda. No education. No mentor. No circle. No protector. She doesn't speak your language. Doesn't know your ways. She has no one to tell her shit. *Nothing.*"

"Yes." He sounded subdued.

Angel's voice hardened. "Those guards would've arrested me, maybe even shot me. Security at that tower where I work wanted to throw me out. Only one thing stopped them. I got the highest of the high looking out for me. Majda. Because Majda *wants* something from me." She shook her head. "Bhaaj had nothing. And she survived. Hell, more than survived. She rose up to the high ranks herself."

Duane met her gaze. "Yes. She did."

Yes. Angel heard the respect he added to that word, felt it in his mind, honoring Bhaaj. Another thought came to her. "You got Majda support too. But Majdas—they don't usually do that for men. Not for fighting."

He shrugged. "I'm good at what I do."

Good answer. He neither boasted nor showed false modesty, just stated the obvious. "Majda give you grief, too?"

He laughed dryly. "Sometimes. I manage."

Angel considered him. "Maybe I'll join this running team of theirs after all."

"Really? Even after what happened today?"

"Yah. I'll smash these arrogant slicks." Quickly she added, "By running, I mean. Not beating them up." Well, probably not.

He seemed pleased by the idea. "You'd be a good addition to the team."

Thoughts swirled in her mind. For one, she wasn't the best runner in the Undercity. "I can bring them a lot of fast dusters." She smirked. "We could overrun their pretty sports palace."

Duane gave a hearty laugh. "I'd love to see it."

"Eh." Angel played it cool, but inside she grinned.

Yah, her people were coming. They'd get dust everywhere.

CHAPTER IX
Red Rash

Ages lost in time.

Located far below the Undercity, the Down Deep included passages older than the history of humanity on Raylicon. Whatever had created this vast labyrinth had vanished like the sea above, its memory lost in the misty passage of time.

The air felt icy on Bhaaj's face. Silence reigned; even the distant sound of dripping water had faded. Blue swirls glowed everywhere, feathering along the walls, the ground and the stalactites that hung far above like giant icicles. Sparkling crystals encrusted every surface, especially the columns that supported the high ceilings. Despite their age, the engravings that graced those pillars remained clear, never eroded by wind or scoured by sand. Great winged lizards curled around them like the mythical dragons of Earth.

Singing drifted into the silence.

Max, Bhaaj thought. *Can you amp up my ears?*

Done, Max answered.

The music became clearer. Somewhere far away, a chorus was singing *The Lost Sky.* Even with no words other than "ah," the haunting melody evoked a dying world where the seas had dried up and the air had too little oxygen. It mourned the loss of the sky for those long-dead empaths who had retreated under the ground to protect their vulnerable minds from a cruel twist of genetics. The song echoed along the aqueducts, magnified by the extraordinary acoustics. And therein lay the other reason Imperial Space Command, or ISC, coveted the Undercity. Something about the unique design of the aqueducts nurtured those who lived here, those Kyle operators who could help them protect the vast numbers of humanity spread across space.

Bhaaj didn't understand. Well, sure, they all knew that whatever alien beings had brought humans to this world had vanished six thousand years ago. They'd left nothing behind but their ruined starships—until that day when the EI called Oblivion awoke in those ancient vessels.

Oblivion.

Humans had learned almost nothing about the massive EI, only that Oblivion destroyed the race that kidnapped their ancestors from Earth. Why did Oblivion stay dormant for so long? One fact became clear: whoever had built the ancient starships had managed to knock out the EI even as it killed them. They protected their human cargo at the cost of their own existence. So humanity survived, stranded on the alien, hostile world of Raylicon.

Six millennia later, the ever-increasing digital signals produced by humanity prodded the EI awake. Oblivion did *not* like competition. It went the EI equivalent of bat-crazy and tried to obliterate what created those signals—by jumping into the Kyle network. From there, it could have spread its tentacles of digital malevolence across settled space and ended every one of its rivals, from the great star-spanning meshes to the tiniest picowebs. In the process, it would've erased almost everything created by the human race—including humanity. It damn near succeeded. In the end, they managed to delete Oblivion before it went on its EI rampage, but just barely. And what gave them that tiny but telling edge?

The Undercity, it seemed.

During their battle against Oblivion, something ancient stirred in the aqueducts. Not a thing, a—a what? The people *sang*, almost every adult and child, their voices rising together. That chorus reverberated throughout the aqueducts, amplified until its haunting music flooded the Undercity, the Maze, the Down Deep. It poured through the forever network of spaces beneath the desert until it reached the ancient starships—where it crashed like a gigantic tsunami of sound into Oblivion.

The flood of sound weakened Oblivion enough that the mesh experts managed to erase it just slightly faster than it could recover. Maybe the effect came from the wave properties of the song, the unique waveforms it created in that vast network of aqueducts. Except it wasn't just sound. It blended with the minds of the people creating it, all those Kyle operators, their neural signatures subtly different from normal humans. Individually their brain waves remained weak, but together their influence became something new, a power humanity needed to understand. On that day, Bhaaj realized the truth, as did the few people within ISC who witnessed the battle. The aqueducts helped protect humanity in ways they had just begun to understand. They couldn't risk destroying this buried civilization that might hold secrets to the survival of interstellar civilization.

Unfortunately, when Oblivion vanished, so did any record of its origins. They had no idea if only one such EI existed or if others slumbered throughout the stars. Its existence became the best-kept secret of ISC. They couldn't risk the interstellar meshes coming alive with speculation or panic, or even worse, that people would search for another such EI. No one knew what might rouse such a sleeping mammoth. They might not be lucky enough to survive the next time.

Today the song drifting in the distance offered nothing so dramatic, just music made by the people for themselves, a creation of beauty simply for the joy of the experience.

"You hear?" Bhaaj asked, speaking to no one in particular.

Paul Franco answered. "Yah. Many voices."

"Maybe." Tower paused. "Pretty."

"I don't hear anything," Captain Morah said.

"I can hear it with my audio implants activated," Lavinda said. "It's gorgeous."

"Yah. Called 'Lost Sky,'" Byte-2 commented. "Ruzik sing. Sounds good."

Bhaaj smiled. "Ruzik sang it for slicks."

"Eh." Ruzik waved his hand in dismissal.

Bhaaj wondered if he realized the importance of what he'd done. He'd only sung it for the woman checking in teams at the Selei City marathon, so the race officials could record an anthem for the Undercity. "The Lost Sky" had played while Angel received her gold medal. Although the Selei City Open wasn't a top marathon, it made the local news and a few offworld sportscasts, which meant now anyone could listen to the song in recordings of the ceremony.

Bhaaj was no expert on the music business, but she'd had enough sense to protect the song. She'd registered "The Lost Sky" with herself as the publishing liaison. That way, no one could claim that spectacular piece of music as their own and make millions on it, giving nothing to the aqueducts. If they wanted to license the piece, they had to arrange it with her. Not that anyone had ever expressed interest, but you never knew.

"Oh!" Captain Morah said. "Yes, I hear it now. Goddess, that's beautiful."

"Lovely," Lieutenant Warrick said. "It's so sad, though. Like weeping."

"The City of Cries," Lavinda murmured.

Bhaaj glanced at her. "Some people think that name originated in the aqueducts."

"I wouldn't be surprised." Lavinda spoke dryly. "The Cries tourism bureau wants to change it. They think it discourages people from visiting."

"A city that weeps," Bhaaj mused. Or it could mean a city full of people crying out. That didn't seem any better for enticing tourists to come and spend their money, though.

Abruptly the music cut off. Silence descended like a weight.

"Why'd they stop?" Lieutenant Warrick asked.

"Know we come," Paul told her.

They continued on, following a tunnel lit by swirls of living light. The passage ended at a room shaped like a perfect octagon, about forty paces across. Each of the eight walls had an archway in its center, offering exits to eight tunnels that stretched away into the darkness.

A man stood in the archway across from them. Barefoot and wearing only a tunic and trousers with their cuffs gathered at his ankles, he looked as if he should be freezing. Yet he seemed unaffected by the cold. His face glowed with the same blue luminance as Bhaaj's skin.

The man nodded to Karal Rajindia with respect. "Welcome, Healer." His gesture took in all of them. "Come with."

So they went with him, increasing their ever-growing troupe to eleven people. The tunnel he followed resembled the one they'd just left, enough that Bhaaj suspected she'd get lost without Max's flair for mapmaking. Good thing they wouldn't be here long; eventually the algae would muck up even his ability to track their route.

The new tunnel ended at an opening that formed a circle in the ground, the entrance to a spiral stairwell descending into shadows. The glyphs engraved around the circle displayed ancient Iotic symbols for the god Azu Bullom.

Jaguar, Bhaaj thought. After Earth's lost children had found the world of humanity's origins, they'd tried to figure out where they'd come from. Even knowing Azu Bullom looked like a jaguar, or maybe another large cat, they had no luck. Six thousand years ago, no known language on Earth resembled Iotic. The planet wasn't even in the right position in the galaxy to match the patchy records in the starship ruins. Maybe the records were wrong. Maybe they'd never know the truth.

They filed down the stairwell one at a time, around and around. The silence seemed heavy with the masses of land above them. Mercifully, they soon stepped into a large open area at the bottom of the well. No dust covered the stony ground; either the Deepers swept it clean or the dust that appeared everywhere in the Undercity didn't drift into levels this deep.

A large cavern stretched before them. Light swirls glowed everywhere in pastel colors, not only blue, but also rose, gold, lavender and pale green. Stone columns supported the ceiling, some built by architects and others created from stalagmites that rose from the floor and stalactites that hung from the ceiling until the formations joined into pillars. High above them, the ceiling formed a mesh of stone lace. All these spectacular formations had to date from a time before humanity came to this dying world; it would take eons for the mineral-laden liquid to create this cathedral-like cavern. Here and there, water still trickled from the ceiling, enough to create a sparkling mist when drops hit the rocks and sprayed into the air.

People were everywhere, talking in groups, walking among the glimmering columns, doing upkeep on the cavern, or coaxing algae into artwork on the stone. Not only did their skin glow, but their clothes also glistened with sparks of light, probably algae picked up from the air. The cavern went on a long way, until the distant people resembled ghostly spirits floating among the pillars. The singing had begun again, and it drifted through the cavern like harmonies from a chorus of angels.

Their group stood together, staring in silence. Lavinda's reaction was so intense that Bhaaj felt her shock even through her mental barriers. She'd never imagined a miracle like this cavern.

It seemed impossible to Bhaaj that any of her own DNA descended from this ethereal world. She was all dust, jagged edges, and fists. Nothing of this grace could exist within her war-torn heart.

Paul Franco motioned to them. "Come. Must hurry."

As they crossed the cavern, people turned to look, watching their group with unusually large eyes, another trait Bhaaj shared with them. Also like them, her pupils could expand until they seemed to fill her irises, gifting her with exceptional nighttime vision. They easily contracted in sunlight, though, letting her see fine then as well. Pure Deepers couldn't adjust to brighter light; they needed shades to protect their vision.

When they reached the far side of the cavern, Paul led them around a stone curtain. Beyond it, they entered the closest equivalent to a hospital in the Deep. The eight beds in the large room consisted of tooled stone slabs softened by rugs and woven blankets, and a wide ledge along one wall that provided room for two more beds. No dust showed anywhere; whoever tended the hospital kept it meticulously clean. Tapestries hung on the walls, rich with abstract designs in blue and lavender, many surrounded with bioluminescent swirls, providing what little light the Deepers needed. The song from the chorus swirled through the room, richer here, as if it laid a soothing balm on any patients who sought help in this lost, buried place.

People occupied every bed. One man seemed all right, sitting up as he drank from a stone mug. Only traces of a rash showed on his skin. The other nine patients, however, looked terrible. The red rash covered their arms, faces, and other exposed skin. Some lay without moving, staring at the ceiling, but most seemed asleep or in a coma.

Karal turned to Paul. "I thought only three were sick."

His face had gone pale. "Yah. One day ago. Only three."

A woman was approaching them from the room. Tendrils of her curly hair straggled around her face and exhaustion darkened her eyes. Walking with a slow tread, she seemed like she hadn't seen a good sleep in days. Her blue tunic and trousers were the same color as those worn by Undercity healers, including Karal Rajindia.

Paul nodded as the healer came up to them, then motioned at the room. "What happen?"

"Bad." The woman's voice cracked. "Two more die."

"Bad water?" Karal asked.

The woman glanced at her with a start. "Must be. Not know where."

Bhaaj pushed her hand through her hair. The last thing this healer needed was a crowd of people hulking around her infirmary. Although the woman wouldn't accept charity from them, a bargain should work here.

"Got prop," Bhaaj said, using the more common word for *proposal*. It wasn't a bargain until the other party agreed the terms.

The healer turned toward her, then jerked and straightened up. "Eh. The Bhaaj."

The three-word greeting didn't surprise Bhaaj. Although most everyone in the aqueducts knew her name, people never used it without permission. Instead, they put "The" in front of it, making it a title.

"Prop what?" the healer asked.

"We help." Bhaaj indicated Lavinda. "In return, let her watch." She had no intention of asking Lavinda to do anything except go home as soon as possible. However, the healer here only had to accept the bargain, not observe it happening.

"Yah. Help good. Queen can watch." The woman didn't even try to negotiate. Nor did she seem to care that Lavinda and her three guards were above-city intruders. That more than anything told Bhaaj just how serious the situation had become.

"Come." With no more ado, the healer turned toward the infirmary, motioning for them to follow. Karal and Paul joined her, bringing their packs with medical supplies.

Lavinda spoke in a low voice to Bhaaj. "What's going on? I didn't get all of that."

"They have a contaminated water source somewhere. It caused an outbreak of the rash." Bhaaj was furious at herself. It shouldn't have taken a crisis like this to convince the Deepers to seek help. She should have tried harder to reach them. Every time it seemed like she'd made progress, something happened to show how far she had yet to go. No one could fix generations of poverty in a few years, but sometimes it felt like she was slogging in quicksand, slowly sinking into its depths.

So how do I go on from here? Bhaaj thought.

Are you talking to me? Max asked.

What? Oh, no. Actually, yes. Any ideas for our next move?

Make sure the army doesn't decide they need to come rescue Colonel Majda.

No kidding. Although most of the brass in ISC had no wish to destroy what made this world unique, a few of them wanted to remove Undercity Kyle operators from the aqueducts, breed them, and raise their kids as government wards. Given a reason, like a life-threatening disease, they might gain support.

I doubt most ISC brass want to kidnap babies, Max told her.

They might think of it as something else. Could they "rescue" psions from here and force them to work for ISC?

It doesn't seem likely, Max answered. **It takes years of study and mental discipline to train a telop. They know an unwilling Kyle can simply refuse to "think." Trying to coerce them can also damage their ability to manage the neurologically intensive demands of the work.**

"Bhaaj?" Lavinda was watching her face. "What is it?"

She focused on the colonel. "We should go back to the Undercity."

"These people need our help."

"Lavinda, listen," Bhaaj said. "This is more serious than I realized. We've gone beyond what your sister approved for this visit. I'll feel a lot better when we get you somewhere safer." In her side vision, she saw Paul approaching them.

"I can help here." Lavinda sounded frustrated. "Let me."

Paul came up to them. "Need new mech to filter water," he told Bhaaj. "I get."

No surprise there. If people were drinking contaminated water, their filtration equipment was probably damaged. "We go with you."

"Wait," Lavinda told her. "At least let me look around. You have my word I won't intrude. Any offers of help I come up with, I'll suggest to you first. We'll figure out if we can make it work." She motioned with her hand, her gesture taking in all the infirmary. "How can we convince your people that I represent anything they'd want to join if I run any time the situation gets a little tricky?"

Well, damn. Lavinda was offering exactly what Bhaaj had hoped this visit would bring, a willingness to meet and understand the people of the aqueducts on their own terms. She spoke carefully. "I greatly appreciate your offer. It's just—I can't guarantee your safety, especially this far below the surface. If something happens, I'm the one who will answer to General Majda."

"Not you," Lavinda said. "Vaj may hate my choices, but she knows they are *my* choices, not yours. And hell, I'm not the heir or even the spare now that my sisters have their own daughters. I'm seventh in line to the throne. If something happens to me, it won't affect the Majda succession. Vaj may not want me in danger, but for her, family plays a close second to duty. If my visit helps convince your people to work for ISC, she won't insist I leave." Wryly she added, "Most of the time she actually trusts my judgment."

"She's a, uh, daunting presence." Bhaaj could think of many other words to describe the general, but daunting seemed the most diplomatic.

Lavinda smiled slightly. "This is true."

"You stay, then?" Paul asked them.

"For now," Bhaaj said. "You go. But leave trail through Maze, yah?" Although both Max and Raja had created maps of their route, it wouldn't hurt to have a backup. The Deepers were even better at hiding from the Undercity than the Undercity was at hiding from Cries. "Make marks with blue swirls. Show path."

Paul nodded, a keen intelligence in his dark eyes. "Is good."

Karal had come up to them, listening. Now she said, "As soon as I finish treating patients who already have the rash, I'm going to vaccinate as many of the other Deepers who will let me." She glanced at Ruzik's gang and the Majda guards who all stood, listening and waiting. "Do any of you have vaccinations?"

"I do," Ruzik said in the Cries dialect. "I got a lot of them when I went offworld."

"I have for red rash," Byte-2 said.

Tower scowled at Karal. "Not got. Not want."

"Need," Bhaaj told the looming Knight. The vaccine wouldn't

instantly protect her; it would take a while to become effective. But it could help.

Tower crossed her muscled arms, presenting a formidable appearance.

Bhaaj met her gaze and said nothing.

After a moment, Tower threw up her hands. "Fine," she growled. "I take meds."

Bhaaj nodded. Enough said.

With no fanfare, Karal took a disk off her belt. One by one, she scanned them all, even Paul, though she'd probably checked him plenty of times. She must have already set her equipment to deliver the vaccine, because after she checked Tower, she unhooked a med-syringe on her belt and gave the dust ganger an air-shot in her neck.

"Fuck!" Tower stepped back fast, raising her fists.

Karal froze, but she didn't give ground, just met her angry stare.

"Eh." Ruzik frowned at Tower. "Not hit healer."

Tower glowered, but after a moment she lowered her fists and grunted at them all.

Karal turned to Lieutenant Warrick. "Your vaccine is old. I can update your meds."

Warrick looked startled. "Thanks. I'd forgotten to get it checked."

The doctor tapped a code into her air syringe, then gave Warrick a shot. Tower stopped scowling and looked satisfied to see the loud guard undergo the same treatment, which apparently Tower considered insulting.

Karal turned to Ruzik and his gang. "You all have the vaccine now, but none of you have a full set of health nanomeds. You should get them. I can do it in my clinic after we finish here."

They all just looked at her. Bhaaj held back her sigh. She'd been working on them for over a year now. Ruzik had agreed to the meds he needed to travel offworld, but it only provided the minimum of what most Imperialate citizens took for granted. Tower and Byte-2 had nothing beyond the vaccine.

After waiting a moment, Karal said, "You're all good for now. Just don't drink any water here unless you're sure it's filtered."

"We ken," Bhaaj said. "Our thanks."

With that, Karal took off, back to her patients, and Paul headed for the Undercity.

Lavinda motioned toward the cavern beyond the infirmary. "I saw a lot of people out there." She hesitated. "Some seemed to have, well . . . I guess you could call them congenital abnormalities."

Bhaaj's pulse surged. *You think?*

Don't get angry, Max thought. **The lack of medical care here isn't her fault.**

Bhaaj waited a moment, then answered in an even voice. "The Deeper population is the most inbred on this world, maybe the most in the Imperialate. The rate of birth defects caused by that is high. Hell, it's astronomical." She lifted her hand, motioning Lavinda toward the cavern. "Karal can help, but she's had trouble connecting with the people here."

Lavinda nodded, her expression thoughtful. Or not thoughtful, exactly. What?

Remorse, Bhaaj realized. Rather than condemning the people who lived below the desert, as did most above-city types, the queen regretted the pain she saw here and felt responsible. Her reaction was like a cool breeze in the desert. Bhaaj ushered her out of the infirmary, accompanied by their gang of guards.

Bhaaj had hoped they'd blend in as they walked through the cavern, but no such luck. They towered over the Deepers. In the Undercity, people didn't grow as tall as in Cries, an effect that became even more pronounced here, driven by malnutrition. Although aqueduct farmers altered plants to survive in the darkness, their crops never flourished. For all that Bhaaj had resented the orphanage, they'd kept her from starving in her first three years of life. Then came Dig. As much as Dig had hated it when her mother pressured her to do cartel jobs, she'd agreed in return for food and water for her circle, more than Bhaaj had realized back then. The spoils of her mother's corrupted wealth had helped feed the circle Dig led, including her dust gang.

Another difference hit Bhaaj. Few of the Deepers carried weapons; the knives on their belts looked more like tools. No guns showed anywhere. In contrast, Bhaaj openly wore her shoulder holster with its pulse gun, and she also had her spy drones, both Red and Blue. Every person in her group came armed. Even with the eight of them bristling with weapons, though, none of the Deepers paid them any heed.

A group of teens had gathered around a rocky stump, resting their bottles of filtered water on its flat top. They laughed, gossiped, and flirted like any other kids. Their voices had a musical lilt, one that matched the distant singing drifting through the cavern, accenting their delicate beauty. One of the girls had only one leg from the knee down and leaned on a makeshift cane. A boy had veins visible on his arms, his appearance as fragile as an aging senior. Another girl had only three fingers on one hand. Yet they didn't seem to notice. They sounded so vibrant, so full of life, that Bhaaj wanted to weep.

"Goddess," Lavinda said in a low voice.

"Yah." Bhaaj couldn't hide the bitterness in her voice.

"How do your people survive?" Lavinda asked. "After a few generations, wouldn't inbreeding kill off the population?"

Bhaaj spoke stiffly. "Changelings. Like me."

The colonel glanced at her. "What?"

"Changeling. It means one parent comes from the Deep and the other from the Undercity."

"And that widens the gene pool?" Lavinda asked. "Less inbreeding?"

Bhaaj did *not* want to have this conversation. She spoke curtly. "That's right."

"Your mother came from here, didn't she?"

"Possibly." Bhaaj steered the topic away from herself. "If a mother comes from the Undercity, she often goes back there to raise her child. It's easier to survive. A Deeper father might go with her, but often not. Sometimes Deeper mothers go with an Undercity father, but they usually stay here. It's hard for Deepers to live in the Undercity."

"The Undercity doesn't seem as inbred, though."

Bhaaj wished she'd let it go. What she wanted didn't matter, though. She'd proposed this trip to help the army better understand her people. If Lavinda's questions bothered her, well, tough. "In the Undercity, we sometimes have children with people from Cries. It happens more often than with Deepers and the Undercity."

"And your father?" Lavinda asked. "Where did he come from?"

Bhaaj's reaction came out before she could stop it. "I've no fucking idea."

"My apology," Lavinda said. "I shouldn't have pushed."

Bhaaj walked in silence until her pulse settled, then said, "My apology. I'm just not used to talking about my ancestry." Or lack thereof. It bothered her more than she ever wanted to admit, that sense of loss that came from having no blood family.

"Do you mind if I ask about your genetic tests?" Lavinda asked.

"You mean the genetic searches the army did when I joined up?" Bhaaj shrugged. "They didn't find anyone who shared my DNA."

"Nothing at all?" Lavinda stared at her. "How could that be? We have access to almost every Skolian alive."

She wondered if the colonel realized the privacy violations she'd just implied. Then again, Bhaaj had no illusions about how thoroughly ISC could infiltrate the lives of their own citizens. She spoke in a casual voice, pretending she didn't care. "It just means my parents came from the aqueducts. Before Doctor Rajindia opened her clinic here, we were off the grid. Even now, almost no genetic data exists on our populations." Before Lavinda could follow up with the obvious question, Bhaaj added, "And no, I've never found any other relatives here, either."

"I'm sorry." Mercifully, Lavinda let it go at that.

As they continued to walk, Bhaaj watched other people passing through the cavern, headed to where they worked, lived, or relaxed. A few groups had gathered in this communal area, socializing among the glimmering rock formations. Could anyone here offer a hint about her parents? Until recently, she'd been too busy repressing her knowledge of her birth to look. In her youth, a few rumors had floated around that her mother came from the Deep, but she'd never heard squat about her father. It was as if he appeared out of nowhere, got her mother pregnant, and then vanished.

Lavinda motioned to several women working on a translucent wall. They were coaxing the algae on its rippled surface into artwork, the colors blending like waves along the stone.

"That's lovely," Lavinda said.

"Yah." The artistry of her people never stopped amazing Bhaaj, given her zero talent. Ask her to solve an engineering puzzle and yah, she could conquer it, no problem. That seemed less, though, than the creations of these painters. What inspiration allowed them to see how those swirls fit together, blending, ending, reforming, drawing your gaze along their lines with such a grace? It was like another language, one she'd never learn to speak.

"Do you think the painters would talk to us?" Lavinda asked.

"Maybe." Bhaaj led her toward the artists with all their guards in tow. None of the Deepers reacted to their abrupt change in path. In the Undercity, dust gangs would've already made quick work of the intruders, mugging them, and then sending them running for the surface. The Deepers didn't even notice.

I think they notice, Max thought. **They just communicate with moods.**

Bhaaj rubbed her aching temple. *I do feel a pressure on my mind. It gives me a headache.*

They may be trying to reach you. You're the only one among your group who looks like them, at least in part, with the way your skin glows.

Bhaaj just shook her head. Even if she'd known how to respond when an empath tried to reach her, she had no desire to open herself up that way.

They stopped a few steps away from the artists. One painter looked up, a woman with the rare green eyes that occurred only among the Deepers. To Bhaaj, she said, "Eh?"

Bhaaj nodded to her artwork. "Good draw."

The woman returned her nod, accepting the high praise, then went back to work. Bhaaj glanced at Lavinda and tilted her head. When Lavinda started to speak, Bhaaj gave the barest shake of her head. They headed onward in silence.

After a while, Lavinda said, "I take it she didn't want to speak with us."

"Actually, she did." With a wry smile, Bhaaj added, "What you heard qualifies as a conversation."

"Oh." Lavinda squinted at her. "Sometimes down here I feel like a bull stumbling around a museum full of porcelain vases."

Bhaaj thought of ISC. At least Lavinda cared. "You're fine. No problems."

They spent several hours exploring the cavern. None of the Deepers spoke with Lavinda, but many "chatted" briefly with Bhaaj. They weren't hostile, just wary of their visitors.

Bhaaj watched a father limping toward the hospital with his small daughter. Both showed signs of the rash. "We should go back to the infirmary. See if Karal is ready to make use of us."

"Yes, let's go see." Lavinda sounded subdued.

The hospital was even more crowded than when they'd left. Patients and equipment packed the room, including the mini-clinic Karal had set up, a square of four consoles and other medical equipment. Karal was leaning over a patient on a bed. Even from so far away, Bhaaj could tell the doctor was upset.

Heartbroken.

As Karal pulled a sheet over her patient's head, Bhaaj's comm hummed.

"Not now," Bhaaj muttered. She stabbed her finger at her gauntlet comm. "What?"

Karal looked up at them from across the room, her gaze going to Bhaaj.

Paul's voice came out of the comm. "Found good filter mech."

Huh. Why call her instead of Karal? The doctor was coming toward them, so Bhaaj said, "Talk to Kar, yah?"

"Can't reach," Paul said. "Not answer talky."

"She here." As the doctor joined them, Bhaaj extended her comm to the healer.

"Paul?" Karal asked.

He answered in a warmer voice. "Eh, Kar. Got good filter mech. I come back."

"Nahya!" Karal's voice shook, and her left fist clenched the cloth of her trousers. "Not come back! Stay away. Stay alone."

Bhaaj stared at her. In the same moment that she said, "What the blazes?" Lavinda said, "Why not?" and Paul said, "Not make sense."

Karal spoke urgently to him. "I check you. When you leave. Not sick. Good. Stay alone now. You feel sick, let me know."

"You not answer talky." Paul sounded baffled.

"Will answer," Karal promised. "Was—caught up in stuff."

"What stuff?" Paul asked.

Good question. Bhaaj said, "Karal, what's going on?"

The doctor glanced at her, but then she turned and spoke to Lavinda. "I'm sorry," she told the Majda queen. "I had no idea."

"About what?" Lavinda asked. "Are you saying this isn't an outbreak of carnelian rash?"

"It's the rash." Karal made no attempt to hide the fear in her voice. "It's a mutation, a strain I've never seen. This version doesn't just spread through water. It can infect people with airborne particles. It's highly contagious." She took a shaky breath. "You've all been exposed."

Bhaaj felt as if the doctor had socked her in the stomach. "How bad is it?"

Karal spoke grimly. "Since we've arrived, five more people have come in and we just had another death. Already we have a twenty percent fatality rate, and we're at the start of the outbreak." Her voice had a ragged edge. "More of these people are going to die, maybe a lot of them."

Lavinda stared at her. "Can't you treat them? Carnelian rash is easy to cure."

"I'm trying!" Karal practically shouted the word, a reaction all the more frightening because in all the years Bhaaj had known her, she'd never seen the doctor lose her calm.

Karal inhaled deeply, then spoke in a quieter voice. "My treatments don't work on this variant. I can slow the progress of the disease, but not cure it. For some people, it barely helps." She watched them with a hollowed gaze. "If we can't stop this, it could wipe out the entire Deeper population."

CHAPTER X
Carnelian Tide

Ruzik stood tensed and on guard with Byte-2 and Tower, supposedly for the Majda queen, but he kept a closer watch on her officers. Although he'd begun to trust Lavinda Majda, her guards were another story. None of them had tats, scars, or cyb to mark their battle wins or build their buzz with other fighters. Captain Morah seemed competent. He'd wanted to dump the loudmouthed Warrick off a cliff, but gradually he'd realized she was more tactless than hostile.

The other guard answered to Lieutenant Caranda. These above-city types had no clue how to protect their privacy, the way they used their names so easily when strangers could hear. Caranda didn't have a mouth like Warrick, but Ruzik *felt* her scorn in a way Warrick had never shown, as if Caranda shouted it through the canals until her malice toward the Undercity echoed everywhere.

Right now, trust or not, they had zero to do, both Majda guards and Dust Knights. They stood a few paces back from Karal, Bhaaj and the Majda queen, surrounding the people they'd been sent to protect. It felt like overkill. What, did they think the Deepers might attack? Yah, big threat. He worried more he might injure one of the fragile Deepers if he tried to nudge them away from the queen. Not that anyone came close. They went about their business as if no trespassers had shown up in their world.

Bhaaj, Lavinda, and Karal sat just outside the infirmary, using sheared-off rock stumps as chairs. Their seats circled a larger stump that acted as a table. Veins of quartz wove through the stone, sparkling in the light, which no longer seemed dim now that Ruzik's eyes had adapted. He listened, ever vigilant, and he liked none of what he heard. He could protect them against violence, cold, starvation, and theft, but how could he defeat the red-sickness, an opponent that attacked with fighters so small, you couldn't see them? He had no answer.

General Majda's voice came out of Lavinda's comm. "Doctor Rajindia, we've set up a holo link so you can talk with specialists at the Cries University hospital. With all that input, it shouldn't take long to solve this. We will get a cure soon."

"Thank you." Karal sounded both exhausted and relieved. "I can set up holobooths here for the links." She paused, then added, "I should get back to my patients."

"Absolutely," the general said. "Put my sis . . . t—omm."

"Sorry," Karal said. "We're getting interference. Could you repeat?"

"Put Colonel Majda back on the comm," Vaj said.

"Right away, ma'am. Here she is." Karal nodded to Lavinda, then stood up and headed back to the infirmary. Although she still looked as if she carried a great weight, her step had lightened. It didn't surprise Ruzik. She'd gone from fearing a plague that might wipe out the Deepers to a medical crisis she could solve.

Lavinda spoke into her comm. "Colonel Majda here."

Vaj spoke curtly. "I want you out of there. *Now.*"

"We're in quarantine," Lavinda said.

"I'll send responders with full hazmat gear," Vaj said. "They can escort you out . . ." A spate of static almost obscured her next words, but it sounded like, "With no risk to themselves or you."

"I don't need anyone to escort me out," Lavinda said. "It won't be long before the doctors find a cure for this variant. Even if it takes more time than we expect, the danger isn't to me, given my health meds. It's to the people here. To reach me, any responders must go through the Undercity. Right now, the disease is confined to the Down Deep, but we aren't sure yet how it spreads. In air? The algae? Us? Your people can protect themselves, but they might carry the disease through the Undercity. It could infect people there."

"Your safety is more important than a bunch of lazy, homeless people in a slum," Vaj said.

"Oh, fuck that," Lavinda muttered.

The general's voice turned to ice. "What did you say to me, Colonel?"

Lavinda changed her tone. "My apologies. Permission to speak?"

"Go ahead."

"The point of my coming here was to improve our relationship with the people. If we take actions to protect me—and only me—and in the process infect or kill those who live in the Undercity and Down Deep, that defeats everything you hope to achieve. They'll hate us."

"Could you repeat that last?" Vaj said. "Your signal broke up. What is this down deep?" She made the words sound as if they were lowercase rather than the title of a city and people.

"They live below the Undercity. Several hundred, I think. None are homeless. They have a remarkable culture." Lavinda added, "They also have the highest Kyle rates of anyone we tested."

"Fine." Vaj sounded frustrated. "We'll drill down through the desert to get you."

Bhaaj stiffened, but before she could protest, the colonel said, "Vaj, no. We're too far below the surface. All sorts of networks support these caves, tunnels, and ruins. Goddess only knows what will happen if you start drilling. You could collapse entire regions."

Silence.

The general finally spoke in a less authoritative voice. If Ruzik hadn't known better, he'd have thought she sounded strained, even upset. Hell, maybe he didn't know better.

"I can't risk your life," Vaj said. "I need to get you out of there."

Lavinda's tense posture eased. "That's what you said when I wanted to join the military without using the Majda name." She spoke with unexpected gentleness. "Vaj, this is no different. We knew I was taking a risk by coming here. If I wasn't your sister, you wouldn't demand I leave quarantine despite the risks it poses to the people we want to reach. Any volunteer knows they might be offering their health, even their life, just as I offered my life to defend the Imperialate when I joined the army."

Vaj audibly exhaled. After another long pause, she said, "All right. Stay. Just be careful."

"I will."

"Very well." The general's voice turned crisp. "Keep me updated."

"Will do. Out." Lavinda touched her comm, cutting the link.

Tower snorted. "Lot of talky just to say, 'am worried for you.'"

Lavinda gave a startled laugh. "True." Her smile faded. "My apologies for the insults."

Tower waved her hand in dismissal. "Not problem."

Ruzik wondered if the Majda queen realized she was speaking Iotic. When he'd first met these high types, they'd seemed like ciphers without feeling. The more he learned, though, the more he kenned that they did care, they just had their own ways of doing and showing.

Lavinda was tapping panels on her gauntlet like a music-maker twanging a lytar. "I need to get this comm working better."

A man's voice came out of Bhaaj's comm. "It's the algae in the air."

Lavinda blinked. "Max, is that you?"

"Yes, and my greetings, Colonel," Max said. "I've updated my systems to deal with the algae, both coding changes and physical redesigns. I can send the updated codes to your EI. Can Raja access any nanobots that work on your tech-mech? I can also send specs for the hardware redesign, if Major Bhaajan agrees."

"Yah, sure," Bhaaj said. "Send anything Raja needs."

Raja spoke in her Iotic accent. "I can manage a simple redesign. Nothing major, but anything is worth a try. The contaminants in the air are indeed affecting my comm function. It's not serious, but if we'll be here for a while, I should clean it up."

"Max, yes, please send her everything you have." Lavinda spoke to Bhaaj. "Do you know any other way out of here besides how we came in?"

"Sort of." Bhaaj looked less than enthused, to put it mildly. "A few kilometers from here, if you go even deeper, you'll find a spiral staircase. It goes straight up, I don't know how far, hundred meters, I'd wager. It's the exit that comes out in the Tikal temple."

Ruzik's interest sparked. Tikal, an ancient pyramid, stood alone in the desert, far from any settlement. He wasn't supposed to know about it, but then, he wasn't supposed to know a lot of things he'd figured out about the slicks and their world.

"You mean the exit you tried to use the last time you came down this far?" Lavinda said.

"Yah." Bhaaj grimaced. "It's a nightmare, one far more dangerous to you than any bout of carnelian rash. It almost killed me, and I'm a weaker Kyle. If you tried, you'd have to turn back." Flatly she added, "Or die."

Lavinda didn't look surprised. "We can sit this out. Once Karal gets the outbreak under control and makes sure we aren't contagious, we'll leave." Dryly she added, "I think that will be enough for this visit."

"No kidding." Bhaaj had a look Ruzik recognized; she wanted to talk about something she knew her listener didn't want to hear, which meant she'd probably take forever to get to her point, going around and around in sand-itching circles.

"I barely survived using that temple exit," Bhaaj said. "It's because our Kyle minds are too sensitive to the Kyle machines there, yes?"

"Essentially," Lavinda said. "Those stairs pass by the rooms with the machines."

"Going that close to them almost killed me, and I have less Kyle brain structure than you."

"Bhaaj, yes, I know." Lavinda sounded irritated. "I realize I can't use that exit. You don't need to keep reminding me."

"I didn't mean it that way." Bhaaj spoke carefully. "Those ancient machines are too powerful for most Kyles, right? That's why it kills us. They overload our brains. It's why the Ruby Dynasty is so important, even if they no longer rule. It *doesn't* kill them. They're strong enough to withstand its force."

"That's right." The colonel studied Bhaaj as if trying to read her thoughts. Ruzik *felt* Bhaaj imagine a fortress to hide her mind. They'd worked together enough that he could sense her at a low level even when she blocked her moods. He doubted, though, that the Majda queen could pick up anything.

Lavinda spoke warily. "Those machines house an ancient EI. Most of the time, it's dormant. If it detects a Kyle operator, though, it tries to reach them. That's what almost killed you. Your neurons fired out of control, causing something called *status epilepticus* or back-to-back convulsions."

Bhaaj met her gaze steadily. "But the Ruby Pharaoh can go there."

Lavinda swore under her breath. "Stop it."

"We both know the pharaoh has Down Deeper DNA," Bhaaj said.

"She had it checked after I told her how much she resembled the people here. Hell, Lavinda, she has *green* eyes. She's smaller than most people, and her skin looks almost translucent."

"What does that have to do with any of this?" Lavinda was clenching her fist on her knee. "Fine, you proved the most revered figure in the Imperialate has Deeper DNA. I'm no confidante of the pharaoh, but from what I've seen, she genuinely doesn't care. The rest of the universe *does* care."

Bhaaj leaned forward. "Why? Because they consider it an insult? It's true about her genetics, Lavinda. No one can change that one little explosive fact."

The colonel just looked at her, but Ruzik had no doubt she felt excruciatingly aware of their listeners. It didn't take a genius to figure out that if any of the guards here repeated what they'd just heard, they'd get whacked for treason. Ruzik didn't care who shared their DNA. He had no doubt, however, that the Majda guards would never "impugn" the pharaoh's good name by revealing her supposedly low ancestry.

"The pharaoh can help the doctors find a cure," Bhaaj said. "The physiology of the people here is different from anything the medical establishment knows. Even Karal hasn't treated Deepers. But one person out there has a similar physiology."

Lavinda met her gaze. "No."

"Why not?"

"Seriously, Bhaaj? Are you going to ask the pharaoh to let them test potential cures on her? Or for her to come *here*?" Before Bhaaj could respond, Lavinda added, "No. You aren't. You have no access to the pharaoh. You think Vaj will ask her? My sister—the Joint Commander of the *Pharaoh's* Army—would rather lie naked in molten lava than acknowledge that Pharaoh Dyhianna traces her ancestry to these aqueducts."

"It's not Vaj's decision." Bhaaj met her gaze. "Only the pharaoh can choose whether or not she wants to help."

"We don't need to bother her," Lavinda said. "We'll have a cure in plenty of time."

"It's a *lie*," a woman said.

Startled, Ruzik glanced at the Majda guards. Lieutenant Caranda, the quiet one, stood with her face twisted into an ugly mask of hatred. Hostility blazed in every line of her features and every tensed muscle of her body. She practically spat her words at Bhaaj. "Undercity DNA? It's a damned *lie*. Pharaoh Dyhianna is so far above you and your kind, she should never even have to hear about your dirty little diseases, which wouldn't kill you if you weren't so much less than real human beings."

For a moment, everyone just stared at her. In the same instant that Tower said, "You want your bat-fucked face smashed, bitch?" Lavinda said, "That's *enough*, Lieutenant Caranda!"

Ruzik barely managed to keep himself from raising his clenched fists. When Bhaaj stood up, he knew what she wanted. She'd spent too many decades listening to this shit. Everyone had a limit, even Bhaaj, and she'd just reached hers. She needed to get away from these people before she destroyed what remained of their shaky truce with the Majda intruders.

Bhaaj walked toward him, facing away from the others, and he gave her the barest nod. As she passed, she spoke in a barely audible voice. "Keep Tower behaved."

Yah, Ruzik thought to her, and unclenched his fists. He'd deal with it.

She strode away then, taking her fury with her instead of letting it explode.

Bhaaj didn't know how long she sat against the far wall of the Deeper cavern. The rock felt rough against her back, rippled rather than jagged. At first, she barely noticed the cold air. Her climate-controlled clothes kept her warm, but she doubted she needed to worry. Her body was better adapted to the temperature here than for most people.

Gradually her pulse calmed. She continued to sit, gazing past the pillars to the distant people who every now and then walked across her field of view.

After a while, she thought, *Max, how long have I been here?*

About twenty minutes, Max thought. **And yes, I'm in communication with Raja. Nothing else has happened with Colonel Majda and crew. Ruzik kept Tower from going nuclear. No one is talking. They're just waiting.**

Bhaaj exhaled. *Thanks.*

He does a good job.

Ruzik?

Yes.

Agreed. Knowing he had matters under control gave her a sense of refuge. She had a circle here, support, people who could help during those times when she wondered how she'd continue. Acting as a liaison for the aqueducts and a universe that hated them— sometimes it felt like it would explode the hidden places where she protected her heart.

Motion stirred in her side vision. Turning, she saw Lavinda headed toward her. Ruzik and his gang walked to her left and the Majda guards to her right.

Lavinda came over and sat next to Bhaaj. They stayed that way, both looking out at the cavern. Their various guards hulked around the rock formations, close enough to do their job but far enough away to give the people they guarded privacy if Bhaaj and Lavinda kept their voices low.

"I'm sorry," Lavinda said.

Bhaaj shrugged. "You were just saying what everyone thinks."

The colonel exhaled. "I fancy myself as a fair-minded, unbiased person, but sometimes I don't even notice my failings until I hear them coming out of my damn mouth."

"What you said is true," Bhaaj answered. "Most people would react the same way as Caranda to the idea that the pharaoh shares DNA with my people."

Lavinda spoke tightly. "The lieutenant will submit a formal apology to all parties."

"Good." Bhaaj doubted it would make a difference, but no matter. She just wished Vaj had sent people more suited to this visit.

"The choice made sense to Vaj," Lavinda said. "Both Warrick and Caranda come from well-placed families. They've progressed through the Majda force faster than most."

"Oh." Big surprise there.

"Bhaaj, listen. I don't know how to fix so many ages of ignorance and neglect. But you and I—we can make a start."

Bhaaj raked her hand through the curls that had escaped her braid and straggled around her face. "I'd like to. I just—I get so tired sometimes."

Raja's voice rose into the air. "Excuse my interruption, but Doctor Rajindia is coming."

Lavinda and Bhaaj rose to their feet. Karal had almost reached them, only a few meters away, but she was walking slowly past the rock pillars. So very, very slow.

As the doctor came up to them, Lavinda said, "Are you all right?"

"Yes, fine." Karal spoke in a subdued voice. "We've lost two more people."

Bhaaj stared at her. "Already?"

"I can't find a way to stop it, not even with help from the university team." Karal shook her head. "The usual treatments don't help. Maybe a little, but it just slows down the deaths."

"Have you had a chance to vaccinate people who aren't sick yet?" Lavinda asked.

"I'm trying." Karal pushed up her sleeves, which promptly fell back down her arms. "I can't keep it up, though, not with so many people who are already sick coming for treatment."

"We can help," Bhaaj said.

"Just tell us what needs to be done," Lavinda said.

Karal shifted her weight. "Your Highness, it's not safe."

"We've already been exposed," Lavinda replied. "And we'll be vaccinating healthy people."

"Maybe not," Karal said. "I don't know the incubation period for this variant. From what I've seen, the delay between when you contract the disease and when you start to show symptoms can be anywhere from a few hours to about thirty." Her voice flagged. "We need more stats. The aqueducts are mostly off grid. The medical EIs don't have any data for us to mine."

"We can test people to see if they have it," Bhaaj said. "Get you more data."

Karal rubbed her eyes. "Normally I'd say no, that only medics should be involved. But saints, I could use the help."

"Then it's decided." Lavinda motioned at the guards looming around them. "You have eight of us. Tell us what to do."

"Colonel Majda!" Captain Morah stepped forward. "We're here to protect you. We can't go off vaccinating people."

"Protect me against what?" Lavinda asked. "All these ferocious Deepers? The only danger here is that we'll contract carnelian rash.

It's too late to protect any of us against that." When Morah opened her mouth to protest, Lavinda raised her hand. "That's an order, Captain."

Bhaaj could just imagine how Vaj Majda would react to *that* statement. Lavinda couldn't supersede an order from her sister. Fortunately, Vaj hadn't given any specific to this situation.

Bhaaj spoke to Ruzik. "You, Tower and Byte-2 give vaccines, yah? And do med-scans."

"Will do." Ruzik glanced at Karal. "Just tell us how."

"Absolutely." The doctor turned to Captain Morah. "For all of you, if you're willing."

Morah glanced at Lavinda. When the colonel nodded, Morah said, "Yes. We'll do whatever we can."

They headed to the infirmary for supplies then, hoping to stem the tide of death.

CHAPTER XI
Song of the Deep

Running track?

Angel wanted to snort. The "track" looked like a big, flattened circle. Seriously? A circle?

She stood with Mason Qazik, the running coach, in the risers above the outdoor track. It amazed her that this huge place existed, open to the sky, inside the sports complex building. Below them, athletes were running around the track, some in pairs, some alone. Mason squinted at them, the pupils of his dark eyes like pinholes in the sunlight. The breezes stirred his straight hair. He stood at average height, maybe a bit less, with a lean build and long legs compared to the rest of his body.

A runner, Angel thought. She had a similar build, especially her legs. Most dust gangers did in the aqueducts.

"Those eleven runners are the ones trying out for the team," Mason was saying. "They won't all qualify, probably. On any other world, a lot of them wouldn't bother to try out." He gave her an apologetic look. "I've so few candidates here, though, they know they might make the team even if they have no chance anywhere else."

"Eleven?" Angel couldn't fathom why so few came to run for him. They weren't even fast. "This team, they always run in loops down there?" She didn't get it. They weren't reaching any useful place, just going around and around in a circle.

"Well, yes." He considered her, looking worried. "I'm not saying

147

you won't be working with good runners. We do have some Olympic-level athletes. You might know Azarina." He motioned to a young woman with a long black braid hanging down her back. She'd pulled ahead of all but one other runner on the track. The woman reminded Angel of Colonel Majda, though younger, with a more carefree manner in the way she moved.

"Majda," Angel said.

"Yes!" Now Mason sounded greatly pleased. "Azarina Majda." In a confiding voice, he said, "She's damn good. One of my best. I don't think she could beat you, but she'd give you a run for your money."

Angel wasn't sure what he meant, but she continued to show respect, which she appreciated. So she said, "Eh."

Mason seemed worried rather than relieved by her reaction. "You'd be working with Tayz Wilder, too. He's our best distance runner." He motioned at the guy out in front, a fellow pounding the track at a good, solid clip. "In the last Olympics, he placed fifty-sixth in the royal marathon, and he was on the young side then, only twenty-two. He'll do a lot better this time around."

Angel almost said *eh* again, but then thought maybe he needed more. So she said, "Sounds like a good runner." He didn't seem that fast, but what the hell.

Mason looked a bit less worried. "Are you staying in the city? Or do you return to the, uh, the Underground after you finish work?"

"Undercity," Angel said. "Yah. I go home to sleep. See husband." She missed Ruzik.

"If you ever need a place to stay, we have quarters for the team here in the complex." He spoke as if he were trying to sell her something. "We can set you and your husband up with a great suite. Whatever you need."

Angel considered him. "You want me to run, yah? Because you don't have fast people."

"Well, I wouldn't put it that bluntly." He winced. "Actually, knowing me, I probably would if you let me blabber for long enough."

Hah! Blabber. Great word. Angel couldn't help but like this guy. "We got plenty of good runners. Some better than me."

He stared at her. "What?"

"Faster runners." Angel could just imagine how the batty robots at this place would panic if a flood of Undercity gangers arrived to run circles in their sports complex. Yah, that would be fun. "You should bring them here, too."

"You and your husband aren't the only ones?" He looked ready to jump up and down. "There are others?"

"Like Tam," Angel told him. "She's faster than a skitter-kit jolting from key clinkers."

Mason squinted at her. "Uh, what?"

"Tam is faster than me," Angel said. "She can go all day like that. Good climber, too." She'd seen Tam Wiens scramble up rockslides so fast, she could outrun the collapse of the rubble.

"Yes!" Mason turned ecstatic. "Please do bring them."

Angel crossed her arms and glowered at him. "The cops won't let them come."

"I'm terribly sorry about what happened." Now he looked ready to have heart failure. "I give you my word I'll take care of it. You and your friends, your teammates, the other runners, they're welcome here. I give you my word."

For about three seconds, Angel felt good. Triumphant. Then she remembered that she had to convince her "teammates" to come here and run pointless circles in the hot, too bright sun with people who didn't like them. Now she felt stupid.

"I can't promise they'll come," she admitted. "A lot will probably say no."

He spoke carefully. "We can offer many incentives. We understand that, uh, amateur athletes need transportation, places to stay, amenities. Perks."

Angel could tell he wanted her to make a proposal. She considered the thought. "You can get snap bottles of filtered water, yes? And food. Meat. Green plants too, the kind you can eat."

He looked confused, like he'd expected her to ask for something else. "That's it? Food and water?"

"Runners get thirsty." Angel felt like an idiot stating the obvious but given all the pure water these people took for granted, she never knew what she needed to tell them. "Get hungry, too." She grimaced. "Always hungry. Never enough food."

He regarded her for a long moment. Then he spoke quietly. "Yes, we can provide as much filtered water and quality food as they want.

We have a nutritionist who can make sure they get everything they need."

They were making progress. "I can't promise they will come," she told him. "But for good meals and filtered water—yah, they might." Dryly she added, "Make sure they run for you before they eat. Not after. You give them lots of food, some will eat too much and get sick." She'd seen it the day they let the army doctors test them for Kyle traits in return for free food and water.

Mason spoke in a strained voice. "Of course. We'll be careful."

Angel nodded, accepting his proposal. She'd bring it to the Undercity when she went home. She'd only been out in this overly bright world for thirty-five hours, but it felt like forever. She found it hard to believe the daylight would go on for ten more hours, and then darkness for thirty-five hours at this time of year.

Although some slicks she'd met said they didn't like working at night, Angel didn't mind. It felt like home. Slicks did their routines in shifts of threes. Their first "workday" came in the morning, eight hours long. They slept in the middle of the day, when the heat reached its people-roasting worst. Second workday landed in the afternoon. Then people had dinner and slept while the sun went down. Later they came back for a night shift, eight hours. Afterward they went home to sleep or do whatever. It all started again at sunrise. Every ten days, they had two free days with no work. Angel had already figured out that more important people with more important jobs got more free days. It had no more logic than other slick customs. The more high-status they considered your job, the less time they expected you to spend doing it. Weird.

She stayed a while longer, talking with Mason. Once he realized she did intend to work with his team and might even bring more runners, he seemed as happy as a kit with a ball of string. And ho, did he like to talk! Angel discovered that if she just stood, nodding every now and then or saying maybe a word, he could carry the entire conversation. Eventually, when hearing all those words wore her out, she managed to get free and head for home. She had no trouble leaving the sports complex; the robots went out of their way to guide her off the premises. She hadn't thought robots had moods, but these seemed delighted to see her gone.

As Angel walked along a blue path in one of the many city parks, her comm buzzed with a familiar tone. She tapped the receive panel. "Eh, Ruzik."

"Eh. Where?"

"In city." She warmed at the thought of him. "Coming home."

"Nahya." He sounded tired. "Not come home. Stay in city."

"Say what?"

"Not come back. Bad here. Sickness. Red rash."

"Got vaccine." She used the Skolian word for vaccine since it didn't exist in their dialect.

"Might not work."

Angel didn't like the sound of it. "You got rash? I come back."

"Nahya." He spoke firmly. "Not have. Am fine. Many others *not* fine. Dying."

"Ruzik, you not die." She had to get back to him, get him somewhere safe.

"Am good. Really." In a softer voice he said, "You not die, either. Stay in city."

Angel stated the obvious. "Need to help. Can't if I not there."

"Yah, help. In city." He spoke with urgency. "You be backup comm."

What? "Not ken."

"Sickness in Deep. Majda party in Deep. Can't leave."

"In Deep?" Angel had never gone that far below the Undercity. "Not get home?"

"Can't. Spread rash." He switched into Flag. "We're in quarantine. It turns out we're all carrying the virus now. This is a new version. We can spread it even though we aren't sick."

"Majda colonel too?"

"Yah." Ruzik took a breath so deep, Angel heard him inhale. "All stuff here glows blue. Walls, floor, rocks. From tiny crits in air. Gets into comms. Mess them up. Max does fixes, but the more backup we got, the better. You backup in city. Need you there."

It was one of the longest speeches he'd ever made in dialect. If he spared that many words to make his point, it had to be important. "I stay." Angel spoke firmly. "You check in each hour, yah?"

"Yah." He sounded relieved. "You good?"

"Fine. Maybe run for city slicks. They want you, too."

He snorted. "Not think so."

"Offer good prop. Water. Pure. Food. Good food."

"Got food. Got water."

It was true; with the work she and Ruzik did, going between the Undercity and Cries, they usually did get enough food and water. Angel didn't push. If she ran for the team, he probably would too. Right now, she just wanted him to stay healthy. "Not drink bad water," she told him. "Not get rash."

"Yah. Will do." His voice sounded odd, as if he were holding back.

"You not sick? That truth?"

"Is truth." Now he sounded like himself. "Bhaaj fine. Byte-2 fine. Tower fine. Majda queen and her dust gang fine."

Angel breathed out with relief. "Talky in hour, yah?"

"Yah." His voice softened. "You stay good."

"You too." She cut the link.

Angel headed to her office in the Selei Tower. Maybe she could discover useful info about the red rash in all those slick networks she'd found to explore.

Bhaaj finished checking the two children with her scanner. "Got virus," she told them, just as she had told everyone else she'd treated in the past hours. "Feel sick? Rash?"

"Nahya," the smaller girl said, a child of about six with pale gold hair. As far as Bhaaj could tell, some Deepers had lighter hair and skin because their bodies had less melanin, which protected against sunlight. The changes seemed deliberate, given that people in the Undercity also lived underground, and they mostly had darker coloring similar to the upper classes in Cries. Whatever the reason for the change, it had faded into the misty history of the aqueducts.

"Not sick," the older girl said. She looked like an eight-year-old version of her sister.

Bhaaj held up her air syringe. "I protect. Give vaccine, yah?"

They shrugged permission, not even asking what vaccine meant. They'd probably overheard this conversation enough in the past few hours to memorize it. So Bhaaj gave them a dose. The vaccine did even less when administered after people had the virus, but since every person Bhaaj had checked already carried it, the point was moot.

"Warning," the air syringe told her in an androgynous voice. "My supplies are down to two percent. I can't synthesize any more of the medicine you are using."

The girls in front of her giggled, young enough to be unfazed by talking things. Bhaaj tried to smile, with little success. "You got home?" she asked them.

"Brother," the older girl said. "Big. Twelve years."

"Hoshma?" Bhaaj asked. "Hoshpa?"

"Nahya," the girl said.

"Saints," Bhaaj muttered. Didn't *any* kids here have parents? Most of the people she'd treated were younger than twenty-five. A few had lived longer, but so far she'd seen no one older than fifty. They just *looked* older, worn by starvation, thirst, and disease, with no medical care beyond the infirmary run by their overworked healer. She'd seen no sign of gangs or punkers. They all took care of each other, children raising children, with great reverence for their "elders" who'd managed to survive past the doddering old age of thirty-five.

"Go home. Stay with brother," Bhaaj told them. "Come back if get sick."

"Eh," the older girl told her. With that, they held hands and ran off, maybe going home, maybe going to play, maybe going to die.

A woman spoke behind Bhaaj. "I need a new syringe."

Bhaaj turned with a start. Lavinda stood there, looking like how Bhaaj felt: exhausted, with dark circles under her eyes. Her black hair had escaped her braid and hung around her face in straight tendrils.

"Yah." Bhaaj held up her syringe. "Mine too."

They headed back to the infirmary in silence. Talking took too much energy. Bhaaj had learned more about the Deep in the past few hours than in the entire rest of her life. The effects of malnutrition and inbreeding, missing limbs, scoliosis, thinning of the skin, malformed organs, and other health conditions—it affected at least twenty percent of the population. Many medical journals also classified the Kyle traits as negative mutations. The genes not only gave rise to the neurological changes that created psions, they also involved other changes, some serious, some fatal. With that included, almost seventy percent of the Deeper population experienced genetic conditions that affected their health and well-being.

Lavinda spoke in a low voice. "Why do they stay down here? They're dying."

"Why does your family live on Raylicon?" Bhaaj asked. "The entire world is dying."

"It's home. Our legacy. The birthplace for all of us, Skolian and Trader alike."

"Yah." Bhaaj lifted her hands, then dropped them. "That's what the Deep is to these people. It's all that most of them know."

Near the infirmary, the hum of machines greeted them, low and even. They walked past the rippled wall that separated it from the cavern—and the scene beyond hit Bhaaj like a fist. Patients lay on every available surface that could be converted into a bed, or in makeshift cots cobbled together out of random supplies. Karal had scooted her mini-clinic to the far side of the large area, giving more space for beds. She stood now before the three holobooths she'd set-up, which glowed with the images of Cries doctors, several of them talking at once. Every now and then, the holos flickered, either fuzzing out or disappearing altogether, then reforming.

"Where is the Deeper healer?" Lavinda said.

Bhaaj glanced around the room, but she couldn't see the woman who'd first greeted them. "Maybe she's out treating people."

"Need water," a man said in a ragged voice.

Bhaaj turned to a man lying on a bed to her left. A worn-out blanket covered most of his body, but his bare arms lay on top the threadbare cloth. An ugly rash covered his arms and face like a distorted map of some planet's continents drawn in mottled red bumps.

"Here." Lavinda slipped a bottle out of the bag she wore slung over her back. Snapping it open, she tilted the bottle to his lips. He tried to gulp down the water, and he did manage a few swallows. "My thanks," he whispered.

Lavinda smoothed his hair back from his face. "Healer treat you?"

"Yah." He closed his eyes, his ability to talk used up.

Lavinda looked up at Bhaaj, her face drawn. "We have to do something."

"We are." Bhaaj couldn't tell whether or not their efforts helped. If the vaccine didn't work, or if Karal and her advisors didn't come up with a better solution, the entire population here could come down with the carnelian rash. She hadn't found a single person who wasn't infected. Some were already showing symptoms, the rash, a fever, chills, nausea, and a hacking cough.

Lavinda was watching her closely. "The people we've treated came here because they or someone they knew is sick. It isn't surprising they're all infected. That doesn't mean everyone in the Deep has the virus."

Bhaaj exhaled. "I hope not."

They headed towards Karal until they came close enough to hear her and the flickering holo-doctors, who seemed as unsubstantial as mist drifting in a desert, about to disappear any moment.

"It's carried by the algae," Karal was saying. "The particles are too small to see when they float in the air, but they spread on surfaces everywhere."

"Air?" a man in one holobooth asked. He was standing in front of a board covered with chemical symbols. Static partially obscured his voice. "It's transm . . . not only water . . . air too?"

"Air, yes, and the algae." Lines of strain creased Karal's face. "The algae are everywhere, on the walls, ground, ceilings, rock formations. Even on the people. It activates receptors in their skin that makes it glow blue."

In another holobooth, a woman sitting at a high-tech console said, "I've been studying the specs you sent." Her image wavered and washed out. When it reformed, she was saying "—the virus can spread even without the algae. That just offers a good substrate where it can breed."

The doctor in the third holobooth spoke, a gray-haired woman in a blue lab coat. "If you aren't meticulous with the quarantine, it could spread to the Undercity." Her voice turned grim. "You have visitors there, Doctor Rajindia. You must quarantine them from Cries."

"We *can't* let it into Cries," the man at the table said. "You *must* maintain the quarantine."

"Yes, absolutely," the glossy-console doctor stated. "We have to protect the city."

Karal regarded them with a sour look. "First and foremost, we have to protect the people here."

"I'm trying alternate versions of the vaccine based on the data you've sent," the man said. If he'd noticed Karal's cold tone, he gave no hint. "I have a lead on a modification that might be more effective against this new variant."

"Good." Karal glanced at her own console. "The algae are getting into my tech-mech."

"Could you repeat that?" the doctor at the high-tech console asked. "I didn't catch it."

"The algae are damaging my equipment." Karal spoke urgently. "Send me any results you have. Don't worry if your tests are inconclusive. Send me a continual stream of your work, thoughts, anything. That way, if we lose our link, I'll have what you've done so far to work with."

"Will do," the man said.

"I'm sending now," the gray-haired doctor said.

Across the infirmary, a woman lying on one of the beds started to cough, a hacking sound that felt explosive in the otherwise quiet room.

"I have to go," Karal told her advisors.

"We'll keep you updated," the man said.

After Karal signed off, she glanced at Bhaaj and Lavinda. "Are you two okay?"

"Fine," Lavinda said. "We need more vaccine."

Karal motioned, her gesture taking in the entire mini-clinic. "Take what you need." With that, she headed toward her coughing patient.

Bhaaj exchanged a look with Lavinda. "Do you know what we need?" the colonel asked.

"We can figure it out," Bhaaj said with far more confidence than she felt. "We should look for air syringes." As she glanced around, her gaze raked across the back wall of the room, which was only a few meters away. "Lavinda, wait." She motioned at a row of stalagmites that bordered the wall like a series of rippled cones standing guard over the infirmary. A person's foot showed next to one of them. "Someone is back there."

Lavinda grabbed a sterile smart-cloth from a tray and headed with Bhaaj to the wall. When they stepped around the cone, they found a woman slumped against the rocky wall behind it. The Deeper healer. She sat with her eyes closed, her legs stretched out, and her arms limp at her sides.

"Healer?" Bhaaj knelt on one side of the woman and Lavinda on the other. This close, Bhaaj could see the telltale rash on the woman's neck, arms, and hands.

The healer opened her eyes and watched Bhaaj with a bleared gaze. "Eh?"

"We help," Bhaaj told her. "Got water. Meds." Except they had no meds. They'd exhausted them, besides which Karal had already vaccinated the healer and treated her for the rash.

The woman's voice rasped. "Just need—rest. Just—a little."

"Here." Lavinda opened her snap bottle and sterilized it with the smart cloth using great care, as if she could protect the healer from the virus even now as it raged through the woman's body. Lavinda tilted the bottle to her lips, and the healer drank in gulps.

After a moment, the woman's gaze focused on her. "The hums—?"

"Hums?" Lavinda asked.

"I think she means the chorus." Bhaaj had become so used to the distant singing, she'd almost stopped noticing. She spoke gently. "Hum still goes."

"Not . . . hear." The woman closed her eyes and sagged against the wall. She laid her hand on Bhaaj's arm. "Sing it, yah?"

Bhaaj felt as if her heart were breaking. "Can't sing." She had no idea which was worse, her inability to do anything even remotely resembling the beauty of that soothing music or knowing that if she tried, she'd sound so horrible that she'd ruin whatever comfort it offered this dying woman.

Lavinda spoke quietly. "Raja, ramp up my ear augs so I can hear the music better."

"How is this?" Raja asked.

"Yes, that works." Lavinda's gaze seemed to turn inward.

Then she sang.

Her voice came out on one syllable, the "ah" favored by the ethereal chorus. She had perfect pitch, exactly on tune for the haunting melody that had continued nonstop since they arrived. Bhaaj doubted the same people were singing now as before; even if the entire chorus had managed to stay healthy, no one with an unaugmented body could go for that many hours and still create such a clear, effortless sound.

Lavinda sang to the dying healer. The purity of her voice was stunning; no wobbles, no slips, no wavering, no scratchiness, none of the errors that plagued Bhaaj when she tried even simple tunes she'd known since childhood. Lavinda's voice was sheer joy to hear, earthy in the lowest ranges, warm and full in the middle, and as clear in the high ranges as water burbling in a mountain creek. The size of her range astounded Bhaaj, and she sounded exquisite everywhere, never struggling for the lowest or highest notes. Bhaaj stayed frozen, mesmerized.

The healer let out a long sigh. She took Lavinda's hand and tightened her hold on Bhaaj's arm with her other hand. "My name... Sarzana."

Bhaaj's voice cracked. "You honor us."

"The Bhaaj." Her voice was low. "You came to help. Brought city queen." She spoke to Lavinda, who kept singing, but low enough so they could hear the healer. "My thanks."

"Your name will know honor." Bhaaj's voice shook. "All will sing the tale. Sarzana saved the Deep." She had no doubt about what would have happened if Sarzana hadn't sent Paul for help. This mutated strain of the rash would have wiped out most if not everyone here. "All will sing your name."

"Words kind..." The healer closed her eyes, and her head rolled to the side.

"No." Bhaaj grasped her shoulders, drawing the woman back up, cradling her body against her own. "Come back." Memories crashed into her mind of that day when she'd held Sparks in her arms, the small girl's body covered with that hideous rash, red and oozing. Bhaaj had begged her not to die while tears streamed down her face, one of the few times in her life she'd openly wept.

No response came from the healer. Her body remained limp in Bhaaj's arms.

Lavinda's voice faded into silence. "I'm sorry," she whispered.

Bhaaj kept holding Sarzana. "Wake up," she pleaded. "Wake up."

Someone laid a hand on her shoulder. Looking up, Bhaaj found Karal kneeling next to her, her motions strained, as if the doctor had aged years in the past few hours. She scanned Sarzana with her monitor. "She's gone." Softly, Karal spoke to Sarzana's lifeless body. "I—I'm sorry."

"She didn't come back here to rest." Still holding the healer, Bhaaj sagged against the wall, too depleted to hold herself up. "She knew she was dying. She didn't want anyone to see."

"I gave her everything I had." Desperation edged Karal's voice. "It should have cured her even if she was showing symptoms. And she wasn't, not when we arrived. Damn it, I should have *found* a way."

Bhaaj lifted her head. "It's not your fault your medicine doesn't cure this variant of the rash."

Karal opened her mouth to respond, then stopped when a commotion came from outside. Someone was calling out. It took Bhaaj a moment to process the Iotic words.

"Please!" That sounded like Captain Morah. "Help us."

"What the hell?" Lavinda let go of Sarzana's hand, careful but fast, then jumped to her feet and strode out from the sheltering row of stalagmites.

Bhaaj straightened up, then stopped, still supporting Sarzana.

"Go ahead," Karal said. "I'll take care of her."

With an exhale, Bhaaj laid down Sarzana's body as gently as she could manage, then sped after Lavinda. The colonel had headed across the infirmary, making her way toward a group entering the room, all three members of Ruzik's gang, plus Captain Morah, Lieutenant Caranda—

And Lieutenant Warrick.

Both Morah and Caranda were holding up Warrick. She sagged in their grip, her face pale.

"Shit," Bhaaj muttered as she made her way among the beds where people slept or had dropped into a coma. *I'm sorry, I'm so sorry,* she thought at them.

"—how long has she had the rash?" Lavinda was asking as Bhaaj joined them.

"I'm not sure." Captain Morah nodded to Ruzik. "He noticed it first."

"Tired," Warrick muttered. They helped her sit on a makeshift platform, and she rested her head against the wall next to it, closing her eyes with an odd look, as if she didn't believe how badly she needed the support.

Bhaaj glanced at Ruzik, who had stayed back with Tower and Byte-2. "You see her rash?"

"I see she too pale," Ruzik said. "Ask her to push up sleeve."

Warrick opened her eyes. "I thought I felt worn out because we were working so hard." She gestured to Ruzik. "If he hadn't asked me to look, I doubt I'd have noticed until I collapsed."

Bhaaj nodded, then turned to Ruzik and his gang. "And the three of you?" *Let them be all right,* she thought to the ancient deities she didn't even believe in. *He's like a son to me. They are my family. Don't take them. I'll give you anything, anything you want. Just spare them.*

"Am fine." Ruzik pushed up the sleeves of the pullover he donned in the chill air of the Deep. No trace of the rash showed anywhere on his arms. "All clear. Not hot. Not cough."

"Same here," Byte-2 said. "All good."

Tower also nodded to Bhaaj.

Bhaaj exhaled, her relief so big that she doubted her attempts to look impassive fooled them.

Lavinda was speaking to Captain Morah and Lieutenant Caranda. "Any signs at all?"

"Nothing for me," Morah said.

"I'm good," Caranda answered. Although she refrained from comments about the Undercity and their diseases, it offered little satisfaction to Bhaaj. She'd far rather hear insults from healthy people than remorse from the dying.

Warrick mumbled, "Can't believe I forgot my last checkup." Her body slumped to the side.

"She needs to lie down," Captain Morah said.

Lavinda looked around the crammed infirmary. "There's no room."

A woman spoke from behind them. "I can clear some of these beds."

Bhaaj turned with a start to find Karal watching them. In a voice aching with pain, the doctor said, "Some of the patients no longer need theirs."

They all stared at her. Finally Lavinda said, "Where will you put the bodies?"

"I—I don't know." Karal took a breath. "I haven't had a chance to think that far ahead."

A woman Bhaaj had thought was sleeping in a nearby bed opened her eyes. "Queen's dust ganger use my bed." She sat up slowly. "I switch with her."

Disbelief flashed across Karal's face, followed by hope. "You get up? You sure?"

"Yah, sure." The woman shrugged. "Less sick now."

"Ah goddess!" Karal yanked the monitor off her med-belt and

scanned the woman. "You're getting better!" She switched into the Deeper dialect, which sounded even closer to Iotic than Undercity speech. "Getting better, yah?"

"Yah." The woman spoke as if to say, *Sure, I've rested, now I can get up.* She had no idea of the import of her words, that it meant you could survive this version of red rash.

A man spoke behind them. "Not need my bed. Give to sick."

Bhaaj swung around. The man who'd been sitting up when they first came to the infirmary now stood behind them, watching their group with curiosity. Traces of the rash remained on his face and arms, but he looked a lot better than when Bhaaj had last seen him. "I go," he said. "Not like it here. Go home. Sleep there."

"Wait." Karal stepped over, scanning him. "Let me check . . . ah, yes, I see. The treatment I gave you slowed the disease enough for your body to fight it off."

"Eh?" he asked.

"Healer meds help," she said. "And you strong. Not die."

He nodded his thanks. "I go now."

Bhaaj felt how much Karal wanted them to stay until she was certain their recovery would continue. But what could she do? The infirmary couldn't handle the influx of new cases unless some people left, either on their own—or as the end of a life-watch.

As Karal went about getting Warrick settled, Bhaaj spoke in a low voice to Lavinda. "We need to find a place for the people who've passed away."

"Is there a burial site near here?" Lavinda asked.

"We don't have cemeteries," Bhaaj said. "Plots of dirt like that don't exist in the aqueducts. We cremate our dead and spread the ashes over a place with meaning to the departed."

Lavinda motioned at her remaining two guards. "We can help carry people."

"Yah." Bhaaj spoke to Ruzik. "Our guards help, too. All work together."

Ruzik and Morah considered each other with a decided lack of enthusiasm. With that mutual dislike settled, however, Ruzik, Byte-2 and the Majda guards went off together to help the Deepers.

Tower stayed behind.

"Eh?" Bhaaj asked her.

Her protégé spoke in a subdued voice. "Not just Majda guard." She pushed up the sleeve of her pullover, revealing a trace of the rash on her lower arm.

Damn! Bhaaj's pulse surged. "How long?"

"Not know. Not look." Tower grimaced. "Then start itch."

Bhaaj wanted to curse at the universe, or at least at the portion of it that had inflicted this virus on her people. "You get more meds from Karal. Fast."

"Too late."

"No. Not too late." Bhaaj *had* to believe the treatment could help. She couldn't lose her Knights this way. They'd trusted her when they'd agreed to protect Lavinda during this visit, but it had all gone wrong. "You strong," she told Tower. "Young, healthy. Get better."

Tower just nodded, nothing else to say. She headed toward Ruzik and the others, including Karal, to get the treatment that just might spare her from becoming one of the bodies they were preparing to take from the infirmary.

"What about you?" Lavinda asked her.

"Eh." It took Bhaaj a moment to put her thoughts in order and push up her sleeves. Her skin looked fine, no rash, just scars from her youth that she'd never bothered to have removed. Or maybe she'd never felt ready to erase those signs of the life that had defined her childhood.

"Is good." She looked up at Lavinda. "And you?"

The queen rolled back her sleeves, revealing clear skin. "Nothing."

"Good." Bhaaj watched her Knights across the room. She wanted to go hover around Tower, Ruzik, and Byte-2 and ask if they were okay again and again, as if repeating the question could somehow improve the answers.

"Come on." Lavinda rubbed her neck, a simple massage that probably didn't come close to relieving her strain. "We should get back to doing scans and vaccinations."

Bhaaj made herself nod. "Of course."

They made their way across the infirmary, moving among beds crammed so close that barely a handspan separated them. People murmured, slept, or stared at nothing. She and Lavinda helped anyone they could, offering filtered water, making them more comfortable, giving words of comfort. By the time they reached the wall that separated the infirmary from the cavern, Bhaaj felt as if she'd aged a year. Stepping around the wall, they looked out—

"Ah, no," Bhaaj said.

People hadn't just trickled into the cavern, they'd flooded it. Patients lay everywhere on rough pallets, some with kin or circle members, some groaning, some silent, some so pale they already looked like death, all waiting for just a few moments with the Deeper healer.

Except their healer couldn't help. She lay dead in her tomb of stalagmites.

CHAPTER XII
Passing to the Light

"You sure?" Karal asked. "Not rash? Fever? Cough?"

Paul spoke patiently, his voice coming from the comm on Karal's med-bracelet. "Am fine. Not have red rash."

Karal closed her eyes, her gratitude almost palpable. She'd sat at one of the four consoles that formed the border of her mini-clinic, but right now she had no interest in her equipment, only Paul. Bhaaj stood with Ruzik outside the clinic, knowing they should go away to give Karal privacy, but too tired to move. They'd treated people for so many hours, they'd run out of supplies. Lavinda was still helping patients, offering water to a woman in a nearby bed. Byte-2 and Lieutenant Caranda both stood by the wall, staring at nothing, as if the simple act of remaining on their feet took what little remained of their energy.

"Is good," Karal told Paul, her voice warming far more than people were supposed to show, but right now who the hell cared. Paul lived. He'd so far escaped the rash. They'd earned the right to show their relief.

"You stay in Undercity clinic," Karal said. "Not go out. Not see anyone."

"Yah," Paul said. "Got food here. Water."

"Good." Karal thought for a moment. "Send me bot, yah? With supplies. I say what need."

"Can do," Paul said. "Tam say she come down. Bring stuff."

"Tam!" Bhaaj smacked her palm against her forehead, finally remembering the runner they'd arranged to carry messages in case their comms stopped working. "I forgot to tell her not to come!"

"I tell," Ruzik said. "She knows." He switched into Skolian Flag. "I also told the Knights about the thieves who tried buzz us. They found all three and have them quarantined." Dryly he added, "With themselves."

Bhaaj let out a breath, relieved at least one of them still had a working brain. "Those thieves probably don't have the rash. Neither you nor Tower ever went near Paul, and we hadn't reached the Deep. You probably hadn't yet been exposed."

Paul spoke over Karal's comm. "Tam say she never get red rash."

"All can get rash," Karal said.

"Tam say that not true," Paul persisted. "Drank water with rash. Long time ago. Others in circle did too. Sister die. Circle boys die. Hoshma die. Tam not get sick."

Karal glanced at Bhaaj. "Have you ever heard of someone being immune to carnelian rash?"

"I don't know." Bhaaj paused. "We've had outbreaks in the Undercity, though I don't recall any this bad. When I was a kid, I never asked anyone who *didn't* get sick if they drank unfiltered water. It didn't occur to me."

"Even now, not everyone in the aqueducts realizes that's where it comes from." Karal spoke into her comm. "Paul, do scan on Tam, yah? I tell how. Send scan with supplies."

"Why?" he asked.

"I find out why she not get rash."

"Better I send Tam," he said, as patient as always.

"Nahya! Not send person! Just robot!"

"I ken." His voice softened. "Stay good, eh?"

"You too," Karal murmured.

After Karal signed off, she glanced at Bhaaj. "Paul knows how to program the bot that the cyber-riders built for me. He can code it to follow the path he marked in the Maze." She sounded like she was trying to convince herself more than anyone else. "We'll have more supplies soon."

"Good." Bhaaj glanced around the infirmary. It was eerily quiet despite the many patients. Mercifully, a few had recovered enough to go home.

Far more had passed away.

✣ ✣ ✣

Temple.

A few healthy Deepers who'd brought their ailing kin to the infirmary offered to help carry the dead to the temple for cremation. Bhaaj did as well when they needed more muscle. The temple felt otherworldly to her, a fitting place to lay those who'd left this world. The hexagonal room had an airy, domed ceiling. Over the ages, the Deepers had engraved the walls with winged spirits. Luminous artwork swirled across the carvings, abstract and otherworldly, as if angels had brushed their wings over the stone and left a glimmering film of light.

Incense wafted from glazed vases in the corners. The smoke drifted to the ceiling and vanished, leaving only a faint scent, similar to sage and rosemary. A maze of conduits networked the stone above the temple all the way to the surface, weaving through tons of rock. That held true all over the Down Deep, indeed everywhere in the aqueducts. It bore witness to the brilliance of those long-vanished geniuses who'd built these ruins, not only that they could coax fresh air from the desert down to a place this deep, but also that their ventilation networks had survived for thousands of years.

The mourning Deepers released their dead here, giving them into the care of the few temple servers who hadn't yet fallen to the rash, gentle monks in drifting robes, pale rose or blue. Afterward, Bhaaj walked to the infirmary in an aching silence, wondering if she should stop giving vaccines and start carrying more of the dead. With her large size and muscular build compared to the Deepers, she could better lift the bodies. It hurt, not physically but on a much deeper level.

As Bhaaj entered the infirmary, she saw Byte-2 leaning against a nearby wall. Even as she approached, he slowly let himself slide to the ground until he was sitting in a slumped posture. She quickened her pace and reached him in the same moment that Ruzik joined his brother.

"Byte?" Ruzik knelt next to him. "What wrong?"

"Tired." Byte-2 closed his eyes. "So tired. . . ."

Ruzik pushed up his brother's sleeves, revealing a full-blown rash. "Nahya!" His voice cracked. "I lead, brother. You do what I say. And I say *nahya*. Not get rash!"

Byte-2 answered in a voice they could barely hear. "Sorry . . ."

One word, and it felt like a punch in the gut to Bhaaj. They only apologized when it no longer mattered if you showed weakness. As with death. She knelt on his other side, across from Ruzik. Smoothing back the hair on Byte-2's forehead, she said, "We get you better. Soon."

"We treat." Ruzik looked up at Bhaaj. "When new supplies come."

"Yah." Bhaaj clung to that hope. Except they'd already treated everyone in their party twice. She knew it and Ruzik knew it. "You?" she asked Ruzik.

He showed her his arms, revealing smooth skin. "Not got rash."

"I have it," a woman said behind them.

Bhaaj jumped to her feet even as she turned to face the speaker. Caranda stood there, her sleeves already rolled back. The rash had advanced all the way up her arms and was sending tendrils along her neck.

"Damn!" Lavinda came over to them. "How do you feel?"

Caranda let out a strained breath. "Tired."

"You had full vaccinations, right?" Lavinda asked. "You were up to date on all of them?"

"Everything." With that said, Caranda seemed to sag into herself. She didn't try to continue, she just went to the nearest empty bed. As she lay down, Lavinda stepped over and helped her stretch out in as comfortable a position as you could manage when a painful rash covered parts of your body.

"The new supplies will be here soon." Lavinda sounded desperate. "We'll be treating you in no time."

Caranda said nothing.

Bhaaj joined her and spoke in a low voice. "Do you have any signs of it?"

Lavinda met her gaze. "Nothing."

"You have to let me know if you show symptoms," Bhaaj said. "Don't try to be strong and ignore it. We need to treat you again if they start."

Lavinda pushed back her sleeves, showing the smooth skin of her arms. "Really. Nothing."

Ruzik stood up, staying with his brother. "What about you?" he asked Bhaaj. "And not say 'I'm fine.' You always say. Never true."

"I really am fine," Bhaaj said.

"You look like you've run a marathon," Lavinda said.

"Yah, I'm worn out. Who wouldn't be?" Bhaaj showed them her arms, then tapped her neck and face. "No rash. No fever. No nothing."

"Good." Lavinda still sounded worried. She tilted her head toward Karal, who'd gone back to the holobooths and was again deep in conference with the Cries doctors. "Look at her hands."

Bhaaj looked. The rash covered Karal's fingers, showing beneath the cuffs of her shirt.

"Damn," Ruzik said. He didn't even try to hide the agony in his gaze.

Bhaaj struggled to make her exhausted brain think. The Down Deep healer had already passed. If they lost Karal, too, what would they do?

Lavinda was watching her closely. "We can get guidance from the doctors in Cries."

"Not for long." Bhaaj gestured at the mini-clinic. The images of the doctors sputtered continually in their booths now, sometimes phasing out altogether.

Lavinda's comm hummed. She stabbed her finger at the panel. "Colonel Majda, here."

"Lavinda, this is Vaj." Her sister's voice snapped out of the comm. She used her *I'm not taking any nonsense* voice. Static overlay her words, but they came through enough to distinguish. "We're going to drill down ... make a well ... extract you. Get doctors ... to these people."

Lavinda stared at the comm as if it had sprouted horns. "Vaj, no! That could collapse this entire place, killing the very people you want to save."

"Not as many as will die from this illness."

"You could kill *everyone*," Lavinda said. "Vaj, think about this. You wouldn't drill a tunnel under towers in the city, right? They might fall. This is no different. Even if you make a small well, you risk destabilizing the spaces around it. Except if they fall, you could start a massive cave-in."

"Those ruins have survived for six thousand years," Vaj said through the static. "One well won't bring them down."

"You don't know that," Lavinda said. "The cartel war collapsed two of the largest canals and they were a lot closer to the surface."

"We'll be careful," Vaj said. "We'll find somewhere with less danger of falling."

"How?" Lavinda demanded. "These people hide with stealth tech-mech that rivals anything the army uses."

"Don't be absurd," Vaj said. "We have better sensors than a bunch of people in a slum."

"Seriously?" Lavinda asked. "We can't even find Bhaaj down here when she goes off grid."

"Damn right," Bhaaj muttered.

"Karal Rajindia still has an open line to the university," Vaj said. "She's on it right now. That's how I knew to contact you. We need to use what remains of her signal to locate you before we lose that link altogether. It can guide us where to drill."

"Vaj, NO!" Lavinda said in the same instant that Bhaaj said, "No! *Don't do it.*"

"You *can't* come here," Lavinda told her sister. "We're in an infirmary and a cavern packed with patients. Only rock pillars hold up this place. Yes, it's brilliantly designed, yes, it's survived for thousands of years. That's because the people who live here take care of it. That all ends if you start forcing new passages. You drill down through that much rock and the whole place might fall. You could bury hundreds of people and our only medical equipment. We're at least half a kilometer below the surface. If that much rock comes down, you'll never get us out."

Vaj swore with a slew of creative oaths. "Then tell everyone in these aqueducts to turn off their blasted tech so we can find a safer access. Damn it, don't they know we can help?"

Bhaaj spoke into Lavinda's comm. "General, it isn't one thing you can turn off. People use black market tech throughout the aqueducts. Even if every person who operates any form of it agreed to turn it off, which is unlikely, it could still take hours to reach enough of them to raise the tech-mech cloak that hides these spaces."

"Major Bhaajan, is that you?" Vaj asked.

"Yah, it's me." Bhaaj kept her tone respectful, instead of cursing the way she wanted.

"Vaj, listen," Lavinda said. "It isn't just a fluke of neuroscience that makes the population here different. Everything about the way they live, their environment, even the algae and lack of light, it all goes into what makes them miracles. If you destroy that, you'll destroy them. Why do you think they've hidden for thousands of years? They're protecting themselves. We *need* them. We need the aqueducts the way they were designed, to do whatever they were designed to do with the people they were built for. You can't endanger all that just to extract your sister."

"You're more than my sister," Vaj said. "You're important to the Imperialate."

"Not really," Lavinda said. "The army has plenty of colonels. I'm no financial genius like our sister Corejida. And I'm seventh in the line of succession. The most important person in our group isn't me, it's the one who serves as our liaison to the people we want to reach. Major Bhaajan."

"Goddamn it," Vaj said.

Yah, well, I don't like you much either, Bhaaj thought. Although she didn't agree with Lavinda about her supposed importance, they all knew the aqueducts needed a liaison, and right now Bhaaj was the only experienced candidate.

"Be reasonable," Vaj told her sister. "If the doctors don't find a cure, everyone will die."

"It isn't one hundred percent fatal," Lavinda said. "People are recovering."

Hope sparked in Vaj's voice. "What percentage?"

"We don't know yet," Lavinda admitted. "At least ten percent."

"Ten bloody percent?" Vaj said. "Are you saying the death rate is *ninety percent*?"

"No!" Lavinda took a breath. "So far, we've lost thirty to forty percent of the people who contracted the disease. But that's only the people who've come here for help. How high it goes depends on how many other people either don't get it or who recover." She spoke unevenly. "Yes, it's still a lot. But if you blast in down here, you could kill everyone, and not just from collapsing the place. Taking these people away from their world might kill them just like taking fish out of the water."

"Lavinda—"

"Promise you won't extract me," Lavinda said.

It was a long moment before Vaj spoke. When she finally answered, she sounded drained. "Very well. You stay."

"I do think you should contact the Ruby Pharaoh," Lavinda added. "She needs to know what's going on."

"She knows," Vaj said. "She's in constant communication with us about it."

"She might be able to help. Her DNA—"

"Enough." Vaj didn't seem angry, just worn out. "Yes, I understand what you want. But what good is any similarity in her DNA to the Deepers? We can't risk testing the treatments on her." She sounded oddly defeated, and Bhaaj didn't think it had anything to do with the pharaoh. Vaj could protect an interstellar empire, commanding one of the most powerful armies in the history of the human race, yet she remained helpless to save her sister's life.

"However," Vaj added. "You and Doctor Rajindia have permission to talk to the research teams at the university about the pharaoh if it helps."

Lavinda's tensed posture eased. "Thank you."

"Keep me updated." That static had grown so loud, Vaj's words barely came through.

"I will." Lavinda spoke awkwardly. "Vaj, if I don't see you again—" She took a breath. "Know that I love you."

The general went silent. Then she spoke with a gentleness Bhaaj had never heard from her, never even known she could express. "And I you, my sister."

With that, they signed off.

As Lavinda lowered her arm, Bhaaj tried to look anywhere else, pretending she hadn't just heard their conversation. Ruzik had been standing back, far enough to give Lavinda privacy. When he saw she had finished, he came over to them. "Angel wants talk with you."

Bhaaj tried to focus. "Angel?"

"Yah." He lifted his arm, extending his gauntlet comm toward her.

"Eh, Angel." It was all Bhaaj could manage.

"Eh, Bhaaj." Angel's voice came out of the comm. "Got idea."

"Idea?"

"Am at Kyle job." Static crackled over her voice. "This place, they are big on Kyle learning. Cries doctors talk to us about rash. About Kyle genes. These genes, they kill."

"Yah. Some." Bhaaj shrugged. She already knew the mutated DNA that gave rise to the Kyle traits could also cause problems. "Why look at this?"

Angel switched into the Cries dialect. "Not all the mutations have a negative effect." Static interrupted her, then faded. "The medical EIs searched ... one found a study ... it shows a better immune response ... a few of the Kyle mutations work against certain types of disease."

"I didn't get all that," Bhaaj told her. "Do you mean Kyle operators don't get carnelian rash?" That made no sense. The empaths were dying just like everyone else.

"Wait ... try make better signal." Angel's voice became clearer. "The scientists who did the studies looked at other viruses, not carnelian rash. But they did find that some Kyle genes stop those other viruses. It's one reason this Kyle biz survives in humans; sometimes it helps keep people alive. If it's true for other types of sick, maybe it's true for red rash."

Karal had come over as they talked. She spoke into Ruzik's comm. "Angel, Karal here. We're looking at the entire human genome, including the Kyle mutations, to see if we can find a correlation between people with an increased resistance and anything in their DNA. We've found nothing so far." Her voice wavered and she sagged against the console behind her.

"Are you all right?" Bhaaj asked. It was a stupid question; the doctor looked ready to pass out.

Karal managed a wan smile. "I'm still going." She spoke into the comm. "Angel, a lot of the people who have the rash are Kyle operators."

"Yah ..." Static obscured Angel's voice. "... but *many* Kyle alleles exist. It's not just a few, it's a whole gang of them. The stronger the psion, the more of these Kyle things they carry. You need to check *all* of the genes."

"We can't," Karal said. "We don't ... don't have the full set to use as a comparison." With that said, she took a faltering step around the console and slid down into its seat. She crossed her arms on the top of the console and laid her forehead on them.

"Ah, damn." Lavinda leaned over to touch the doctor's shoulder. "Karal?"

"Need to rest," Karal mumbled.

"Angel, I've got to go," Bhaaj said. "We'll keep checking the Kyle idea. You, too. Keep us updated, yah?"

"Yah. Talk later." With that, Angel cut the link.

Straightening up, Lavinda met Bhaaj's gaze. "Karal needs a cure. Now."

"We can check the DNA of the people who've come in but aren't sick," Bhaaj said. "See if something in their Kyle alleles correlates. We need a template with every Kyle allele that exists to compare with theirs." They both knew someone with Deeper DNA who also carried the full set of Kyle alleles. "Vaj gave her okay for us to talk about it with doctors."

"That assumes the doctors are willing to ask the pharaoh for help." Anger edged Lavinda's voice. "Some people would rather let everyone here die than admit Pharaoh Dyhianna traces any heritage to the aqueducts."

"We still need to try."

"Raja, can you still hear me?" Lavinda asked.

Her EI answered. "Yes, of course."

"How much longer will you be able to contact anyone as far away as the surface?"

"Not long," Raja said. "A few minutes, maybe."

Lavinda swore under her breath. "I need to comm Paolo and my children."

Max spoke. "I'm having similar problems. Bhaaj, you should comm Jak."

Bhaaj watched Karal, who hadn't moved. "One of us needs to talk to the research team at the university. Doing a comparison of the Dyhianna Selei's DNA with the patients who've shown the most resistance wouldn't put the pharaoh at risk."

"Go talk to your husband," Lavinda said. "I'll comm the university."

"Jak understands." Bhaaj wanted to comm him so much it hurt, but this took precedence. "You should talk to Paolo." Although Lavinda's family had arranged her marriage, forcing her to comply with customs that the rest of humanity considered extinct, she and her husband had formed a deep friendship. It would never be love in the traditional sense; given the choice, Lavinda would have rather married a woman. She and Paolo made it work, though, and they had several children.

"I wish I could talk to him." Lavinda spoke with regret. "But I need to be the one who contacts the research teams. The request for Pharaoh Dyhianna's DNA analysis won't work unless it comes from me or Vaj."

Well, yah, there was that. Bhaaj withdrew then, leaving Lavinda to work her Majda magic. She checked on Tower, on Warrick, on the other Majda guard. None of them responded or even opened their eyes, but all three still breathed with a steady rhythm.

Bhaaj watched Ruzik helping his brother to a cleared bed. *Please,* she thought. *Let them be all right.* For all her experience, all her expertise as a PI, a fighter, and a liaison for the Undercity, she couldn't fix this. If she lost the people she loved, she'd lose a part of what made her whole.

Stop it, Bhaaj told herself. *Your wallowing helps no one.* Seeking privacy behind the stalagmites by the far wall, she tried not to think about how Healer Sarzana had also come here. After she sat on the floor with her back propped against the wall, she tapped a code into her comm.

Jak answered with no delay. "You good?" Static blurred his voice.

"Yah. Fine. Not have rash."

"Say again?" He still sounded urgent. "Not get that."

"Am good," Bhaaj said. "Not got rash."

"Ah." Relief suffused his voice. "I come down there."

"Nahya!" Her fingers spasmed as she gripped the ground. "Stay away! Not safe here."

"Not care."

"Not come. Swear it, Jak." Goddess, what if he caught the rash and died? No, she couldn't think of that. "You come, you get sick, I can't help anyone. Jak, swear. Not come."

After a long silence, he let go with one of the most creative streams of curses she'd ever heard, better even than Vaj's outburst. When he stopped, she said, "That mean you not come?"

"Damn it, Bhaaj."

"Swear."

"I already swear plenty," he growled.

She smiled wanly. "Give me oath. Not come."

Another long silence. Then: "Fine. I swear. Not come."

"Good."

Static came from the comm, covering his voice.

"Jak?" Bhaaj asked. "Not hear you."

"Now you swear."

"Swear what?"

His voice cracked, and she didn't think it had anything to do with static. "Be careful."

"Always. I swear."

"Not get sick."

"Do my best." She meant it.

More static came from the comm.

"Jak?" Bhaaj asked.

No response.

"I'm sorry," Max said. "I've lost the line. I can't get it back."

"I ken." Bhaaj laid her head against the wall, too spent to hold it up. She could almost feel how much Jak wanted to come here. He'd given her his oath, though, and his word was good. She let her eyes close. Maybe she could rest for just a few moments.

"No," Bhaaj muttered. She had to get back to the infirmary and help treat the sick. She tried to get up, then sagged to the floor.

"You need to rest," Max said. "You've missed the last two sleep periods. I'm surprised you're still moving."

Bhaaj tensed. "Are you sure that's all?"

"That's *all*?" Her supposedly emotionless EI sounded incredulous. "You've hardly slept for fifty hours. You're going to kill yourself." Before she could respond, he added, "And yes, I've been monitoring the health nanomeds in your body. They've found no symptoms of the disease."

Bhaaj let her head rest against the wall. "Good." Just a few moments of rest . . .

"Wake up!" Ruzik's panicked voice intruded into her drowsy blankness. Why so upset—

It came back to Bhaaj in a rush. She jerked upright, knocking Ruzik over.

"Damn it, Bhaaj." He fell against the wall. "Guess you alive," he muttered.

She looked around, disoriented. "I sleep?"

"Yah. Like rock. Two hours." Ruzik shifted his weight, moving to sit against the wall. He bent his long legs and rested his elbows on his knees. "Thought you dead."

"Not dead," Bhaaj informed him.

"Yah. Figured."

"Feel fine." Even just a couple hours of sleep had recharged her. "Byte? Tower?"

"Same." His voice sounded shadowed. "Byte maybe worse."

"Ah, goddess," Bhaaj murmured. "I go help."

"Already did. Robot came." Ruzik was speaking too slowly. "Brought supplies. Told me how to use. I treat Tower. Treat Byte. Treat Majda guards."

Bhaaj looked him over, really looked now. He had rested his head against the wall and closed his eyes. A horrible feeling started within her, threatening to grow until it consumed her. She spoke in a low voice. "Ruzik, look at me."

He opened his and regarded her with a bleary gaze.

Bhaaj swallowed. "You too?"

"Gave myself more meds," he said. "Just need—sleep."

"Ruzik, no." Tears threatened Bhaaj, making her eyes hot. She kept reliving that day when she'd cradled the dying Sparks in her arms. They should never have drunk that unfiltered water. But goddess, they'd been so miserably, horribly thirsty. Sparks had died for that mistake. Now Ruzik, too? No. *No.* She couldn't bear to keep outliving the people she loved.

"I get help." Bhaaj pushed to her feet and looked past the stalagmites. The holos of the doctors in Cries no longer played in any of the booths. Someone was sitting at one console, tapping various panels. Every now and then one of the booths flickered, but nothing else happened.

She turned to Ruzik. "You rest now, yah?"

"Is good," he murmured, his eyes still closed.

Bhaaj strode out to the mini-clinic. Ah. Lavinda was the one typing at the console. As Bhaaj came over, the colonel glanced at her. "You're awake."

"Yah. I'm good." Mercifully, Bhaaj saw no rash anywhere on Lavinda's skin. "You?"

"I'm not good," Lavinda grumbled. "I can't get these damn booths to work." She motioned at the consoles. "The robot brought supplies to repair the mini-clinic, but I don't know how."

"What?" Squinting at the console, Bhaaj realized the edge of a robot stuck out from behind it. Moving closer, she found a tray-bot stacked with new supplies. "Hah! This I can do." Engineering problems she could solve. As she knelt by the robot, studying its wealth, she said, "Can you give me a hand here? I need to move all these parts to the consoles."

"I can try," Lavinda said.

Eh? The Lavinda she knew would have said, *Of course. We'll make it work.*

She stood up, regarding the Majda queen. "Are you all right?"

The colonel wouldn't meet her gaze. "Yes. Fine."

"Lavinda, look at me." Bhaaj felt as if the roaring started in her ears again.

Looking up, Lavinda spoke quietly. "Raja, tell Major Bhaajan what you told me."

Raja answered in a neutral voice. "Colonel Majda's nanomeds have detected the illness in her body. Although she does not yet show symptoms, it won't be long. She has the two-three variant of carnelian rash."

No, Bhaaj thought. "Two-three?" she asked, as if that could somehow change the truth, that Raja would say it meant something else, not the fatal outbreak sweeping the Deep.

"It's the variant we are trying to treat here," Raja said. "The twenty-third version of carnelian rash ever detected."

Bhaaj came back and sat in a chair by Lavinda. "How do you feel?"

"I'm all right." Lavinda gave her a wan smile. "A slight fever. I can still help."

From what Bhaaj had seen of the variant, it wouldn't be long until Lavinda needed to lie down and let her body fight the disease. Bhaaj wanted to rage against whatever cursed pantheon of deities had wreaked this suffering on the human race. Instead, she spoke in the gentlest voice as she could manage. "I'll bring the supplies closer. As long as you can work, I can show you how to help with the installations. When you need to rest, tell me."

"That sounds good." She watched with Bhaaj with undisguised concern. "And you? How long do you have?"

"Max has been monitoring my meds. He says I'm fine."

"No trace of the illness at all?" Lavinda asked.

Max spoke. "Major Bhaajan is carrying the virus, as you all are. She's contagious. She just hasn't contracted the disease."

"Goddess," Lavinda muttered. "What's your secret?"

"I've no idea." Bhaaj forced herself to continue. "When I was young, a small girl in my circle and I were dying of thirst. We drank unfiltered water from a stream." With difficulty, she said, "Sparks, my circle-sister, died. I—I tried to save her. I couldn't."

"I'm sorry," Lavinda said. "And you?"

"I had no idea then why Sparks caught the red rash. I didn't realize it came from the water." Her voice cracked. "Afterward, I couldn't think about it. I pushed down the memory. But it's coming back to me now. I drank the water that day, too. I didn't die. I didn't just survive the disease. I never showed any symptoms."

Lavinda sat up straighter. "That's the same thing this runner of yours, Tam Wiens, says. And Paul Franco should have developed the rash by now, given how much he was exposed. The last time we checked, he still showed no signs."

"Tam and Paul aren't here, but I am. Maybe we can use me to figure out a treatment."

Lavinda leaned over the comm. "Mini-clinic, if someone is immune to the virus, can we use their antibodies to form a vaccine?"

"That's a more complicated question than you may think," the console answered. It had an androgynous voice, one soothing to hear. "The EI called Max has shared medical data from Major Bhaajan's nanomed system with me. The Major isn't immune. She isn't making antibodies for the current variant of carnelian rash."

"Then why am I not sick?" Bhaaj asked.

"I don't know," the Med EI said.

"Surely other people must have resistance to the virus," Bhaaj said. "Why am I the only healthy person here?"

"You're in an infirmary purposed to treat people with carnelian rash," the EI said. "Healthy people aren't patients."

"Oh. Yah. Of course." Duh. She needed to think better. "Okay. Step one: I get the comms working. Step two: I find more healthy people and send our scans to the team in Cries." She paused. "Did the robot bring medical data for Paul Franco and Tam Wiens? We can send their info, too."

"I don't know if Paul is still without symptoms," Lavinda said. "I can't reach him. I think the robot brought the scans for both him and Tam Wiens, though."

"All right." Bhaaj looked around. "Where is Karal?"

Lavinda motioned to a bed across the infirmary. "Sleeping. She wore herself out." Her voice sounded scratchy. "I don't know how much longer she has."

Another wave of fear hit Bhaaj. She had to get help, somehow, but she couldn't leave all these people to die, including some she cared about more than almost anyone else alive.

"I'll get started on the booths and comm," she muttered.

"Wait." Lavinda caught her arm. "You need to prioritize."

"No!" Bhaaj yanked her arm away. "No one gets special treatment." She wanted to use the remaining supplies on Ruzik, Byte-2, and Tower so badly, it was killing her. And Lavinda, too, not because she was a Majda but because, well, she was Lavinda. But she couldn't choose favorites.

"I don't mean people." Lavinda paused to gather strength. "I mean actions. You have supplies that will help you reconnect with the doctors in Cries, that will help treat people here, and that will prolong lives. But as soon as you remove those supplies from their protective covering, the algae will start to corrode them." She raised her arm, showing Bhaaj a medical scanner she still held. Then she let it drop into her lap. "These scanners are the most resilient tech we have against the algae, probably because they're the simplest. And even they're showing signs of damage."

"Oh. Yah. Of course." Bhaaj tried to organize her plodding thoughts. "First, I should get scans from people who haven't come down with the rash, so I have them ready to send the doctors. Then I'll repair the holobooths and send the doctors everything I can before the system starts to degrade. Next, I'll contact Paul at the clinic. Have him send another robot with more supplies."

"I thought the clinic only had one robot," Lavinda said.

Damn. She was right. "The cyber-riders can build him another." It wouldn't take them long if they knew the urgency. "Then I can start treating more people—" Her voice cut off as she thought of the many patients outside the infirmary, throughout the cavern. How many others lay elsewhere in the Deep, dying, unable to make it this far? She couldn't reach everyone, not in time to stop the toll exacted

by a disease spreading this fast with such a high fatality rate. "I'll
just—I'll do what I can."

"I help," a man said.

Bhaaj looked up with a start. The man stood on the other side of
the mini-clinic console. She didn't recognize him, neither as a patient
nor anyone else she'd seen. He had the classic features and coloring
of the Down Deepers, with one huge difference.

His hair was white.

Ho! Bhaaj had seen no other Deeper who looked older than fifty.
This man was probably into his seventies, a rarity anywhere in the
aqueducts, but especially here. Like the other Deepers, he didn't seem
to feel the cold. He wore a shirt with short sleeves and a pair of old
but well-tended trousers. No trace of rash showed anywhere on his
exposed skin.

He waited a moment more, then said, "You are The Bhaaj, yah?"

Stop gawking like an idiot, she told herself. "Yah. Call me Bhaaj."
He deserved her name for so many reasons, she couldn't count them,
but certainly for surviving so long in a world where the bruising
fatality rate left many children without even parents, let alone great-
grandparents.

"Not sick?" Bhaaj asked.

"Not sick," he said. "Not this time. Not last time."

Bhaaj felt as if her stomach dropped. "Last time?"

"Last time a big sick came." He spoke simply, as if he related a
normal occurrence. "Young man then. Sick took many. Not me." He
motioned at the infirmary. "I help. Hear what you say. Need not-sick
Deepers." He lifted his hands out from his body as if to show himself
to her. "Here."

"My thanks." Just how many plagues had decimated the Deep,
killing entire generations? Bhaaj felt ill, and it had nothing to do with
carnelian rash. "I scan, yah?"

"Yah." He indicated the scanner Lavinda held. "Use that?"

"This one is a mess," Lavinda said. "Better to use a new one."

"Yah, of course." Bhaaj stepped past the consoles and knelt by the
tray-bot. It formed a tiered affair, like a rolling set of stacked trays
controlled by an AI brain. Supplies crammed its every surface, not
only the trays, but every hook, nook, and cranny. Its robot arms held
even more, like a child who'd crammed their hands full of candy in

a sweet shop. Bhaaj found a scanner and ripped off the protective covering. Standing up, she stared at the small circle in her hand. It blinked, telling her something, though she had no idea what.

"This is different from the other scanners." She turned to Lavinda. "I'm not sure how to use it."

The colonel spoke slowly. "When I sat down here, I knew I wasn't getting up again. So I've explored the mini-clinic. Trying to learn. I can show you."

Bhaaj went over and stood while Lavinda fooled with the edge of the disk. "Let's see—yes, one tap on this arrow turns it on. And this—wait, no this—two taps here sets it to scan a human body. One more tap and it will record as much medical data as it can get from your subject and store it in a file." She handed Bhaaj the disk. "That's why it doesn't have even a simple AI brain. It leaves more memory to store data."

Squinting at the scanner, Bhaaj saw a green arrow pointing toward its center. She stepped over to the man and held out the disk the way she'd seen Karal do. Another green light blinked on its surface, and it gave the familiar hum of a working medical monitor. As Bhaaj scanned it over his body, it lit up with more green lights.

File compl . . . , Max thought. **Na** . . . ?

Bhaaj stopped scanning. "What?" *Max? What's wrong?*

"My apology," Max said. "I'm having trouble with the exterior sockets where the bio-threads in your body link to your gauntlets. The algae has damaged them. The medical monitor sent me a wireless signal. It finished its scan. It wants to know what to call the file with the data."

"Uh, how about 'Healthy Man One'?"

"Can use name," the man said. "Callin."

Bhaaj nodded to him, acknowledging the honor he'd offered. "Max, call the file Callin, Healthy Subject One."

"Scan done?" Callin motioned to the infirmary crammed with patients, some awake, most sleeping or in comas. "I go back to work."

"You help treat?" Bhaaj asked.

He spoke gently. "I pass to the lights."

Pass to the lights. Ah, goddess, he was moving the dead to the crematorium. No one else in the infirmary remained healthy enough to do it. "My thanks," she managed. "Any others who can help? Those not sick?"

"Most stay with circle. Not leave loved to die alone."

"Yah. Of course." She hesitated. Where was his circle of loved ones?

Watching her face, Callin said, "I outlive." Moisture showed in the corners of his eyes.

"My sorry," Bhaaj murmured. She didn't give a damn right now about the pressure never to apologize. This incredible human being—who had outlived his loved ones by decades—responded to the nightmare of another plague by coming here to help the dying. He deserved every honor she could offer.

Callin gave her a slight bow, then went back to work. Too drained to move, Bhaaj watched him walk across the infirmary. He stopped often to talk to patients. He wasn't only taking away the dead, he was also doing his best to gentle what time remained for the living, offering sips of water from the dwindling supply of snap bottles, finding them blankets if they shivered, or rolling up clothes to make pillows.

"This is a nightmare," Bhaaj said.

Lavinda gave a grunt. "Then wake me the hell up."

Bhaaj turned to see the colonel slumped to one side, practically falling out of her chair.

"Here." Bhaaj helped her sit back up. "I'll get you a bed."

"Damn it." Lavinda pulled away from her. "Prioritize, Major!" She spoke with a snap of military authority that Bhaaj instinctively responded to. "Get your duties done in proper sequence."

Bhaaj answered wryly. "I'm retired, Colonel." In a softer tone, she added, "I'll come back when I get a chance, Lavinda. I promise."

With that, Bhaaj headed out to the cavern, to see who she could find with that elusive resistance to the carnelian rash.

If anyone still lived out there.

CHAPTER XIII
The Last Voice

Bhaaj had known too many battlefields scarred by war, those haunted places where combat had ended and left in its wake only the injured—and those who'd passed beyond the violence. It wrenched her soul more than she could ever process. Her memories had become tangled in the hell of post-traumatic stress that started in the aqueducts before she'd enlisted and inflicted new layers of pain on her psyche throughout her combat service. Yet none had struck with the heartbreaking sense of futility that ground her down now, as she moved among the patients in the cavern.

These fragile Deepers weren't combatants, just people struggling to survive in a world most of humanity couldn't imagine existing. They lay in makeshift beds they'd cobbled together before they became too sick to move or that someone else had set up for them. Most were still, either asleep or in a coma from the virus raging through their bodies. A few coughed convulsively, a wracking protest that sounded as if it was tearing apart their throat.

With great care, Bhaaj stopped at each person, speaking words of comfort if they were conscious and offering them water. Saints, they *needed* to drink. Dehydration could kill them as fast as illness. Food had become a hopeless goal; no one could keep down more than watery soup. Using medical equipment from the clinic, she scanned each patient and administered whatever treatment she could give. For those with a cough, she injected nanomeds to relieve that hacking misery. Nothing she offered could cure the disease, but she desperately hoped she could ease their suffering.

As Bhaaj stood up after treating a patient, she saw a flash of color behind a pillar. Red. She peered in the direction where she'd glimpsed the swirl of cloth.

Max, are you there? Bhaaj asked.

No answer.

"Max?" she asked. "Can you talk?" Even though she spoke in a low voice, the sound seemed to echo in the cavern. Until the moment, she didn't realize how quiet it had become. No one spoke. No one even snored. If not for the rare coughing, silence would have hung like a pall over the entire place.

"Yes, I'm here," Max said. He'd turned the volume on her comm way down, but he still sounded too loud.

"Can you access my optical systems? I'm looking at a pillar with some red cloth."

"Yes, I see it. And yes, I'm getting healthy life signs for someone behind that column."

"Good." Bhaaj headed toward the pillar. As she came closer, she saw a woman standing there, leaning against the column of rock, the only other person on her feet anywhere in view. She wore a filmy red tunic with many layers of cloth and loose pants of the same color gathered at her ankles. As Bhaaj came up to her, the woman turned with a jerk.

"Eh." She relaxed when she saw Bhaaj. A man lay on a blanket at her feet, staring at the distant ceiling with a blank gaze. He gave no sign he saw or heard either of them.

Bhaaj tilted her head at the man. "Your circle?"

"New handfast," the woman said, her face anguished. "Need help."

Handfast. If she and this man had just become handfasted, they were married, aqueducts style. What malicious demons controlled their fate, that they found it fitting to give this young couple such a gruesome wedding gift.

"I treat." Bhaaj knelt at the man's side, and the woman knelt with her. The plea in her gaze—or her thoughts—felt so strong, it pulled at Bhaaj like an invisible rope. When Bhaaj laid her hand on the man's forehead, he seemed like a furnace, burning with the disease.

"He gets worse." The woman twisted her fingers in the loose cloth of her tunic.

I'm sorry, Bhaaj thought, wishing she could do more. She injected him with meds that could have cured known variants of carnelian rash. It wouldn't stop this ruthless version, but it might give him more time.

The woman nodded as if Bhaaj had spoken aloud. She offered her husband water, and he took a sip, but then his head rolled away, and he didn't respond again. The rash showed everywhere on his exposed skin, yet his wife seemed perfectly healthy, with no trace of the illness.

"Not sick?" Bhaaj asked her.

"Nahya." Her voice cracked. "Rest of circle—all sick. Or dead."

"Ah, goddess." Bhaaj felt so damn useless. She had only one pebble of hope to offer. Showing her med-disk to the woman, she said, "I scan you?"

The woman frowned at the disk, then at Bhaaj. "What?"

"Scan. Find why you not sick." She shook the scanner. "Maybe help with sick."

"Ah." The stiff set of the woman's shoulders eased. "What I do?"

Bhaaj rose to her feet. "Just stand."

As the woman stood up, Bhaaj scanned her body. When she finished, she nodded and the woman nodded back, a flicker of hope in her gaze. Or in her mind. The longer Bhaaj spent here, the more sensitized her mind became to the Deepers. If she tried to block them out, her head ached. The pain only went away when she relaxed her mental barriers.

She moved on, searching for sparks of hope among the dying.

"I'm sending you the scans for one woman and two men who aren't sick." Bhaaj spoke into the comm she'd repaired in the mini-clinic. She'd gotten the holobooths working again, sort of, and all three doctors had come to consult with her.

"A third man had four children with him," Bhaaj continued. "One was so sick, she couldn't move. The man and two of the other children were also sick, but it didn't seem as severe for them. The fourth child showed no symptoms at all. I'm sending data for them all. I've also included a scan for the man who guided us here. He was exposed well before the rest of us, but he still shows no sign of the disease. And I've included my own data, as well as that for one of our runners, a woman who seems immune to prior variants of carnelian rash."

"Your files are coming through." That came from the woman with gray hair and a lined face. Bhaaj thought of her as Doctor Gray. "The data looks good, not corrupted or fragmented."

"I'm getting it, too," the male doctor said. He was sitting at a desk in front of a holoscreen. The last time Bhaaj had seen him, the symbols that covered his screen had shown a chemical synthesis. This time, they displayed DNA helixes, not just floating in front of the screen but above his desk and all around him. They looked like ladders twisted into spirals, with different-colored balls for different atoms. Bhaaj thought of him as Doctor Helix.

Bhaaj's last talk with Angel remained vivid in her mind. "My contact at the Kyle Corps says you think our immunity might link to our Kyle DNA."

"It's a possibility we're looking at," the third doctor said, seated at her gleaming console. Doctor Tech. "It's resistance rather than immunity. Now that we have these new DNA samples, we can compare them with the full complement of Kyle genes to see if any mutation shows up in all of you with resistance."

Bhaaj's hope surged. "The full Kyle complement?"

"Actually, yes." Doctor Gray spoke carefully. "Pharaoh Dyhianna granted us access to her DNA records."

Doctor Helix snorted. "*After* the army had us sign top secret clearances, nondisclosure agreements, and any other damn contract they could come up with."

It didn't surprise Bhaaj that the pharaoh had come through for them—and that Vaj made doubly, triply, quadruply sure they'd never breathe a hint of any similarities with the Deepers they found in the pharaoh's DNA.

"If you do find a mutation that's the same for everyone with the full resistance," Bhaaj asked, "then what happens?"

"We figure out what it does," Doctor Tech said. "Then we figure out how to replicate that effect in everyone else who is sick."

Bhaaj suspected that was a lot easier to say than do. She shifted her weight in her chair. "I don't know how much longer we'll have functional comms or holobooths. I'm trying to get more repair materials, but it takes time for our people in the Undercity to gather the supplies and get them here. The more you update us with your results, the better off we'll be when we lose contact again."

"Understood," Doctor Helix said, echoed by the others.

After they signed out, Bhaaj sat with her head hanging down.

"Bhaaj?" Max asked.

She raised her head. "Your voice sounds scratchy."

"A little," he said. "I've lost contact with Cries, but my immediate systems are functional."

"Good . . ." After a moment, she said, "How much have I slept in the past few days?"

"About five hours." He spoke firmly. "You need sleep. You'll kill yourself from exhaustion just as surely as if the carnelian rash finished you."

"And when I wake up?" She felt so heavy. "How many people will die while I sleep?"

"Bhaaj—" For the first time in all the years she'd evolved with Max, he seemed at a loss for a response. "I'm sorry."

"Don't be sorry. Help me." She stood up slowly, rolling her shoulders to work out the stiffness in her muscles. "Have my nanomeds release more stimulants into my body."

"Done." He didn't even castigate her for overusing the meds.

She turned to where Lavinda still sat in the chair she'd sunk into. When Bhaaj shook her, Lavinda stirred and sighed, then slumped forward. Bhaaj barely managed to catch her before she fell off the chair. Pulling her upright, Bhaaj put an arm around her shoulders, keeping her from collapsing. "Raja? Are you still here?"

"Yes," Lavinda's EI said. "Colonel Majda's nanomeds are working to keep her alive, if that is what you were going to ask."

"How is she doing?"

"Not well," Raja said. "She would be better off lying in a bed."

Bhaaj looked around the infirmary. Far on the other side, Callin and a woman with wispy gray hair were tending to patients.

"Eh!" Bhaaj called, waving her hand.

No response. They continued to treat people.

Hear me, Bhaaj thought.

Callin lifted his head, then waved at her. Both he and the woman headed toward the clinic.

Lavinda stirred in her chair. "Where . . . ?"

"You're still in Karal's mini-clinic." Bhaaj strained to keep the colonel from toppling onto the floor. "How are you doing?"

"Not great," Lavinda mumbled.

"We're getting you a place to lie down."

"That'd be...good." Lavinda fumbled with the snap bottle hanging from her belt. After Bhaaj helped her drink, she murmured, "The singing...it soothes."

It took a moment for Bhaaj to realize she meant the distant chorus. Concentrating, she listened. Yah, they still sang, fewer people now, a ghostly sound. "It's beautiful." With difficulty, she added, "Like when you sang it for Healer Sarzana's passing. Your voice is incredible."

Lavinda sighed, opening her eyes. "I wanted to be a singer. Not a colonel." She spoke slowly. "In a universe where I had choices, I'd have become a vocalist and married my artist lover who painted such beautiful pictures."

Bhaaj wondered if Lavinda had ever admitted that painful truth to her family. "I'm sorry."

"Ah, well." Her eyes dropped closed again. "I've had a privileged life...can't complain..."

Why the hell not? Bhaaj thought. Lavinda had given her life to the family "business" and accepted an arranged marriage with a man she didn't love. Yes, she made an excellent colonel, with intelligence, political savvy, and an ability to lead. But she also had an exquisite voice, a gift she'd never used, at least not in any public way. What did the military fight to protect, if it didn't include those pursuits that elevated human existence to more than just survival? Bhaaj couldn't help but wonder which they needed more, another cog in their military machine or a singer with the voice of an angel. She had no answer.

"We help?" a woman asked.

It took a moment for the words to sink into Bhaaj's deadened brain. Turning toward the speaker, she felt as if she moved in a fog. Callin and the gray-haired woman had come to the other side of the consoles. They stood watching her, two people worn and wrinkled by their years in the Deep, their hair gray, their bodies weathered with age—and both healthy. They'd outlived almost everyone else born here in the last few generations.

Bhaaj stood up, keeping her hand on Lavinda's shoulder to steady the colonel, and also herself. "Find Majda queen a bed, yah?"

"We do," Callin said.

He and the woman came around the consoles, taking care as they joined Bhaaj. With an exhale of relief, she gave Lavinda into their care. As they helped her stand, the colonel mumbled, "My thanks." They nodded to her with a respect that Bhaaj had never dreamed she'd see the Deepers show anyone from the above-city. They took Lavinda to one of the few open beds in the infirmary, a ledge softened with rugs they'd just changed. If it bothered Lavinda to lie down where someone had died only moments before, she gave no sign. She seemed past caring.

Watching them, Bhaaj felt as if she'd sunk into a pit of molasses. *Cut it out,* she told herself. *Get your act together.* In silence, she left the mini-clinic and squeezed between the beds of sleeping or comatose patients, pausing to treat anyone who needed a booster or water. It felt like it took ages, but she finally reached the platforms where the Majda guards lay. Although she gave them both medicine from her new supplies, neither responded nor opened their eyes.

Tower slept on a bed beyond the Majda officers, stretched out on her side, turned away from Bhaaj. *So still.* No sign even showed that she continued to breathe. A chill went through Bhaaj as she leaned over the Dust Knight.

"Tower?" she asked. "You hear?"

No response.

"Tower!" Bhaaj grasped her shoulder and rolled the ganger onto her back—

"Go away," Tower grumbled. She opened her eyes. "Am tired. Need sleep."

Bhaaj gulped in a breath, hit with a relief so intense it hurt. *That* sounded like Tower. She took the nanomed syringe from her belt and gave her another injection. "Thirsty? Hungry?"

"Yah, water," Tower admitted.

Bhaaj unhooked a snap bottle from her belt, sterilized it, and gave Tower as much water as the fighter could swallow. She drank a lot, more than the other patients Bhaaj had treated.

"It's good she's getting fluids," Max said. "But *all* these people need that much water. No way do you have enough supplies for everyone."

"Aren't the Deepers still filtering it?" Bhaaj said. "They have the new equipment Paul sent."

Max paused. "I don't think anyone has brought more in the past few hours."

Bhaaj couldn't recall any recent deliveries, either. If the equipment had broken down, taxed beyond its ability to meet the demand, they were in trouble. Or the supply might have dwindled for a different reason. "Maybe no one is left who's healthy enough to keep doing the work."

"I hope it hasn't gotten that bad."

"Paul will get us new supplies," Bhaaj said. "He will." She didn't know who she meant to convince, Max or herself.

"Yes." Max sounded neutral. Somehow that worked better than if he'd given her platitudes about how everything would be all right. The longer this went on, the less all right anything seemed.

Ruzik and Byte-2 slept on beds beyond where Tower dozed. Bhaaj made her way to them and checked their breathing. Yes! Both exhaled against the skin of her hand. Neither opened their eyes, though, nor showed any other sign that they noticed when she gave them another dose of nanomeds.

"Live," Bhaaj spoke in a low voice. "*Live.*" It felt as if someone had reached inside her and gripped whatever vessel held the love she gave her circle, slowly crushing it until her heart ached.

Neither Ruzik nor Byte-2 responded to her voice, but their chests continued to move, in and out, their breaths shallow but steady.

They still survived.

For now.

Again.
Kneel. Inject. Water.
Kneel. Inject. Water.

Bhaaj plodded through the cavern, trailed by the dutiful tray-bot, which she'd reloaded with medical supplies and the last of the filtered water. Sunk into a trance, she moved without thinking, following the same procedure again and again and again. Kneel next to the patient. Give water. Inject them with meds. She kept draining the syringes. She didn't know how to reload this new type Paul had sent, or if it was even possible, so she placed each empty syringe on the cart and took a full one.

She'd expected to run out of water, but Callin showed up several times to replenish her supply. With snap bottles. Where did he get them? As far as she knew, no one in the Deep had bottles like those from Cries. The cyber-riders from the Undercity must have helped Paul Franco build more robots to ferry in supplies. That only raised another fear, however. Where did *they* get these life-saving bottles? She feared they were raiding what remained of the stores Weaver had traded to the medical clinic. She didn't have time to ask; she had to treat all these patients who'd managed to get as far as the cavern before they collapsed . . . so many . . . more than a hundred . . .

Kneel. Inject. Water.

Kneel. Inject. Water . . .

The ground slammed into Bhaaj. With a groan, she tried to lift her head.

"Bhaaj?" Max sounded upset. "Are you all right?"

"What happened?" She sat up, rubbing her forehead where she'd hit a nearby pillar. At least she'd missed the young girl she'd been giving a drink. If the child realized what had happened, she gave no sign. She just slept. Or more likely, she'd slipped into the coma that sometimes marked the last stage of the disease before death exacted its unforgiving toll.

"You passed out while you were helping the patient," Max said.

"Need to rest . . ." She took a breath. "I need more stimulant."

"Sorry. But you're already topped out on what your internal health meds can provide."

"Oh." Bhaaj rubbed her eyes. In the distance, she could see Callin and the gray-haired woman carrying a body out of the infirmary. "Max—how many people have we lost?"

"I don't have anything close to accurate data." After a moment, he said, "If it helps to know, I'm sure you've slowed the fatality rate with the medicine you're giving patients."

"I hope so." Bhaaj climbed to her feet, hanging on to the pillar for support.

"Eh," someone said behind her.

Turning with a start, she saw the young woman in the red tunic. After Bhaaj had treated her husband, the woman had alternated between looking after him and helping however she could manage.

"Eh," Bhaaj said.

"Ghosts need talky with you," the woman said. "Have to do it now. They not stay long."

"Ghosts?" She must mean the doctors in the holobooths. "They flick off-on?"

"Yah." The woman grimaced. "A lot."

Damn. Despite her repair attempts, Bhaaj couldn't outrun the spread of the algae. It saturated the air, the caverns, everything. As perilous as it was beautiful, it had already mucked up both batches of new supplies Paul had sent them.

"Here." Bhaaj nudged the tray-bot toward her and motioned to the patients. "You do, yah?" She'd already shown the woman how to use the syringes, both the meds that slowed the disease and those that soothed the hoarse cough.

"I help." The woman motioned toward the infirmary. "You go. Do talky."

Bhaaj headed to the infirmary.

"It's one of the Kyle genes!" Doctor Tech's voice boomed with excitement. "A rare one. Besides coding for a few minor Kyle traits, it also causes the production of a protein that doesn't do much of anything. But it does affect viral replication. The lymphocytes and monocy—"

"Doctor, slow down!" Bhaaj struggled to focus. "I've hardly slept since this all started. My brain is on autopilot. Simplify it as much as you can. Please."

"Sorry," Tech said. "You know how a virus works?"

"Sort of," Bhaaj said. "It makes more of itself in your body. To do that, it needs your cells."

"Essentially." That came from Doctor Helix. "Cells in the human body are like tiny factories that can copy molecules. The virus has none of that factory equipment, so it sneaks into the cells and hijacks what it needs to make more of itself."

"Your body produces a protein that stops the virus from entering the cell," Tech said. "It's like a key that locks the door into the cell."

"If the virus can't invade your cells, it can't multiply in your body," Doctor Gray added. "In most people, the virus reproduces faster than I've ever seen with carnelian rash. It's outstripping the ability of the body's immune system to deal with it."

"But it doesn't in your body," Helix said, "so the virus doesn't overwhelm your immune system. That's why you don't get sick."

"Can we give the protein to everyone?" Bhaaj asked. "Why do so few of us have it? And why do some get a much less deadly version of the disease?"

"The Kyle allele that codes for the protein is recessive," Helix said.

"Allele?" Bhaaj knew the word. Maybe in some previous life she'd understood it. Right now, her worn-out brain refused to think. "What?"

"Genes come in pairs," Gray said. "You get one from each parent. Alleles are different forms of a particular gene. If an allele is recessive, that means you need it from both parents for you to show the trait."

Bhaaj struggled to focus. "I thought most Kyle genes were recessive."

"All of them," Helix said. "Kyle traits don't manifest unless you inherit the alleles from both parents. A *lot* of Kyle genes exist, and each codes for more than one thing, not just Kyle traits. Many of the mutations they cause are negative, which is why Kyle operators are so rare."

"But you say this protein they make in me isn't bad?" Bhaaj asked.

"It doesn't do much of anything, good or bad," Tech said. "When the carnelian virus infects you, however, the protein blocks it. If someone has only one copy of the allele that produces the protein, it doesn't work so well, but it still helps. Their body makes enough to slow the virus and give their immune system a fighting chance. That's probably why a few people get it and then recover."

Bhaaj's mind was finally absorbing their words. Her unknown parents had each bequeathed her one bit of genetic wealth that she'd never noticed—until it saved her life. "How do we use this to help the people here?"

"We're working on it," Doctor Tech said.

Doctor Helix started to answer, but her holobooth flickered. A spark jumped from the floor to one of the screens and the booth went dark.

"What the hell?" Bhaaj asked.

"Major Bh—" Static filled Gray's voice, growing so loud it hurt Bhaaj's ears. Her holobooth went dead, followed a second later by Tech's booth. Two of the clinic consoles crackled and then went dark. Lights flickered on the third. It recovered, some of its lights turning green again. That one moment of hope was short-lived, however. Its green lights blinked off one after the other, like a wave of darkness sweeping over the unit. With one last sputter, it died, leaving only one of the four consoles still working.

"No!" Bhaaj said. "Not now!" She jumped to her feet and leaned over one of the dead consoles, stabbing at its lifeless panels.

Nothing.

"What's wrong with it?" She banged her fist on the console. "Max! Can you link to these?"

"Not anymore," Max said. "My functions are degraded. That's why I'm not communicating with you using our neural links. Even if I could, it might not be safe. You shouldn't link me to anything. I might corrupt their systems."

Bhaaj swore as she stepped over to the one working unit. "Console, can you respond? Can your EI talk?"

A woman's voice came from the console. "Yes to both questions. I am the EI called Med Three. Consoles One, Two, and Four stopped working because the central CPU for Console Two is corrupted from the algae. The others were already damaged, and Two pulled down their systems when it failed."

"Can you protect yourself from whatever knocked out the other three?" Bhaaj asked.

"I've removed myself from the link," Three said. "However, my CPU is also corrupted. It will cease to operate soon."

"I fixed all of you!" Bhaaj gripped the edge of the console. "I replaced your boards."

"Yes, that helped." A sputtering came from the console. "However, it isn't enough—" Static blanketed whatever else it had to say, and then Console Three followed its brethren into oblivion.

"No," Bhaaj groaned. "Max, can you fix them?"

"I've too much damage to my exterior elements," Max said.

"We have to do something." She looked around, searching for—for what? How did they treat a cavern full of dying people who had only her and two survivors to help them? It wouldn't be long before she and the elderly Deepers ended up alone, the three of them left to mourn in a bruising silence, surrounded by more bodies than they could carry to the heartbreaking radiance of the temple.

"Bhaaj, listen." Max spoke in a calming voice. "The university team knows now why you aren't sick. They'll work overtime to translate that into a treatment."

"They still have to get it to us," Bhaaj said. "In time." Of which they had almost none.

"They will." He spoke with assurance, but it sounded fake.

"Yah. Sure." They had only two ways to get the medicine here. They could use the route Paul had taken through the Maze, or they could send people with no Kyle ability down a staircase that went more than half a kilometer deep. It would bring them out in a remote and isolated area nowhere near this place.

"They won't reach us in time." She felt so damn tired. "Even if they find a treatment soon enough, even if they break quarantine to bring it to us—which is a big if, Max, because anyone from Cries who comes here has to stay until this virus is no longer contagious. If they come anyway, they still have to *find* us." Her voice scraped, ragged. "The Undercity will never let them in. They'll think Lavinda betrayed her promise to bring only three guards. Even if the medics convince the Undercity to let them through, who will show them how to get here? Paul is quarantined in Karal's lab—" She broke off as desperation rolled over her. "We're hidden—no one can find us—"

"Bhaaj, stop," Max said.

"I can't stop." Only adrenalin kept her from crumbling. "I have to *act*." She wanted to rage at someone, but she had no one to curse. "I can't rebuild the CPU for an EI mesh node. Who the blazes can? You need a fucking doctorate in computer-mesh science."

"Bhaaj, take a deep breath," Max said.

"Stop humoring me."

"Breathe."

She wanted to growl, but instead she gulped in a breath.

"Again," Max said.

"Enough," she muttered. She did take another deep breath, though. Her mood began to calm.

"Angel can get them into the Undercity," Max said.

"No!" The idea of Angel coming here—*no*. She was the only one in Bhaaj's innermost circle beyond the reach of this mess. Ruzik and his Dust Knights were here, dying in the Deep, and Jak was in quarantine with Paul, risking his own health and maybe his life so he could help send medical supplies. Only Angel remained safe.

"She can't come here." Bhaaj spoke with defeat, knowing Angel would come in an instant if she believed she could save her husband's life.

"It will work out," he said. "All this—"

"Max, shut up."

The EI went silent.

"Ah, hell, I'm sorry." Bhaaj knew he just simulated emotions, but she had long ago decided that if the sim became so convincing that even he couldn't tell the difference with the real thing, who cared how he experienced them? "I didn't mean that."

"I know," Max said. "It's all right."

She looked across the infirmary to where Ruzik lay in a bed near Byte-2. Tower slept in another to their left. Lavinda was over there, too, and her guards. Bhaaj turned her attention back to the dead consoles and glowered, as if her anger could wake them up. No such luck.

Standing up, she tried to take stock of her situation. Her mind was falling apart the way rock crumbled under the constant blows of a hammer, pulverizing her ability to think. She kept breathing as Max had recommended, even and full, until she gathered her scattered thoughts into something coherent. Then she left the mini-clinic, headed out to the dying patients. She couldn't stop trying. If she dared sleep, even for a few moments, what would she find when she awoke? Given *any* chance that she could help even one person stay alive until help arrived, she had to follow through. Sleep wasn't an option.

She reached Caranda first. The guard lay on her stomach with her head turned the other way. Bhaaj touched her shoulder. "Lieutenant?"

No response.

Bhaaj tried to run her scanner over the guard. The disk, however, had gone dark. Frustrated, she dropped it on the ground and shook the guard's shoulder. "Caranda? Can you hear me?"

No response.

"Max, do my ear augs still work?"

"Yes. They are fully within your body." Then he said, "Activated. I do have a warning. Even when you're rested, you need to take care using your biomech. Right now, you're too depleted to run on enhancements for more than a few minutes."

"Understood." Bhaaj realized she could hear the singing again. She'd thought it stopped, but now she realized one person still sang, a man gifted with a rich baritone. His voice seemed to ache with the haunting song. Taking a deep breath to steady herself, she leaned over Caranda and listened. Yes! The guard's faintly rattling breath came to her.

Relief flooded Bhaaj. Hard on its heels came a much less welcome thought. "Max, you said the algae hasn't reached my ear augs. But I'm breathing in algae all the time. Isn't it in my lungs?" She felt cold. "If it gets into my body, couldn't it overcome even this protein that keeps me healthy?"

"Possibly. It would take longer that way, though, than when it affects exposed surfaces or gets into tech-mech." He paused. "You need to go somewhere without algae."

"Yah, right."

"Maybe it can't overcome your resistance. You've found survivors here from a previous outbreak. A good number of them must exist, or else all these children and young people wouldn't be here."

"Yah, but that was a different variant."

"I don't know the answer. I'm sorry." Wisely, Max changed the subject. "Do you want me to leave your audio augmentations active?"

Bhaaj straightened up. "For now. If they start to show signs of damage, deactivate them." Inching past Caranda's bed, she made her way toward the place where Lavinda lay, a makeshift platform built from stone struts that someone had carried into the infirmary. A man in the bed on her right opened his eyes, but before she could ask if he needed anything, he sunk into a comatose silence. The patient in the next bed asked for water, his voice so low, she'd have missed it without her enhanced hearing. She sanitized a bottle from her belt, then offered him a drink. After a few swallows, he let his head roll to the side, his eyes closed, his breathing shallow.

Bhaaj laid her palm on his forehead. "I'm sorry I can't do more." She moved on then, pushing her hand through the curls that had escaped her braid. After what felt like eons, but was probably only a minute, she reached the bed where Lavinda lay on her back, her eyes closed, her body limp.

"Lavinda?" Bhaaj asked. "Can you hear me?"

No response.

Leaning closer, Bhaaj could barely hear the colonel's strained breaths.

"Max, how long do you think she has?" Bhaaj asked.

"I'm not sure," he answered. "An untreated patient at her stage would probably die soon. However, she has the best medical protections a person can get. If anyone can survive this, it's Colonel Majda."

"Yah." That might be enough, at least for now. Lavinda had more time.

Warrick, the other Majda guard, lay in the adjacent bed. With care, Bhaaj moved to the guard, squeezing past Lavinda's bed. The lieutenant lay on her side, facing away from Bhaaj.

"Warrick?" Bhaaj shook her shoulder. "Do you need anything?"

No response.

"Lieutenant?" Bhaaj gently rolled the guard onto her back—

The moment she saw Warrick's face, she knew the truth. "No," Bhaaj whispered. In a louder voice, she said, "Max—?"

He spoke gently. "I'm sorry."

"It can't be." Bhaaj couldn't believe how flat her voice sounded, because inside she wanted to scream. She laid her hand against Warrick's cheek. Judged from the stiffness of the guard's body and the pallor of her face, she must have passed away some time ago. Bhaaj's mind refused to accept that truth.

Even as she tilted back the guard's head to give her CPR, Max said, "She's gone, Bhaaj." His voice showed a strain no EI was supposed to feel.

"Maybe you just can't pick up her life signs because—because—" Because he was also dying, the algae eating away at him within her gauntlets.

"I'm sorry," he said in a low voice.

She looked past Warrick's body to where Ruzik lay several rows away. Watching him, she felt a great hollow spreading inside her heart, not the organ that beat in her chest, keeping her alive while everyone around her died. This cavity existed in the place where she put her joy in the treasured people who formed her circle.

"Keep going," she muttered to herself. "Move." She pushed on, easing between the beds that blocked her path.

"He's strong," Max didn't need to ask where she was heading.

Bhaaj felt as if she were cracking. "Max, I have the answer *inside* of me. My blood is full of those life-saving proteins. Can't I give them to these people?" She couldn't donate enough blood to save everyone, but she could for Ruzik, Byte-2, and Tower. And yes, she hated knowing that about herself, that she was willing to sacrifice even Lavinda to save the people she loved, but it changed nothing.

"You don't know if your blood type is compatible with *anyone* here," Max said. "You're A-positive. You can only donate to people with A-positive or AB-positive blood, and not even a lot of them, because your blood has other differences. It's probably your Deeper heritage. They don't have the same blood types as other humans. But you're only part Deeper. Who knows what would happen if you gave a full Deeper your blood. You also don't know if giving the protein to dying patients via a direct blood transfusion will help them or kill them. Your blood also carries other Kyle proteins, some of which can be fatal in certain conditions." He continued, relentless. "You also don't know how to do a blood transfusion. You don't have anyone to tell you how, and the mini-clinic no longer operates."

"I have to do *something*." Bhaaj stopped at the next bed that blocked her progress. She felt as if she'd run into a wall. After a strained moment, she realized Tower lay there on her back, her eyes closed, no rise and fall of her chest.

"Be alive," Bhaaj said, shaking Tower's shoulder. "*Live.*"

Nothing.

"No, no, *no.*" She leaned over Tower, straining to hear or feel *anything*, the faintest breath—

"Bhaaj, go way," Tower muttered. "Let me sleep."

Bhaaj gave a startled, raspy laugh that sounded more like tears. "Yah, fine." She eased past Tower's bed to where Byte-2 and Ruzik lay, the brothers side by side, just as they had stayed their entire lives, running, fighting, and existing together like two parts of a whole.

Breathe, she willed them. *Keep breathing.* She leaned over where Byte-2 lay—yah, his breath brushed her cheek. "Good job," she murmured as if he had achieved a great success. Laying her palm on his chest, she felt its rise and fall. He didn't stir under her touch.

"Breathe," she murmured. "Don't give up."

Bhaaj turned to Ruzik, the closest she had to a son, maybe the only child she'd ever have—he would be breathing surely. Almost everyone else still lived, and he had better meds than Tower and Byte-2. Yah, he'd pushed himself harder than the others, always a leader, but he was young and strong, full of vibrant, vital life.

Bhaaj listened for his breathing.

Nothing.

She leaned closer.

Nothing.

She set her hand on his chest and felt—nothing. No rise and fall.

"*No!*" Bhaaj shook Ruzik. "Breathe!"

"Bhaaj—" Max started.

"He's still warm!" Moving fast, she gave Ruzik CPR, uncaring that it meant breathing in and out of his mouth and pushing on his chest, uncaring that even her enhanced resistance might not be enough if she inhaled the full force of the virus. None of that *mattered*. She kept on, kept on, kept on, thirty compressions, two breaths, thirty compressions, two breaths.

Over and over.

Over and over.

With a ragged gasp, Ruzik gulped in a breath.

"Ah, goddess." As Bhaaj grabbed the edge of the bed, holding herself up, Ruzik took another gasping breath.

"Thank you," she whispered.

Ruzik didn't answer. He remained in a coma. But he kept breathing. He *lived*.

"Max." The roughness in her voice felt like relief, like desperation, like agony. "How long does he have?"

"I don't know." He sounded false somehow.

"You don't know, or you don't want to tell me?"

"Bhaaj—I'm sorry."

"Don't tell me your sorry! Help me *fix* this." She grabbed the syringe on her belt. "I can give him another treatment."

"No! It's too soon. If you give him too much, it will hurt, not help."

"We're so damn close to a cure." She looked around, searching desperately for something, *anything* to help. Karal Rajindia—yes, there she was, across the infirmary, in a bed by the wall.

Bhaaj inched past the beds and their silent patients, bit by bit, making her way to where the doctor lay, as motionless as everyone else. On and on.

On and on.

Sometimes Bhaaj wasn't even aware she still moved. Several times, she jolted awake when she fell against someone's bed. She had no idea how much time passed until she reached Karal Rajindia, but finally she stood looking at the doctor. She found what she'd dreaded. The rash covered Karal's face, shoulders, and arms, so bad that the red patches blended together. It looked horrible, worse than she'd seen on even Ruzik and Byte-2.

"Karal," Bhaaj said. "Can you hear me?"

No answer.

"Don't die!" She leaned over—and heard the rattle of the doctor's breath. "Ah saints, thank you." Bhaaj had no idea who she thanked, some long-dead saints, fate, or a pantheon of mythological deities. It didn't matter. Karal lived. She couldn't help anyone, but she still survived.

"Bhaaj, your vital signs show you're in trouble," Max told her. "You need to stop moving. Stop using your biomech. Stop being *awake*. You need to sleep."

"I can't sleep." Tears ran down her face, those forbidden signs of pain, what you never let show, because if you let yourself cry, you'd never stop. "If I can help even one person, I have to stay awake. And if I can't—" Her voice broke. "I need to be here when they go, Max. I need to say good-bye."

His words came out with kindness. From an EI. "I understand. But destroying yourself won't help anyone."

Bhaaj headed across the infirmary again, moving on autopilot. Her mind slowly formed a thought. She had to reach Ruzik, Byte-2, Tower, and Lavinda, too. That idea kept her going, pushing her beyond the demands of her body that she stop. When she stumbled, when she fell, even when she went to sleep on her feet and lurched awake, she kept going, kept struggling because she knew no other way to live. Or to die.

Sometime during that endless trek across the infirmary, the last voice in the chorus—the last man singing the lament for his people—stopped.

Silence descended on the Deep.

Bhaaj groaned. A thought formed in her mind. "Maybe this is what I deserve."

"What are you talking about?" Max asked.

"I'm *part* Deeper and even I didn't know how many people lived here." She stumbled and nearly fell across a patient. Grabbing their bed, she propped up her weight with her arms until she regained her balance. She stared down into the person's face, a man, a woman, she couldn't tell which. They looked so pale, their hair lying in damp curls around their face, their eyes closed. They hadn't even stirred when she banged into their resting place.

"My sorry," Bhaaj mumbled to them. She continued on, moving doggedly, her steps uneven.

The singer resumed his music, his voice drifting through the air.

"It's my fault," Bhaaj said to no one in particular, since not a single human remained in the infirmary to hear her words.

"Why is it your fault?" Max sounded genuinely confused. "The people of the Deep chose to remain hidden. They may even need isolation to survive."

"They never asked for help." Bhaaj grunted as it soaked into her brain that she'd finally reached the narrow space between Ruzik and Byte-2. She planted one palm on the edge of Byte-2's bed and the other on Ruzik's and let her weight sink into her arms. She barely held herself up, sagging between them.

"Their isolation is killing them," she said. "Why do they choose to live that way even if it's killing them?" The answer lay in the wash of moods from the empaths around her. In her fatigue, her mental barriers had crumbled. She'd become so attuned to the Deepers that even when they lay unconscious, she picked up a vague sense of their minds. It wasn't much, but with so many of them here, it was enough.

"They stayed away to *protect* us," she said. "They've been dying for generations, centuries, who knows how the bloody hell long, alone here, so they wouldn't spread the disease."

"It's heartbreaking," Max said, "But it isn't your fault."

"I repressed my identity." Bhaaj couldn't stop the words, those thoughts she'd pushed down until she barely knew they existed—except for now, when exhaustion and uncompromising reality forced her to look at the truth. "I denied the part of me that came from the Deep. I never tried to search for my family." Her voice felt ragged. "If I'd come here more, if I'd understood better, I could have brought them help sooner. Before this happened."

Max spoke firmly. "You looking for your parents wouldn't have stopped carnelian rash from decimating these people."

"These killing sicknesses, they've happened here before. Carnelian rash, other diseases." The words wrenched out of the mental prison where she'd hidden them for so many decades. "Is that how my parents died? I'll never know."

"You were a newborn," Max told her. "You couldn't have done anything."

"I'm nearly fifty, Max. I've had plenty of time to come here."

"For flaming sake, you're *one* person. You can't fix everything. It's impossible."

"No, I can't. But I can help." Her voice cracked. "It's just—I keep trying and I keep failing." She slumped against Ruzik's bed, listening to the rattle of his breath.

In the distance, the man singing "The Lost Sky" faltered, then picked up the music again.

"It grinds you down," Bhaaj said. "I try to move forward, to solve problems, to make life better for my people. Just when I think we've made progress, it falls apart again."

"Listen to me," Max said. "When the Deepers realized they might have another outbreak, this time they didn't stay isolated. They sought help because you've reached out to them. They knew about Karal Rajindia because of you. And why is Doctor Rajindia in the Undercity? Because of you. How can you say you've done nothing?"

"I know you mean well." Her words felt like shards of glass that cut her emotions instead of her skin. "But I'm the one who brought everyone here, all of them, Karal, Lavinda and her guards, Ruzik and his Dust Knights. I *invited* them." Her hand slipped off Byte-2's bed. With a grunt, she grabbed Ruzik's bed with both hands, barely catching herself before she fell to the floor. Somehow she held herself up, her hands braced on the stone platform under the blankets that softened its surface. Ruzik never stirred or gave any hint that he knew she stood vigil over him.

"It's my fault they're dying," Bhaaj said.

"Stop being an arrogant asshole," Max said.

"Why not?" Bhaaj muttered. Then she realized what he'd said. "What? Screw you, Max."

"Since when did you control the decisions made by Doctor

Rajindia, Ruzik and his crew, or Majda royalty? They make their own choices. Them, Bhaaj. Not you. Stop being self-indulgent."

"I know what you're doing. It won't work. Insulting me won't shake me out of a guilt I deserve." Bhaaj straightened up. "We're so close to a solution, so *close*—and it's too late. I'm losing almost everyone I care about." Her voice grated. "I have what will save them in *my own blood,* and I can't do a damn thing."

In the bed behind her, the rattle of Byte-2's breath ended.

Bhaaj spun around, lost her balance, and grabbed his bed. "No, Byte, no. *Breathe.*" She started CPR, leaning over, starting compressions, bracing his head, breathe, compressions—

Behind her, barely audible above the noise of her efforts, the rasp of Ruzik's breaths stopped.

"*NO!*" Bhaaj whirled to his bed and started CPR on him. Next to her, Byte-2 still wasn't breathing. She *couldn't* choose. She couldn't let Ruzik die, but he would never forgive her if she let his brother die.

"Max." She stopped her compressions on Ruzik. "Turn on my full biomech. Everything."

"Combat mode on." That he didn't protest, despite knowing she was too spent to use her biomech at full force, told her more than any warning he could give her. He saw no other choice.

The world jumped into sharp relief as her senses heightened. Her bio-hydraulics activated, along with her augmented skeletal and muscle systems, increasing her speed and strength. As often happened in combat, everything seemed to slow down, every second stretched into eons.

Bhaaj raced to the mini-clinic. Even with her speed pumped up, her steps felt excruciatingly slow. Her altered time sense let her to judge how to edge past other beds even at her enhanced speed without knocking over their fragile patients. When she reached the clinic, she leaned over a heap of equipment left on a chair by someone who'd become too sick to finish organizing them. She raced through the pile, tossing aside what she didn't need—there! With a grunt, she grabbed two oxy-booster units and sped back to Ruzik and Byte-2. Stepping between their beds, she set up the oxygen boosters, one for each of the brothers. Sleek and compact, each unit had a screen that displayed data, including oxygen flow and heart rate.

"Max, link to the boosters." Her voice seemed to echo, slowed and deep compared to her enhanced speed. "Do they work?"

"The oxygen delivery function is available." His voice also sounded drawn out. "They can't do chest compressions, however. You'll have to provide those for both patients."

She laid one palm on Ruzik's chest and the other on Byte-2. "Control my pushes so I don't shatter their ribs."

"Optimizing force and speed."

Bhaaj began compressions on Ruzik and Byte-2, her action controlled by Max's routines. She could only hope that his functions hadn't become too damaged by the algae, that he could still judge well enough to keep her enhanced strength from injuring either brother.

"Start oxygen flow from the boosters," she said.

"Activating—no, damn it. The delivery system isn't working on either of them. You'll have to pump the bags manually."

"I can't!" She kept on with the compressions. "I only have two arms."

"If their brain and vital organs don't get enough oxygen, they'll die."

"Link to my beetle-bot drones," she grunted. "Have them squeeze the bags."

"They can't. They just fly and spy."

"So have them fly up and down on the bags." Her words came out in disjointed pieces as she kept up the compressions, her motions more machine-like than human. "If you link their AIs to the booster, they can monitor the oxygen level and adjust their pushes." She had no idea if it would work, but she had no other options, short of suddenly growing two more arms.

A hum came from the mini-clinic. Startled, Bhaaj realized she'd left her jacket hanging on a chair by one of the consoles, with her beetles in its pockets.

"The blue beetle can't fly well enough," Max said. "Our tampering to weaponize it left the drone more susceptible to damage from the algae. However, Red has enough control to do what you want. It will have to alternate between the two booster units."

"Will it be enough?"

"It might."

The red beetle flew past Bhaaj, headed for Ruzik's bed. It

descended onto the booster, pushing down into the bag, then rose up again, letting the bag inflate.

"Good," Bhaaj grunted. "Are my chest compressions working?"

"Yes. I'm controlling your hydraulics to provide what I've calculated as the best rhythm and force. I can't guarantee you won't break their ribs, but I'm doing my best to avoid it."

"Thanks." She kept going—

Again.

Again.

Compress.

Again.

Again.

"Breathe," she whispered as she worked.

"Bhaaj, your body can't maintain this," Max said. "You're past the recommended limits for using your biomech systems. You need to stop."

"No! You keep me going. You hear? Even if I'm unconscious, keep my biomech going."

"It isn't safe—"

"Do it, damn it! Swear."

After the barest pause, an eternity for an EI, he said, "I swear."

"Good." They both knew he had no choice. The biomech web implanted in her body by the army allowed her to override the EI's mandate to save her life at all costs. A soldier couldn't let their EI interfere with their ability to fight during battle. It meant Max couldn't stop her from using full combat mode no matter what price it demanded, even her own death. She'd done civilian updates to her systems in the years since she retired, but she never changed that aspect of his coding.

Bhaaj kept going.

Her mind gave up any attempt at coherence, driven too far by the bio-electrodes firing her neurons. Her thoughts disintegrated until she stopped thinking, just kept doing compressions.

Again.

Again.

The distant voice of the man singing "The Lost Sky" faded into silence.

Silence.

Silence.

Compress.

Again.

Again.

Silence.

Bhaaj lost her sense of how much timed passed. Minutes? Hours? Drowning in the ocean of her exhaustion, she began to hallucinate, her brain creating fragmented visions that haunted her with their approach. Ghosts gathered in the cavern, far in the distance but coming toward her like the spirits of death.

"Not yet!" she rasped. "You can't have them."

Compressions. Keep going.

The ghosts continued their relentless approach, resolving into darkly glimmering forms.

Closer.

Closer still.

Bhaaj ignored them.

Compress.

Compress again.

Every time she raised her head, the hallucinations had drifted closer, come to demand their tribute, the dead she refused to let go.

Compress again.

Her red drone kept inflating and deflating the oxy-boosters, and she kept up the compressions, forcing her body to the highest level she could reach during battle. She fought no soldiers here, carried out no orders, faced no attackers intent on obliterating her. No, this enemy was different, an uncaring, unthinking molecular invader that took life without firing a shot.

Wracked by lack of sleep, her failing mind formed the images of four figures, like the four riders of the apocalypse. They came on, relentless. Merciless. Bhaaj kept going, robbing them of their prizes, the two brothers they sought to claim.

Compress.

Compress. Again.

The ghosts never stopped, but they never rushed either, they just kept moving in their own slowed time.

Stop, she thought to them. *Now. Stop.*

They ignored her disjointed thought and entered the infirmary, invading the no-longer-safe space, seeking to break the invisible barrier Bhaaj had raised to block their approach. She refused to let Ruzik and Byte-2 pass into their realm. As long as her biomech system would move her arms, she would deny these spirits their demands for tribute.

Compress.

Compress. Again.

Closer still, the ghosts came, only a few beds away—

And then Bhaaj saw it.

The shimmer.

On their bodies.

Decon sheaths.

Decontamination.

Protection against the red rash.

?

Spirits didn't need a shield against the virus.

"Ah, saints al-damned-mighty," Bhaaj whispered.

Help had come.

Too late.

Too late.

She continued her compressions, literally unable to stop. Footsteps scraped on the stone floor as the human ghosts approached her, so close now. Time stretched into torturous seconds.

Her vision blurred.

Her arms weakened.

Her rhythm faltered.

Someone kept saying, "Bhaaj, if you don't stop, you'll die."

A voice. Max's voice.

She kept going.

Going . . .

Someone touched her shoulder.

She lifted her head. A ghost. A woman. Bhaaj couldn't focus, only gasp, "*Help them.*"

Another ghost reached them, a man who scanned Ruzik even as Bhaaj worked. When he looked up at the woman and shook his head, Bhaaj said, "*No!* You can't give up!"

The woman carefully grasped Bhaaj's upper arm and tried to pull her away from the beds.

"No." Bhaaj held her ground. "You give them CPR," she scraped out. "I'm trying—not enough left in me."

The woman spoke with great caution, as if Bhaaj were a primed weapon that could explode at any moment. "Major, you must let go of combat mode. You'll kill yourself."

"Can't..." Bhaaj groaned as her body strained—

And then Max betrayed his promise and did the supposedly impossible, defying her order. Instead of forcing her biomech to keep her going, he let her body fall.

Bhaaj collapsed forward, plowing into the medic. The woman grabbed her, and Bhaaj just barely glimpsed her air syringe. Bhaaj tried to jerk away, but it was too late. The medic injected her. With a moan of protest, she fell into a darkness that took away the world—

And left only its unforgiving death.

CHAPTER XIV
Legacy

"Bhaaj?" the voice repeated. "You hear? Wake up."

What...? Bhaaj opened her eyes, bleary and confused. Maybe age was setting in faster than she'd realized, faster than even her supposedly healthy body could handle. She ached all over. No, wait, her muscles hurt because she'd fallen asleep sitting against a rock barrier. She was on a stone ledge, leaning on the wall behind her. Except that made no sense...

"Eh," a young woman said. "You alive?"

Bhaaj focused on the person standing in front of her. Woman? Man? No, woman. She had bleached hair that she'd razed off the sides of her head, leaving only the top standing up in a stiff brush. Her black leather jacket hung open, showing a ripped white shirt underneath. She wore dark trousers, worn and faded, and heavy boots. Her ears stuck out from her head a bit, not enough to seem strange, just enough to accent her stunning looks. She had the gift of smooth skin, not yet scarred by life in the aqueducts. As with most Undercity natives, she had larger eyes than normal for other humans. The aqueducts hadn't yet stolen her beauty.

"Yah," Bhaaj muttered. "I'm alive."

"Good." The woman sat on the ledge next to her. "About time."

"Tam?" Bhaaj asked. "Tam Wiens?"

"Eh." Tam gave her the once over. "You look like shit."

Bhaaj tried to focus—

And it all came tumbling back, everything, the rash, the desperation—

The deaths.

"No!" She lurched to her feet, then lost her balance and dropped back to her seat.

"Not move," Tam admonished. "Not ready."

Bhaaj thought of Ruzik and Byte-2. "No. I have to keep going." She tried again to stand, and nausea swept over her. She toppled like a broken pole.

"Ah!" Tam caught her before she hit the ground. With a grunt, she hauled Bhaaj up and set her on the ledge with a thump. "Stay put."

Another factoid sunk into Bhaaj's sleep-deprived brain. "Tam, nahya! Not come here!"

"I come." Tam sounded unruffled. "Not get rash. Never." She then added, "Bring Angel."

Angel? "Nahya," Bhaaj repeated. "Not bring Angel." She already couldn't live with herself. She wanted to fold up and die or keen forever for Ruzik and his brother and goddess only knew who else. If she'd gotten Angel killed as well, she might as well go jump off a tower in Cries. "Not Angel too."

"Angel come." Tam grimaced. "Bring slicks. We not want them. Gangers want to take tech stuff, beat them up, throw them out. Angel say nahya." From her look, she might as well have bitten into a sour fruit. "Knights guard slicks. Angel tell Paul. Paul tell me. I go on path he make."

All that? Bhaaj's voice scraped. "Max, how long was I out?"

Static came from her gauntlet, but then it stopped and Max's voice came through, scratchy but understandable. "About two hours."

"*Hours?*" No. It couldn't be that long. Ruzik and Byte-2, they'd be long gone by now. She forced herself to look toward where they'd died. A medic stood at Ruzik's bed, scanning the body and—

And talking to him.

"Ruzik?" Bhaaj's voice scraped. "Byte-2?"

"Not good." Watching her face, Tam quickly added, "Not dead. You keep alive. Sort of. Enough."

"Ah, goddess," Bhaaj whispered. "Max?"

"Here," Max said. "And yes, I'll turn on your ear augs. *Only* for your senses. No hydraulics. Your body can't take it. No amped-up muscles or skeletal system."

Bhaaj scowled. "You broke your oath. You let me pass out."

"True." Max didn't sound the least bit remorseful. "That's why you're alive."

He had a point. Bhaaj grunted at him.

"You're welcome," Max said. "Hearing magnified."

The sounds of the infirmary intensified, the clink of equipment, the rolling tread of the tray-bot, the murmur of a few voices. Bhaaj strained to focus, blocking out as much as possible except for the beds where Ruzik and Byte-2 lay. Sounds there became more distinct...

Breathing.

"Optical augmentation activated," Max said without her needing to ask.

Her vision focused on Ruzik as if she'd jumped closer to him. He lay on his back—and his chest rose and fell in a slow, steady rhythm. His face looked pale, so pale, but he *lived*. His eyes were open as the medic talked to him and he even gave a slight nod, so very slight, but enough to show he heard and understood.

And Byte-2? He lay on his side, still unconscious or in a coma—and *breathing*. Farther away, Lavinda was sitting up in bed, talking to a medic.

Bhaaj's voice cracked. "Thank you." She didn't know who she meant, Tam, the medics, Angel, Karal, Paul, the doctors at the university, the Ruby Pharaoh, Vaj Majda, everyone and anyone who'd helped save their lives.

She let out a long, slow breath as her pulse calmed. Tam waited, not pushing.

"You brought the healers here," Bhaaj finally said.

Tam nodded, accepting her thanks. She understood what Bhaaj didn't add. The Dust Knights had become Bhaaj's circle in the Undercity. Everyone knew Ruzik served as her second, that if anything happened to her, he would lead the Knights. It made no difference that she'd never given birth to him or Byte-2 or Tower; in all ways that mattered, they'd become her family.

As Bhaaj's surge of adrenalin eased, she looked around the infirmary. Three medics in the uniform of Cries emergency responders were going from bed to bed and injecting patients with med-syringes or otherwise treating them. Angel stood a few meters away, clutching the mattress of an empty bed while she stared past several other beds to where Ruzik lay. She looked ready to explode.

"Eh, Angel," Bhaaj said.

Angel jumped and spun toward Bhaaj, her body as tense as a board. "Eh?"

"Why stand there?" Bhaaj asked. Didn't she want to be with Ruzik?

"Medic send me away." Angel squinted at her. "I am maybe too much worked up. Not good for Ruzik, eh? Tam say go calm down."

"Ah." Bhaaj smiled wanly. Then she realized whose empty bed Angel stood by. Her pulse surged again. "Tower?"

"Am good," a woman said to her right.

Bhaaj turned with a jerk. Tower stood a few paces away, beyond Tam, her hand braced against the wall for support. Lines of fatigue creased her face, she'd lost weight, and her hair curled in a crazy mane, but she stood firm. Bhaaj wanted to shout with relief, go throw her arms around the hulking Dust Knight, or do some other embarrassing business that would mortify them both.

"Eh, Tower," Bhaaj said.

"Eh." Tower left it at that. She obviously didn't have the energy for anything else.

Bhaaj motioned at the packed infirmary. "Slicks came." Four of them, it looked like. "Need room to move around." She tilted her head toward Tower's empty bed. "Maybe stay there. Give healers more room, eh?"

"Eh." Tower didn't look fooled by Bhaaj's attempt to get her to lie down, but her voice warmed. "Checked on Kar."

Bhaaj peered across the infirmary—yah, Karal still lay in bed there. "Alive?"

A woman on Bhaaj's other side spoke in the Cries dialect. "Doctor Rajindia will live. It was close, but we caught her in time."

Bhaaj blinked, startled by the unexpected language. As she turned, she also stood, slow and careful this time. A woman in the scrubs of a Cries emergency responder stood there, watching her with that intent stare medics got when they wanted to see if you really felt as "fine" as you claimed. A translucent shimmer covered her body, the membrane known as a molecular air lock. Normally those protected against air loss in spaceships, but a tech could change the thickness and permeability for other uses. This one fit the medic like a second skin, including her face, which meant they must have altered it to let in air but keep out the algae. Down here, the membrane would probably only last a few days before it started to break down, but for now it served the same purpose as a decon suit and gave the medics more flexibility to treat patients.

Bhaaj's voice sounded as rusty as she felt. "Thank you for coming."

"I'm sorry it took us so long," the woman said. "We had, uh— trouble getting here."

"My Dust Knight told me you got attacked." It didn't surprise Bhaaj; the medics must have shown up with Angel but with no advance warning to the Undercity. Angel had apparently reached the other Knights in time, though, to let them know what was happening.

Now that she looked more closely, she realized Angel also wore one of the decon shimmers. Bhaaj nodded to her, wishing she had a better way to express both the immensity of her gratitude that Angel had reached them in time, and her anger that Angel put herself at risk. She said nothing, though. She'd have done the same.

Bhaaj spoke to the medic. "And the rash? Did it spread to the Undercity?"

"We've seen no sign of it," the woman said. "We left a monitor with Goodman Franco at the clinic. He's still slightly contagious, but he never contracted the illness. The three thieves didn't contract the virus at all. They were able to help give our EIs a map here."

"Good." Bhaaj decided she wasn't so pissed at the thieves after all. Who'd have thought they'd end up helping to save so many lives? She hesitated with her next question, hating to ask but needing to know. "How many—?"

The medic answered in a subdued voice. "We estimate that twenty to twenty-five percent of the population in what you call the Deep have already died or will soon."

"Goddess," Bhaaj murmured. She felt ill again.

"We can't be sure," the medic said. "The fatality rate for patients here in the infirmary and cavern, the ones you treated, is only about twelve percent. That's for a population of about one hundred and fifty people." She motioned toward Callin, who was tending a recovering patient. "He says only half the people who live here managed to come for help. That's why we predict a higher mortality rate. We'll get a better idea as we spread out from this area." She sounded stunned, but Bhaaj doubted it came only from the disease. Anyone connected with the doctors who'd worked on the treatment would've known what to expect with the rash. But a population of three hundred living this far below the surface? Even Bhaaj hadn't realized that many people called the Deep their home.

"Several members of Callin's team are acting as guides for our medics," the woman added. "He's taking them to patients who never made it here."

Bhaaj wasn't sure what she meant by Callin's team, but she could guess. He must have gathered other Deepers who didn't get the rash. She wondered if the Cries medics had any idea of the honor he did them by revealing his name. Probably not. It didn't matter. They deserved that honor.

The woman continued in a quiet voice. "Major—"

Bhaaj focused on her again. "Yes?"

"If you and your Undercity team hadn't come to help, the death rate would have gone much higher." She took a deep breath. "From what we can tell, only about ten percent of the population here has full resistance to the rash. Another twenty percent has partial resistance because they carry one of the recessive genes. For everyone else—" Her voice scraped. "The fatality rate could have gone as high as seventy or eighty percent. And that's just here. We think fewer people in the Undercity have the gene that gives resistance. If this had spread up there—" She shuddered. "A disease as simple as carnelian rash could have wiped out a substantial portion of your population. Over a thousand people."

Although Bhaaj had never known of an outbreak with this high of a fatality rate, they'd weathered many endemics. "We live knowing that can happen." And died knowing it. "That's probably why the Deepers didn't ask for help in previous outbreaks, those before Doctor Rajindia came here. They must have realized they could spread it to the Undercity and kill most of us."

Bhaaj stopped then, unable to say more. Somehow, she had to deal with the realization that had hit her while she stood alone only a few hours ago, in desperation, amid the dying. The last time such an illness struck the Down Deep, two generations ago—and who knew how many other times in the more distant past—the people here had kept their population isolated. Rather than seek help, they'd protected the Undercity from illnesses that could have wiped out substantial portions of the people.

The Deepers had given their lives so their brethren could live.

"Paul has both recessive genes," Karal Rajindia said. "That's why he never showed symptoms." The relief that suffused her voice said as much about her relationship with Paul as any words could have revealed. "So do you and Tam Wiens."

Bhaaj was sitting with the doctor in the mini-clinic chairs while the med-tech worked on the consoles, replacing the trashed CPUs and healing their EIs. For the first time in days, the infirmary wasn't full, with patients leaving when they felt well enough to walk. The Cries and Deeper team had also reached many in the caves, tunnels, and smaller caverns scattered throughout the Deep like an intricate maze. As word spread, more people came to the infirmary, both ailing patients who could still walk and those who needed stronger members of their circle to carry them. Those few who remained healthy helped treat the remaining patients, clean the infirmary, and carry their dead to the temple. Over the past hours, the brutal death toll had finally, mercifully dwindled to nothing.

"How much longer long do you think Paul will have to stay in quarantine?" Bhaaj asked.

"I'd say about seventy more hours." Karal looked around the infirmary, her gaze pausing at a medic from the university. "All of us, including the ERs from Cries."

Bhaaj didn't know who'd dislike the wait more, the medics or the Deepers acting as their hosts. No one protested, though. Four Cries medics had come, including one who specialized in mini-clinic tech. They never complained or spoke down to anyone. The Deepers expressed their thanks with nods, and a few gave their names. Some refused to see anyone from Cries, but they allowed their own people to treat them. With the loss of Healer Sarzana, several younger Deepers stepped up to fill the void. They watched and listened intently to the quartet from Cries. Although the medics seemed confused by that silent attention, Bhaaj had no doubt the new healers were taking in everything they saw, heard, and experienced, not only how the medics treated this new version of carnelian rash but also anything else they could absorb.

A rustle came from behind Bhaaj. Turning, she saw Lavinda coming up to them. The colonel carefully let herself down into one of the mini-clinic chairs.

Karal spoke in Iotic. "My greetings, Your Highness."

"Thank you." Then she added, "Lavinda, please."

"How are you feeling?" Bhaaj asked.

"Slow. Fuzzy." Lavinda smiled wanly. "Alive."

"Good," Bhaaj said, ever the queen of understatement.

"How did you do it?" Lavinda asked. "My understanding is that toward the end, you were the only one here still functioning enough to keep treating people."

"It wasn't just me," Bhaaj said. "Two Deepers who didn't have the rash helped." Quietly she said, "I'm sorry we weren't able to save Lieutenant Warrick."

Lavinda's expression became shuttered. "We all knew this visit involved risks."

"Oh, hell." Bhaaj wasn't having any of her canned phrases. "None of us expected this."

"True." Lavinda exhaled. "I thought I was coming to understand your people and civilization. I had no damn idea."

Bhaaj met her gaze. "Know this, Lavinda. Everyone here realizes you rank as a queen in the above world. They may not fully understand what that means, but they know it implies the highest of the high. They all saw you working side by side with us just like anyone else. They know you told your sister to stop when she wanted to pull you out no matter what it cost us." She regarded Lavinda steadily. "You were willing to die for my people. They won't forget." Nor would Bhaaj.

Lavinda shifted her weight, seeming as uncomfortable with emotions as a native of the aqueducts. "I'm just glad it didn't come to that."

A beep came from console one. The med-tech working on it straightened up and glanced at Karal. "I think it's working again. See if you can get anything."

"Good!" Karal scooted her chair over to the console. Within

seconds, she was deep at work, bringing up holicons to float above the console and flicking her fingers through them.

A woman with hair bleached the color of white-gold was approaching them. Tam. Bhaaj would never forget her iconic appearance. Stories were already spreading about Tam Wiens in the ever-evolving Whisper Mill of the aqueducts. Without Tam to recognize the cryptic markers that Paul had left in the Maze, and her ability to lead the medics here, it would have taken them far too long to find the Deep, perhaps too late to save anyone.

"Eh, Tam," Bhaaj said.

"Eh." Tam stood on the edge of the mini-clinic. "Mean Jak wants talk with you"

Bhaaj blinked. Why would Jak contact Tam's EI instead of hers?

"Jak try your talky," Tam added. "No answer."

Max spoke. "I still can't get incoming messages. I can't keep this algae out of my systems."

The med-tech, who was working on console two now, looked up. "I brought several tech-mech sterilization kits. Would that help?"

"Absolutely," Max said. "Thanks."

Bhaaj took off her right gauntlet, undoing its fasteners on her lower arm. As she handed it to the medic, she spoke to Tam. "Jak still on talky?" She'd already commed with him several times, to let him know how they fared, and she wanted nothing more right now than to collapse in his arms. Except she couldn't, not until this damn quarantine ended. In truth, what she needed most right now was just to sit for a while.

"I tell him you're fine," Tam said. "He says comm when you can."

Bhaaj nodded, relieved. "Will do."

With that, Tam headed off to help with patients. Watching her, Bhaaj was struck by how self-confident she seemed. It hadn't always been that way. In the greater culture of the Imperialate, no one blinked at the idea that more than two genders existed or that some people might feel their biological sex didn't match their identity. In the aqueducts, however, they'd never heard of gender dysphoria. When Tam decided to transition, it didn't go well, to put it mildly. For survival, she'd formed a dust gang with three of her friends; soon after, they became Dust Knights, the top tier of the fighting hierarchy in the Undercity. After that, no one bothered her. Tam once confided to

Bhaaj that she'd asked Karal for help. Not long after, she began to change, looking more like a woman, a process that evolved over several years. For a time her ability to run had slowed, but she'd gradually recovered. She seemed happier now, more at peace.

Karal suddenly spoke. "Bhaaj." The doctor was squinting at the holos flowing over her newly operating console. "I'm getting some data here you might want to see."

Bhaaj glanced at her. "Anything useful?"

Straightening up, Karal glanced at Lavinda.

"Uh, well, I should probably go rest," Lavinda said. With that, she stood up, moving slowly, and left the mini-clinic.

Bhaaj rolled her chair over to the console. "What's up?"

"We're doing a genetic analysis on everyone we've treated," Karal said.

"Well, yah." Bhaaj wondered why the doctor had wanted Lavinda to leave. They all knew the doctors needed to analyze the genetic makeup of every patient, both survivors and those the rash had claimed. It was intrusive, yes, but the Deepers had decided the benefits outweighed the loss of their anonymity. They wanted to develop a genetic map to warn them who was at risk from this new variant, who was partially protected, and who had full resistance.

Karal continued to look at her.

"What did you find?" Bhaaj asked.

"You told me once your mother was a Deeper," Karal said.

The world suddenly seemed to go silent. Into that void, Bhaaj heard herself say, "Yes, I think so."

Karal spoke her next words—her impossible words—in a perfectly calm voice. "You have a cousin here. A woman."

A cousin? *Family?*

"Bhaaj?" Karal said after a few moments.

"You're sure?" she asked. "A cousin of mine? And she survived the rash?"

Karal nodded. "They found her in a cavern with several kids. The children took care of your cousin when she caught the rash. By the time they also got sick, she'd recovered enough to care for them."

Bhaaj felt as if a roaring filled her ears, the pound of her accelerated pulse. She closed her eyes, trying to calm her adrenaline-fueled response.

Karal said nothing, waiting.

After a moment, Bhaaj looked at her again. "If she's my cousin, and she recovered, does that mean she has the protein that protects us from carnelian rash?"

"Yes, she got one copy of the allele from her father. Genetically, her father was your mother's brother."

Her mother's brother. Her uncle. "Is he still alive?"

Karal spoke with sympathy. "No. I'm sorry. No one else survives in your cousin's family."

A hotness gathered in Bhaaj's eyes. It couldn't be tears. She never cried.

Like hell. She'd wept like a damn baby when she'd seen the people she loved dying. She said only, "I'd like to meet her."

"I'm sure we can arrange that."

"And my father?" It stunned Bhaaj how calm her voice sounded despite the emotional explosions going on within her brain. "Did you find any trace of him?"

Karal hesitated. "Not here in the Deep."

That didn't surprise her. "In the Undercity, then. He must be there. He isn't in any Skolian database the army searched."

The doctor spoke carefully. "No, he isn't in a Skolian database."

Bhaaj didn't trust this odd tone Karal was using. "What aren't you telling me?"

"Of course the army checked their databases. That's also what we used for this endemic." Karal paused, then forged ahead. "We were looking for such a rare Kyle allele, though, that I expanded the search. I found some anomalies in your DNA, enough that I took the search to secured military databases we don't normally use for our citizens." Her gaze never wavered. "Those databases have greatly improved since you enlisted over thirty years ago."

Bhaaj waited. "And?"

The doctor spoke quietly. "Your great-great-grandfather was a Trader Aristo. A Highton, their highest caste. We might even identify him if ISC will check their dossiers on Aristos." She met Bhaaj's incredulous gaze. "I'm no expert on Trader slaves, but I've worked with ISC intelligence to compile stats on those with Kyle ability. Your father had to be a Kyle slave. His grandmother was almost certainly sired by a Highton with one of his female slaves. The Aristo probably bought her to breed for Kyle traits. They're always doing that, trying to create a Ruby psion. That could explain why your father had some of the rarer alleles, like the one that protects you from carnelian rash."

Bhaaj stared at her. "That's impossible! How could a Trader slave even get to Raylicon, one of the most protected worlds of the Imperialate?"

Karal lifted her hands, then dropped them onto her thighs. "I've no idea."

"I am *not* a fucking Aristo."

"No, you're not." Karal met her gaze. "You do have about six percent Aristo DNA."

Bhaaj spoke tightly. "Six percent of a monster is still a monster."

"Genetics don't work that way." Karal waved her hand through the holos floating above her console. "I've done a lot of research for the military on the genetic profiles of Kyles. Aristos were a genetic mistake by Skolian scientists more than three centuries ago. They tried to alter Kyle DNA so empaths could better protect their minds against negative emotions. It worked, but not in a way anyone expected or wanted. It created the Aristos. When their brains detect pain, especially from empaths, who send stronger signals, it shunts that response to their pleasure centers. They're essentially anti-empaths."

Bhaaj gritted her teeth. She had to force herself to stop so she could speak. "They're a bunch of egomaniacal sadists who prey on empaths."

Karal grimaced. "We've compiled their genetic profiles. We know which genes contribute to their traits, the sadism, the narcissism, their tendency toward totalitarian government. It's a relatively minor fraction of their total genome."

"Minor?" Bhaaj stared at her in disbelief. "You call what they've inflicted on the universe *minor*? They enslave nearly two trillion people. They torture empaths. They consider it their gods-given right to make us scream in agony. They commit *genocide* if a population pisses them off."

Karal met her gaze. "Yes. They do. What I'm telling you is that the genes which code for those traits are only a small part of their DNA. You didn't inherit any of it. As far as I can tell, your Aristo genes code for strength, independence, and intelligence. Nothing else."

Bhaaj clenched her hands on the arms of her chair and stared at a console so she didn't have to meet Karal's too-knowing gaze. Aristo. *Aristo.* Her great-great-grandfather had been a psychopathic monster.

Bhaaj, Max thought.

You're working again. She still had on one of her gauntlets, enough for him to reach her.

The tech-mech sterilization is helping my repairs, including via wireless links. His supposedly neutral thoughts felt odd in her mind. She wasn't sure of the right word . . . compassionate, maybe?

If you are six percent Aristo, Max thought, **that means you are forty-four percent Trader slave.**

Is that supposed to make me feel better?

Yes. Somehow a Trader slave escaped his owners. You studied the Aristos as an army intelligence officer. You know how well they control their populations. For a slave to escape at all would be remarkable. To make it to a Skolian world, in particular Raylicon—it would take an incredible person to manage such a feat.

Bhaaj didn't know what to think. *So why did he desert me in that godforsaken orphanage?*

I don't know. Perhaps he had no choice.

She exhaled, a long, controlled breath. Karal continued to sit, neither pushing nor speaking. After a moment, Bhaaj said, "And you haven't found anyone else here with DNA that could match my father?"

"None." The doctor hesitated. "I can't guarantee we've checked everyone. But if he's here or if he has other children, I've found no trace. I haven't checked as many people in the Undercity, but I do have records for a good number there, too, and none show your DNA." Karal paused, started to speak, then closed her mouth.

"What?" Bhaaj asked.

"How old are you?"

Bhaaj blinked at the question. "Forty-nine."

"You look younger."

She shrugged. "I have good health nanomeds. They delay aging. I also stay in good shape, eat a good diet, all that stuff doctors pester you about." Belatedly, she remembered she was talking to one such doctor. "Which of course I greatly appreciate," she added.

Karal met her gaze. "From what I can tell, forty-nine years ago, an outbreak of carnelian rash killed a substantial portion of the population here."

"You're sure it was exactly forty-nine years?" That didn't add up. "The survivors had to be resistant, even immune to the rash. But only about thirty percent of the current population seems to have the genes that fight off the rash."

"It was a different variant," Karal said. "The resistance some of you show to the current variant probably helped fight the previous, since the allele you carry is more common here than in the Undercity." In a musing voice, she said, "It looks like the previous variant also interfered with the methods of birth control the Deepers use. They had a flood of births after they recovered from the outbreak. It prevented the population from becoming so decimated, they died out." She thought for a moment. "That doesn't surprise me. Any mutation that helps increase the birthrate will survive." Dryly she added, "Not that humanity's overpopulated selves are otherwise in danger of dying off. That could be why the mutation is almost unheard of beyond the aqueducts."

Almost unheard of—except for the Ruby Dynasty. Bhaaj thought it the ultimate irony that she—a woman who came from the lowest of the low, a child of the worst slum in the Imperialate and a Trader slave—also shared DNA with the highest ranked people in two empires. Yah, great, what a laugh. Goddess, she wanted to punch something.

Why? Max asked. **Nothing Karal said reflects badly on you.**

Yah, well, you never had to live in poverty and watch your loved ones die because you had no resources to help them. Lot of good it did me, sharing DNA with those exalted types. And quit eavesdropping on my brain. His repairs were going a bit too well.

My apologies. I can't help but detect your increased neural firings when your thoughts become this intense.

Neural firings indeed. Only Max would talk that way when trying to make someone feel better. It did have the effect he probably wanted, though, distracting her enough to ease her reaction to Karal's revelation.

Although Bhaaj still knew almost nothing about her father, Karal had given her a scrap to hold, the knowledge that whatever his history, he'd been remarkable. As far as her Aristo ancestor, well, if she'd managed to take what little good he carried within his DNA, then she could find a way to live with the knowledge of her heredity. It seemed fitting that the strength, intelligence, and independence he'd bequeathed to his distant progeny helped her become a military officer who could fight the horrors his Highton caste inflicted on the rest of humanity.

She regarded Karal. "If it's possible—I'd like to meet my cousin."

The woman stood by a sheared-off rock formation that served as a table in an alcove of the cavern. She wore a swirling yellow tunic and loose pants gathered at the ankles. Soft boots warmed her feet, so different from the heavy protection Bhaaj wore. Silver bracelets with sparkling yellow and gold stones adorned her wrists and similar chains hung around her neck, jewelry that Bhaaj could never in a million years imagine wearing herself. Her curly hair looked almost identical to Bhaaj's, though. It poured around her shoulders and down her back in a gloriously wild mane.

When Bhaaj approached the alcove, the woman was looking the other way, staring across the cavern. Bhaaj recognized that gaze. Many thoughts occupied this woman's mind as she tried to sort them out.

"Eh," Bhaaj said.

The woman turned—and Bhaaj almost gasped. It was as if she stared into a softer, younger version of her own face.

"Eh." The woman nodded as Bhaaj came up to her.

They stood for a moment, taking each other in. "Good meet," Bhaaj said.

The woman reddened, and unlike with Bhaaj, whose flushes rarely showed, this woman's cheeks turned pink due to the translucent quality of her skin. She and Bhaaj also both glowed with the blue luminescence the algae created when it interacted with receptors in their skin.

"You are The Bhaaj," the woman said as if she faced a great person.

Well, that was embarrassing. "Is nothing."

"Is much. All know of The Bhaaj." The woman hesitated. "I am part like you?"

"Yah. Your hoshpa, he brother to my hoshma."

"Is honor."

Bhaaj grunted. "This Bhaaj biz, it means not even a little."

"Maybe not. Maybe yah." The hint of a smile showed on her face. "I am Barin Da." She spoke shyly. "Many call me Barinda."

Three syllables. People must like this woman a great deal, to honor her with such a name. Bhaaj inclined her head with respect. "I am Bhaaj." Realizing she was taking the name of this woman's aunt, she added, "Bhaajan."

"Bhaaj's jan," the woman murmured. "My hoshpa—he was small when his sister is lost. He knew only a little. He tell me this: she had great beauty. Outside. Inside. Great caring for people."

Bhaaj felt as if a lump formed in her throat, making it difficult to talk. "He tell you about my hoshma?"

"Some."

"How—how is she lost?"

"During rash last time. She worry about baby." Barinda reddened. "About you. Worry you get sick. She and her man, they go. She give birth some other place. Not Deep."

Bhaaj had heard the rumors that her mother gave birth in the Maze that separated the Deep from the Undercity. Those stories had never included a husband. "Her man? My hoshpa?"

"Yah." Sorrow showed on Barinda's face. Or maybe it poured from her mind. Bhaaj felt more attuned to her than she'd ever experienced with another empath, even more so because of the way her barriers had softened here, submerged in the flow of empathic moods among the Deepers.

"He never come back," Barinda said. "Die of rash, we think." She paused. "We think you all die."

Bhaaj spoke with difficulty. "Hoshma die." She lifted her hands palms-up in the Undercity gesture for *I don't know.* "Hoshpa gone. Go above-city? Die?" She lowered her arms. "Not in Undercity."

"Maybe someday find," Barinda offered.

"Maybe." Bhaaj pulled off the pack she'd slung over her shoulder and withdrew two snap bottles of filtered water along with some exquisite blue-glass tumblers. "Come with?" She indicated a ledge along the wall that offered a bench for the table. Geodes showed in the rock, sparkling with color, purple, pink, and green crystals all overlaid by the shimmering blue luminance. The walls also gleamed with embedded crystals, and lines of algae swirled in pleasing patterns across them. It was so beautiful, it felt painful to Bhaaj, knowing this all existed in the darkness, lost from the rest of humanity, tended only by these remarkable people who never saw the sky or felt the wind.

"Eh." Barinda smiled. She slid a pouch off her shoulder and gently removed two blown-glass plates graced with green and gold curves, followed by a bag of spice biscuits. "We talk, eh?"

They sat at the table, spreading out their wealth of food and drink. Barinda's spice biscuits were small cubes hollowed out with intricate designs. Whoever made them had used sugar powder, a rare delicacy in the aqueducts. The cook would have needed a 3D printer to place the powder in such delicate, complex designs. Although the printers weren't rare in the aqueducts, the talent to use them with such artistry came about far less often. When Barinda picked up a cube, Bhaaj followed suit and popped one into her mouth. Ah, heaven indeed. She offered Barinda a snap bottle of filtered water.

So Bhaaj spent the afternoon dining with a member of her birth family for the first time in her life.

EPIL☉GUE

"Do you think any of them will come?" Coach Mason Qazik asked.

"Some." Bhaaj expected at least a few Undercity runners to show up at the sports complex for the track-and-field practice. Angel and Ruzik both seemed curious about the team, and a few other Dust Knights had expressed interest when they learned the bargain involved above-city food, including sun-grown vegetables and snap bottles of water.

She and Mason were standing in the lowest row in the bleachers that bordered the oval track. The spectacular facility offered the best support and equipment that Cries could offer elite athletes. Too bad they had almost no such athletes to use said facilities. About ten Cries runners were on the track, warming up for the upcoming practice. Bhaaj and Mason watched them closely, mainly so they didn't have to look at each other and feel awkward.

"Our runners don't really know what to think of your invitation," Bhaaj admitted. "They almost never come to the surface. The sun feels too—" She searched for the right word. "Harsh."

Mason glanced at her. "When I talked to your protégé, Angel, she said I needed to make a bargain with your athletes. It's hardly the first time I've heard an elite athlete imply such. A new hovercar, high-level club memberships, a daily 'per diem.'" Dryly, he added, "Can't call their per diem a salary, after all, not for amateur athletes." He shook his head. "In all the years I've been doing this, though, I've *never* had an athlete ask for what Angel wanted. Food and drink. Simple, healthy meals and filtered water."

Bhaaj remembered all too well the days in her youth when she'd snuck onto the Concourse, intent on stealing enough food to stave off starvation. "Yah," she murmured. "Sometimes it's worth more than gold."

Mason motioned at a table set some distance away from the track, near an inner wall of the complex. "We have a buffet for the runners. Also, a nutritionist who can help them, uh—well, decide what to eat."

Bhaaj spoke gently. "It is well chosen, sir." She'd never forget the time in her childhood when Dig had stolen enough from her mother's supplies to keep their dust gang from starving during a particularly rough time. Bhaaj had gorged herself and thrown up later, sick from overeating.

Mason awkwardly. "It doesn't matter if all the kids who come here try out, either today or, well I don't know, some other time. They don't have to be ready for an Olympic team." His face reddened. "Not that qualifying for this one requires much skill. But I don't care about that. Major Bhaajan, if they'd like to come, and eat afterward, or even before, while the other athletes run—it's fine. Any who want to come are welcome."

Given that aqueduct natives were forbidden even from approaching the sports complex, let alone coming inside, it had never occurred to Bhaaj that this track-and-field team would consider Undercity athletes. That was before she knew Mason Qazik, however. "Thank you, Coach. And please, call me Bhaaj."

He blew out a hearty gust of air, making no attempt to hide his relief. "Well. Good." He squinted at the sky. "If they do show up, I hope the sun doesn't bother them too much. It's bright today, even for me."

"Yah, true." Bhaaj doubted anyone from the Deep would come. They couldn't bear sunlight without darkened glasses, salves for their skin, and clothes to protect their skin. No one even knew how it would affect them to go places without the algae of their world, a part of their lives as common to them as the air they breathed.

At least they still lived. In the season since the endemic had swept through the Deep, the survivors had recovered. They'd lost twenty percent of their population, but it could have been much, much worse. Ruzik, Byte-2, and Tower had no lasting side effects, and the same for Karal, Lavinda, Morah, and Caranda. Neither Paul nor Tam had ever shown any signs of the rash. The army held a memorial for Lieutenant

Warrick, one attended by the Majdas. General Vaj Majda herself gave the Selei Medal to Warrick's family to honor the lieutenant.

Ruzik's entire gang had come to the memorial, the first time they'd attended an above-city event with people from Cries. Nor were they the only Knights who'd ventured to the surface lately. A good number had shown up when Bhaaj ran track-and-field practices in the desert. They'd come out of curiosity, also in respect because she was their tykado teacher and mentor. Going to the sports complex for a Cries coach they'd never met, however, was an entirely different story.

"We'll see what happens," Bhaaj said.

The comm crackled on the band Mason wore around his wrist, and a woman's voice rose into the air. "Coach, this is Tena down at the track entrance to the complex. Mason! There's a bunch of Undercity gang members here. Are you sure you want me to let them in?"

Mason glanced at Bhaaj with a look of apology. "Sorry," he muttered. He tapped the transmit panel on his band and said, "Yes, of course, let them in. Escort them to the track."

"But Mason—*a lot* of them showed up. Forty almost. Some are little kids, like nine years old. No way could they be trying out for the team. And the older ones look like—I mean, they've got tats and scars and ripped clothes and—*shit*, that girl has a huge knife on her belt."

Bhaaj scowled. "Goddamn it. I told them not to bring weapons."

Mason glanced at her, then spoke into the comm. "Uh, Tena, tell her she has to leave the knife with you."

"Are you kidding? That woman looks like she's ready to murder someone. No way am I telling her anything."

"Here." Bhaaj motioned to Mason, indicating his comm. He extended his arm toward her.

"Tena," she said, "this is Major Bhaajan, the coach of the Undercity team." That overstated it, given that the Undercity had no official track-and-field team, but never mind. "Could you please allow the runner with the knife to talk to me on your comm."

"Uh, um, okay. Just a minute. I have to go back over there."

After a moment, a gravelly voice came out of the comm, what Bhaaj recognized as Rockjan, one of her older Dust Knights. "Eh," Rockjan said.

"Not bring fucking knife," Bhaaj growled at her.

"Not safe here," Rockjan growled back.

"You got knife, you go home," Bhaaj said.

Silence.

Bhaaj waited.

"Fuck," Rockjan muttered.

"Stay or go?" Bhaaj asked.

After a moment, Rockjan grumbled, "Stay."

"Good," Bhaaj said. "Give knife to slick. She give to me. I give to you after run."

Silence.

After a few moments, Tena's voice came over the comm. "I have the knife." With a surprised wonder, she said, "It's gorgeous, like a work of art."

Rockjan's voice came distinctly in the background. "Not pinch my blade, bitch."

"Stop it," Bhaaj said, using the Undercity dialect so Rockjan would know exactly who she meant. "She not steal your damn stab-em. And you not insult slick."

Silence. That offered a good sign, since if Rockjan really believed the fragile Tena intended to steal her knife, they'd have heard her beating up the beleaguered assistant coach.

Mason spoke awkwardly into the comm. "You okay, Tena? All set?"

"Yes, we're, uh, good." She sounded as jumpy as a softpaw kit. "We're on our way."

"Good." Mason hit mute on his comm and regarded Bhaaj uneasily. "Do you think they have any concealed weapons?"

Of course they did. Bhaaj doubted anyone had come unarmed despite her warnings. But they hadn't displayed their weapons, except Rockjan, who'd probably forgotten it was on her belt.

She said only, "They know they're welcome here. They don't intend to attack anyone." That assumed no one tried to attack them. What startled her more than Rockjan's knife was that so many of her runners had shown up today. "They *are* welcome, right?"

"Of course, of course!" His look turned earnest. "Even the nine-year-olds. They can eat if they prefer, instead of trying out."

"They gave their word they'd try out." Bhaaj didn't know what

Tena meant by nine-year-olds, but Bhaaj had encouraged a few preteens to come. Even if they weren't ready for the team, they could start training for the future. "They'll try out. They won't accept food otherwise."

"Ah." Mason nodded. "I understand." He even sounded like he did get it.

They stood side by side, waiting.

Mason's comm crackled again. "We're here, Coach," Tena said.

Bhaaj gazed across the long track to the other side of the stadium. Yah, there, she saw them, Angel and Ruzik walking with the young woman who served as Mason's assistant coach, all three of them leading a group of dust gangers out of the building and into the streaming sunlight. Bhaaj recognized most of them from their desert workouts. She'd spent the last season getting them ready for this practice. Except—who were those other two kids?

Max, activate my eye augs, Bhaaj thought.

Done.

Her view of the group jumped closer. Not all the runners were Dust Knights; a few came from circles protected by the Knights, including a couple of eleven-year-olds that Bhaaj knew loved to run. Tam Wiens stood out from the rest with her bleached hair and perfect runner's build, more lithe than most Dust Knights, not as tall, more suited to marathon distances than the heavily muscled gangers. All the runners, however, had the Undercity trait of unusually long legs compared to the rest of their body. That included a teen-aged boy and girl she didn't know. They looked familiar. It tugged at her mind . . .

Ho! The *cartels*. Cutter Kajada and Hammerjan Vakaar had sent the two oldest kids from the group they'd introduced to Lavinda when they asked if her offer extended to the cartels. She'd said yes— and so today a Kajada girl and a Vakaar boy came to Cries. Lavinda hadn't meant this; she'd invited them to train as Kyle operators. It didn't matter. They were *here*, two children of the warring cartels come to Cries, not as criminals, but as hopefuls for a sports team, of all things.

"A new day," Bhaaj said. A small step, sure, but maybe someday it could be more.

Mason glanced at her. "What?"

"Just glad to see them." Bhaaj straightened up, watching the runners gather on the track a few meters from where she stood with Mason.

The Cries athletes gaped at the Undercity team, and some of them turned to Mason with panicked looks. He lifted his hand, acknowledging the runners as if this unprecedented event was perfectly normal. Ruzik kept his group organized, motioning them to the starting line. When they'd practiced in the desert, Bhaaj had made sure they all recognized the bang of a starting pistol—that they knew it meant *go*, not that someone had tried to shoot them. She hoped that training stuck today.

Angel nodded to her and Bhaaj nodded back. For an instant Ruzik grinned, but he doused the look before it barely registered. Bhaaj understood. It hadn't been that long ago that he'd lain so close to death, she thought she'd lost him. Yet here he came, for an afternoon of doing what he liked best, even more than martial arts practices. For him, for many of them, this was pure fun.

"Everyone set?" Mason called out.

One of the Cries athletes raised his hand, a fellow with black hair and the build of an elite runner. The athletes all crouched down, taking their starting positions, though the Undercity runners seemed puzzled. The concepts of a "starting" and "ending" point in a race didn't make much sense to them. They had, however, agreed to do this in return for food and water, and they would respect the bargain. If it made no sense, well, who cared.

Mason lifted his pistol and called out in a voice loud enough for everyone to hear. "Ready, set—*go*." In that same instant, he fired, and the shot rang out across the stadium.

The runners took off.

Tam, Angel, and Ruzik immediately pulled into the lead. The only Cries runners who came close to them was the fellow who'd raised his hand and a young woman who looked like a Majda, Azarina probably. Within moments, Tam left even Ruzik and Angel behind, stretching out her long legs in the sheer joy of running.

"No, no!" Mason was practically wringing his hands. "Didn't you tell them this is ten kilometers? Don't they understand? They have to *pace* themselves. They can't give everything they have right out of the starting gate. They'll wear out long before they finish."

Bhaaj glanced at him, surprised, not so much by his outburst but that he genuinely seemed to care if his Undercity runners did their best. She spoke amiably. "What makes you think they're giving it everything they have?"

Mason gestured agitatedly at the large scoreboard high above the track. During meets, when crowds filled the stadium, the board displayed stats for whatever event was taking place. Right now it showed how each athlete was doing, taking its data from a monitor they wore on their arm that synched to the stadium system. Not only did it show a continually updating list of their times, but it also included a comparison with their best times, if known.

"That woman in front!" Mason said. "She's going way too fast."

Bhaaj almost laughed. She felt good. Too fast indeed. "That's Tam." She'd given Bhaaj permission to tell the coach her name, at least if she showed up for the race.

"Yes, yes, Tam." He pointed to her evolving stats. "If she could keep that pace, she'd come close to beating the record set on this track by Tayz Wilder, my best runner." He motioned to the man who had raised his hand, the one with the look of an elite athlete. "He placed in the top fifty at the Olympics three years ago. I don't see how an untrained athlete could keep that pace." He hesitated. "I mean, well, she doesn't *look* untrained. But still. That's a grueling speed for anyone to maintain. The same for Angel and her husband. How will they keep that pace?"

"Oh, I'm sure they won't," Bhaaj said.

"You should have *told* them, warned them—"

Bhaaj stopped him by laying her hand on his shoulder. "They *are* pacing themselves. They can all go faster than they are now." She couldn't keep the pride out of her voice. "You wanted good runners, Coach." She motioned at the field of athletes. "I brought you some good runners."

He stared at her, then turned and stared at the scoreboard, at the runners, at the board again. A light seemed to kindle within his gaze. "Hot damn."

Bhaaj couldn't help but smile. "Yah."

They watched as the runners went around the track again, again, and again, working toward the twenty-five laps they needed to complete the event. All the leaders, including Angel, Ruzik, Tayz, and

Azarina, kept a steady pace. Tam, however, stayed out in front. She excelled at distance runs, as did Ruzik. Although Angel could do marathons fine, enough to win the Selei Open, her forte was shorter distances, where her strength and more muscular build worked in her favor.

The scoreboard continued to evolve, comparing their times to various records. Bhaaj recognized the name of the person who held the all-time record on this track: Garnet Jizarian, a noblewoman who wasn't even native to Raylicon. A few decades ago, Mason had recruited her with the help of the Majdas and their connections among the noble Houses, convincing Jizarian to relocate to Raylicon for a few years so she could join his team. She'd become an Olympic gold medalist in track and field. Back then, Bhaaj had only recently enlisted, and she'd followed Jizarian's successes with interest, inspired that a runner on the team from her home world could do so well. Tam wasn't going to beat that record today, but she had a chance of beating Tayz's all-time best on this track.

As Tam, Angel, and Ruzik neared the end of their run, each kicked up their speed, sprinting for the finish. Bhaaj knew they used a bigger kick than many above-city athletes; a lot of her runners did it without even thinking. It was a survival mechanism. They ran to outpace their enemies, and that final kick could separate those who were caught from those who prevailed. Tayz and then Azarina kicked next, and they all pounded past the finish line in the order of Tam, Angel, Ruzik, Tayz, and Azarina, the top three all beating Tayz's previous record.

"Ho!" Instead of being pissed, Tayz shouted with what looked like joy. He jogged a cool-down lap around Tam, Angel, Ruzik, and Azarina, gulping in air even as he raised his fingers in the V victory sign to each of them. The Dust Knights looked disconcerted, but Azarina grinned. She seemed almost as happy as Tayz despite her fifth-place finish.

Tayz jogged past the bleachers where Bhaaj stood with Mason and gave a joyous shout. "Coach, we've got a *team*."

"Hell, yes!" Mason lifted his thumb in a universal sign coaches used to say *good job*.

Bhaaj nodded to them all, her version of shouting approval. "Tayz seems happy." She hadn't expected that, given that three Undercity natives had just pounded his record into the ground.

"You've no idea," Mason said. "He's been incredibly frustrated. He wants to do better, to be pushed by his teammates. Being the undisputed ruler in your own little sphere isn't good if you want to challenge yourself." In a confiding voice, he added, "Scouts from other teams have sniffed around, especially this past year as his race times kept improving. I feared I'd lose him to some recruiter from a bigger team." He straightened up, making no effort to disguise his satisfaction. "Now I'm not so worried."

Interesting. Apparently winning even superseded accepting Undercity kids. Bhaaj suspected at least some Cries athletes who lost their potential place in the Olympics to an Undercity native would complain, but that was a worry for another day. Her protégés had done well today.

The other runners were passing the finish line, many of the Undercity athletes ahead of their Cries competitors, including the two eleven-year-olds. No coach she knew would take twelve-year-old runners to the Olympics next year, but they showed Mason the talent in the aqueducts. He had years to work with these kids, and this only scraped the surface of what the Undercity could offer.

The athletes milled around, talking, drinking water, meeting each other. They'd eat later, after they cooled down. Neither Tayz nor Azarina showed any hesitation in talking to the Undercity runners. Angel and Ruzik conversed easily with them while the others listened, both the Undercity and Cries athletes taking their cue from the behavior of their team leaders.

Bhaaj turned to Mason in almost the same moment he turned to her. She couldn't help but smile. "We've got something happening here."

"That we do." He grinned with undisguised delight. "That we do."

Lavinda showed up after the practice, waiting by the entrance to the main building. Bhaaj assumed she'd come to meet Azarina, but when Bhaaj came near, Lavinda said, "Walk with me?"

"It would be my honor." Bhaaj meant it. She'd seen the true measure of Lavinda's character during the colonel's visit to the aqueducts.

They entered the complex and walked down the spacious corridor that ran around the perimeter of the building. Bhaaj said, "Azarina ran well today."

Lavinda's voice lightened. "Yes. She gets better all the time." She glanced at Bhaaj. "I thought you might like to know what we've found about your father."

Bhaaj's pulse jumped. "Yah. Yes. I would."

"We've tried to match your DNA with known Aristos." Her look turned apologetic. "We don't have enough data, at least not to find a match."

"Ah." Bhaaj tried to push down her disappointment.

Lavinda paused, then said, "Raylicon isn't known as a leader in many things aside from its military and governmental centers."

"That could change." Bhaaj had just spent more than an hour listening to Mason's thoughts on how he could improve Raylicon's less than stellar track-and-field team. That man could *talk*.

"The thing is," Lavinda continued, "we do have a few stars. The Cries City Ballet, for one. It's known everywhere. Dancers come from all over the Imperialate to audition. It's considered on par with some of the best dance companies anywhere."

"I can imagine." Bhaaj had seen the Cries troupe perform, and they'd stunned her with the beauty of their artistry. Then again, anyone who could do anything artistic tended to leave her gobsmacked. "Why do you bring them up?"

Lavinda pulled her to a stop. "The top dance troupes in all three of our civilizations—Skolian Imperialate, Trader Empire, and Allied Worlds of Earth—they all tour."

The distant sounds of activity in the complex suddenly seemed to fade away. Bhaaj could only hear Lavinda. "And?"

"Fifty years ago," Lavinda said, "The Cries City Ballet and the Qox Ballet Theatre had a cultural exchange. The Cries dancers went to the planet Glory in the Trader Empire to perform. The Trader company, the Qox Ballet—they came here."

"Fifty years?" Her breath caught. "That was one year before my birth."

Lavinda nodded. "Something happened during that trip. The Trader who owned the ballet got upset. He was furious at my family actually, because we're the main patrons of City Ballet. He said we tricked him." She shook her head. "He refused to leave after the ballet finished its shows. Most everyone associated with the troupe stayed under lockdown in his ship in the port, but he and his security people insisted we let them search the city. He didn't tell us why exactly, but it sounded like he thought someone in Cries had stolen some jewelry."

"Jewelry?" Disappointment flooded Bhaaj. "Oh."

Lavinda spoke dryly. "I should rephrase that. He implied a possession of his with great value went missing. We assumed he meant jewelry by the way he spoke. Now we aren't so sure."

Bhaaj stared at her. "You think a dancer from the Qox Ballet defected? My *father*?"

"It could be anyone associated with the troupe. From the way he talked, though, we think it was a dancer."

"Why wouldn't he just say his dancer was missing?"

Lavinda spoke firmly. "By interstellar treaty, if a Trader slave reaches our territory and asks for asylum, they become free. We won't return them to the Traders." She grimaced. "Since we didn't know what the Aristo lost, we let him search all he wanted. We even helped. We didn't want any diplomatic incidents."

Bhaaj turned the thought over in her mind as if she were meeting someone for the first time. "A dancer as my father? It seems unlikely. I don't have an artistic bone in my body."

"You're an incredible athlete, though," Lavinda said. "Dancers are some of the most athletic, physically fit people I know. Also, dancers are known for their mathematical talents and spatial aptitude, especially in ballet. They have to incorporate the patterns as they dance until it becomes innate, all those algorithms of movement, the geometry of the choreography, and a spatial awareness of people moving in a three-dimensional area. According to your army records, some of your strongest traits are math, geometry, problem solving, and situational awareness."

"Huh." She'd never thought about it that way. "Did the Aristo find what he'd lost?"

"We don't think so." Lavinda paused, frowning. "It's odd. With all of us looking, we had the resources to find any person or thing in the city."

"In Cries, yah." Bhaaj spoke with a sense of opening, as if Lavinda had unlocked a door and said *let's see what's in here.* "There is a place someone could go that even the army can't monitor. A place that deliberately hides not only from Cries, but also from the rest of the aqueducts." She spoke with difficulty. "A place even I didn't know much about, though my mother came from there."

Lavinda lifted her hands, perhaps unconsciously copying the aqueducts shrug. "It didn't even occur to the brass back then. We had no idea what existed in the aqueducts. Did your father take refuge there? It would explain a lot."

"Yah," Bhaaj mused. This offered the first theory anyone had posed that made sense. "Except what happened to him? He isn't in the Deep."

"I don't know." Lavinda snorted. "We do have a Trader embassy here in Cries, supposedly."

"Supposedly?"

"It's small. They mostly use it in attempts to spy on us."

Bhaaj spoke wryly. "As we do with our embassies in Trader territory."

"Well, yes." She paused. "Perhaps they found your father. I don't know why he would bring you aboveground, but if your mother died, he may have sought help. He probably knew almost nothing about the Undercity, given the isolation of the Deep." Her voice turned thoughtful. "If he came back up to Cries, the Traders could have located him. Slaves carry identifiers within their bodies, and the embassy was probably always on alert for him. If he realized it in time, he must have been desperate to put you someplace where they wouldn't find you."

"Like the orphanage."

"Possibly." Lavinda sounded apologetic again. "I know it's not much to go on."

"Maybe it's enough." Bhaaj felt oddly lighter. Her father might not have died or deserted her after all. Maybe he even still lived somewhere. She smiled at the colonel. "Let's take our athletes home."

"Indeed." Lavinda grinned. "The team is looking good."

"Yah." Satisfaction rolled over Bhaaj. They'd taken steps forward this time, maybe even some strides. Today she could look toward the future with optimism.

TIME LINE

The original settlers of Raylicon were moved in time as well as space; they came from around 900 AD in their own universe. The times given here refer to the time on Earth that corresponds to when they ended up, after their time shift.

Circa 4000 BC	Group of humans moved from Earth to Raylicon
Circa 3600 BC	Ruby Dynasty begins
Circa 3100 BC	Raylicans launch first interstellar flights; rise of Ruby Empire
Circa 2900 BC	Ruby Empire declines
Circa 2800 BC	Last interstellar flights; Ruby Empire collapses

✤ ✤ ✤

Circa AD 1300	Raylicans begin to regain lost knowledge
1843	Raylicans regain interstellar flight
1866	Rhon genetic project begins
1871	Aristos found Eubian Concord (a.k.a. Trader Empire)
1881	Lahaylia Selei Skolia born
1904	Lahaylia Selei Skolia founds Skolian Imperialate and becomes first modern Ruby Pharaoh
2005	Jarac born
2111	Lahaylia marries Jarac
2119	Dyhianna Selei Skolia born
2122	Earth achieves interstellar flight with inversion drive

2132	Allied Worlds of Earth formed
2144	Roca Skolia born
2161	Bhaajan born and abandoned at Cries orphanage
2164	Bhaajan runs away from orphanage and returns to Undercity with Dig Kajada
2169	Kurj Skolia born
2176	Bhaaj tries to enlist in army, but is too young ("Children of the Dust")
2177	Bhaaj enlists in army; they send her to school ("Children of the Dust")
2178	Bhaaj ships out with army
2182	Bhaaj makes jump to officer ranks
2197	Bhaaj retires from army as a major and returns to Undercity on Raylicon
2198	Bhaaj moves to Selei City on world Parthonia and works as PI
2203	Roca marries Eldrinson Althor Valdoria (*Skyfall*)
2204	Eldrin Jarac Valdoria born (*Skyfall*) Jarac Skolia, patriarch of the Ruby Dynasty, dies (*Skyfall*) Kurj Skolia becomes Imperator (*Skyfall*) Lahaylia Selei Skolia dies, followed by the ascension of Dyhianna Selei Skolia to the Ruby Throne
2205	Bhaaj returns to Raylicon. Hired by Majdas to find Prince Dayj ("The City of Cries" and *Undercity*) Bhaaj establishes the Dust Knights (*Undercity*)

2206	Althor Izam-Na Valdoria born Bhaaj hired to solve killer Jagernaut case (*The Bronze Skies*)
2207	Del-Kurj Valdoria and Chaniece Valdoria born Major Bhaajan hired to solve the vanishing nobles case (*The Vanished Seas*)
late 2207	Major Bhaajan hired to solve technocrat case (*The Jigsaw Assassin*)
2208	Carnelian Rash threatens to wipe out Down Deepers (*The Down Deep*)
2209	Havyrl (Vyrl) Torcellei Valdoria born
2210	Sauscony (Soz) Lahaylia Valdoria born
2219	Kelricson (Kelric) Garlin Valdoria born
2220–2222	Eldrin and Althor change warfare on planet Lyshriol ("The Wages of Honor")
2223	Vyrl and Lily elope and cause a political crisis ("Stained Glass Heart")
2227	Soz starts at Dieshan Military Academy (*Schism*)
2228	First war between Skolia and Traders (*The Final Key*)
2237	Jaibriol II born
2240	Soz meets Jato Stormson ("Aurora in Four Voices")
2241	Kelric marries Admiral Corey Majda
2243	Corey assassinated ("Light and Shadow")
2258	Kelric crashes on Coba (*The Last Hawk*)
2255	Soz meets Hypron during New Day rescue mission ("The Pyre of New Day")
early 2259	Soz meets Jaibriol (*Primary Inversion*)

late 2259   Soz and Jaibriol go into exile (*The Radiant Seas*)

2260   Jaibriol III born, aka Jaibriol Qox Skolia
(*The Radiant Seas*)

2263   Rocalisa Qox Skolia born (*The Radiant Seas*)
Althor Izam-Na meets Coop ("Soul of Light")

2268   Vitar Qox Skolia born (*The Radiant Seas*)

2273   del-Kelric Qox Skolia born (*The Radiant Seas*)

2274   Radiance War begins (also called Domino War)

2276   Traders capture Eldrin; Radiance War ends
(*The Radiant Seas*); Jagernaut Jason Harrick
crashes on world Thrice Named
("The Shadowed Heart")

2277-8   Kelric returns home (*Ascendant Sun*);
Dehya coalesces (*Spherical Harmonic*); Kamoj
and Havyrl meet (*The Quantum Rose*); Jaibriol
III becomes emperor of Eube
(*The Moon's Shadow)*

2279   Althor Vyan Selei born

2287   Jeremiah Coltman trapped on Coba ("A Roll of
the Dice"); Jeejon dies (*The Ruby Dice*)

2288   Kelric and Jaibriol Qox sign peace treaty
(*The Ruby Dice*)

2298   Jess Fernandez goes to Icelos ("Walk in Silence")

2328   Althor Vyan Selei meets Tina Santis Pulivok
(*Catch the Lightning*; rewritten as
Lightning Strike books)